Cool Hand

An Amber Farrell Novel
Book 4 of the
Bite Back series

by
Mark Henwick

Published by *Marque*

Series schedule, reviews & news on
www.athanate.com

Bite Back 4 : Cool Hand
ISBN: 978-1-912499-16-8

First published in December 2016 by Marque

Mark Henwick asserts the right to be identified as the author of this work.

"Sometimes, nothing can be a real cool hand."
Paul Newman as *Luke Jackson* in *Cool Hand Luke*.

Cover design: CreativeEdge, Andrew Dobell
Cover model: Maria Askew

Author's note:

Series continuity:
The Bite Back series is a continuous story rather than a string of episodes. It's not advised to start anywhere but at the beginning, with Sleight of Hand, and read through in order.

Asian names:
Throughout this series, I use the Western sequence (First, Middle, Last Name) to depict names, so as to match with the majority of characters in the books. Most Asian societies would put the Last Name first.

Were Pack Territories
in Cool Hand

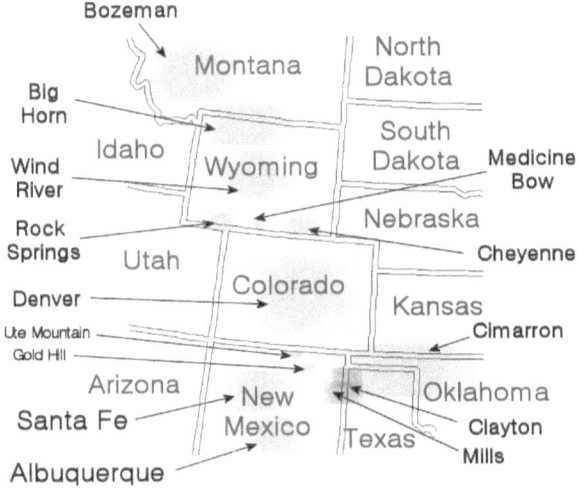

Bozeman

Montana

North
Dakota

Big
Horn

Idaho

South
Dakota

Medicine
Bow

Wind
River

Wyoming

Rock
Springs

Utah

Nebraska

Cheyenne

Denver

Colorado

Kansas

Ute Mountain

Cimarron

Gold Hill

Arizona

New
Mexico

Oklahoma

Santa Fe

Texas

Clayton

Albuquerque

Mills

Chapter 1

WEDNESDAY NIGHT

"If you don't believe your whole life has been a path leading to this one point, you're not focused enough."

That had been Top, while I was training in Ops 4-10.

But he'd also said: *"You're every second of training we've hardwired into you. Focus on the big picture and your instincts will handle the rest."*

What happened if my instincts led me down the wrong path?

It was just after midnight. I was burrowed into a thick layer of snow, peering through a gap in a field of winter wheat, scoping out the hideout of the last remaining Matlal Athanate in Denver. Or rather, an hour east of Denver in a remote location on the high plains—one reason why the place had been so tough to find.

In fact, I wasn't the one who'd found it. It was Nick Gray, the skinwalker, who'd sent me the intel. I was grateful, but also wary. He'd already gone above and beyond the terms of his original contract in helping me rescue Emily Schumacher from Dr. Noble. In my current exhausted, foggy state, I couldn't even remember what I'd promised him if he could hunt down the remaining Matlal. Anything he wanted, probably. With a bonus of extra 'anything' if we managed to rescue the *toru*—their blood slaves.

Which brought me to my next question: where the hell *was* Nick? All I had was a series of texts—the first one simply saying *Matlal hideout, Bow Creek Ranch*—with a set of GPS coordinates.

The others had read:

Have to hit them tonight—they're moving out.

Toru inside, proceed with caution.

And the final:

Meet you there. One hour. Cashing that check.

Yeah. My blank-check promise. No way that could go wrong.

Maybe it already had. It had been longer than an hour, and no further word from Nick. That was making me antsy. What if this was a trap? What if the messages weren't from him? It would be a dangerous business attacking the skinwalker, but what if someone had, and had then used Nick's cell to send us out here into an ambush?

The cold of the snow was already working its way into my hands and feet; the thought that we'd been tricked made me feel as if all that cold had frozen into a lump in my belly.

No. Only Nick would have made the comment about the check. I scooped up some snow and smeared it over my face, the chill clearing my head a little. I'd been trained to run risk assessments, but I hadn't been trained for running an op with half-rogue wolf and maybe-half-Basilikos Athanate yammering at me inside my head. My brain was running off in all directions. Too much sensory input; too many competing instincts.

Focus.

I scanned the area once more. We'd timed our arrival for just after sundown and done preliminary recon before settling within striking distance of the ranch buildings, but I still felt like we were missing something. The house was dove-gray clapboard with small, white-silled windows. No lights and minimal heat. Pale fingers of snow reaching up the walls.

It felt abandoned, though the word that came to mind was older and darker: *forsaken*.

We were downwind, of course, and my wolf nose could taste the scents of House Matlal in the cold night air. Mostly coming from the barn—a huge, tarred wood structure that loomed ominously behind the ranch house. Beside it, the top of a yellow backhoe poked out of the snow. There were other vehicles parked in the yard between the house and the barn—a truck and several cars. Both yard and vehicles had been cleared of snow. The access road, too. More evidence that the Matlal intended to leave tonight.

The barn was our target. In contrast to the cold, empty house, to my wolfy eyes its heat signature lit up the night, leaking through every gap as if it were smoking in the cold night air. That's where everyone was—but why? Were they feeding? Was that where they kept the toru?

My vague feeling of unease grew stronger. Something felt wrong here.

I checked my phone again. *No signal.* Damn. No way to tell when or if Nick was arriving—or anybody else. With most of Altau concentrated on building defenses against wide-scale military attacks from Basilikos, it had fallen on me to track down the last of Matlal's broken House—a lesser threat, relatively speaking. I had almost no resources—most of House Altau was scattered across North America, among the newly formed sub-Houses. Haven was an empty shell.

Even House Farrell/Pack Deauville were spread too thin. Alex was still recovering from the injuries he'd gotten fighting Noble, and Olivia was busy with Larimer's pack, helping them deal with Noble's betrayal. Pia was back at Manassah, guarding Jen. I hadn't been able to reach Tullah. I was down to David and Julie, who were stationed at strategic locations around the ranch buildings. Bian was on her way with the few reinforcements Altau could presently muster. And Nick was still MIA.

Whitetail deer stirred on the far side of the ranch, about a half-mile away. I started twitching and salivating. The wolf wanted to go hunting and taste raw meat.

Eww.

I pushed that down.

My wolf and Athanate gave me great advantages, but they set each other off, too. Taken in isolation, it was kinda like riding a tiger—exciting, if you don't fall off. But this wasn't in isolation. I was praying that at some point they'd reach a balance and I'd still be in control. Until then, I had a job to do and their distractions were dangerous.

Bian also distracted me as she came alongside like an eel, making her own Bian-sized burrow in the snow.

I didn't turn. "About time," I muttered.

Her breath felt hot in my frozen ear. More distractions. "You do bring me out to the most wonderful places, Round-eye. But it could have been anyone sneaking up on you," she murmured. "With all sorts of bad intentions."

I smiled in the dark. Her intentions were always bad. Or wicked.

"Julie's got my six," I said.

"And?"

"You probably had a little red dot on the back of your head the entire time you were sneaking up on me."

She huffed quietly and twisted around to see if she could spot Julie.

Good luck.

I'd managed to find a white ski jacket and pale jeans that didn't stand out too much in the snow. Bian was in full zebra-pattern snow camo. Instead of her usual katana, she had a futuristic-looking, matte-black blade the length of her arm and a shorty shotgun strapped to her back. Julie was behind us somewhere, invisible in white workman's coveralls.

"Who else have you got?" I whispered.

"Tom and Paul are over there." She pointed. "And we've got some backup. Elizabetta and three other kin who insisted on coming." She sighed. "At least the kin are staying back. There's one on the road as lookout."

Tom and Paul were good, but that still made only six of us. Seven, if Nick ever showed. The kin had no real training and they lacked Athanate strength and speed. Neither Bian nor I would want to involve them unless we were desperate.

"News on Nick?" I asked Bian.

"About ten minutes behind us, last update I got."

"I was starting to worry."

"He came across a couple more Matlal guys downtown. Sounds like he ripped their heads off." She shivered delicately. "I like him."

I snorted and took the comms set she handed me. Bian had bought tactical gear that allowed me to talk to everyone, just like on operations back in my days with Ops 4-10. One of these days I'd have to get some of this for House Farrell.

"Paul, join David behind the barn," I said into the set. "Tom, Julie, come up in line with me. Elizabetta, hold back and wait for Nick."

They called off acknowledgments. Tom and Paul had been in the military, and David had worked with me before. They weren't anything in comparison to a fully trained team, but with luck, we would have surprise on our side. And I had Julie with me. Not to mention Bian, who was terrifying when she really let loose. It should be enough. *Should.*

"Listen up, Round-eye." Bian shifted until she was resting against my back and could whisper straight into my ear. "These toru, they've probably been held by Matlal for a long time down in Mexico. The ones they brought up here with them would be the safest ones. Habituated to being toru. Not looking to escape."

She paused, and I nodded understanding. We couldn't expect any help from them. I twisted around until I was breathing into her ear.

"I'm sure there's lots of things you can teach me, little sister, but hostage rescue isn't one of them."

"Mmm. Sounds like an invitation." She paused. "You're blushing."

I was. I hadn't thought through what I was going to say before I said it. Again.

"It's pitch black, Bian."

"Yes, but your face just got hotter."

"Increasing noise from the barn," David said on the comms, interrupting us.

Julie slithered into the snow beside me.

BOOM.

"What the frigging hell's that?" I asked.

BOOM.

"Drum." David said. "Big one. Inside the barn. They're chanting, too."

Drum? Chanting? Oh, shit.

All the cold that I'd been trying to ignore suddenly reached hard, icy fingers deep into my chest, and squeezed.

"People, it just hit the fan," I said into my mike as I got up. "We go now. Julie with me. Tom with Bian five yards behind us. Paul with David—you two stay out of the barn and stop anyone from leaving. Elizabetta, stay clear and wait. This is going to be hard and fast, team. No arguments."

I was already running, high-stepping through the snow, gripping my HK MP5 submachine gun, with Julie half a step behind.

BOOM.

"I want that C-4 against the barn door like yesterday," I grunted.

"Gotcha." Julie didn't waste words.

We slithered across the space between the ranch and the barn. I pointed off to the side, where I wanted Bian and Tom to wait.

Mercifully, Bian followed orders.

Good. No time to explain.

BOOM.

Julie and I shucked our packs. Working quietly but with frantic haste, we pressed the malleable C-4 explosive into the gaps between the sliding door and the frame, and around the fixtures that held the rails.

BOOM. The drum spoke again, and this close I could feel it in my chest—a liquid hammer thumping on my heart. As the sound of the drum died, the murmur of voices swelled and a wave of cold, prickling dread ran down my body. They were doing what Adepts called a 'working', a manipulation of paranormal energy. And it wasn't a good one.

"Done." Julie beat me by half a second, and rammed the timer and detonator package in. "Primed."

"Primed," I answered. "Set three seconds on my mark. Two, one, *mark.*"

We pressed the timers and dove out of the way. No opportunity for a single primer setup; I hoped the timers were close enough. And that the door wasn't as tough as it looked.

It wasn't.

BOOM.

BOOM.

The plastic explosive obliterated the sound of the drum, and the edges of the barn door simply disintegrated into a mist of fire and splinters. I reached in and tore at the remains. They collapsed outward and I was through, leading with my MP5. Julie flowed into the barn at my shoulder, a lethal shadow, snake-cool and quick.

Gods, it was good to work with her again. I could ignore everything on my right-hand side; she had it.

But we both skidded to a halt. For a long moment, it was impossible to grasp what I was looking at.

The barn was filled, floor to ceiling, with a tiered, Aztec-style pyramid. In fact, from *below* the floor—it'd been dug out. Bursting through the entrance, we'd nearly fallen into a kind of narrow moat around the pyramid. The air stank of cloying wood smoke, paraffin and blood. There were oil lamps on small, floating platforms in the moat below us, and smoking braziers fixed on the corners of every tier of the pyramid. Their flickering light barely reached the walls, though there was still plenty of light for my wolf eyes to see.

And it was hot, but not hot enough to explain why everyone in there was buck naked. The sense of cold dread I'd felt outside surged through me again. This place oozed with evil energy.

Julie fired. *Tap-tap-tap.* It jerked me out of my daze. One down.

A man jumped down from the second tier to the first, body shiny with sweat and a knife the length of my arm raised up to strike. A golden mask obscured the top of his face, but his mouth was ugly with hate. As he tensed to leap the moat, I raised my MP5. *Tap-tap.* His knees buckled and my second shot hit him in his throat, angling up into his head and making the third shot redundant. He fell into the moat. Another Matlal came at me, a woman this time. Same kind of knife and mask. My ears were recovering from the noise of the explosion, but I could hear her shrieking like a jet engine spooling up. *Tap-tap-tap.*

I felt rather than saw Bian lunge between me and Julie, leap the moat and launch herself up the tiers of the pyramid. Her black blade wove a path around her; men and women fell away, leaving smaller, frightened figures cowering on the steps.

Smaller?

God. There were children here! The toru were children!

Heart in my mouth, I leaped across the moat and up two tiers, where another Matlal was holding a knife on two children, their faces pressed down. I vaulted over the children and killed him. Their screams shrilled in my ears. Another Matlal. Up a tier. Everything slowed as the bodies got closer together, and it was harder to keep the children safe. Another Matlal. Another.

Some of the Matlal ran for the side door. I let them. David and Paul would take care of them.

We had hit them like runaway trucks, throwing them back. Just like the manual said, we rode the shockwave, moving faster than they could organize. Bian had bolted up the steps of the pyramid like a startled horse.

And still we were too slow.

The apex of the pyramid was a gray stone slab the size of a small bed. It had dark streaks down its sides and fresh blood starting to trickle over the stains. A man stood there, big golden helmet and full face mask giving him an expression of cruel horror. Some kind of high priest. A sheen of sweat made him gleam like an oiled snake. A body—a child's body—was lying on the stone in front of him. His hand was arcing down, the wicked blade in his fist flashing gold in the firelight. We were too late.

And then his severed arm was tumbling end over end down the steps, spraying blood.

His eyes widened with shock behind his mask, unable to comprehend the swift justice of the blade that Bian had thrown at him.

Tap. I shot him right between those startled eyes and the bullet punched bits of his mask through his brain.

Then Bian was there, hurling his dead body away and bending over the child in frantic haste.

Julie and Tom shot one more each. As suddenly as it had started, it was over.

Chapter 2

I stared around the barn in amazement and repulsion. The renegade Matlal had built an Aztec temple out of railroad ties, earth and massive stone slabs, with five great tiers sliced through by a flight of steps leading up to the top. The moat it sat in looked regular and concreted beneath a layer of the sort of liner used for pools. The tiers themselves were edged with the railroad ties and filled with concrete. The steps leading up the side were rough dressed stone.

All hidden on a ranch, out on the cold, high plains of Colorado.

I'd researched Luc Matlal, the former head of House Matlal. I knew there were radical political groups in Mexico who claimed he was part of them. Their common theme was the reestablishment of a Nahuatl state. It fit with the arrogance of the man I'd met.

It didn't explain this.

Matlal hadn't struck me as the type of military commander who'd use building projects to keep his troops occupied. The backhoe outside would have done the heavy digging, and they could have used some of the earth they'd dug out for the core of the pyramid, but they'd have needed rubble and supplies—stone, concrete, railroad ties. That meant trucks visiting. Dumps in the farmyard. Site vehicles going back and forth.

I guessed that this far out on the plains, no one was around to notice the activity. But at a minimum, it had to have taken them three solid weeks to build this thing.

Why do all this work? Just to indulge Matlal's fetish for Nahuatl history? Including sacrificing children?

My stomach twisted. I wanted to vomit. It was evil and insane, beyond even what the rest of Basilikos did. There was a cloud of malevolence clinging to the structure. Like the noonday desert sun on unprotected skin, it made me feel that my skin was getting drier—itching and stretching and burning.

It'd only been a few minutes since we'd cleared the building, and everyone had followed us inside. I would have had trouble organizing my thoughts enough to give instructions over the comms set, but Elizabetta and the other kin just swept in and took over. Frightened, panicking children were being given sedatives, wrapped up in emergency blankets and carried back to the house. Minor injuries were being dealt with. Elizabetta stopped in front of me long enough to check me for wounds, and then passed on to help Bian in her grim struggle on the altar.

The child had been sliced on her chest, but the priest—or whatever he called himself—hadn't had time for the next cut.

I left Bian and Elizabetta to it. There was nothing I could contribute and I was scared the blood was going to set off my wolf.

David stood below, next to a huge drum made from an eighty-gallon rainwater butt. He looked as baffled as I was by the sight of the pyramid, but he gave me a nod. Everything had gone well outside.

Tom and Paul came back in.

"Ranch house is empty," Tom said. "They were packed and ready to leave."

The way he said it gave it away. "Not the children, though," I said.

"No." He wiped his hand against his shirt as if touching anything the Matlal had touched soiled him. "You okay?" he asked.

I nodded, my mind skittering around again, trying to grasp it all.

Killing the children before escaping made a sick kind of sense for the Matlal. They'd have planned to split up into smaller groups, each making its way south and trickling across the border back to the safety of Matlal's domain in Mexico. Children might draw attention to them. And if they went across the desert, the children might not be able to keep up.

But why this elaborate setup? What on earth was the purpose of this?

I couldn't get rid of the feeling that this was somehow an imperfect copy, maybe of another temple.

What had Luc Matlal been doing on his hidden estates down in Mexico? What had he found? When I first read the briefing notes on him, and had seen the Nahuatl political party affiliations, I'd dismissed that as opportunistic political maneuvering on his part. What if it was more?

Whatever it was, I'd *felt* it first; from outside the barn I'd sensed the shape of evil in my mind. And even though that feeling was less now the Matlal were dead, it persisted, like the after-image of a bright light when you shut your eyes. That image wasn't just a still shape; the surface swam with pale electric movement as if fluorescent snakes were climbing the tiers.

I'd seen none of that when we'd come in, but reaching out a tentative hand to touch the steps, I somehow expected a shock.

Nothing.

My brain seemed slow from the smoke. I wondered if they'd put something mind-altering in those braziers.

I used a discarded gold helmet to scoop up some moat water, and doused the flames. The smell of paraffin began to cover the odor of whatever had been in the braziers. I left the floating lamps; there didn't seem to be anything in them.

With the reduction in light, menacing shadows seemed to ooze out of the wooden walls and steal down them to pool at the bottom.

I shuddered. Too many lungsful of crazy smoke.

Tom ended a call on his cell, and with Bian busy, he reported directly to me.

"Nick Gray's a couple of minutes away. We've got a few more kin coming," he said. "I also put in a request to the Pack. Hope you don't mind. A dozen of them will come out and help clean up." He kicked the side of the pyramid. "Need to clear the whole site."

Felix had been adamant about the pack not getting involved in fights between Athanate, but all the paranormals understood the need to destroy evidence of us.

I nodded. "There'll be other bodies somewhere close. Find them. I guess they would have used the backhoe to dig a pit, so it shouldn't be hard." Saying it like that made it just business. Nothing to do with what those small bodies would look like, in the cold, dark embrace of the earth.

I took a breath, pushed all the visions away. "Once you've done that, clear out any evidence in the house as well, and finish up by burning the buildings down."

Tom grunted, turning around to take in the pyramid and calculate the effort required to destroy it.

"Anyway," he said, "I guess that's all of the Matlal remnants accounted for now."

I shook my head. I'd checked the bodies here, and there was still one missing. The silver-haired woman who'd been kicking my ass at Cheesman Park until the FBI showed up and saved me. I guess that confirmed she was the one who'd given Nick the information on how to find this place. He'd told me earlier in the week she was willing to provide insider intel—in return for joining House Farrell. Had that been part of the 'anything' I'd promised him? My head was still fuzzy, but no, I remembered Nick had asked for me to talk to her. I'd agreed to that. Then he'd said she was looking to join House Farrell. I was sure I hadn't agreed to that. How had we left it?

Crap. I was getting into enough trouble as it was. If I couldn't remember important stuff like this, things were only going to get worse.

Tom and Paul moved down a tier to talk with David.

"This is bad. It's not just that they weren't running—" Tom started.

"Hold it." I stopped him.

As the smoke cleared from the barn through the gaping ruin of the door, my brain was clearing too. My wolfy nose was still in shock from the smells and the smoke, but my wolfy ears had recovered.

Over in the back corner of the barn were some tool cabinets, looking so ordinary they were out of place. Something had rattled over there.

As soon as I took one step toward the cabinets, a girl—maybe a year or so older than the other children—slithered out from the narrow gap between them and sprinted for the door, clearly terrified.

Tom held his hands up and moved to block her. Julie was at the door. They'd catch her as gently as they could.

I stayed focused on the cabinets, my nose twitching. Something drew me there.

There was no one hiding between them, or on top, or under them.

Still.

Away from the smell of the braziers, my wolfy nose told me they weren't empty.

I put the HK down and knelt beside the right-hand cabinet. It was an old wooden cupboard that had been pressed into service to store tools. The right door hung a little ajar, and I slowly pulled it open.

He was jammed in what had been the bottom drawer space. It didn't look possible, but he'd managed to squeeze himself in there and half turn so he was stuck. It looked like we'd have trouble getting him out.

His face was only a few inches from mine, partly obscured by an old wooden-handled screwdriver he was clutching like a knife. He was shaking with fear, his eyes staring, round as an owl's.

The last thing I wanted to do was reach in and drag him out, or traumatize him any more.

I eased back a couple of paces, bending low so I was level with him and he couldn't see the gun lying on the ground behind me. I watched him, ignoring all the stuff going on in the rest of the barn. This one little guy was my save.

"You're safe now," I said, talking slowly. "I'm here to help you, and we can walk out of here together just as soon as you're ready. Everything will be fine."

Had his terrified stare relaxed just a bit?

Did he understand what I was saying, or was it just the tone?

I said it again, in Spanish. Nothing.

"Hablo español como una gringa," I said with a smile.

The tiniest nod.

Progress.

There was more noise, and his eyes looked fearfully over my shoulder.

"De nada," I said. "Estás a salvo." *It's nothing. You're safe.*

He was trying to see what was happening on the altar. I could hear Elizabetta and Bian. Was there some triumph in their voices? Could they stitch the girl up and save her? How much blood had she lost?

When he stretched his neck, I could see the scars. Some old, some partly healed, looking red and sore. Some fresh.

My jaw clenched.

He whimpered and I realized my face had gone bleak as a rock. I screwed it up and tried blowing out a breath to relax my expression.

"Not you. The people who did that to you." I pointed at him and then touched my neck. "Matlal. They're dead. Todos muertos. They can't hurt you now."

He shook his head—a short, violent motion. He understood some of that.

So what did he mean, shaking his head? What would he be thinking?

I was going to get him out, but I wanted to do it without touching him. He'd been touched enough by the Matlal.

How to manage it?

His mouth worked, but the sound was too distorted.

"Say again?" I said, leaning closer.

"K...kill me," he stuttered, his accent thick.

He was still frightened. I bit my lip. Maybe he thought we hadn't gotten all the Matlal.

"They can't kill you. They're gone. You can come with us and we'll protect you." I looked at his thin body. "We'll take you to get some food. You like burgers?" His eyes went round again. "Tacos? Milkshake?"

That seemed to have registered. Maybe I was getting through to him. I had a moment of wondering whether he had ever tasted a milkshake or a burger. What had they fed him on? Did he remember anything from before Matlal? Where had he come from? Had he been stolen from his parents?

Too many questions, and none I could ask him yet.

At least I was getting some kind of response.

What else did eight-year-old kids like?

"We'll take you to a place where they have toys and games. You know, like video games? You can play. Would you like to play video games?"

There was definitely a reaction to that. He knew what a video game was. Maybe House Matlal had let them play games in between feeding sessions.

There was shouting behind me and he flinched. If anything, he seemed to trying to squeeze himself deeper into the cramped space.

More shouting, louder now.

What the hell is going on?

I stood up and turned around.

"Hey guys," I said. "Keep it down—I've got a scared kid here."

"Amber!" David shouted as he rounded the base of the pyramid and ran towards me, one hand stretched out as if he were trying to warn me or stop me from doing something.

And that was the moment when the kid came out from the cabinet and stabbed me with his damn screwdriver.

Chapter 3

THURSDAY

"It's not funny."

The more I insisted, the funnier everyone thought it was, until I had to start laughing as well.

There was more than a little hysteria in some of the laughter.

We'd killed the Matlal. Regardless of the fact that they deserved it for what they'd been doing, it wasn't something to be dismissed and shrugged off.

We'd saved the children, every one of them that'd been alive when we hit the ranch, even the poor kid on the altar.

And we'd taken no casualties, except for one stupid bitch who'd managed to get herself stabbed in the butt with a screwdriver.

Yes, all in all, a success. But all of us would remember the streaks on the altar at the top of the pyramid.

If laughing at me stopped everyone from thinking about that, I'd take the hit.

It was coming up on dawn. We were back at Jen's house, Manassah. Bian was there. Nick had arrived at the site after I'd been stabbed and then disappeared again without explanation. Tom had stayed at the ranch to supervise the destruction of the site. Elizabetta and the rest of the Altau had taken the children and gone on to Haven.

Their charges included Gerardo, the little rat who'd stabbed me, now doped into submission with strong sedatives.

Turned out I should have listened to Bian. The children had been brainwashed into believing a twisted travesty of the world around them, where only House Matlal were their friends, and suffering was their holy path to redemption. Everywhere else, they were told, other children were being lured into a path of eternal damnation by the temptations of the world. Burgers and video games were the worst things I could have offered Gerardo. Those hoarse words he'd whispered to me—he'd been asking me to kill him to spare him from damnation. And I'd gone and hit every one of his preprogrammed buttons until he'd thought I was the Devil herself.

Those deaths: sacrifice on the altar made them messengers to the gods, guaranteed rebirth as the blessed Matlal Athanate if they went bravely.

Which explained what the children thought was going on. What the hell had the Matlal troops thought they were achieving?

Unfortunately, they were beyond answering now.

Jen was trying to get me to drop my jeans so she could put some antiseptic on the wound.

"Of course it hurts," I argued. "But I'll heal. That's what Athanate do."

Bian, of course, was also trying to get me to drop my jeans.

"I did say I could kiss it and make it better," she said, draping herself over a long-suffering David and looking at me with smoky eyes.

"It'll get better on its own," I insisted.

"Butt," she drawled, stretching the word out till everyone was laughing again, "it could get better quicker."

"At least let's have a look at it," Jen said.

"Hell, yeah," Bian said, earning herself a glare from Jen.

Pia was being no help at all; she was falling around giggling.

"For goodness sake." Jen grabbed me around the waist from behind. "Alex, give me a hand here."

Oh! Now that was different. My kin were cooperating.

It surprised me enough that they managed to capture me between them. Alex held my wrists, and I didn't want to struggle too hard. His own wounds weren't healed. He'd taken a lot of damage from fighting Noble's magically-enhanced wolf a couple of days ago. All of which he'd made worse by dragging the corpse the whole way down the mountain.

Kin cooperating instead of arguing...I'd go along with that. It was a start.

While he held me from the front, Jen reached around and opened my jeans, to catcalls and hoots of laughter from everybody else.

"Stop it!" I yelled. No effect.

She pulled the side down, just enough for everyone to see the wound in the middle of my right cheek. Blood had caked in my jeans and panties. It stung as Jen pulled the fabric clear. Of course, now it started bleeding again.

Thanks to my Athanate immune system, infection wasn't going to get a hold. The tear to skin and muscle would knit together in a couple of days. In a week or so, my body would have completed the repair so you'd never have known I'd been stabbed.

Tonight, however, it hurt.

I didn't care. Everyone was winding down. That felt great. I decided to surrender to whatever indignities they wanted to heap on me and relaxed against Alex.

Deep breaths. He smelled so good. Wolf and man.

Kin. Purr.

I gently pulled free of his grip and snaked my arms around him, burying my face in the crook of his neck. His arms went around me in return and held me.

I closed my eyes. It felt so damned good. Even if my head was too screwed up to take any more advantage of him, I could just drown in this feeling.

I stopped caring what they did to me. My eukori reached out and tangled with his. His dark aura seemed to shiver, then lost its shape and flowed over mine.

Together we reached out a little further.

Jen's eukori was clamped down; she'd had a heated argument with Bian before conceding that Athanate healing would be better than standard medical antiseptics and analgesics.

Bian's eukori was tight and secret as usual.

The others were open. Not all the House was here, and among the missing was the aching void where Melissa should have been, with her quick, sharp observation—forever silent now. Pia and Alex sensed my sorrow and filled it with their peace and love.

While I nuzzled Alex's neck, Jen wiped the wound down with a wet cloth and reluctantly let Bian have her way with me.

"The things I do for you, Round-eye." Bian laughed.

I could smell the bitter-fruit scent of aniatropics, the bio-agents she was producing in her saliva which would help heal me quicker.

Her tongue touched me and I flinched.

"If anyone dares take a photo of this, I'll have their hide." My words were muffled against Alex's neck.

The pain in my buttock eased away. I could sense the aniatropics seeping into the damaged muscle, speeding the process of knitting it back together.

Then the door burst open and Julie stood there.

"Ahhh! Nooo," she yelled, covering her face. "I can't ever un-see that." She was blocking the doorway and turned to speak to someone in the hallway outside. "No! You can't come in yet," she said to whoever it was.

Yet another person lining up to witness my humiliation. I tried to care, but I was too comfortable. It felt like I had no bones at all. If Alex hadn't been holding me up I'd have ended up as a puddle at his feet. I hadn't felt this relaxed in ages.

"If this is some kind of initiation ritual for House Farrell," Julie turned back to watch, "I think I just lost my application form."

I chuckled and reached a little more with my eukori. The combination of relaxing and mingling eukori with Alex's seemed to boost the range a little. I could feel Jen and Bian. David and Pia. Gary and Leon, Pia's red-haired kin twins. Julie, happy colors drifting through her. And…

I jerked my jeans back up. My heart went into overdrive.

"That wasn't so bad, was it?" Bian said.

"I don't even want to know about that," Julie said. "But guys, guess who Agent Ingram just dropped off."

She stepped out of the way and Keith came in, grinning broadly and managing to look a bit shy at the same time.

Keith. Her husband. My ex-boyfriend.

Julie was part of my House. Whether she knew it yet or not, I knew it.

Keith… *Oh, yesss*.

My fangs came out, aching with hunger, and I lunged toward him.

Chapter 4

Bian and Pia had me backed up against the wall.

"She's coming back."

There was a moment's confusion, but I knew I had a real problem when I heard them speaking about me instead of to me.

Then I remembered. My guard had been down. Keith had come in and I'd lost it. If it hadn't been for Bian, I'd have reached him.

Great way to welcome him.

I squeezed my eyes shut and made sure my jaws were clamped closed. The fangs were gone, but I was still getting the throbbing in my jaw. It felt like anything could set them off again.

I wasn't fighting now. I wasn't doing anything but breathing and trying *not* to think of Blood. Which was hard. My body ached for it.

"Amber?"

"Here," I muttered.

"You're fine." Bian was using her Diakon-serious voice. "You've had a slip. No big deal."

"Can't," I said. "Can't bite. Promised Diana. Wait for her. Dangerous."

"Yeah, and don't forget, invitation only."

All of which was a problem.

"What happened?"

That was Jen, her voice sharp with worry.

"She's passing through crusis. It's a phase—" Bian began.

"She knows what crusis is," Pia interrupted. "I've explained it to her."

"Okay. Everyone calm down and back off," Bian said. She waited. She was putting out pacifics in her pheromones and her voice had the force of command. I could feel the tension dissipate a little. I kept my eyes closed; it felt like it helped. David got the others to sit, and Bian led me to the sofa. Alex and Jen sat on either side of me. More than anything else, that made me feel better. Bian knelt in front of me, still holding my hand.

"You hearing me, Amber?"

"Yeah."

"Towards the end of a normal crusis, Aspirants get periods of irrationality we call crusis mania. Now, your crusis is all bunched up, unpredictable and—how do I put it—complicated with you being hybrid Were as well."

I huffed. She wasn't overstating it. The Were side of me seemed to thrive on letting go and following instinct. The Athanate was all about maintaining control. I was a hybrid that the Athanate told me they'd never seen before. Athanate and Were don't cross-infuse, yet here I was. I'd successfully changed to wolf and my Athanate fangs had manifested.

Unpredictable? More accurately, they had no idea what I was going to do.

"On top of that, you're the leader of House Farrell, with an additional set of expectations and urges."

"Got that," I muttered.

Pia moved around behind the sofa and her thumbs began to press down into my shoulder muscles, forcing me to loosen up.

"You want to walk me through what happened?" Bian said.

It wasn't a request. I opened my eyes to look around. Everyone else was gone. It was just my kin, David, Pia and Bian.

"I was feeling great," I said, "leaning on Alex and just soaking up a good feeling from everyone."

"You mean literally?" Bian said. "Using eukori?"

I nodded.

"You could reach everyone in the room?"

"Yeah."

She seemed surprised. "Okay. So, you were all relaxed. Then what happened when Julie and Keith came in?"

"I don't know exactly. It wasn't Julie. I just saw Keith and I thought...he's not House Farrell. He'd be a great addition to the House. Then it felt like a sort of insane jealousy and I had to have him in the House."

That moment of lost control might cost me Julie. I'd have a hard time convincing Keith to stay now. And that was before I got to start worrying about how Alex was reacting to this.

"Easy," Pia murmured, sensing my mood and digging the thumbs in even harder. "We excuse people who have lapses when the mania hits. It happens."

Much as I appreciated the support, Pia was wrong. She meant that Athanate going through crusis in a safe, controlled environment were allowed lapses. I wasn't in that environment. I had to be out here in the human world, and I couldn't afford a lapse like that in public.

I *had* to get myself under control.

Alex's hand slipped onto my thigh and squeezed gently. A little of the tension eased.

"Let me guess," Bian said. "You two were an item back in the army?"

I nodded miserably.

Alex squeezed again, and Jen took my hand in hers. My kin were upset, but not more than I was with myself. What if that'd happened outside, on the street?

"Okay," Bian said. "Let's look forward. We've dealt with the last of the Matlal. You've reached a compromise of sorts with the pack. Until Basilikos actually does something major, or something else changes, there's no immediate call on you. Sounds like an opportunity for recovery time."

"That sounds like a great idea," Jen said.

Yeah, it was. Unfortunately, my paranoia didn't think this recovery time was going to last more than a couple of hours.

"Just like Alex needed recovery time to heal his wounds," Bian was continuing, "it's the same sort of idea with crusis. You need to rest, you need to sleep, to let the brain deal with all the changes that are going on inside you."

"Amber's not sleeping well," Jen said.

"I bet," Bian snickered.

"No, it's not that—"

"I'm fine." I stopped. "I don't need a lot of sleep."

"You need it to integrate the changes, Amber," Pia said.

"And to keep you sharp."

"I'm fine," I said again. "Never been better. My reactions are quicker, all my senses are stronger, my body—"

"Really?" Bian dropped my hand and walked across to the door. The others were in the hall outside. Bian grabbed Julie and pulled her back in.

Julie's face was still pale with anger at the stunt I'd pulled on Keith.

"I'm sorry—" I started to say, but Bian cut me off.

"Deal with that later," she said. "Julie, Amber reckons she's operating at peak performance. What do you think?"

"Tell them," I said. She was quiet. "Julie?"

Her jaw was set in a hard line and her eyes were unflinching.

"Sorry, Boss. Not only what just happened. You're off your best. A long way off. Second guessing yourself. Erratic."

"What?" I couldn't believe it. "Gimme an example."

"Last night. No way the kid should have caught you like that. Wouldn't ever have, back in the unit. Not focusing. It's as if you're burning out."

"That's not fair. He was just a scared kid, and I was distracted by David calling me. And I'd been breathing in that wacky smoke…"

If I kept talking, I might convince myself. I could see the rest of them, however, weren't buying it. I shut up.

The trouble was, even if they were right, no matter how much I needed a rest, I couldn't afford it. And I didn't want to talk about what happened when I tried to sleep.

I was already a dangerous dilemma for House Altau.

Once I'd committed to becoming Athanate, I'd shot through into the final phase of crusis quicker than they believed possible. Athanate could not give birth. The only way to increase numbers was by infusing humans. The process of infusing caused the crusis, which normally lasted months, every Aspirant having to be shepherded through by a skilled Mentor.

If some Athanate variant in me had reduced that period to days, it was an enormous gain for the Athanate. If it reduced the risk of the process failing, it was an even bigger gain.

But now I was also infused with Were.

If I, in turn, infused a human, would they become a hybrid like me or an ordinary Athanate? Would it be quick? Would it be safe?

What if I bit another Athanate? I had to, as House Farrell; all the members of an Athanate House exchanged Blood.

Was this variant Blood I had a huge new opportunity or a dead end?

Diana had said she would run some controlled tests on me. I didn't trust anyone else to guide me through this, not even Skylur—and certainly not Naryn. Skylur's newly returned Diakon and I didn't see eye to eye on—well, anything. Bian and Pia, as skilled as they were, weren't skilled enough. And Diana had gone missing down in New Mexico, where House Romero might have crossed over from Panethus to Basilikos.

If House Altau couldn't trust me not to go biting humans, there was one obvious way to deal with it. Lock me up. I'd had enough of that in the army Obs unit, after I was bitten—not to mention my little stint in the psych ward, thanks to Noble.

And Altau didn't even know the full extent of my problem. In addition to the Athanate and Were, I had a spirit guide, Hana. That made me an Adept as well.

I didn't know what Athanate thought about hybrid Athanate and Adept. I did know the Adepts' opinion, which was that this mixture would be as volatile as the rest of it.

Jen and Julie were right. I wasn't sleeping. I dozed, but every time I sank down toward deep sleep all the monsters in my head came out to play.

I was fifteen when my dad died. He'd been a practical man every bit as much as a great father, and he'd helped me imagine a strongbox in my mind, where I could lock up everything bad that happened to me. Like him dying.

It'd worked from that time on, and I had lots of stuff that went in there. But two years ago, during that night in South America when I was bitten, things had started to happen that didn't fit so well into the strongbox. That'd been made worse by being used like a magic lightning conductor by Tullah's dragon spirit guide, Kaothos, when we rescued Jen. And then I'd used Athanate healing powers on Jen without really understanding what I was doing.

All on top of mind tampering that Petersen had used on me when I was being experimented on in the army observation unit, Obs.

If I understood Pia and Bian right, I needed sleep to recover, but now whenever I tried to sleep, the strongbox failed and all my nightmares came out to haunt me.

The rest of the room continued talking, unaware of the circling thoughts in my head.

"So what can we do?" Alex asked. "We're Amber's House. That has to count for something. We have to be able to help."

"You can," Bian said. She started to count things off on her fingers.

"Biting anyone isn't a good idea for Amber at the moment. She's not in control of herself and the sensations would make that worse. So keep Keith away from her, for instance. Anyone who you think might be a good candidate to join the House. Amber would probably agree and Athanate instincts might kick in."

They were all nodding. I wished they wouldn't talk as if I wasn't there.

"Same goes for sex," Bian said.

"What?" Both Jen and Alex.

"Guys, along with being a really fun thing, sex is important for Athanate. It lights up parts of the mind that bypass controls. Inhibitions get lowered and for new Athanate, there isn't much distinction between sex and feeding. It could get out of hand real quick."

Jen and Alex looked shocked, but they didn't argue.

"Pia, David, if she's not in bed and asleep," Bian said, "I want one of you with her at all times. I know you work for Jen now, but you'll just have to schedule it somehow."

"This is just a phase, isn't it?" Jen said. "Diana will come back, and Amber will be all right?"

Bian's lips pressed together in a thin line. "Diana is the one to fix this," she said.

Neither Jen nor Alex missed the evasion, but they didn't say anything.

What if Diana couldn't fix me? I'd go rogue or turn Basilikos. Either way, I'd made Diana swear to kill me if I did.

The rest of them looked at each other and nodded again. It was like a club I was excluded from.

"Okay, I—"

Bian's cell bleeped at her and she frowned at a message on the screen.

"It's Gray," she said to me. "He wants to meet both of us as soon as we can. I guess that's going to be when we're done with Naryn."

"Naryn?" I said.

She sighed. "Look, even though crusis mania isn't unusual, we still have to report any incidents. And the pair of you need a meeting to clear the air anyway."

Great. I wouldn't have minded Skylur knowing about the mania, and I only wished Diana was here for me to tell. But Naryn would love to have an excuse to lock me up, and/or disband House Farrell. Bian read my face. My relationship with Naryn—or lack thereof—was no secret. "Give me a couple of hours with him first," she said. "You rest. Chill. When I call, have Pia bring you out to Haven. If you're still in one piece after Naryn's finished with you, we can go together and see what Nick wants."

Chapter 5

Why Jen decided shopping would be a good way to keep me chilled while I waited to go see Naryn, I didn't know.

Alex had decided he suddenly felt too weak to come out with us, even when Jen said there was plenty of room to lie down in the back of the Cadillac limousine while we were in the mall.

Jen called in to the office and had them rearrange her schedule for the day. Pia's too. Then she'd switched off her cell. She'd made an effort, and I felt guilty that I was having trouble responding.

I was nervy. The people wandering through the mall seemed threatening in some way I couldn't quite pin down. I worried because I wasn't carrying a weapon, and I found myself rubbing my sweaty hands down my jeans.

Julie and Pia walked just behind us. Both of them were discreetly armed. I kept reminding myself I'd trusted Julie with my life more times than I could count. There was no reason to worry. However upset she'd been that I pulled fangs on her husband, she'd managed to put it aside like a pro for the moment.

Keith was another matter. I had spoken to him for a few minutes and apologized, but it was going to take much more to make things better between us.

He'd been angry. Angry that I'd genuinely frightened him. Angry that Julie might be in danger from me. Angry that Julie still felt a commitment to me and Jen.

I wasn't sure what I could do to fix things with him. But if I didn't, I couldn't expect Julie to stay. That thought really hurt.

Sensing my mood, Jen laced her arm through mine and guided me towards a casual clothing shop.

"Not more jeans?" I said. She'd bought me some last week.

"Can't deny, you're surely hard on clothes, honey," she said, exaggerating her twang.

We came out after only ten minutes, so I couldn't really complain. I even carried our purchases so Julie and Pia could keep their hands free.

"Home?" I asked, turning back hopefully.

"Oh, no."

I groaned, only partly joking, but I couldn't manage to be miserable for long. Not with Jen.

Sure enough, within minutes her wicked humor had wriggled its way under my mood until I was laughing. Shopping with her was certainly different. More fun than with anyone else, and after a while I was following her blindly, shopping bags hanging off me like a hat stand, not even bothering to look at the store fronts.

The snickers from Julie and Pia snapped me out of it.

I blinked and saw the dimly-lit, near-naked mannequins that were artistically posed on the walls like a frozen ballet. We'd just walked into *Tenero e Intima*, the ritziest, sexiest Italian lingerie shop in the entire state of Colorado.

The kind of lingerie I might like to take a look at alone. Secretly.

But with Jen, and in front of everyone? This was supposed to keep me calm? I gritted my teeth and forced a smile.

No one ever died from embarrassment, said Tara in my head.

We walked out twenty minutes later with me carrying Jen's distinctive, pink and black *Tenero e Intima* shopping bag front and center.

For such skimpy little clothes they sure came in big packages. No one would be in any doubt where we'd been.

"What were you laughing about with the cashier?" I asked, nudging her with my hip.

"She was just saying that these would be wasted on a guy. They don't really appreciate them…"

Oh no.

"Jen. Quiet."

"…so I just said they weren't going to be wasted at all."

She realized I'd stopped and looked up.

We were standing in front of Mom.

"Mrs. Farrell." Jen recovered first. "Jennifer Kingslund. Jen, please."

"Yes, of course," Mom said. They shook hands awkwardly. "Stacy."

"Um. Look, why don't you try the coffee at Pietro's?" Jen nodded at the café across the way. "They do a great macchiato. We'll take these back to the car, and see you in a little while."

She left with Julie escorting her. Pia's eyes met mine and she strolled a few yards away. Close enough to keep an eye on me, far enough to give us some space.

Mom frowned and hugged me. "Does she have to hang around?" she whispered.

One of my sister's ideas was that I had fallen in with a cult. And yes, just like it would be with a cult, Pia was there because I couldn't be trusted on my own. The cult theory would get a boost from this. I'd have to find a way to defuse that, obviously without saying 'actually, I'm a vampire'.

"It's a security issue, Mom."

"I guess we could have coffee," Mom said eventually. "I hoped you'd drop in at home."

"It's—"

"Busy. I know." Her lips made a thin line of exasperation. "Dangerous as well, no doubt. Oh, come on."

We went into the café and sat down at a table in the window with our coffee. Pia sat a few tables away. A human wouldn't have been able to eavesdrop, but Pia could, of course.

Not that there was anything to eavesdrop on.

"How are you?" we both said at the same time. It broke the silence and we could smile.

"Well," I said. I felt awkward.

"You look tired," Mom replied. She was being tactful.

"There's a lot going on. Too much." And so much that I couldn't tell her.

Mom looked out the window at the stores outside. "This morning—"

"I'm waiting on a call," I said, on the defensive. "Jen needed to do some shopping."

"Yes, I could see that," she said. "Essentials."

She stopped, visibly biting off any more comments in that direction. She didn't approve of rolling eyes, but she had this Mom way of doing it without actually moving her eyes.

"They weren't for me," I said. I winced inwardly. I sounded like a teenager.

That got the non-moving eyeball roll again. "I heard what she was saying, and believe me, Amber, those..." she waved a hand, "underwear things *are* for you."

She bit her lip, her face screwing up as if she were about to burst into tears.

"What's wrong, Mom?" I knew I was causing her worries, and I just couldn't bear the thought of making her cry in front of everyone.

But she wasn't hiding tears. She started giggling.

The relief at seeing that set me off as well, and then the pair of us couldn't stop.

Curious looks from the other people in the café only made it worse.

"Oh, that's better," Mom said finally, blowing her nose. "Almost as good as a really good cry."

"I miss you, Mom," I said. "I really do, and I'm sorry I can't be around more."

"How are you really, my big little girl?" she said. The name she used to call me when it'd been just the three of us—Mom, Kath and me.

"Okay. Just okay. It's hard at the moment."

"I know." She sighed and wiped her eyes with a tissue. "Your friend from the FBI stopped by."

My heart missed a beat before she went on: "You know, Agent Ingram, that nice man from Texas."

"What did he want?" If he was trying to pressure me by hassling Mom—

"Oh, it was a courtesy call. Isn't he a wonderful old-fashioned southern gentleman?"

When he wants to be.

Mom didn't see any of that. "He couldn't tell me any more than you, of course. But he made a joke out of it—*if ah tol' you she was helpin' with inquiries, you'd get entirely the wrong idea.*" She got the accent quite well. She patted my hand. "I understand. You've gotten caught up in a federal operation because of that drug smuggling ring you helped the police with. Gangs and guns and big criminals. Horrible. You can't say anything without breaching their protocol."

I owed Ingram, big time. And he would know it. He hadn't told her anything she couldn't have found out reading between the lines in the paper, but because he'd said it, it was official.

"I suppose I should thank him for the extra security." Mom's eyes flickered across to Pia, who was carefully not smiling as she listened in.

"Ahh...yeah. Not everything is being provided by the FBI. Jen's funding full-time security, and running that is one of my main jobs at the moment." Well, not exactly a lie. I was officially Jen's head of security, but Pia was not part of Victor Gayle's security team.

"Well, that's so much better than being a PI," Mom said.

Hmm. My life had become much more dangerous than when I was getting half my income from tracking wandering spouses and the other half from reading clients' account files to figure out where their money was being stolen from.

I let it pass.

"I suppose, after this is all sorted out, you won't actually need to work?"

Mom made it a question, and we were back on awkward ground.

She meant that, as Jen's partner, any salary I made would be insignificant against Jen's money. If anyone else had said that to me, I might have bitten their heads off, but she was saying it because she preferred me to be safe. Trouble was, I'd be bored being safe, and that was something else I wasn't going to be able to explain clearly to her.

But, on the other hand, she hadn't come at this in the way my sister Kath had, calling me Jen's whore.

"I can't tell when it'll be finished." I evaded the question, which she noticed, but didn't follow up on.

"I'm concerned you're vulnerable at the moment." The way she said it, so carefully, showed it was something she'd spent a lot of time thinking about. She paused to sip her coffee and looked away. "I don't mean the physical danger, though God knows that's bad enough. I mean you might be in a place, you know, emotionally. You could be making some mistakes because you're confused."

"I'm not confused about Jen," I said gently.

"You'd think a mother would have some idea about her own daughter's true sexuality—" She stopped. "I'm sorry. I didn't mean to talk about this. She sat up straighter. "It's your decision, your personal life, Amber. I'm fully supportive of you. It's just I didn't see this coming." She faltered a bit. "That you would end up in a...a relationship with a woman. And it's fine, of course. I'm sure Ms. Kingslund is a wonderful person, despite what you hear."

"Jen *is* a wonderful person." It felt as if it should have been harder to say something like this to Mom, but with everything hitting me over the last couple of weeks, there was an element of becoming punch drunk. And for my Athanate, the issue was clear; there was no denying my kin. Not even to be kind to my Mom. "And I love her."

I knew Mom would have difficulty understanding. From her point of view, I'd known Jen for a month and it would be very quick for a human to make a commitment like that.

"Of course," she changed tack, "after meeting Alexander, and getting along so well with him, I have to say I thought you two would have been good together. And it's great that you're still friends, that you share interests. You should never turn your back on friends."

What she meant was that when I came to my senses, Alex would still be there. I could see the tracks in my mother's mind. Jen gets tired of me, Alex and I pick up. Little church marriage, white picket fence, grandchildren. Bang, bang, bang. Result.

Damn. This part was going to be even harder. There were things I couldn't tell Mom. Alex is a werewolf. I'm a vampire. But there were things I could tell her, difficult as they were. And better that she found out directly from me, rather than Kath picking up some gossip and telling her.

"Yeah. About that. About Alex." She looked at me as I hesitated. "It's not that simple."

"Simple!" She stopped herself from snorting and finished her coffee.

"No. You see, I love Alex as well."

"You can't. Oh, Amber! I mean, I understand that you think you love two people, but it's not possible. It'll only—"

"No, Mom. I'm different, okay? It's not one or the other. It's both. I can't explain. I know it sounds crazy, but it's the way it is."

"Everyone goes through a phase of thinking they're different. This *is* crazy. This sort of thing can't work. I mean, does Alex know? What does he think of it?"

"Both of them know, and they both understand."

Well, that was true as far as it went. I was working on the rest.

But Mom didn't understand. And it looked as if I'd convinced her I was unstable.

I should be telling her that I couldn't have children. I knew that would be her next question. But I was lucky; I was wrong about that.

Instead, her eyes strayed across to Pia. She edged her chair closer to the table and dropped her voice.

"I read up on it, you know," she said.

I missed the connection and blinked in confusion.

"PTSD," she said the initials slowly, with the carefulness of unfamiliarity. "And I looked up lots of information on women in the military, too."

I sat back with a little hum of acknowledgment. I guessed this meant that she accepted that Kath had been lying when she'd told everyone I had never been in the military. But where was she going with this?

"I understand things happen to women in the military." She hurried on as I started to frown. "Also that combat experiences affect women badly. And how some unscrupulous groups recreate the sense of regulation to take advantage of the institutionalization of some veterans."

"Whoa, Mom. Hold it. Please." I reached across and took her hands. "Listen. I wasn't raped in the army. I loved my life in the unit. Yes, there was something that happened in combat, but like all the operational stuff in my unit, I can't tell you anything about it. I wish I could, but I can't." I felt a prickle of sweat on my brow. This was getting close. "I can't say it hasn't permanently affected me, and it's part of the reason I'm living an…unconventional lifestyle. But I'm okay with that. And I'm not in the clutches of some weird cult. Honestly."

She squeezed my hands, tears glistening in her eyes. I felt them too. I wanted so much to tell her everything, knowing she'd find a way to reassure me it would all end up well.

"I know how hard this is for you," I said. "Believe me, it's hard for me, too. I know I don't say it often enough, but thanks for just being you. Thanks for going and reading up and finding ways to fix your crazy daughter."

She managed a smile at that. "You're so strong," she said. "I'm worried I'm no use to you any more."

"Mom, if I'm strong, it's because you always were."

"I wasn't strong. When Blane died, you were always the one—"

"No. All I did was work hard. I couldn't have done that if I hadn't known there was something there to work for. Us. I knew you were there, all the time, holding us together."

It hurt that she was so upset, and it hurt even worse that I couldn't do anything about it, and the feeling that the distance would grow between us, unless I could tell her.

I couldn't tell her, and I wasn't going to outright lie either. The best I could do at the moment was to control the flow of bad news.

I took our cups for a refill while she sat there. I glanced across and saw sympathy in Pia's watchful eyes.

The whole situation made me angry, and even more in favor of Emergence. If I could explain to Mom about being Athanate and the changes I'd gone through, at least she'd know the reasons why I was acting the way I was.

"That wasn't really what I wanted to talk about," she said when I returned.

I suspected that there was only one other topic that would be on her mind, and I was right.

"What's happened between you and Kathleen?"

"We had a discussion about her recent behavior. It's best if we don't talk to each other. Same goes for talking about each other."

"It's not just that. She's stopped talking to me as well."

I shrugged and avoided her eye.

As far as I was concerned, that was an improvement on spreading lies about me, but it would be upsetting for Mom. I knew I should be more upset, that I should do something, but Kath had gone too far.

"I think she's drinking again."

She never stopped, I thought. *Just drinks less sometimes.*

It'd never gotten to be a problem at her work, but I'd been aware for a long time that she drank too much.

Despite my silence, Mom knew what I was thinking. "No, Amber, listen to me. She went through this once before. It was just after you left to go into the army. She was so upset about that and she fell in with the wrong crowd."

"She snapped out of it," I said. However badly she'd fallen behind in her schoolwork that year after I'd joined the army, her final results were excellent.

Despite my outward indifference, this conversation was upsetting me, and I could see Pia was picking up on that, shifting nervously in her seat. This wasn't at all what Bian had suggested I should be doing.

Why was it so annoying? Because I didn't want to be concerned. I didn't want to care about whatever mess my sister was making of her life. And it wasn't quite that easy.

"Or maybe you talked her out of it, last time," I added as an afterthought.

"I had the chance then, because she lived at home. I never got to the bottom of it all, but I know it was something that was set off by your leaving."

"All my fault, then?" the demon in my throat said childishly.

From the corner of my eye, I saw Pia take a call.

"No!" Mom said. "Stop that."

"I'm sorry," I said. "I didn't mean it."

Mom took a deep breath. "It wasn't your fault, but she missed her big sister so much she made some bad decisions."

And when her big sister came back, what did she do? Made even worse decisions.

"Mom, she's a grown woman now. I'm not my sister's keeper." I felt awful for saying it. Not for Kath, but for Mom. "I'm not responsible for her. She's done everything she could to drive me away."

"But can't you see? She was so worried, she got that nice psychiatrist you're seeing—"

"No!" I snapped. "She had me abducted off the street—"

"Amber!" Mom's face stopped me from blurting out everything that had happened. Waking up strapped down to a gurney with that 'nice psychiatrist', Dr. Noble, leering at me.

"It was just a deprogramming treatment he recommended. They didn't abduct you really. You're upset and you're exaggerating. Kath was only doing what she thought was best for you."

I was upset, but I wasn't exaggerating, and I couldn't talk about this anymore.

"I wasn't seeing Dr. Noble about psychiatric issues. And he wasn't nice in any sense of the word."

Pia had finished her call. She stood and tapped her watch.

"Mom, I've got to go," I said. There were tears in her eyes again, and that hurt. It hurt even more that she was trying to hide how upset she was from me.

However upset I'd been today, I loved her and my heart ached. I needed to fix this, but I couldn't until I got out from under everything else, and maybe not even then.

"I'll talk to Kath when I can, but that's not going to be soon."

I didn't mean that the way it sounded. Or maybe I did. I didn't want to talk to Kath, and I wanted soon to mean any time up to the slow, cold death of the sun. I'd made it worse by saying that; it would have been better to say nothing. I was losing the art of talking to my own mother. Did all Athanate go through this?

Right now, I had Naryn to worry about.

"I'm sorry," I said, which felt completely inadequate. "Love you." I gave her a kiss. It made me even more miserable.

I had to turn my back on her tears.

Chapter 6

We met Jen and Julie coming back, turned them around and trotted to the car.

I turned my cell back on. Missed calls, one of them from Agent Ingram.

I grimaced. He'd want some payback for releasing Keith and talking to Mom. I was okay with that.

It had become clear to me that Ingram was considerably more senior in the FBI than he let on. Diana had identified him as a possible ally in the plans for Emergence—someone who could get us meetings with senior levels of law enforcement, and ultimately to a meeting with the president. I needed to keep him happy, but there wasn't much more I could do without Diana.

A couple of calls from Olivia about an hour ago.

The other call was from Ricky, Olivia's lover, and it was followed by a text message.

URGENT! CALL ME!

As well as being Alex's friend, Ricky was one of Felix Larimer's lieutenants, and an urgent message from him was something I needed to respond to. Beyond that, I also felt I owed him. I'd encouraged Alex's secretary, Olivia, to act on her feelings for Ricky, and then Alex and I had recruited Olivia into our pack, which had to have put Ricky in an awkward position with Felix. It hadn't been intentional; Olivia was one of those werewolves who were unable to change and I'd promised to help her. That, and her being present when Alex and I formed a pack, had sealed the deal for her.

Pia was driving, so I had time to call Ricky. Whatever was urgent wouldn't trump explaining myself to Naryn, would it?

"It's Olivia," he said immediately when I called. "She's in danger."

Pia had just taken the car up the ramp onto the interstate. I signed her to keep it slow; we might be coming right back off.

"Tell me," I said to Ricky.

"She got into an argument with some of the pack."

"They wouldn't hurt her, would they?"

Pack on pack? They were rough with each other, but not dangerously so. And which idiot in the pack would antagonize Ricky?

"They wouldn't have, but she panicked. She couldn't get hold of you or Alex, I'm out of town, and Felix and Silas are busy."

"Where did she go, Ricky?"

"Nick Gray."

I laughed. "Good call. She'll be fine. Nick won't let anyone hurt her." It'd take a lot of pack members to threaten the skinwalker. His Kodiak bear form must have weighed in at half a ton.

"No, it's not good."

I knew this was only going to get me into more trouble, but Olivia was part of my Were pack and my Athanate House. I couldn't ignore this.

"Tell me where to go," I said, "then explain why it's a problem while we get there."

Talking pack issues made me open my Were senses. I'd kept them suppressed, afraid that it'd trigger something in me. Opening up, I got an immediate touch on my pack's Call.

The Call was a communication that a pack shared. It had a vague sense of direction, and emotions leaked through it. Emotions like the fear that Olivia was feeling at this moment. And Nick was there too; more a presence than an emotion, but touching me through the Call.

Ricky's voice distracted me. He gave me the address of an apartment building next to the railroad tracks in Arvada, not half a mile from where Detective Clayton had been killed in his single-wide last week. Luckily, we were already heading in the right direction. It felt right in the Call as well.

Pia fed the address into the GPS, while Jen called Bian to tell her what was happening. I winced as I imagined Naryn's reaction.

"Okay, we're on our way," I said to Ricky. "Now, what's this all about?"

"It started out with her old boyfriend and a couple of his friends wanting to persuade her to come back into the pack."

"What right do they have?"

"None. They're boneheads."

But it did show that the pack wasn't completely happy with the arrangement that Felix, Alex and I had managed.

I understood the old boyfriend complication. Alex had explained it to me. Guys that brought their girlfriends into the pack felt a sense of ownership. Given the ratio of male to female werewolves, some female wolves had a couple of partners. But Olivia hadn't made that choice. She'd decided Ricky was plenty for her. The old boyfriend would have been pissed to lose Olivia, but he couldn't do anything about it. Ricky was senior.

But losing Olivia from the pack—it might have made some twisted sense to him that he could be the one to try and get her back.

"Nick picked her up and took her to his apartment, thinking that would defuse it. It didn't. The other guys followed. That's when Olivia called me." I heard Ricky take some deep breaths. "Here's the situation, from my point of view. Getting Felix or Alex involved as pack alphas would make it official, and then everyone will want to have their say, and everything will be talked about. That brings the focus back on having two packs sharing territory. Now, I'm talking out of turn here, but my advice is that the longer you let it go, the more used to it people get and the easier it'll be to keep it going."

"Okay. I'm listening."

"You're not your pack alpha. You're an alpha pair, but Alex is dominant in wolf form. You deal with these boneheads, and it remains unofficial. Kick their asses and those guys won't want everyone to know what they did. I'm on my way back now, and when I get there, believe me, they'll be sorry they started this. It won't happen again. But none of that applies if someone gets killed, or Nick gets any more involved. Or anyone from outside the pack. Better if there's no one else, in fact—that'll give no reason for Felix to be involved."

"I can understand killing would make this official. What's that about Nick? He's not an alpha."

"He's a skinwalker. Were don't trust skinwalkers, and why should we? Noble was a skinwalker and he tricked us for years. The pack's all about belonging, and skinwalkers don't. If the boneheads make it about Nick, and he's part of your pack, we're back to square one."

"Okay." I sighed. I just had to work with it. "Got it. What's the situation now?"

"Nick and Olivia are in the apartment. The boneheads are outside, working themselves up or waiting for reinforcements. We don't know. They aren't answering calls from me, not surprisingly. Nick understands, and he's trying not to respond, but he'll have no choice if they break in."

Pia turned off toward Arvada.

"We're there in five," I said.

I was about to end the call when Ricky cleared his throat. "Look, there's something else you should know," he said. "Olivia doesn't want to talk about it."

"What?" It came out sharper than I intended. I had enough on my plate.

"She's next up."

I had to strain to hear him. "I don't understand," I said.

"Kyle, last week. He was the longest surviving of the halfies."

Halfy was the ugly name they had for Were who couldn't manage the change. And a Were that couldn't change died from it, in appalling pain.

Kyle Larsen had been a halfy. He'd died. He'd tried to change; almost the whole pack had been with him up at Bitter Hooks for his final desperate attempt, but their support hadn't helped. In the end, they'd had to kill him, as a mercy.

My breath caught in my throat.

"She's the longest surviving now?"

"Yeah. And this kind of thing doesn't help."

The cell went quiet.

I'd made a commitment to Olivia to help her. It wasn't anything to do with being Were or Athanate. My great-grandmother had been an Arapaho shaman called Speaks-to-Wolves, and I believed she'd helped Were who had trouble changing. Felix didn't believe it, but he'd given me a clue to chase: a necklace handed down through the family that was involved in the ritual. Unfortunately, I had found out a couple of days ago that my sister had thrown it away.

Had that ruined my chances of helping Olivia? Was it too late to find an alternative?

Pia turned into the road leading to Nick's apartment.

I needed to say something. "I'll do everything I can, Ricky."

"I know," he said, and his voice lowered. "She believes in you. Really does."

I ended the call and bit my lip.

No one had ever told me life had to be fair, or promised that problems would come at me one at a time. I just had to do what I could. And pray it was enough.

Chapter 7

"Amber, I gave Bian your message and she's on her way to help," Jen said as we came to a halt.

I groaned. "Ricky said no one else should get involved. I'll have to make this quick."

I had a head start on Bian and maybe ten minutes to deal with this. Me against three hyped-up werewolves. No killing them. Piece of cake.

The apartment building was old red brick, a rectangular block three stories tall and a half-dozen apartments wide. Dark rust stains from the iron balconies ran down the brickwork, looking like dried blood.

Ricky had said Nick was holed up in 312, on the top floor facing the railroad tracks.

The Nissan pickup truck that Nick had rented was parked on the side of the building, with a brand new Dodge Ram 1500 behind it, blocking it in. The Ram had tinted glass, a custom paintjob in gleaming midnight blues, and a bulging air scoop erupting out of the hood. I'd bet my last dollar that belonged to someone in the pack. There was no sign of them, but the building's front door was open and the lock busted.

One way of breaking things up would be to put a brick through that pretty truck's side window. They'd be down investigating the alarm quickly enough.

But this had to be kept private. The fewer witnesses the better. And catching them inside might work in my favor; narrow corridors would prevent them from getting behind me.

I wanted Julie with me so bad I could taste it, but Ricky had been clear. No one else.

Pia was unhappy. Bian had told her to stick with me and it took a direct order for her to stay in the car.

I slipped into the building's lobby and stopped dead.

This was like a nightmare that wouldn't go away. I could smell Matlal.

No! The Matlal in Denver are dead. This isn't a trap.

This must have been where they were staying when they were in Denver. Nick had tracked them down. He'd seen the boneheads following him and he'd decided to come here for a reason.

No witnesses?

It made sense. The place felt unused. Floors were bare concrete; the walls had marks and gouges where furniture had been moved carelessly. Along with Matlal, dust and decay, I could smell mold. And fresh scents of the pack.

I could hear them as well, screaming at Nick and Olivia and hammering on the door, swearing they were going to break it down if Olivia didn't come out.

I sprinted up the stairs, pausing only to check the echoing hallways. I didn't want a surprise coming up behind me, but the place seemed genuinely empty.

They were making so much noise they didn't hear me. They didn't even smell me until I was standing in the hallway.

I growled. I wasn't trying to change to wolf, but my throat made sounds that I couldn't normally. I had to swallow before I could speak, and even then, my voice was an octave lower.

"Ricky is going to be so pissed at you boys," I said.

"Farrell! You jumped-up bitch. We're going to fix this for good now." He was a big guy, body sculpted like a boxer, with a strut like a farmyard rooster. I made him as the ringleader, so he got Bone One as his target name. Neither Ricky's name nor my status seemed to have any effect on his intentions.

"Time for you to leave Denver," he snarled, and started stalking at me as if he were confident I would turn tail and run.

Bone Two followed. He was tall and gangly, with arms like a wrestler. He moved with a loose assurance in contrast to the tight, controlled actions of Bone One.

"Time for you children to learn manners," I said, and backed up till I had the stairwell on my right. Nothing like gravity and some hard steps to deliver a pounding to the unwary. They were still restricted by the width of the hallway to come at me one at a time, or lose the mobility of their arms.

Bone Two worried me. Bone One was too worked up to think straight. I couldn't see enough of Bone Three to make a judgment.

I didn't have any time, either. Bone One launched himself at me.

He showed he had experience fighting. In a bar, or on the street, especially given his Were strength, he'd be formidable. He relied on that strength, speed and aggression. Most opponents would be overwhelmed and quickly defeated.

Good thing I wasn't most opponents.

In this close-quarter roughhouse, the odds were against me: I was smaller and lighter than them; I had less reach; I wasn't as strong as they were. In my favor, I was quicker and stronger than they were expecting. Best of all, I was far, *far* more violent than they'd come up against before. Not wild violence. Studied, deliberate violence.

I couldn't avoid his grab for me, so I went in and met him, hard and fast. I shattered his nose with my forehead, while the heel of my right hand punched upwards and broke ribs. Then my left fist came up and slammed into his throat.

His arms flailed around to grab me. It was a bad idea to let him turn this into a trial of strength. I'd lose that. But I was too close to get away, and besides, the momentum was with me. So I kept straight on, shoving him back into Bone Two. When he stumbled and lost the opportunity to protect himself for a second, my knee went into his groin.

And when he doubled over in pain, I stiffened my hand and drove my knuckles into his eyes.

Bone One was out of it, and I lost a second pushing him down the stairwell.

In that second, Bone Two caught me.

This was bad. His arms pinned mine to my sides. He was too tall for me to hit him with my head and too smart to let me kick him in the balls.

I'd started to drop as he caught me, so I straightened my legs, using his grip on me to lift him. That surprised him, even more when I ran. He was off balance, but light-footed enough not to trip. We crashed into the wall behind him. His breath rushed out, but his body was braced.

I tried to stamp down on his foot. He nudged me off line, then he returned the favor, lifting me and running at the opposite wall.

We both grunted at the impact. It felt like a horse had fallen on me.

Short of dancing backwards and forwards like drunk teens at the prom, he had a couple of options. His best one was to wait for Bone Three to help him, but I was sure he was going to try and slam me into the floor. Until he did something like that, I was out of options.

Very, very bad.

There was a thud down the corridor that distracted him and I got my legs going, pushing him backwards again. He half tripped and I twisted in his grip and lowered my shoulder. When we hit the wall, the point of my shoulder went into his belly and then up at his ribcage.

He grunted again, but this time I screamed. That was the shoulder that Frank Hoben had damaged just before the Assembly. Even with Athanate healing, it wasn't a hundred percent, and it *hurt*.

There was another thud that I could feel through his body, and his grip loosened even more.

I heaved him away.

Olivia's third blow with the wooden chair leg broke it in two over his arm.

With his arm out, and his head wobbling dazedly around, he made an easy target. My punch to his jaw snapped his head to the side and he dropped to the ground, folding silently like an old coat.

Bone Three was cursing and struggling to stand up. Olivia had only hit him the once.

I kicked him onto his back and bent over him.

This time, my growl was pure liquid rage. It poured down onto him and pinned him to the floor. His eyes bugged and he started to shiver uncontrollably.

When I got my voice back, it came out low and cold. "Take your friends and get the hell out of here. Stay away from Olivia. If I ever see you again, I'll rip your throat out."

I stood back and let him scrabble to his feet.

Nick had come out of the apartment after Olivia, and now he lifted Bone Two up by his jacket like he was a trash bag. He dragged him downstairs. On the way he picked up Bone One, who was waving his arms feebly and croaking unintelligibly. Bone Two was completely out of it, his body hanging limp and his boots thumping down from step to step. Bone Three scurried after them.

I didn't think I'd see Bone Two or Three again. I wasn't sure about Bone One.

I watched them as far as the next floor and then turned to Olivia.

Of course she wouldn't have crouched and cringed in the room. She'd been waiting for the best time to come out and make it count. Nick couldn't get involved in the fighting, but she could. The pack probably expected her to.

I hadn't factored that in. I hadn't thought of it at all.

"That was great," I said, still panting from the effort. "Good work with the chair leg. Thanks."

She nodded jerkily, stepped in and hugged me.

I slowed my breathing, suddenly feeling dizzy.

She nuzzled against me, wolf-submissive, her spiky red hair tickling my cheek and her body trembling with adrenaline aftershock.

This was a good thing for the pack; it comforted her, reinforced the pack dynamics and fed my alpha ego. But it was more than that; it was mainlining werewolf feelgood into me. My lips pulled back in a silent snarl of pleasure and I struggled to get air into my lungs.

A good thing for the pack; not a good thing for me at the moment.

A thought bubbled up from my murky hindbrain: *There might be a way of saving Olivia without any Adept magic or rituals. Make her a hybrid like me.*

I felt the Athanate fangs pulse in my jaw.

She sensed my body stiffening and looked up.

"Oh." She gulped. I could feel her willing herself to stop trembling, and very deliberately, she rested against me, head tilted back and throat exposed. What was she doing?

"I understand pack means House as well for you, and I understand about the Athanate side of things," she said, voice strained. "I'm just nervous. I want you to know I'm cool with it."

"Huh?"

"The Blood…and the other stuff."

Not content with feeding me werewolf crack, she was now doing the same for the Athanate. She hadn't been willing to share herself in the pack, but she was committed enough to my pack and House that she was willing to be kin, with all that entailed.

She was safe from me in bed. Her neck, though, maybe not so safe.

Pia was following Nick up the stairs. She could feel what was going on, and she was worried I was going to lose it and start biting.

I forced a brief laugh, and managed to put the fangs away.

"Thanks." I kissed Olivia's forehead. "The Blood, yes, in time. The rest? It's not going to be like that. We'll have to talk it through sometime."

Bian came up the stairs as well.

She was wearing her college girl hoodie and jeans. She had a long sports bag slung over her shoulder, hiding her katana no doubt, and she carried her laptop. Prepared for anything.

"Just saw the cutest little truck take off in a hurry. Did I miss all the fun?"

"Yeah. *Pack* business all concluded."

"Hmm." Bian stood in front of me and looked thoughtfully between my face and Olivia's. "I have the impression Olivia's part of your House."

"She is."

"Then that makes it House Farrell business, Amber, and it makes it House Altau business too."

I nodded. Yup. Complications everywhere. Nothing in isolation.

"If it hadn't been important in the Athanate sense," she went on, "you'd have had no grounds for delaying your talk with Naryn. It was only because I convinced Naryn it was House business that he's not angry. Uh, let me rephrase that. Not any more angry."

"Thanks. I guess we should hurry out to Haven then."

"No." Bian turned her gaze onto Nick. "Since we're here, we might as well deal with your request for a meeting. That's Athanate business too, I'm guessing."

Her nose flared. "We could start with why this building smells of Matlal."

Nick shrugged.

"It belonged to them. This is one of the places they stayed when they were in Denver itself."

I'd expected Matlal's troops to be somewhere more luxurious, but it was well hidden.

Of course, Nick had warned me before what he wanted to talk about with the pair of us.

I'd let him introduce it. I'd pissed Bian off enough for one day.

Chapter 8

I guessed he wanted some privacy, so I sent Pia and Olivia down to the car.

"Let's sit down," Nick said, and led us back into the apartment.

It was clean and tidy—no mold or scuff marks, and it smelled of pine-scented cleaner and lemony air freshener. Doors off the main room were standing ajar, and showed a small bedroom and bathroom. French windows opened onto a tiny balcony which looked straight down onto the railroad tracks. A breakfast bar cut the room off from a cramped kitchen area, and the main space was taken up by a glass-topped coffee table surrounded by an old leather sofa and chairs.

It was cool, the windows open a crack to let the air in.

Nick detoured through the kitchen area and emerged with an icy six-pack of Fat Tire beer and a beige folder. He dropped them onto the coffee table and sat on the sofa.

I sat opposite him.

"Thanks for protecting Olivia," I said. "And thanks again for finding Bow Creek."

He nodded and offered us the beers. No glasses, of course. I twisted the cap off and took a swallow while I watched him and Bian try to outstare each other.

His long black hair was held back with a leather tie. That made his bronzed, sculptured cheeks look even more prominent. His marque was as unrevealing as his brown eyes. It felt a little different somehow. Between the apartment's cleaning products and the building's background scent of Matlal, I couldn't get a good fix on it. I shifted uneasily.

"About finding Bow Creek..." Bian left it hanging.

He snorted. "Insider information, of course."

"How?"

"In good time." He pulled a list out of the beige folder. "This is the list of names and faces that Correia handed over, which you passed on to me at the first briefing when we set up the hunt for the remainder of Matlal."

Bian glanced at it and nodded.

"Everyone on it is accounted for." He ran his finger down the list. "These are all dead, except for the six highlighted, who took flights out of the country immediately after Matlal's attempted coup failed at the Assembly. That includes Vega Martine, who traveled to Panama under a false name. She used a private jet from Centennial. In typical Basilikos fashion, Correia didn't bother to list the toru when she gave it to us, but I believe they were all at Bow Creek."

"Fine," Bian said. "The contract is concluded. Your fee will be paid as agreed. "

"Hmm. There's one more."

"Your informant?"

He nodded.

When Nick had first approached me, he'd said that informant was requesting asylum in House Farrell. I was dreading Bian's reaction.

"What does he want?" Bian said. "Safe passage?"

"That'd be kinda dumb. They couldn't hide in any Panethus domain, and Basilikos would have a price on their head."

"Oh, crap," Bian said. "Stop right there."

She pulled her laptop out and fetched a breakfast bar stool while it woke up. Then she perched it on the stool and checked that the webcam got all of us.

Damn. My meeting with Naryn was about to start with a videoconference on the subject I felt most unsure about—a Matlal renegade asking for asylum from House Farrell.

The laptop screen cleared and showed us Naryn. He was seated at a desk, wearing a headset. It looked as if he was working a couple of other computer systems at the same time.

He didn't look any more pissed than usual, but all we got was a nod of acknowledgment; most of his attention seemed to be focused elsewhere. Bian spoke to him briefly in Athanate before turning back to Nick.

"Okay. So for the record, you have performed according to the contract we set up, and exceeded it in the assistance you provided to House Farrell at Coykuti. Formally, thank you for that. You also found one of the Matlal willing to tell you where the others were, including Bow Creek. Now, what does he want in exchange?"

Bian still hadn't picked up on who it was.

"Asylum," Nick replied, and Bian nodded. That was what she'd been expecting. That was why she'd wanted Naryn linked in.

"With House Farrell," he finished.

It was the first time I'd seen Bian at a complete loss for words.

Naryn wasn't. "Asylum's not hers to give," he said. "This is Altau's mantle."

"I understand there is a way," Nick said. He looked calmer than he was underneath. Of course, he knew he wasn't fooling Bian and me; we could measure his heart rate.

"Sanctuary," Bian said, frowning.

"Sanctuary?" Naryn snapped. "That custom predates the Assembly."

Bian cleared her throat. "Well, I can't see there being any more meetings of the Assembly for a while. Maybe that puts us back to the old customs."

Naryn grunted. "Killing unwelcome visitors is an old custom too." But he didn't seem to turn it down outright.

"Could someone please explain to me what providing sanctuary means for an Athanate House?" I asked.

"It's the same basic structure that Skylur described when he allowed you leeway over having the colonel and his wife as part of your House without them needing to be kin," Bian said. "You remain entirely responsible to Skylur for all the actions of your House."

"So I take on someone Basilikos in a Panethus House…"

"You become responsible for them acting entirely as if they were Panethus. Or face the consequences."

"Great."

Yeah. I couldn't even be sure *I* wouldn't start behaving like Basilikos or turning rogue. If I took this on, I'd have someone else to look out for as well.

Nick took a sip of his beer. "I'm prepared to waive all my costs."

"Why?" Naryn beat Bian to it.

Nick shrugged. "Personal beliefs."

He'd talked to me about this kind of thing before. He'd been interested that I'd found a solution that scared the Confederation out of Denver without killing any more of them than we had to. He wanted to know why I'd done it and whether I'd do it again.

I guess I'd attracted this problem to myself.

But this attitude fit him; I believed him, I trusted him. He seemed to trust me. Maybe there was a way through this.

I noticed Bian and Naryn didn't argue his waiving of his fees. But would it influence their decision?

"So…where is this Matlal who's asking for asylum?" Bian said.

"Close by. Waiting for the all-clear."

Naryn stopped what he was doing on the side and turned to look right into the webcam. "Secured?"

"Not going anywhere, Diakon. But also not going to be handed over to be killed. I'm waiting for assurances."

Standoff.

I sat uncomfortably on the fence here. *Kill them all* had been my knee-jerk reaction after Bow Creek. But what would I have done if one of them had surrendered to me? What if that person wasn't part of what was happening at Bow Creek? Or they'd been compelled?

"Who is it?" Naryn said.

Nick flipped open the beige folder on the table. Inside was one of the flash cards that Bian had printed up for Nick and Verano to use in door-to-door searches.

I already knew it was the silver-haired woman. The one I'd fought in Cheesman Park when Larry had been captured. She'd been beating me until I was rescued by the arrival of the FBI.

It was news to the others.

"Oh, shit," Bian said, and grabbed her laptop. She started clicking and the screen split between a scowling Naryn and a database application. "Sex?"

"Female." Nick frowned in puzzlement.

Bian glared at him, while her fingers continued to click and type. "I got that, idiot. I probably have her bra size and favorite food in my files. I'm asking if you've had sex with her."

"That's not relevant," Nick said. It was the first time I'd seen him knocked off his stride.

"I'll take that as yes, then. And it's very relevant, because if she's screwed with your head, that's when she did it."

Alice Emerson, the Adept that served House Altau, had warned me about that. 'Aural sex', she had joked; sex with eukori.

"I am not under a compulsion," Nick said. "She didn't try anything like that."

"You say." Bian stopped hammering away at her laptop. "We're talking about Yelena Belyevolosova?"

On the laptop screen, Naryn frowned even more and leaned in toward the webcam. "Russian? Belyevolosova? Is that a real name? Yelena White-hair? How did that not raise an alert?"

Bian queried her computer again. "Files say she's a transfer from a Russian Basilikos House, Volkov. Before that, Chazov in Kursk." She snorted without humor. "Who did she piss off?"

Then she went still and clicked away for a couple more seconds, looking more and more unhappy at what she found in her intelligence files. "These entries were approved, but there's no certification. What the hell? Where is this information from?"

Basilikos Houses transferred members occasionally as a sign of good faith. I remembered Matlal had wanted me to be transferred to his House in Mexico when he first met me at the McIntire-Harriman charity ball. It made my skin crawl to remember. I felt the first shiver of sympathy for this woman, Yelena.

"Shit," Bian said, reaching some deep level of detail in her data. "Marlon."

Marlon Pruitt, her second-in-command, who'd sold out, or been duped and then compelled by Matlal's Diakon, Vega Martine. Everything he'd done in the last few days before the Assembly was suspect.

"Shit," she said again. "We can't assume we know anything about her."

"What can we deduce?" Naryn said. "Why has this woman named you, House Farrell?"

"I don't know. I guess it's because of Larry." Naryn might not have been completely up to date, so I went on. "Before the Assembly, I found one of Matlal's Athanate was House Romero, working under compulsion. I was trying to get him out, but it went wrong. He died. I guess making the attempt might show I'm open to alternatives."

"I'm aware of that situation." Naryn sat back. "One more thing we need to discuss."

Crap. I thought that had been accepted.

"Assuming she's from Russia and she was transferred into Matlal..." Bian and Naryn started to dissect what that might indicate about her intentions and reliability.

I sat back and thought about the tiny amount I knew about her. She was better than me at fighting. If Agent Ingram hadn't come along that night at Cheesman, I'd have been caught. That made her both a danger and an opportunity.

She'd given us the information about Bow Creek, if you looked at it one way. Or she'd sold out her companions, looked at another. Difficult weighing that.

"There's one other thing," Nick interrupted. "You've kinda assumed I was the one responsible for killing the last two Matlal in Denver while you were out at the ranch. That's not what happened. Those two were from the elite squad, coming here to kill her. They found me instead and they were damn good. She saved me."

Bian and Naryn took that on board and went back to their quickfire discussion in Athanate.

I stood up, restless.

Put myself in her position.

You're not supposed to do that. It messes with your objective assessment of the situation.

There's nothing objective about killing someone who's trying to surrender. That's what Naryn and Bian are talking about.

What should I do? I owed Nick. He owed her, and he'd made some kind of commitment to her. Why should I pick up that commitment?

Because Nick is Pack. Well, sort of. We hadn't discussed it; it just felt right.

Because if I'm co-alpha of the pack, his commitments are mine. Yeah, if.

Because I owe Nick for what he did at Coykuti. And the pair of them, him and this renegade, put their trust in me.

Damn it! I had enough going wrong.

I could feel the decision in my gut: I couldn't let Naryn hunt her down, or order me to do it. I had to take this on and forestall any decision by them.

As for where she was...

What would I do? Where would I be?

I knew. And it was time to get off the pot.

I walked to the French windows that led to the narrow balcony. The windows that had been left open a crack to let the fresh air in. I opened them all the way.

There was a sudden silence behind me as Bian and Nick looked around at what I was doing.

"Providing you had nothing to do with killing Larry or what went on at Bow Creek, I accept your request for sanctuary, Yelena," I spoke to the uninterested railroad tracks below. "Might as well come in now and swear. But I warn you, if you were part of either of those, I'll hunt you down and kill you."

I stepped back inside, turned and waited, my back to the cold air wafting in from outside. And any weapon that came through those windows.

Nothing like making a grand gesture.

Bian's katana was out and she'd risen to her feet. Nick remained seated, tension in every muscle.

A faint sound confirmed my guess had been correct. A whisper of cloth against brick as she slid down from the roof and onto the balcony, moving slowly and tensely, cat-cautious.

I could *feel* her, unfolding like some dark, poisonous orchid behind me. The brassy scent of Matlal and...*something* followed her in. The hairs on my neck stood up. I refused to turn around.

Naryn was asking what the hell was happening. Bian swung the laptop around until the webcam pointed at us.

When the woman spoke, her voice was quiet, controlled, with a slight Slavic accent.

"Your data is compromised. My name is not Belyevolosova. No more lies and disguises," she said. She sank down on one knee beside me, took my hand and bowed her head over it. "I am Yelena Vylkove. On my Blood, I had no part in the death of Larry Dixon and I was never at Bow Creek. I never used the children. I so swear, and I request sanctuary from House Farrell."

She spoke the truth. I knew it somehow.

Or she was a sociopath, able to lie undetectably like Noble.

Bian placed her katana deliberately on the chair. Her laptop keyboard started to rattle as her fingers raced across it. In his corner of the screen, I could see Naryn turn to his systems to hunt for information on the new name they'd been given.

I felt tension ratchet up in Yelena. Nick caught it, coming to his feet.

"We have to exchange oaths." Yelena pressed her forehead against my hand and spoke quietly a short version of the oath I'd given Skylur at the Assembly. "I petition the protection of House Farrell. I offer my Blood, life, loyalty and obedience to the House. I will honor the obligations and responsibilities of the House. I submit to the absolute rule of the House."

Yesss.

My Athanate was *way* ahead of the rest of me.

I remembered Skylur's closing sentences of his oath at the Assembly like they'd been carved on my heart. "Faith for faith. Blood for Blood. Life for life. I grant the rights and privileges within my gift."

"My Blood is yours," Yelena whispered. She sounded shocked.

"It is done," I finished.

I took my hand away before she could kiss it or anything like that. She rose silently to stand behind me.

I had a moment to wonder what I'd done before Bian won the race for digital information.

"Oh, shit," she said again, her voice barely a whisper as she grabbed her katana and swung it to face us.

Chapter 9

"What?" I asked.

The bright blade of the katana had my attention, but from the corner of my eye, I could see Nick frown and shake his head. He didn't know either. He was up on the balls of his feet now, but I didn't know if he was fast enough to stop Bian, if she took it into her head to attack.

Yelena knew why. I could feel it, but I didn't want to turn my head with that katana pointed at us.

"Step away, Amber." Bian's voice was strained and she had to clear her throat. "The new name she's given isn't Russian. It's Ukrainian. A small town in the delta of the Danube river, on the Black Sea."

My geography wasn't that good, but the mention of the area triggered it; Diana's briefing about the Athanate groups that weren't aligned with Panethus and Basilikos. The western reaches of the Black Sea were part of the oldest of the Athanate Domains, the deadliest, the most secretive: the Domain of Carpathia.

Shit.

Yelena was *not* what she appeared to be. There was only one reason I could think of that she'd have been pretending to be Basilikos.

I'd just given the sanctuary of my House to a Carpathian spy.

But then why tell us her real name and reveal that?

Bian wasn't waiting for her to clear that up. Her eyes had gone serpent-sharp and fixed.

I couldn't fight Bian, but I couldn't put my oath aside either. Blood for Blood: it wound its way through my veins like razor wire. Yelena was my House. Without thinking, I edged in front of her.

"Bian! Wait!" Naryn shouted from the little laptop speakers, following his order with a volley of Athanate.

The whole world seemed to hold its breath. Then Bian's blade tilted up gracefully. Not all the way. Just enough.

A little air made its way down into my lungs.

"Vylkove," Naryn said. He spoke a short question in Athanate.

I held up one hand. Yelena remained silent. Good, because that told me she was obeying me. Bad, maybe, because Naryn wouldn't like his authority challenged.

"I need to understand what's being said."

"He asks if I am *syndesmon*," Yelena said. "Sorry, there is no word for this, not even in your Athanate. Only in old Carpathian dialect. It means things like envoy and liaison." She huffed in frustration, her accent getting a little thicker. "Like ambassador, but responsible to both sides."

"As in Carpathia and Panethus together? I guess this would be a good thing?"

I wasn't watching Naryn. He wasn't the one standing in front of me with a katana in his hand.

Bian nodded, a tiny bob of her head. The tip of the katana floated up a few more inches.

"And are you this syndesmon thing?" I risked turning my head to look at Yelena.

"No. The last one was over five hundred years ago."

"So what are you?"

"House Farrell," she said without hesitation.

I frowned. I'd only given sanctuary, hadn't I?

Bian saw my puzzlement and her laugh was chopped off and humorless.

"She's right," she said. "She petitioned sanctuary, but the oath you used was for acceptance into your House. Congratulations, Round-eye."

"Does that work?"

Bian nodded.

Damn. I couldn't be trusted to tie my own shoelaces.

Yelena had gone very still. "If you didn't understand," she said slowly, looking down, "I do not think it is binding. I release you."

That made me smile. I wasn't the only one who could make grand gestures.

I stepped in front of her and waited till her eyes rose to meet mine. They were gray, like slate in the rain. Wary, watchful. Not scared. *That* was something to keep in mind. Bian's reputation intimidated people, but not this woman.

"I don't release you," I said.

She was keeping her face carefully blank, but she dropped her eyes again and nodded.

"What would make you syndesmon?" I said.

"Only the Domain of Carpathia can elect syndesmon."

The Domain. That meant all of them. A political issue right there I'd need to know about if I was to understand exactly what I'd just accepted into my House.

Naryn had kept his silence, and I wondered what to make of that. It'd been him who stopped Bian. Did he see some advantage here?

Bian wasn't happy with his intervention.

How to move this forward?

I turned back so I was standing half in front of Yelena.

"You say you didn't use the Matlal toru," Bian said, and the katana wove its hypnotic path lower again. "How could you avoid it?"

"I said I hadn't fed from the children. In Mexico, at the Matlal ranch where I was based in Sonora, there were no child toru. Those at Bow Creek were from his headquarters in Yucatán. For his use, and his lieutenants."

"But you fed from toru in Sonora?"

"I did."

The words made the room feel colder. In truth, I wasn't sure which made me feel worse, Basilikos for being monsters and feeding from the fear of their human Blood slaves, or a Carpathian spy who could go along with the practices to disguise her true origin.

The briefings I'd had so far hadn't progressed to telling me how Carpathians treated their human Blood donors. I wasn't sure anyone in Altau knew anything beyond old tales. And old tales in Athanate terms meant really old.

Yelena didn't seem to think feeding from toru was so bad. As House Farrell, that upset me, but it was something I would have to explore later.

"And here, in Denver?" Bian continued. "If you didn't use the toru, how have you survived?"

"None of the team at this apartment used the toru. We were the first to be here, in deep hiding. We had to make our own secret arrangements to begin. Then, once the rest arrived, there would have been too much traffic out to Bow Creek. We had small jobs that gave us chances with marai." She paused. "With humans."

She'd slipped into using a Basilikos name for humans. *Marai*. It was the Athanate word for cattle which didn't belong to anyone. I wondered if that showed how deep that Basilikos mindset had gone. I knew about working undercover from my time in Ops 4-10—the danger that the way you had to behave became the way you believed.

"What about you specifically?" Bian wasn't going to let her evade the question. "What did you do and where?"

Bian waited. I felt Yelena look at me, but I didn't offer support. I understood what Bian was doing—putting her under pressure, trying to catch Yelena in a lie.

"I was…a dancer at a club called Platinum Eye, not far from here."

A dancer. Could mean anything.

"That gives you money," Bian said. "What about Blood? You couldn't risk biting people in the club."

"No." Yelena turned her head away. "Sometimes, men at the club wanted a date."

Bian just stared at her until she went on, her voice getting more accented and harsher with anger. "Yes, I worked as a whore. Is that what you want to hear? Men who were visiting Denver, men who had too much to drink. They took me to their hotels and paid me. They got what they wanted; I got what I needed. Was honest exchange. No killing."

"And afterwards, they remembered nothing about being bitten?"

"Of course."

I tried to watch Nick as well. He didn't look as if this was new to him, but that wasn't the only thing I was looking for. He'd known the places to look. He understood the way hidden teams of Athanate would need to operate, what choices they'd have. The skinwalker was full of secrets.

"So much for Blood," Naryn said. "What about *Rahaimon*?"

Yelena's face was frozen, but her eyes grew even more angry. Still, she looked first at me. "He uses the Athanate word. You know it?"

I did. Athanate fed from humans, not just their Blood, but also their emotions. That's what Rahaimon meant. This was the big difference between Panethus and Basilikos. Panethus loved their kin and fed on that love returned. Basilikos despised humans and fed on fear and hate.

That's what I'd been told.

Naryn seemed to be trying to get Yelena on the defensive. Whatever he expected, she wasn't going to take a backwards step. She got progressively angrier as she spoke.

"Yes. I fed. Lust and ecstasy are easy to cause, like fear and hate. And next you will ask me if I have fed on fear. You want me to lie? They are all frightened at the start. I cannot help that. I fed on it, as any Athanate would. Rahaimon does not make difference between love and fear. Even your kin are afraid sometimes. Tell me this is not true. Tell me you do not feed on it. You train Aspirants how to hold new kin on their first bite to stop them struggling in panic and tearing their flesh when your fangs are in the neck. You Panethus make such a virtue of your kin and their love for you. The truth is that it is easier to make your kin love you than fear you for a long time. Your great virtue is simple practicality."

Bian's katana had returned to her side. Something in what Yelena had said, or the way she'd said it, had convinced Bian.

Not Naryn.

"It might seem so, from the outside," he said. "Tell me, Carpathian, what way do you think humans would choose?"

"What choice do kin have? You say you don't compel, but you do. Not with telergy, not force, but with the promise of long life and pleasure and desire."

Yelena had moved forward until she stood shoulder to shoulder with me. I put out my arm to stop her. Any further forward and Bian might reevaluate where that katana should be.

"What's the difference?" Yelena said. "Why does one way make a monster and the other does not?"

"Enough," I murmured. I was surprised when she subsided and slipped back behind me.

"Sorry, Mistress," she whispered.

A warm pulse of pleasure ran through me at her complete acceptance of my authority.

When she'd come through that window, I'd sensed danger from her. Now, her presence behind me was comforting. My Athanate had overridden my normal caution.

"Interesting philosophical questions," Bian said. The edge had gone from her voice. Her katana, however, still had the same fine edge to it and it hadn't gone away yet.

"It isn't philosophy," I said. "For Emergence, there is only what will be acceptable and what will not. New truths."

Bian's eyes flicked to mine.

"Speaking of which, has Vylkove told the truth, Bian?" Naryn said.

"I'm no Truth Sensor, but I don't think she's lied."

"She hasn't," I said.

They looked at me skeptically.

"I acknowledge your new member provisionally," Naryn said. "We're overdue for a long talk, House Farrell. Bian will bring you here. You better introduce your House to its new Matlal addition, then come to Haven and explain yourself."

Naryn's gaze went past my shoulder. His face remained blank and he said something in Athanate.

Yelena cleared her throat. "He's asking for a gift. It was traditional for petitioners who came for sanctuary to bring some sign of their good intentions."

"You're in my House now," I said. "But I guess you were hoping for sanctuary when you came in. If you had something prepared you might as well tell him."

I looked over my shoulder at her. She was very close. There was a frown marring her face.

"I did, but…" she stopped.

"What?" Bian said.

Yelena's eyes came up to mine. The dark had chased the gray out.

"It's okay," I said.

She leaned forward, her nose flaring. A chill spread across my chest.

"Please," she said. Her head tilted slightly, reaching.

I managed to keep still. It wasn't easy. I couldn't be sure whether it was Were or Athanate that was so concerned at letting her near my unprotected neck, but my body tensed. I overruled it. Yelena was House.

"No harm, Mistress," she whispered. The tip of her nose touched my skin and she inhaled slowly. Without my willing it, my eukori reached out and touched hers.

Eukori was always there. The part of an Athanate's marque that I felt in my head was the edge of eukori. With my House, I'd touched deeper. The bonds between us had allowed our eukori to merge. And with Jen and Alex, there were no boundaries. It had been as if our eukori became one.

Yelena's eukori was open to me. She was like lazy smoke, swirling around. Strangely familiar.

Then she rocked back on her heels, looking dizzy. Her eyes had become black river stone, dark as wells, glossy as sunlight on still water. What was she seeing? I sensed her fangs had manifested, but she kept her mouth closed.

"What?" Bian said again.

"It was difficult to be sure," she said. She opened her mouth. Fangs glinted and disappeared. Maybe that was Carpathian custom, to show good intentions. A little shiver went down my spine. What on earth was this all about?

She squeezed her eyes tight shut and then blinked and looked at Bian.

"This is my sanctuary gift to you. I have heard the Assembly argued about the Athanate that infused my Mistress: forgotten Panethus hiding in jungles of South America; outcast Basilikos; lost Theokos. All wrong."

"They were rogue, wherever they'd come from," I said.

Her eyes stayed fixed on mine. "Hmm. That may be important, or not."

"So? What are you saying?" Bian was getting impatient.

"That my Mistress was infused by an old, old House. A House lost to the world for two and a half thousand years. If I were still Carpathian, I would say welcome back. I would go down on bended knee and say welcome back House Chrysos, the Golden House, the lost House of Carpathia."

Chapter 10

Mayhem, predictably.

Bian hadn't even heard of Chrysos, but a Carpathian spy in Denver was enough to worry her.

Naryn had heard of them, but from what I could make out, what he'd heard lifted them into the realm of myth. He seemed unsure whether Yelena was telling the truth.

The more they asked, the more Yelena clammed up. She wouldn't answer in Athanate at all, and from her point of view, this was something she needed to discuss with me as her House first.

I was in the awkward position of defending her until I knew what it all meant for us.

Of course I had questions, too. Would the connection to House Chrysos affect my crusis mania? Did it explain why I'd become hybrid? Was there anything I could do that would help me get over crusis quickly and with more control?

I'd ask them as soon as I could, but that wasn't going to happen right now.

Eventually, Naryn sent a message to Skylur and he told Bian to bring me in to see him. Now.

Yelena was to be left with my House, not brought to Haven.

Downstairs, I took Yelena's arm as we left the building, Nick following us.

Across the lot, Pia got out of the car, nervous at the sudden appearance of Yelena with me. Julie was already standing outside, hand with pistol hidden in her jacket pocket, and scanning the area. Jen was stuck inside the car, no doubt fuming, but Julie could be quite adamant about security protocols.

I waved at them and stopped. This was unfair on the others, but I had no choice but to leave Yelena with them as their first introduction. Before I did that, though, there was stuff I wanted to get straight with Yelena. "Do you believe everything you said to Naryn about Panethus?"

"Not exactly." For the first time, she wouldn't meet my eyes. "I apologize, Mistress. I allowed Diakon Naryn's attitude to provoke me."

I snorted. "Works for me too. And tell me you aren't two and a half thousand years old."

"No." She understood my question immediately, which was a good sign. "All the scent marques of every major House are kept in the Library of Hutsul. We're not allowed out into the world without being able to identify every one of them, including the ones everyone thinks are lost, like Chrysos."

"And you didn't know until now?"

"No. I felt something when we fought in the park, and later when we were chasing you. There is a feel to your marque, not like other Panethus or Basilikos. But I didn't think anything more until we were standing so close."

"So I'm supposed to be House Chrysos?"

She shook her head. "Not unless the Domain officially adopts you as Carpathian." A hint of a smile twitched the corners of her mouth. "And although my…former House and association in Carpathia would welcome you, others would not."

"Okay. Well, good. I like being Farrell and I've got more than enough to handle at the moment. The rest will have to wait until later, when I get finished with Naryn." I had a million questions to ask, not least of which was how do you 'lose' a House, but the Diakon had been quite specific. I go to see him *now*.

I turned and poked a finger into Nick's chest. "Are you her kin?"

Yelena's eyes darkened again. Nick pushed his hands deep into his pockets and hunched his shoulders.

"I can't provide the right Blood."

"Neither can Alex for me. Come on, Skinwalker, in or out? And what about Ursula?"

"It's complicated."

I laughed. "Tell me about it. What about House Farrell, or Pack Deauville if you want to think of it like that?"

Nick's eyes slipped focus and he was looking far away. "I spent my life hiding what I am because none of the other Were trust skinwalkers. It's not easy. You're…different, but you need to be sure as well."

That surprised me. As far as I was concerned a skinwalker was a kind of Were, and I'd been expecting the usual Were enthusiasm. *Hell yeah*, or something. High fives. Then again, there was something far more deliberate and thoughtful about Nick.

"Aspirant then," I said. "Ursula?"

His eyes came back to me—beautiful brown, patterned like old walnut furniture, and as secretive as his eukori.

"You really need to talk this through with Larimer."

"You're telling me. So looking forward to it." I sighed and turned back to walk to the car. "I'm going to have to leave you with Pia to explain how the House works while I go crawl to Naryn. But first rule, Yelena, is that I'm Amber, not Mistress."

"There are things I need to tell you...Amber." She touched my arm.

"Well, we'll do it with the others. I don't keep secrets from my House."

"It's maybe not a good thing to do it too openly, too quick—"

"I understand that. But I want to be open with the rest of the House."

She glanced quickly, nervously, over at Pia. Was she having as much trouble reading me as I was reading her? Was she genuine? A huge advantage for my little House? A curse? A gift horse?

I squared up, right in front of her. "Listen to me, Dancing Girl. I've made my commitment to you, just the same as I have to every other member of my House: Athanate, Were, Adept and human. Don't abuse that and nothing you've done or been should be a problem. I expect honesty, not just to me, but to everyone in the House. You'll be judged on what you do from now on, not back whenever."

She nodded.

"And that honesty will include the reason you stayed here in Denver and decided to try and get adopted. If I believe what you say about that, I'll start to really trust you."

She nodded again.

Then she tilted her head back and offered me her throat.

I'd laughed about Skylur and Felix both wanting me to do that for them. Now that it was offered to me, the shock of the gesture rang through my body. My Athanate had formed a bond with Yelena as I'd spoken that oath, but this seemed to cement it in place.

It was too intense to handle now. I turned and pulled her with me to meet the gang.

Pia's eyes widened as she caught the Matlal marque. Julie, sensitive to Pia's signals, suddenly had her Sig out, not quite pointed at Yelena, but ready.

"Calm down, everyone," I said. "I'm sorry to spring this on you, but it's as much of a surprise to me as it is to you. This is Yelena Vylkove, the newest member of House Farrell, and formerly a Carpathian spy in Basilikos."

Yelena gave a little bow. "Greeting to House Farrell." Her voice had gone husky.

Pia recovered first. She stepped forward and spoke stiffly. "Pia Shirazi. Be welcome to House Farrell, Yelena Vylkove."

Not *twice welcome*. I wasn't an expert, but as I gauged it, she was being minimally polite.

It's not all my fault, I wanted to say. *I didn't realize what oath I was using.*

But I *had* wanted to give her sanctuary, and I *had* realized there might be more of a problem here.

When I was a sergeant in Ops 4-10, I'd been trained up to the point where I could rely on my instincts. Becoming an Athanate, then hybrid, then an Athanate House meant that my instincts were no longer safe. The trouble was, the Were side of me *liked* instinct, and as I'd shown a couple of times today, the Athanate side *liked* acquiring interesting members to my House.

Yelena and Pia exchanged stiff Athanate neck kisses.

Jen got out of the car, ignoring Julie's glare.

"Jennifer Kingslund, kin-Farrell." She put her hands on Yelena's upper arm. There was the tiniest hesitation as she leaned forward for the neck kiss, but whatever she saw seemed to decide her. "Twice welcome, Yelena."

They kissed necks, even though it wasn't the official Athanate custom for kin.

I could see the surprise in Yelena's eyes as she processed Jen's scent, and I could imagine what was going through her head. *Kin? Unbitten?*

Olivia didn't have any problem with Yelena; she just trusted the judgment that Nick and I had both made: "Olivia Todd. The Were don't do formal much. I guess Pack Deauville, and kin-Farrell? Welcome anyway."

I cleared my throat. "Ahh, no. Kin-Farrell means something more specific. Just House Farrell is fine."

Olivia ducked her head and blushed.

"Julie Alverson, security. Hi." Julie stuck her hand out. Minus the Sig, thankfully.

I tried not to grin. No neck kissing for Julie.

Yelena took the hand. I caught the quick flare of her nose again.

"And Nick Gray, who you all know already," I said to try and lessen the tension a bit. "Altau would prefer everyone to be in little Athanate boxes, so I'll be calling Nick and Olivia Aspirants."

Julie persuaded Jen to get back in the car. We were reasonably sure there weren't any more Matlal in Denver, but that wouldn't be much comfort if we got shot. Nick stayed outside with Julie to help keep the whole area under observation.

I gave Bian a wait-one-minute wave. She tapped her watch and frowned while I climbed in.

Pia was in the driver's seat; Olivia, Yelena, Jen and I were in the back.

Yelena's eyes were roaming over the shopping. The *Tenero e Intime* bags had to be on top, naturally. There was no judgment in her face, though, just a slight bewilderment.

I could imagine her asking herself what she'd landed in. Tough—she was in it now.

"Okay, practical things. Have you got documentation? American ID?"

Yelena nodded and pulled a passport and driver's license from her jacket pocket. I wasn't an expert, but I'd seen my share of fake documentation. These looked good.

I handed them back.

"Have you fed enough recently?" Her reactions made me suspect not.

"No." Her voice was strained.

Her eyes slipped to the side. Jen. Julie. Maybe even Olivia, not fully Were. None of them bitten.

It was very quiet in the car. Jen understood exactly what we were talking about.

Yelena had fed on Nick recently. Away from the confusion of smells in the apartment, I could tell she'd bitten him. But whatever it was in Blood that Athanate needed, Were couldn't provide enough of it.

A problem I would have to face with Alex in the future.

Today's problem was much sharper: Yelena needed Blood, now or soon. Pia's kin were already supplying Pia and David, and they weren't enough for those two, let alone another Athanate.

In a normal Athanate House, there were expectations of kin. The Master or Mistress of the House had Blood rights on everyone, including the kin. In fact, it was expected for him or her to exercise those rights regularly, to confirm the marque. Individual Athanate might bond, like Pia and David, and share kin. A Mentor would share kin with his or her Aspirants. Any kin might be called on in an emergency. Or when a new member arrived.

And of course, with Athanate, Blood and sex twined together. When was I going to pick that thorny knot apart, and how complex did it make this situation?

Echoes of Yelena's rant against Naryn rolled around in my head. In theory, in any Panethus House, a kin could refuse. That wasn't good enough for me. I'd had Pia working on a charter for House Farrell, where it said explicitly that kin chose to give Blood, or not, and the same for sex.

How should I treat Yelena?

I could tell her to go off and find her own Blood. She'd survived in Denver doing just that, and I wasn't worried about her running off. She could have done that at any time. Instead, she'd stopped feeding on unknowing humans. Even more important than that to me, she was in House Farrell now. To send her out would give a completely wrong message.

"It's a fundamental principle in House Farrell that kin are informed and consenting," I said. *Gods, I sounded like some pompous lecturer.* "Not drunk, high, dosed with pheromones, ordered by me, or plain compelled."

Yelena nodded acceptance.

I was expecting some kind of push back, but all I got from her was a look full of patience and trust. She was expecting me to sort this out.

Jen and Olivia both started to speak at the same time and stopped. They laughed in embarrassment, and Olivia got back in first.

"No, Jen, you're doing so much already, and…well. Time I did something, even though I'm half wolf. This one's on me." She slid across the seats, trying to make a joke of it, but the stress making her voice harsh. "Bite me, babe."

Joke or not, Yelena's eyes went dark and glittery, her face paled and her lungs began to labor. Her arm slipped sensuously around Olivia, whose eyes went wide. Yelena half-turned, pulling Olivia closer. Her breath rushed through lips that had gone soft in anticipation. Fangs appeared in her open mouth. Olivia looked at them as if hypnotized.

Oh, hell, it's going to happen right now. What if something goes wrong? Even if nothing goes wrong, what the hell am I going to tell Ricky?

"No." Pia leaned over the seat and reached out a hand to Yelena, speaking in the formal Athanate style. "My sister, wait just one hour. The hunger is deep upon you and Olivia's first should be gentle. With my kin, Gary and Leon, you can drink your fill."

I started to speak, but she anticipated my argument and turned to me.

"When I became a Mentor, it was a decision for my kin as well as me. They expect to be called on for this, and they would be offended if they weren't. Also, they're trained."

Trained. She meant that if Yelena got a little out of hand the twins wouldn't start thrashing and panicking, which would only make things worse. Trained also meant being able to read her signals and calm her down. And with two of them, they had a slim chance that they might be able to. On top of that, Yelena would need to take only half from each, making it easier for them to recover.

If it went the other way, if Yelena indulged herself with the attractive twins, mixed sex and Blood, how angry would Nick be? Damn, but running an Athanate House was hard enough without additional complications like these.

I'd seen Bian recover from Blood arousal. Diana had been there and warned me that many Athanate would not be able to control themselves. Yelena could. She shuddered and turned her head away, as if Olivia's face had become painfully bright to her eyes.

Then she came off the seat and knelt in the central space, surrounded by all the shopping bags. She took Pia's outstretched hand and pressed her lips to it.

"Thank you, sister."

She returned and sat back. I expected Olivia to move away, but she didn't. She threaded Yelena's arm around her and snuggled her head against her. "Rain check, I guess," she said brightly.

For all her bravado, her heart rate hadn't returned to normal. I couldn't decide whether it was brave or foolish.

Yelena liked it. "I will look forward to it, and I will not be rough, sister," she said. She kissed the redhead's hair gently and then tilted her head back and closed her eyes. It looked as if she was concentrating on her breathing.

Everyone was doing things for the House. Putting themselves in danger. Welcoming Yelena.

And everyone was relying on me, on my judgment, even though I was constantly getting everything wrong.

What if I was wrong about Yelena?

What damage might she do to my House?

How long could I go on making mistakes before I made one we couldn't come back from?

Chapter 11

Speaking of mistakes, I had a date to be dressed down by Naryn, one that I couldn't delay any longer.

"How deep is the shit I'm in?" I tried to make a joke of it with Bian in the car.

"This isn't funny." She shook her head. "You're not getting it. Put yourself in his shoes. He's been given the Denver mantle. That means he's responsible for what happens in Denver, but not in the human meaning of the word. In Athanate terms, Panethus can demand he receive the punishment due anyone in his mantle. You go rogue, and Panethus can have him executed."

I knew the way the Athanate law went; I was responsible in exactly the same way for members of my House. I just hadn't thought about it from Naryn's point of view.

"He knows you've been given a difficult task and your House needs a leader," she went on. "He also knows you've achieved a lot under difficult circumstances for Altau."

"But…" I prompted her.

"But he can't accept the risk of him and Skylur getting the blame for what you might do because of a crusis event we can't predict. Or because your wolf tips your Athanate over the edge. Or you simply do something wrong because you don't understand all the Athanate laws yet."

Yeah, what would I do in his shoes? I was silent as I let that sink in.

"I argued him back on the mania, based on Keith being an ex. I've pointed out you're a liaison with the wolves and a pack member, so this isn't just Athanate business and he doesn't want to upset Larimer if he can help it."

I cleared my throat. "Is that going to be enough?"

"With you taking a Carpathian spy into your House?" She sighed. "I don't know. It may depend on what Skylur thinks of it. *If* he's had time to respond to Naryn's messages."

Okay, Naryn had a tough job to do. I got that.

But was the way he behaved toward me solely because of that? I wasn't so sure.

This was going to be a helluva meeting.

We drove the rest of the way without talking.

Only a week ago, in the aftermath of the Assembly, the grounds of Haven had been a tent city. The need to absorb new Houses into Panethus in the shortest possible time had overridden the security issues. Every security team from every House had visited. Every inch of the property had been used.

Today it was silent and empty, still covered in snow from the freak storm we'd had.

We walked in through the main doors, and the place felt as empty inside as out.

"What's happened to the Bow Creek children?" I asked.

Bian grimaced. "About to be sent to Ireland. We negotiated a deal with House Glandore. They're…" she searched for a phrase, "specialists in dealing with trauma."

"Wasn't there anyone closer?" Some of the children didn't even speak English.

"We have Houses in North America that deal with this sort of thing, but everyone is on maximum alert against an attack by Basilikos."

"And here?" I gestured around. "By now, Basilikos knows where this place is."

Bian snorted. "Think of it as the Empty Fort Strategy, from Wang Jingzé's Thirty-Six Stratagems. Basilikos knows we know they know. They see a valuable location left obviously undefended. Therefore, it must be a trap."

"That's great," I said. "Except when it goes wrong. Don't we still have the Lyssae for protection?"

In the depths of Haven there was a room with living statues, the Lyssae. When they weren't being statues they were defenders of House Altau, and I'd guess each of them was worth as many as thirty Athanate. I'd met them and I wouldn't want to go up against them, not with all of Ops 4-10 at my back.

"Only Skylur or Diana would be able to control them," Bian said with a scowl.

So that would be a 'no'. I hoped the empty fort bluff worked. Losing Haven would be a huge blow for Altau.

The house wasn't as empty as it seemed. The children were in the main library, being looked after by Elizabetta's team, and Bian let me go in and see them.

It was a mistake; there wasn't anything I could do. Most of them were heavily sedated, asleep or staring blankly into space. It was eerily quiet.

There was food. Some of them had been awake enough to eat. No hamburgers or spicy tacos: rice, grains, bread and water. There were some plain fruits and nuts, which was good.

Gerardo and the girl who'd been hiding in the tool cabinets with him were awake.

They looked listlessly at us, but Gerardo's face changed when he realized who we were. He fought the drugs in his system to speak. "Devils," he whispered. "Devil women."

They were both wearing rough robes, which was all that had been found at Bow Creek. A supply of clothing was on its way, but I wondered if Elizabetta was going to be able to persuade them to get dressed. Would they even know how to tie shoelaces?

And worse, Gerardo and his friend didn't seem to have any idea of modesty or proper clothing. Their robes were hanging half open. Maybe they were dazed by the drugs, but I got the impression they just didn't care.

"Nos reuniremos de nuevo. I hope we will meet again," I said gently. "Nosotros puede habla. And we can talk."

"I will kill you," he slurred. "You steal my chance to be Matlal. I will kill you."

If he'd been able to, I thought he would have spat at me.

Bian pulled at me, her face utterly blank.

I bit my lip and turned away.

Was Matlal the worst of the Basilikos? Or were there other children like this, all over the world in Basilikos domains?

We got into the elevator.

"How long?" she said. She didn't press a floor button; she entered a code on the pad. Her fingers stabbed at the numbers, missing them. She had to do it twice.

I waited.

"How long," she said again, "after he was kidnapped, did it take him to stop crying for his parents? To realize that they weren't coming? To become that?"

I had no answer.

I'd seen glimpses of the Bian beneath the faces she projected to the world, but today was the first I'd seen of a pain like this.

She was still facing the elevator panel, her face hidden from me.

"Naryn's going to test you, Amber," she said. "He's going to need to know how things are going with the pack. About Larry and Yelena. About Keith and your kin. About obeying orders. He's going to pressure you and see how well you handle the stress. He'll give you orders you won't want to follow. How you handle all that is his overriding concern at the moment. If you don't pass, then he'll order me to put you in one of our security cells." She paused and half-turned her head to me. "I can't go against him in that situation."

I didn't feel there was anything I could say to that, so we went the rest of the way down in silence.

When the doors opened, it was to a dimly-lit cavern.

It was the first time I'd seen the Altau command center.

It looked like an abandoned TV news studio. There were the rows of tables with computer screens. Headsets, keyboards and mice lay on the tables. Rolling chairs were neatly docked against them. All the workstations were empty.

At the far end was a raised circular dais holding a huge desk shaped like a C. Naryn sat there in the middle of it, backlit by a curved wall of monitors. His head was bowed and he was listening to something on a headset. His eyes flicked dispassionately to us for a moment before he returned to concentrating on whatever he was listening to.

He was a short man, with black hair, olive skin and intense eyes. Even sitting, he managed to convey the impression of balance and power. He was dressed in tan chinos and a rumpled, pale blue shirt. A plate of drying sandwiches and a tall coffee mug sat forgotten on the desk.

As we neared, he pulled his headset mike away from his mouth and covered it with his hand.

"The facial recognition system isn't working again," he said quietly, without raising his head.

"Probably the same reason as last time." Bian woke up one of the closer workstations and her fingers danced over the keyboard and mouse. A vertical bank of screens behind Naryn began to display a changing selection of video feeds from airports and transportation hubs.

My mouth twisted. It looked like they were hacking all the security cameras in Colorado.

Naryn spoke Athanate quietly for a minute more before finishing the conversation and slipping the headset off.

He rubbed his face. He looked like I felt.

With Bian distracted, I decided to get in first.

On Tuesday, despite Haven being practically unmanned, not to mention completely snowbound, Naryn had come in to Denver to help against Noble and Colonel Petersen's troops. He was too late to join in the battle on Coykuti Mountain, but given the freak snowstorm, I was amazed he'd been able to get in at all. Also, once he grasped the situation, he hadn't wasted any time in arguments; he'd just concentrated on where he could make the most difference. A very different side of him from the angry Diakon of our previous meeting, who wanted nothing more than to lock me up.

"Thank you for your help with Emily and her family," I said. "It was a huge relief, being able to focus just on the problems with Larimer's pack."

"Working as a team can do that," he said.

I had enough of a feel for the way he came at things to realize the quiet start didn't bode well for the rest of this conversation. The longer he spoke gently, the rougher it was going to get.

"What I did," he said, "I would do for any member of Altau."

And *that* was a neat reminder of what Bian had said: I might be House Farrell, but I was still part of Altau, and as Diakon, he represented House Altau in Skylur's absence.

"That's how Athanate Houses work. The least of us can call on our resources, and expect support to the utmost of the House's abilities." He leaned back and motioned me to pull up a chair before concluding. "The justifications and accounting come afterward."

Ouch.

I sat opposite him. Bian continued her work on the computer systems. A second bank of monitors started displaying freeze-frame pictures of faces from the security cameras. The faces were progressively overlaid with patterns of neon-green triangles. At the end, they looked as if they'd been reconstructed from green wire.

"I understand there's been no challenge for the leadership of the pack," Naryn said. "How have you left the situation with Larimer?"

"We are, temporarily, a sub-pack."

"Who's we?"

"Alex and me. An unchanged Were called Olivia Todd. Maybe Nick Gray, the bounty hunter. Maybe Ursula Tennyson."

"That's Ursula Tennyson as in his lieutenant? And what about the person who I understand is Olivia's lover, Richard Olsen? He's a lieutenant as well, isn't he? As Alex was. Why not make a clean sweep of all Larimer's lieutenants, and try for Silas Falkner as well?"

I swallowed my anger. He was just trying to provoke me. Trying to see how much I was in control of myself.

"Because that's not what I'm trying to do, and this is not part of any plan," I said. "We don't want to challenge Felix or take over the pack. Felix is the right person to lead it. We just want to be an affiliate pack in the same territory. And my entire House qualifies as my pack. From my perspective I don't see a difference between House and pack."

His eyes didn't move to look at Bian, but I could almost see the way he was thinking. Naryn had been the Altau Diakon before Bian. Then he'd been in charge of Altau's clandestine spread of sub-Houses across the whole United States. One of the reasons he was back as Diakon in Denver was that Skylur felt I'd damaged Bian's integrity as Diakon; I'd made her too sympathetic to me. Naryn was making absolutely sure not to fall into that trap.

Bian had argued that my links to the pack were one reason for not locking me up.

If Naryn thought leaving me free was undermining the pack's stable structure, that argument failed. The thought of being locked up again spiked my adrenaline. I tried to take deeper breaths without being obvious about it.

Naryn noticed the change in my heart rate. He already thought I was a hair's breadth from rogue, and this wasn't helping.

Calm.

I forced my pulse back down again. Was it enough to convince him I could keep control?

His eyebrow arched, but all he said was, "How permanent is this arrangement with the pack?"

I wondered what he wanted to hear. That the situation was stable, and Pack Deauville would be staying in Denver? Or that we'd have to leave the area to remain a pack? I had a feeling Naryn wouldn't let me loose in the world without supervision.

"I don't know. When we met, the pack was in shock from the news about Noble. We made a case that we belonged in Denver just as much as they did. We refused to challenge and we submitted to Felix in front of them all. It worked, but what they're thinking now after they've had a chance to sleep on it, I'm not sure."

"Obviously, from today's incident, not everyone's happy. Can Larimer manage them? Is he secure?"

He was asking if Larimer was likely to have challenges that might split the pack. A fair question.

"Felix is still the alpha; they're doing what he says. But he can't go against fundamental things that affect the whole pack. The Call is like a..." I struggled to think of a way to describe it.

"Democratic voting system," Bian said, joining us. The software glitch had apparently been fixed.

"Yeah, but with a kind of feedback as well. Once the majority makes a decision, the rest of them feel pressure to come into line, and they will. At that point, Felix can't go against them. It hasn't been decided yet."

"And Larimer is in favor of this new structure?"

"Yes. I think he was trying to steer us toward it." After he'd offered to marry me as a way around the confrontation. I was still feeling dizzy from that. Kind of flattered, yes, but more bewildered. He'd been serious. Felix didn't do things halfway...

"If he moves too openly on something like this," Bian added, "he risks creating a counter effect. They might feel he was only doing it to avoid a challenge, for instance, and the pack wouldn't like that."

Naryn tilted back and drew a deep breath.

"Let me see if I've got this straight. There's an outcome on the fundamental structure of the pack still teetering in the balance. The Confederation threat has not been dismissed and was possibly made worse by your preemptive action in claiming an association between the pack and Altau. The pack has an ongoing internal problem of new Were who can't change, which you've stuck your nose into. All you have on your side is an alpha whose command structure you've compromised and who has to be cautious about his management of the pack in the structural changes you've proposed." Naryn paused, and my guts went into in free fall. "How do you think Larimer will feel about your taking a Basilikos into your House, which, as you've claimed, is the same as your sub-pack, and so part of his now?"

Oh, shit.

I hadn't seen that. I'd been so focused on what it felt like to me, as House Farrell, and then what Altau would say, I hadn't gotten around to thinking of the pack ramifications of Yelena. Dammit, Felix's wife and son had been killed by Basilikos.

Others might have the luxury of considering one thing at a time. I wasn't ever going to have that again, and it was time I got used to it.

"Not strictly Basilikos," I said as a delaying tactic while I tried to get my head around the depth of the mistake I'd made.

"No. *Strictly*, a spy from the Domain of Carpathia, the Athanate group whose standard operating procedure is to kill all Athanate intruders, which practice they are apparently now extending to formerly free cities like Istanbul."

I was in trouble on all sides.

Stop digging, said Tara in my head. *Stop reacting. Think about what will be necessary to fix this. Think!*

Tara was right. *I'm trying*, I replied testily. But my brain synapses were firing too slowly, like thick syrup was running through my neural pathways. A quick glance at Bian told me she agreed with Naryn.

But Larimer's reaction wasn't Naryn's primary concern. He was watching me, his eyes hawk-bright, seeing how I reacted.

My wolf wanted to snap at him, but I couldn't. I fought to get myself under control. "I'm sorry I acted without discussing it with you and Bian first," I said. "And I need to apologize to Felix as well, but I can emphasize to him that she's Carpathian rather than Basilikos. I'm confident I can manage that face to face."

Out of Naryn's line of sight, Bian's head dipped a fraction. Enough encouragement for me to go on.

"Taking it from where we are now, I can't go back on my word—"

"Yes, and neither can Altau. Not to you, not on the commitments you've made for Altau." He scowled and made an impatient gesture to sum it all up. "You've responded with knee jerk tactical decisions to complex situations and landed the whole of Panethus in a piss pot."

He was deliberately flipping between Were problems and Athanate problems.

And he was watching how I handled it, not listening to the arguments I made.

I'd underestimated him. Because I'd seen him angry before, I'd expected angry. But whatever his expression, he was ice-cold underneath. Well, I could do that too.

Keep telling yourself that.

Instead, I went on the attack. Maybe not the wisest action. "If you're talking about claiming an association with the pack to get the Confederation to stand down, I'm not backing down on that. House Tarez didn't think it was a problem, and since I haven't had Skylur on my back, I'm guessing he didn't think it was either. What would you have done? Gone in with all guns blazing in the middle of Denver?"

He couldn't deny that would have landed the whole paranormal world in the piss pot, as he put it. So he ignored it.

"Skylur hasn't had time, and Tarez knew nothing of the circumstances, so his opinion is of dubious validity," Naryn said, his tone deliberately dismissive. Baiting me again. "What do you think the Confederation is going to do? By now, they'll know the threat was empty. There's no way Altau can defend against the Confederation while we're completely committed to fighting off Basilikos."

"But Skylur himself talked about an association with the Denver pack."

"He didn't. He said they were allies. There's a big difference."

That was news to me. I was taken aback. "You abandon your allies?"

Naryn tightened his lips. He didn't like me questioning him. "If necessary. But Athanate cannot *ever* abandon associations. You've committed us to a fight with the Confederation that we can't—"

I could feel the heat rising in me, and I wanted to snarl. I opened my mouth.

"It's done," Bian interrupted both of us. "We can't go back and undo it. We have to focus on the threat from Basilikos before we can look at solving the crisis with the Were. Amber is right in one respect—it's fundamental to Emergence. We can't announce ourselves to humanity while we're having a war with the Were, or the Were are fighting each other, any more than we could while we're having a war with Basilikos."

Naryn turned to her. He surely hadn't missed her timely rescue, keeping me from shooting my mouth off. I didn't know if that would count against me or not. "Exactly how do you propose we avoid having a war with the Were?" Naryn said.

My turn to take the heat off Bian. "Make associations," I said. "The Confederation can't rely on a conflict between Basilikos and Panethus lasting forever. If they attack us while we're fighting Basilikos, that's as good as a declaration of an alliance with Basilikos. I don't think they want that."

"She has a point," Bian said.

Naryn waved it away. "It would be a better strategic decision to ally ourselves with the Confederation and impose them as a government on all Were, including Larimer."

"No!" It felt like he'd kicked me in the stomach. He couldn't be serious. Inside, my wolf scrabbled in panic at the thought. I had to fight her down.

"Why not?" Naryn said. "Put emotions aside and explain to me why we are better off associated with a pack who don't like us and who are in a vulnerable position?"

I couldn't answer rationally. But my Were side wouldn't let me consider an association with the Confederation. I was stuck. Right where Naryn wanted me.

"This is an order: put the case to Larimer," Naryn said, closing the topic. "Tell him we're not abandoning our association, but there's simply no assistance we can give at this stage. He has to make his peace with the Confederation, or face the consequences alone. Once he's within the Confederation, Altau can assist in peacefully preventing the encroachments on his authority or territory that he seems to be concerned about."

My hands clenched out of sight beneath the table, and I ground my teeth.

There was *no* chance of Felix making peace with the Confederation. I knew that through my Were side, but I couldn't explain it. And Naryn's sweetener about assistance wouldn't sway the argument an inch.

Naryn moved on before I could say anything, and he caught me by surprise again with something I hadn't seen coming.

"You've initiated a contact with the Empire of Heaven," he said. "That's completely unauthorized."

"You're wrong," said Bian. "Skylur wanted me to open a conversation with the Empire. His instructions were to make it tangential."

"And a discussion about dragon spirit guides is tangential?"

I took a deep breath. *Calm.* "That part was my fault," I said, trying to keep my voice even. "Bian didn't know, and I didn't realize it was such a sensitive topic."

"How could you—"

"Enough!" Bian interrupted him. "We cannot have this discussion without Skylur."

"You're no longer the Diakon of House Altau," Naryn said. "And I prefer to hear House Farrell answer for herself. Unless you feel she's incapable of taking responsibility for her own actions?"

The room went silent. I could feel the tension thrumming between the three of us.

This time it was Bian who reined herself in. "I had my instructions directly from Skylur. I have his full authority on contact with the Empire. You don't."

They stared at each other, but Bian wasn't backing down.

Naryn was far older than Bian, and far more dangerous. Skylur was out of communication, dealing with whatever problem had required him to rush down to LA. They'd have to live with any conflicts of authority Skylur had left.

Rather than let them build it any bigger than it was, I tried a diversion.

"If you don't want me talking to the Empire, I have a good idea."

They both looked at me.

"I make myself temporarily unavailable by going down to New Mexico to find Diana," I said. "I need to anyway—"

"No!" Naryn said. "You're barely under control as it is—"

"That's exactly why I need to go there!"

A slight sign from Bian. *Enough.*

"I'm not authorizing that." Naryn ignored my interruption. "Diana went there with Skylur's forbearance, not his permission. We know Matlal had a project to undermine House Romero—Correia told us that. Even if you were fully through crusis, while we still have no idea of the outcome, you can't just walk into potentially hostile territory."

"No potential about it. If Romero were still in control, they would have contacted us." Bian said. "No reports, no responses to our messages, nothing. After his message supporting the Basilikos arguments at the Assembly, I believe Jaworski's turned traitor and New Mexico is now Basilikos."

I frowned. Jaworski was an asshole, all right, but Diana hadn't thought he was a traitor.

So much for a diversion. They'd just found something else to argue about. At least it kept Naryn from baiting me.

I tried to break in again. "I could be in and out without Romero realizing it."

Naryn snorted and jerked his thumb at the screens behind him. "Those facial recognition systems? They were originally developed by Romero's IT division. You wouldn't even get out of the airport."

He sat back, looking tired, and I found I had some sympathy for him. He'd been handed an impossible task, running the Haven HQ with no one but Bian and a handful of kin to help, and he was making the best he could out of it.

I was one of the things making it impossible. It wasn't as if I didn't have experience dealing with authority when I wasn't in agreement—lots of that in the army—but I couldn't seem to find a way with Naryn. I understood the testing he was trying to achieve with me, but in doing that, he'd lost sight of the full picture. And I worried he was edging close to making one of the worst mistakes of command—giving orders he should know couldn't or wouldn't be obeyed.

"In my opinion, Diana behaved irresponsibly," he said, "but she's powerful and respected in all Athanate communities. If she really does need help, it would be even more irresponsible of me to send anyone alone. Doubly so for you." He stabbed a finger toward me. "And if she doesn't need help, if she's in the middle of some delicate negotiations, for instance, an uninvited intruder could ruin everything."

He ran his fingers through his hair. "It's not just that," he said. "We've just gotten a message from House Cooper in Bozeman. That Confederation lieutenant, Iversen, you sent packing from Denver—the one who's tasked with negotiating for the Confederation—he's been flagged at Bozeman airport. He, and several others, were boarding a flight down to New Mexico."

"They're skipping Colorado?"

Naryn looked bleakly at me. "I doubt it. More likely setting up a pincer attack. But in any event, New Mexico combines an unknown and volatile Athanate situation with a hostile Were presence. No way I'm sending you down there."

"I need to warn Felix about the Confederation."

Naryn's eyes hooded. "Yes. It's appropriate and within our capabilities at the moment to *inform* him. It'd provide pressure on him to do a deal. You shouldn't reveal that Haven is empty, while talking to him about our lack of resources."

There was silence for a minute. Every topic I'd brought up seemed to open another argument, so I waited it out.

Naryn had eased back from the confrontational style. That could be because he was finished testing me. But it could also be that this was the eye of the storm.

"Your...lapse this morning with your former lover," Naryn said. From the looks he and Bian exchanged, I gathered the conversation they'd had was heated. I was getting the toned-down version. "Any other Aspirant, under normal circumstances, would be under the supervision of a Mentor, in semi-isolation with trained kin attending. Any other Aspirant wouldn't be liable to turn wolf, wouldn't have been fighting rogue skinwalkers and rescuing toru," he waved his hand, "and so on. Putting all that aside, you're entering a critical phase. You're a heartbeat away from going rogue."

If only he knew how complex it was. And getting worse.

I needed Diana to help sort out my head. I needed her now.

"You're showing borderline stability on your Athanate side. What if you come across other former lovers? What if there's no one present to restrain you?"

I didn't have any other former lovers in Denver, but I knew that wasn't the point. I kept my mouth shut—barely. Top would have been proud.

"Anyway," Naryn went on, "it's my understanding that in wolf form, any tendency to go rogue is controlled in the presence of the alpha."

I nodded. Bian had gone very still, and I got a cold feeling down my spine.

"So you should be safer spending more time in the pack environment. Your House will have to do without you from time to time. Since you haven't bitten any of them yet, that's not such a problem."

"But I've just taken on Yelena. I have to make sure she's okay."

"Yes, your Carpathian recruit. I still haven't had an opportunity to discuss it fully with Skylur," he said. "We've exchanged a couple of messages. He approves Vylkove's incorporation into House Farrell on the same basis as the rest of the House—it remains your responsibility to ensure your whole House acts in the manner of a Panethus sub-House of Altau."

"It's asking a lot of her, without her full-time leadership and availability for her House," Bian said.

Naryn gave her a long, cold, *stop interfering* look. "I'm not taking her away completely." Naryn leaned on the desk, his voice going deceptively quiet. "But if you're saying they can't handle this, then I'll need to take over the running of the House myself. Would you prefer that?"

"No, Diakon," I said. My mouth had trouble forming the words. The Athanate hormone elethesine was pumping into my system. My body had gone still, but coiled tight like a spring. My jaw throbbed.

Naryn would know exactly what was happening.

I had to sit still and stay calm. I wedged my hands beneath my thighs to hide the trembling.

He waited.

Finally, he shook his head.

"You're barely under control. Go and stay at Coykuti. Your House can visit you there. Hopefully, Larimer will keep you stable from the wolf side. Tell him the situation and persuade him to make a deal with the Confederation. Maybe he'll even be able to come to terms with you having a Basilikos in your House."

I could hardly breathe.

I had a flashback to killing a Naga while I was in wolf form. The feel of his neck under my jaws. The crunch of bone and cartilage. My body felt like a thin wrapper around my wolf, and she wanted out. She wanted to leap across the table and attack Naryn.

Stop!

From his point of view, Naryn was being reasonable, even if he didn't realize Alex was my alpha, not Felix. Getting me to stay at Coykuti reduced the chances of my losing control and put me with people who could do something about it if it happened.

He hadn't ordered me locked up.

And if the Denver pack joined the Confederation, the problem with being allied to one side in a Were war disappeared. Neat solution for Altau. Not going to work. He didn't understand the Were at that fundamental level. When the Denver pack said *no*, I wasn't going to sway Felix.

But, as Diakon, it was his right to order me to try.

Even if that order was the trigger that sent me rogue.

I couldn't hear for the roaring in my head.

My vision narrowed down to a tunnel.

Bian was lifting me up.

I couldn't speak, which was a good thing.

She'd gotten me halfway to the elevator—halfway to safety—when he spoke again, calling out after us. "One last thing, House Farrell."

Something about the way he said it set off alarms. Bian felt it too. Her hand clamped on my arm so tightly I couldn't pull away.

"Haven is, as you've seen it, empty," said Naryn. "With this emergency, all our kin have been deployed elsewhere, including mine and Bian's. The last of them will be escorting Matlal's child toru to Ireland. That'll leave just Bian and me."

I knew that. It was a plain statement of fact, delivered casually, and it sent shivers down my spine.

"House Farrell has retained kin," he said.

Bian's hand tightened even more.

"They're not—" I managed to say.

Naryn surged to his feet, eyes narrowed in anger.

"Don't try that, House Farrell. You have a charter for an Athanate House. Skylur's decreed that your House operates like an Athanate House, whatever arrangements you make internally. You have human members, and as far as Athanate law's concerned, they're kin. I'm forced to remain here at Haven. I can't go hunting for Blood. I'm calling on you as a subordinate house to share kin while we're operating under this emergency."

Damn him. I wanted to scream. Instead, I focused on the pain in my arm from Bian's grip. Naryn's voice seemed to come from very far away.

"Your choice, Farrell. Either the humans in your House are kin, in which case I can call on them, or you're breaking the terms of the charter. Whether you've bitten them or not is irrelevant." He stared at me, challenging me to defy him. "Bian and I will need Blood tomorrow evening. Send your choice of kin."

Chapter 12

Bian's grip on my arm was like leopard claws digging into the flesh. My legs were rubber and my vision grayed out as I struggled to stop fangs or fur manifesting. I couldn't remember walking the rest of the way to the elevator.

I started to speak. "I don't want to hear it," she snapped.

Inside the elevator, as the doors were still closing, she thrust me against the side and pinned me there with her body.

"Let me go," I yelled.

Bian was stronger and quicker than me. My body, however, knew I was bigger than her, and I had more reach; I instinctively tried to struggle. A blur of a stomach punch, even one she held back on, was enough to stun me into gasping submission.

"Listen to me, Round-eye," she hissed in my ear. "We have about forty seconds where he can see us on the security camera, but he can't hear us. I'm sorry he's doing this to you, but he has every right to make this demand. You have to suck it up. If you fight him head on, he wins."

She wrenched my head around and planted a hard kiss on my lips, before pulling me closer so that our faces were pressed against each other's necks.

"Make it look good," she whispered.

Look good?

For the camera, dummy, said Tara.

I hugged Bian. I grabbed her ass. I wasn't sure what might look good to Naryn if he was watching, but if this was Bian's idea of a joke…

"Oh, that *is* good," she purred, rubbing herself against me and chewing my ear. "Now, ignore every frigging thing he told you to do. My gut says he's making the wrong call about Diana. However you do it, get Felix to cover for you. Go find Diana and bring her back. Call me if you need anything. If it makes the difference in getting her back, I'll disobey him and come down. Understood?"

I knew she and Diana were close, but the enormity of what she was offering still stunned me. "What if we're wrong?"

"We'll get locked up."

"And what about my House?" My voice sounded shaky. My whole body was burning with a white-hot anger that Naryn could order me around like that and there wasn't a thing I could do to stop it.

"I get tired of saying it, but *trust me*. I'll find some way."

"Wha—"

"Shut up. Fifteen seconds. I'm doing this because you and I have a legal loophole here. We're entitled to access to our Mentor, Diana. Whether that overrides everything else is a matter for discussion, but it's enough for the moment. Last message: Naryn's being an ass, but you're not helping. You've got to get yourself under better control."

"But—"

"Outta time."

The doors opened with a *ping*.

I followed her out into the corridor. My legs weren't any less rubbery. I was still burning with rage, but in a short elevator ride, Bian had turned it around in my head. Now there *was* something I could do. Something I could focus my anger on.

The feeling of wolf trying to claw herself out through my skin stopped.

The pulse in my jaw died away.

Bian didn't head for the front door.

"I've messaged David to collect you," she said, pulling me deeper into Haven. "You can talk to Vera while you wait."

At the door to the west conservatory, she stopped. She took my arm again to hold me back for a second.

I frowned. "What is it?"

"About Vera. Look, humans have differing reactions to Athanate healing. When you have someone as badly wounded as she was, the problem is twofold. You've got to heal the physical damage first, but you also have to deal with the mental damage."

"Like Jen?"

Bian waggled her hand. "Sort of similar. That was your way of healing for that type of injury; to literally strip out the emotional side. But in Vera's case, the problem was her mind *knew* she'd been shot fatally; there wasn't any emotional side to take out. I didn't want to screw with her memories without a lot more time to study her, which I didn't have."

"So…"

"The alternative was to flood her with euphorics, which is what I did."

I knew what they were. The Athanate glands in me pumped out happy scents when I was contented, and everyone around me got a bit of feel-good. With Bian's greater control, she could deliver a more potent version in her bite.

"It wears off though, doesn't it? She seemed okay…"

"It does wear off," Bian said. "But in different people, the aftereffects can be very different. Even taking that into account, Vera's recovery is...unusual. I'd call it post-euphoric mania. She's fine almost all the time, but every now and then she doesn't make complete sense."

We stepped inside, and I could see Vera dozing peacefully on a chaise, surrounded by lilies which nodded gently in the breeze from the open doors.

"You've been warned," Bian said. "I'd better get back."

Before she could go, I pulled her into a hug, and this time she decided it was her turn to grab my ass.

"Thanks," I whispered.

It was Leopard Bian looking up at me, grinning like a devil. Screwing up my courage, I kissed her. She let me off lightly; there was barely any tongue involved.

I watched her stride away, Leopard Bian turning back to Diakon Bian with every step.

She was scary. She was infuriating. She wasn't Jen or Alex. She wasn't kin. She was...great. And I did trust her, even with my House. She understood the principle I wanted in House Farrell—that all of us should do things because we wanted to, not because stronger people compelled us to. Not even because there were rules. What Naryn was trying to get me to do, to pick people out and order them to give him Blood, was against that. If it could be done, Bian would find a way to deflect Naryn.

If the cost of that was getting humped against a wall in the elevator, I'd take it and count it worth the price.

Vera woke as I approached.

"Amber, how lovely." She touched the coffee pot on the table beside her. "I'm afraid that's cold, but I know my way around Haven now. Should I make some more?"

"Not unless you're thirsty."

"Come on. It must have been a couple of hours since my last cup."

I carried the tray. I was proud and surprised that I'd gotten my reactions to Naryn under control to the point where the cup and saucer weren't rattling.

Vera led us to a kitchen area I'd never visited before. Somewhere, hidden below, there had to be an industrial kitchen for catering for Haven when it was full. The one on the ground floor was for show and light refreshments.

She decided against making a fresh pot and opted for the barista machine, which she clearly knew her way around.

"Leave it out—I'll make some for Naryn and Bian later," she said as I cleaned the pot.

She saw me flinch, and she'd probably already figured out exactly who'd upset me anyway.

"Not your favorite person?" she said.

"No." I glanced around. The whole house had security cameras, but I guessed he wouldn't learn anything he didn't know already.

Vera spotted that twitch too. Whatever mysterious symptoms Bian was referring to, Vera had made a remarkable recovery. In fact, she was looking better than ever, and certainly wasn't missing anything.

"He's a strange man," she said, handing me my mug of latte. The mug was one of Bian's little jokes; the print on the side advertised one of the blood donor operations down in Denver. "Naryn doesn't care for me, but since Jari's recruitment plan has started to come together—"

"I thought the Colonel was with Skylur in LA?"

"No, he's in Wyoming. The affiliate House in Cheyenne has a couple of ranches there, out in the middle of nowhere." She thought about that for a couple of seconds. "He's there with about fifty former members of the unit, and another hundred say they'll be there in the next month or so."

"It's going well?"

"These things are never quick enough for some people, but it looks like we'll have a couple of companies recruited to Altau. It'll be wonderful to see them again. Jari runs them through stages of revealing what's going on. If they commit fully to join, they get to learn about the Athanate from a couple of Altau he has with him from the local House. It looks like about eighty percent are joining. With their training, it improves our situation so much that even Naryn hasn't complained that they're not formally kin."

I didn't miss that she'd said 'we'll have' and 'our situation'. Vera wasn't one for sitting on the fence. If she was in, she was all in.

She typed a code on the security pad and opened the door to the gardens.

"Let's walk outside. The snow's still melting, but the paths are clear."

I was afraid she might think that there weren't any listening devices in the garden, but she didn't make any comments about Naryn. She chatted instead about the unit, what had happened, and her worry for the colonel's staff.

We sat on garden chairs in a little pavilion sun-trap, surrounded by snow-covered lawns.

"I'm amazed at how calmly you're taking what's happened over the last month," I said. She'd gone from being a respectable army wife in North Carolina to a fugitive from the FBI, and finally to hiding out here in the headquarters of the Panethus Athanate—a people she hadn't even known existed a few weeks ago.

She smiled. "Not a complete surprise. Of course, I knew Jari's concerns. And since arriving here, I've had nothing to do but doze and think. I had Bian to talk to for a couple of hours, as well." She sighed. "For Jari and me, this is wonderful. He doesn't see that yet, but he will."

"How do you mean?"

I got the distinct feeling she was going to roll her eyes, but she was too dignified to do that.

"Only someone who's never faced growing old could possibly ask that," she said instead.

"What, is that it?"

She laughed. "I rest my case." She flexed her hands, eyes intent on them as if she couldn't quite believe what she was seeing. "When every month takes another thing away from you, when every week sees another compromise with your body, when every day is a struggle, then the offer to be healthy again is more precious than gold. You're Athanate now. You'll never understand that, and you'll never understand how lucky that makes you, Amber."

"But…"

"Ah, yes. I make it sound as if we're being bought. How wonderful to be so fortunate to have that option, and how cynical I must sound. Let me put it another way. Think of all the other things we value from further up the hierarchy of needs—esteem, honor, friendship, trust, love, morality and that shabby old carry-all, self-actualization. They all seem devalued somehow when there's the constant threat that today your hands are going to be so painful that you can't open the bottle of pills." She lifted her hands again and rolled her wrists, delight written all over her face. "And that's before I get to talk about the growing silence, the numbness, and the way that faces, even familiar ones, seem to get vague around the edges, so you're not sure whether it's your eyes or your brain that's getting duller."

She laughed again; a bright, happy sound on a gloomy afternoon. "Heavens! No wonder Skylur is worried about how to reveal this to the rest of the world. The stampede!"

"Bian seems to have done a good job on you." It sounded rude and I wished I could snatch the words back, but Vera just laughed. "I mean you're looking fabulous," I finished lamely.

"She has. Holes mended, scars fading, body working properly and arthritis just *gone*. I know that's only a side effect of my treatment from Bian, and it's not permanent. What I really need to do is to persuade some poor, hapless Athanate that I am worthy to be kin." She flushed slightly. "I understand the term is, umm, encompassing. We'd have to see how that turns out. And I can't...well, Jari, you understand. I couldn't if he didn't feel completely happy with it."

She sat straighter and folded her hands precisely in front of her, looking out over the snowy lawns. I knew the colonel was fang-phobic. He was okay working with Altau, but he had a problem about being bitten.

And I believed her. If he said no, she'd turn down an offer to be kin. Give up all the health benefits she'd had.

As House, it was my responsibility to get my damned head out of the sand and plan for that. To deal with it, one way or another. Naryn had made that crystal clear.

Despite Bian's warnings about post-euphoric mania or whatever, it seemed to me that Vera was thinking more clearly than I was. Was there some way I could utilize that? If she was recovered, maybe it would be okay to move her to Manassah. How should I get her working with my House? I didn't have an established command structure like Altau. I had no Diakon, no lieutenants. I had no strategy, no plan for growth, not even an idea about how to increase the number of kin to a safe level. Maybe she would have ideas about how that structure and strategy should form.

At that moment, David came around the corner of the building.

"Mrs. Laine, Boss." He knelt casually in front of us, his eyes focused on me. "I have orders from Naryn to get you out to Coykuti, like right now."

His mouth twisted. He didn't think much of being ordered around by Naryn either. Unfortunately, we were all going to have to put up with it for a while.

"Okay. In a minute." I looked back at Vera. "Yeah. I understand what you're saying about the colonel. Being kin is a big step. He needs time. I'll do what I can to hold off on that."

Like what?

I had to stop making promises.

"I guess the relationship of Athanate and kin has developed over time, and Athanate aren't anxious to change what works," I said. "I suppose that shows how different we are."

"Oh, my dear, no," Vera said. "We're all human. There's more that we share than makes us different. And what makes us different is so wonderful. You see, Athanate are the great hope of humanity. You are angels who will lift us to the stars." She smiled and blinked. "That's except those that are devils, of course."

Ah.

Chapter 13

I tried not to think too much about whether I was a devil or an angel as David drove me to Coykuti. On the road, I called Pia using one of my secure cells, and talked her through everything that had happened.

In return, she gave me some insight into the dilemma Skylur and Naryn faced regarding Diana and the current political situation.

Skylur had to keep control of Panethus in order to counter Basilikos.

If a group of Panethus Houses were to leave the party, it could send a sign to Basilikos to escalate from their current probing assaults to an all-out attack.

When Skylur had claimed all of North America, he'd given an ultimatum to all other Houses in the area—become an Altau sub-House by giving him their personal oaths or leave the continent.

Some of those Houses had welcomed the inclusion in a larger Altau. The trouble was, not all of them had, and the ones that weren't happy were already diverting more effort than Altau could afford. Everyone knew there was a problem with House Romero in New Mexico. Everyone was watching to see how it was resolved.

Diana *might* be handling it, and my appearance in their mantle, uninvited, would almost certainly damage that. Diana was known for not communicating when she wanted to allow Skylur the option of denying any involvement in what she was doing, or how she was doing it.

If, if, if.

Bian and I didn't believe Diana was down there negotiating without communicating.

Maybe I could rely on the Athanate loophole Bian had mentioned— access to my Mentor. It wasn't as if that was a lie. I needed Diana to overcome my crusis. Maybe I could be there on Were business. That depended on Felix.

I didn't have a good enough grasp of what it would take to persuade Felix, however much I turned it around in my head as we sped toward Coykuti.

David had collected me in Jen's lovely pink Merc. He'd been looking for an excuse to drive it, and as far as he was concerned, you didn't notice the color so much when you were sitting inside. It did look completely out of place when he parked in front of the ranch house at Coykuti.

I just sat for a minute. I was looking at the midnight-blue Ram with the overdone air scoop that was here too. The Bonehead's car. I'd expected to see Ricky's fire-truck-red Ram maybe, but that wasn't here.

Crap.

I'd followed Ricky's advice. I hadn't made it official. I hadn't killed them. Only Olivia and I had been involved in the fighting, and Bian hadn't arrived until after the Boneheads had left. Why were they here? Had I given them a legitimate reason for complaining to Felix? Had I broken another obscure paranormal rule that I knew nothing about?

David gave my arm a squeeze. "Want me to come in?"

"No. This is wolf stuff for me alone, I think, but thanks anyway."

Ursula's van was here too. I wasn't sure if that was a good or bad sign.

I got out and closed the Merc's door gently. Coykuti's uncanny quiet seemed to reach out and crush the sound. There was no one in the work yard and the farm buildings' doors were all shut. I swiveled to the left, where the pack's ancient barn stood tiredly in the meadow. Nothing moved. I might have been visiting one of the mining ghost towns up in the mountains.

The ranch house felt empty, smelled empty. I could hear a noise from behind it, and I walked slowly around to the back. It was the sound of snipping—like garden shears. The air stirred and the scent of Felix's sister drifted down the slope. I couldn't see her, but the only place she could be was the little family cemetery.

Felix's sister, Martha, had driven me back to Denver once. I think we'd exchanged about twenty words on the half-hour drive. I'd started off thinking she was just uncommunicative, but by the end of that time, her watchfulness made me think I was being evaluated. That she'd talk when she decided whether I was worth talking to.

Have I passed, ma'am?

"Hello," I called out before I got too close. It was usually her son, Duane, that carried the shotgun and I couldn't see him, but I didn't want any unpleasant surprises.

Her head appeared over the dark arms of the yew hedge that held the little cemetery in its embrace. Her hair was bound up in a pale cotton scarf and she wore oversize dungarees. She waved me forward.

"Hello, Amber. Come on. I need an excuse to stop."

"Bit late to be pruning," I said.

"Yeah. Shoulda listened to Duane," she replied. "Needs doing in the fall. Winter's come early this year."

"It's beautifully kept."

"One of my jobs." She snipped a last branch and laid the shears down alongside the bags of clippings at her feet. "I do it for Candy."

Felix's first wife. *Candace Lis Larimer:* the name was etched in crumbling letters on the headstone behind her, along with the date of her death—*Jan 5 1918.*

Something stirred in my mind as I looked at the headstone. Another frigging important thing that I should be doing or asking. I felt too tired. Either it'd come to me or it wouldn't.

"Felix said he didn't know why it's called the tree of life," I said, stroking my fingers through the yew leaves.

"That's because he's dumb," she said. She took a brush and began to work gently on the headstones. I went around the semicircle of the hedge, picking up clippings that had gotten away and waiting for her to continue.

"Candy didn't want headstones," she said quietly after a while. "She planted the hedge, made it like it is: a mother's arms reaching out to comfort. She wanted all the pack's dead to be buried here, one on top of the other. No markers, because we're all just pack in the end. And she wanted this tree."

She sat back on her heels.

"You know, parts of the yew die and rot and feed the rest of it. It lives off itself. It makes itself new from all it has ever been. The pack's like that. It's all the things it's ever done, all its loves and hates, all its desires and fears, all its triumphs and failures."

The sum of all the things it's ever done...

I got goosebumps. I'd finished the circuit of the hedge and put all the bits I'd collected into the bags. Then I went over to Candy's headstone. Martha had moved on to the next one, and I traced the fading dates with my fingers, like I'd done the first time I saw them. And I kicked myself.

"Martha? You're the same age as Felix, right? So, you were around in 1910, weren't you?"

"Course I was. Why?"

"My great-grandmother—"

"Speaks to Wolves," she said. "Sarah, I called her."

"You knew her, then?"

"Oh yes. I got along fine with the Adepts."

Oh, my God. She'd been here all along, and with a bit of thought I could have realized it. Bian and Julie were right; I was way off my game.

"But Felix said he didn't know her," I said hurriedly. "He said he doubted she had anything to do with helping Were change."

"Yup."

Well, that wasn't reassuring. I wasn't sure how I stood with Martha. If I asked something that the alpha had already dismissed, was that some kind of Were insult? Could I try just one more question?

"Did Sarah help the pack?"

"The honest answer is, I don't know." She finished brushing the last headstone and frowned. "First change was more private then. If a newbie was having trouble changing, they'd go into the hills with Candy. Did they meet someone up there? Candy didn't say, but she never claimed to be the one who helped them."

She got to her feet and looked around the little cemetery, hands on her hips. I waited, disappointment heavy on my shoulders. So close and yet no further forward.

"After Candy died, Felix changed things. He said that encouragement from the whole pack would help and they were there to support each other if it didn't." She looked at me. "I mean the mercy killing if it gets too much."

I'd spoken with Alex about when his girlfriend, Hope, had failed to change. I could understand how he'd have wanted others there. To be able to tell yourself that you couldn't be sure whether it was your bite that killed your friend or lover.

I tried again. "Are there any more left from that time? I mean ones who had trouble. Anyone who would've changed back then?"

She shook her head. "We'd have told you if there was. Even if Felix is a hardass about it. We almost never had a failure when Candy was alive." She sighed. "I don't know. All the packs are having trouble, far as I can tell. Maybe it's become harder for other reasons. More new wolves, less space, more stresses."

Something Mary had said to me about how hard it might be for a werewolf to change stirred in the depths of my mind. What had she said?

Everyone has a connection to the energy, even humans. A million people in the broad daylight who believe you can't change into a wolf would make it difficult for a Were in the middle of Denver. But at night, out in the woods…

So, a newbie having difficulties would try out in the woods at night. But too often, it still wasn't working. What was going wrong? Something was teasing me, just beyond reach, like that word on the tip of your tongue.

But Martha hadn't finished. "My opinion? The pack needs a female alpha. *He* needs an alpha mate. Pack's not rightly balanced without one. I had hopes for you."

"I'm sorry."

"Don't be. Either it was going to be or it wasn't. Can't force things like that. Tried with Donna and that didn't work. He never stopped loving Candy. Oh, he would have loved Donna too; she was sweet. Too sweet to become an alpha maybe, but she didn't make it anyway. It was a mistake to go for someone who hadn't made the change."

It was quiet for a while; a companionable quiet.

But I was curious about something she'd said earlier—too curious to let it go. "You said Candy wanted this as a cemetery for the pack, but it's only the three graves, isn't it?"

"Hmm." Martha came to stand by me. "Pack don't much hold with the cemetery. Living is with the pack, but dying is private, I guess. The pack kinda swallows us whole. It gives and it takes away. If it needs you, it feeds you. It needs Felix. He's strong like an ox. But me? I'm just around, and I been around for a long time. That means I'm getting old for a werewolf. Time to think about it."

She plucked a couple of the last dead flowers at the base of the hedge. "Some just stop changing and die. Some take up dangerous sports until their reflexes let them down. Mostly, and that'll be me too, we start to listen to the wind and we hear the last call."

She went quiet, listening. I found myself listening too, holding my breath, not sure if I wanted to hear what she meant, or what would happen if I did.

Martha could see I didn't understand. "Come here," she said, and pointed up the hill. "Look over there, beneath the trees. Tell me what you sense."

"It's dark."

"Go on. Feel. Smell. Just say the words as they come to you."

"The wind from there, it's colder." I drank the scents in, rich and sharp. The more I concentrated, the more I could untangle them. "There's cool pine, dry timber, wet earth."

"More! Smell it. Taste it." Her fingers clamped on my arm.

"Earth. It's slow. It's cold. It's full of life. Just...paused."

"Yes. Cold earth. All still, underneath. It seems to us that life bleeds away into the earth, but that's nature's trick. You never die, but you're gathered up. Like the yew feeds on itself, the pack remembers and you never die."

"Now, close your eyes, and listen. Listen with your whole heart."

Silence that had form and movement, nebulous as cloud, came rolling down the hill.

My eukori reached and blended with the Call and stretched and stretched, thinner and thinner.

"Listen!"

Trembling. Something just beyond my reach. Sighing—no, *singing*—there were words on the wind. Too soft, too faint to understand.

She shook me and my eyes snapped open.

I was leaning into the hill. I'd forgotten to breathe.

"That's where I'll go," she said. "I'll follow the song. Next winter or the next or in ten years' time. Who knows? I'll go to my wolf and I'll run and run until I'm so tired I can't run any more. Then I'll lay down beneath the open sky and rest. And by and by, I'll be part of that song."

With my senses stretched out like a fishing net, I felt something then, something echoing through the Call. Not my pack's Call; Felix's Call. It was nails scraping on a blackboard, shocking cold water down my back, a knife slicing flesh.

"What the hell?"

Martha didn't answer. She was looking up into the mountain, a terrible sadness in her eyes.

"They'll come back soon," she whispered, but she wouldn't say any more.

We started taking the bags of clippings to the recycling heap. On the second round, I felt Felix returning. I stopped to look up the slope at the forest.

The shadow beneath the pines was a hard blackness that pulled your eyes to it and drank in light. Parts of the darkness separated out into shapes that seemed to float down the hill. At the front, a huge wolf, silver and black. Felix. Behind him, the bulk of Silas and Ursula, with two smaller wolves scurrying after them. The pair held themselves low, heads and tails down, their whole body language cowed. Another large wolf was herding them. Although I'd never seen him or Felix furry, I could tell the last one was Duane.

Closer, I could see blood on Felix's muzzle.

And there were only two of the Boneheads.

Felix stopped beside me. I'd never felt the full force of his alpha dominance; he'd obviously had a way of toning it down. And suddenly he wasn't. My legs simply gave way, and I was kneeling on the grass.

Even Silas and Ursula lowered their bodies as they ghosted past, heading for the ranch house.

The Boneheads slunk down the hill like beaten curs. Felix didn't snarl. He barely looked at them, but their bellies were dragging on the ground. It was difficult to tell, but my guess was they were the ringleader and the third guy, the one Olivia had hit over the head.

So what did that mean for Bone Two, the gangly guy I'd been fighting with?

Duane followed them down to their truck, where he watched them change to human. They were still getting hurriedly dressed as they climbed in and drove off.

I took a breath and looked around, my head instinctively ducking.

Felix had changed back to human too.

He didn't seem to care, but I kept my gaze on the ground.

"Give me a couple of minutes," he said softly, folding the alpha presence away. "I'll see you in my den."

Martha patted my shoulder and we walked slowly and silently down to the house.

The long, low building blended in with the landscape, which was only right. It was made from the hill: red clay fired to make the tiles, timber from the flanks of the hill and stone from its deep bones. It belonged. A peacefulness drifted up from it, like smoke from a chimney, and completely at odds with what seemed to have happened on the high slopes above it.

Ursula and Silas were in the kitchen already, dressed but not talking, staring into the distance.

Martha had a pot of coffee brewing. With the couple of minutes requested well past, I filled two of the handmade mugs and followed her directions to Felix's den.

Chapter 14

Even with his dominance pulled back, Felix seemed to take up a lot of space in the little room. He'd changed into black denim, a blue T and plain cowboy boots. He'd cleaned the blood from his face and was combing his hair back with his fingers. He just looked tired now, relaxed in his big leather recliner. He motioned me to an easy chair facing him.

"What happened?" I asked quietly.

"Lance Evans," he said. "The ringleader, the idiot who owns the truck, decided he didn't like being knocked around. Worked himself up and was trying to get some of the others worked up as well."

"*He* didn't like being knocked around? What did he claim he was trying to do to Olivia? Talk to her? With his fists?"

Felix just waited for me to get myself back under control before he went on.

"In a way, he's lucky. If you hadn't stopped it, Ricky would have come back and killed all three of them, and I would have backed him." He sipped his coffee. "As it happened, Silas and Ursula stepped in, brought them out here. I still might have been able to keep it low level, but Evans started arguing. Then he brought up Gray."

Felix stared at me. "You're so new to this, I can't really expect you to understand all the complexities."

"Lay them out Felix, or we'll never get anywhere."

"By submitting to me, you and Alexander have actually strengthened my position as alpha."

"And that was what you were trying to work us all towards," I said, "rather than a challenge."

Which Alex and I might have lost, given the wounds he'd received from Noble, and my lack of experience in fighting four-legged.

Felix nodded, giving no indication of his thoughts on the challenge. "While the pack is healthy and happy, I'm probably as firmly in control as it's possible to be. The trouble is that we're not animals. Every member of the pack knows we're under threat from the Confederation. Everyone knows we're losing too many who can't change. As individuals, they'd probably just let me handle things. As wolves, they'd trust their instincts. But the real curse of the werewolf is they're human as well. Humans have doubts and the Call lets them feel that doubt in the minds of their fellows. Doubt feeds on itself. What if we went with the Confederation, would it be that bad? What if we're doing something wrong for new members that's causing the problems? That's the kind of thinking humans always engage in."

He'd leaned forward as he spoke. Now his chair creaked as he sat back in it.

"I can handle the Confederation. I can handle the loss of new members. I think I might be able to handle having an associated pack in the territory. But it doesn't stop there; the load keeps growing. This associated pack includes Athanate and humans, and that's bad enough. But by now every pack member knows that this associated pack has a skinwalker."

"Can I ask, Alpha, what the problem is with other Were? I mean, those who aren't wolves?" I tried for humble, and I think it almost amused Felix. He didn't bite my head off, anyway.

"Other Were..." Felix stared into his mug. "I guess other Were don't like the pack dynamics. They feel it's claustrophobic. But we don't have a problem with them, they just don't mix with us. They keep to their own kind. Skinwalkers, now, they don't belong anywhere. They can't be trusted. They don't mix with their own, and they don't mix with us, unless they want to use us as cover."

"Like Noble." I wasn't sure that was fair on skinwalkers, to use Noble as an example, but I could see how the Denver pack would have him in mind.

"Like him. I'm not saying Gray's that bad, but if he really is part of your House and that makes him part of your pack, well, we have a problem."

Felix paused. I waited him out. I was getting a feel for the way he built a case, and I was sure there was more where this had come from. I was right.

"That's before we get to the part where Evans started spouting off about the stink of Basilikos all over Gray."

Shit. Just what Naryn had warned me about.

I forced my attention back to the here and now. Felix could tell that I knew about the Basilikos smell. His eyes narrowed.

"I'll explain," I said, "but first, I have a question. There were three of the Boneheads. Wasn't Evans one of the ones I saw crawling off? What happened to the big gangly guy?"

"I killed him."

Felix's face was empty of emotion, but I could feel anger and sorrow behind that mask.

"His name was Peter Young, and he was the only one I thought was worth spit in that group. But Evans had him wound up till he couldn't think straight. He refused to back down. Refused to back down from me! In the end, all I could do was make an example of him."

Felix put the mug down and walked over to his sideboard. He poured bourbon into a couple of tumblers and brought them back.

Not my drink and too early in the day, but I wasn't going to refuse the alpha.

"The other two?"

"I've exiled them. There's shame in that. In some ways exile is worse than fighting your own alpha. Silas and Ursula will tell the pack what's happened, and the best I can hope for is the shock will bring them all back into line for a while."

"Where will they go? The exiles." I was stalling and he knew it, but he answered me.

"If they had a lick of sense, they'd head for Cimarron or Glen Canyon. Sound alphas that might take them in. But Evans will head south and end up with Ute Mountain or Gold Hill."

Both those names were just across the border into New Mexico, which pricked my interest.

"What's wrong with those packs?"

"New Mexico outcasts," he said. "When I say outcasts, it means the psycho head cases running the main New Mexico packs don't want them, and that tells me they're seriously bad. If they were in Colorado, I'd have to deal with them."

He meant kill them, as a pack would do with a rogue on its territory. He didn't seem to hold the rest of the New Mexico packs in much higher regard.

"New Mexico Were are a problem?"

He just nodded.

"Altau have a couple of messages for you," I said. "One about New Mexico: Iversen has been seen heading down there."

He nodded again. He'd been expecting that.

"Naryn also wants me to say that Altau can't spare the resources for a fight against the Confederation at the moment. He advises to make a deal with them and then use Altau as a balance to keep them in line."

Felix snorted.

He wasn't going to be distracted anymore. "What I expected," he said. "Now, about that Basilikos marque."

I sipped the bourbon. The whiskey was hot orange in color, but underneath the bite, the taste was almost sweet, with caramel and toffee. And the smell: a little like new leather. Maybe I should be more adventurous in my liquors now that my senses had been sharpened.

"So. Basilikos," I said. "We'd never have found out where Matlal were holding their toru without inside information."

Felix would know all about Bow Creek—some of the pack were out there now getting rid of the evidence.

"Gray found one of the Matlal willing to help. It turns out she's not Basilikos."

Felix frowned. "Then what the hell is she?"

"A former spy for the Carpathians."

I'd managed to shock him. There wasn't going to be a better time. I bowed my head in sort-of wolf submission.

"The price for her help was accepting her into House Farrell."

He sighed and closed his eyes, leaning his head back on his seat.

The situation wasn't getting any better. I thought I'd better go for broke.

"I'm in trouble," I said, and he grunted without humor. I let it all blurt out. "I haven't had time to learn everything about the Were and Athanate. That means I have to rely on my instincts. They're normally good, but not for paranormal stuff. Even if they were, I'm not sure there are any right instincts for what I am. When I go to my wolf, and Alex is there, everything's under control, but that's not helping my Athanate. The wolf and the Athanate are fighting each other. That sends the Athanate too close to rogue. Skylur's not around, and the one person left who I think can really help me is Diana, but she's gone missing down in New Mexico. I need to go find her, but Naryn told me not to go and sent me to you instead to control me through the wolf. I can't do that. I need you to cover for me while I get Diana back from New Mexico—"

"No!" His head snapped back upright, and all that carefully-packed-away dominance came leaping out. I was suddenly down on the floor, on my knees and shaking like an aspen leaf.

"No, no, no!"

He stood up abruptly to pace, and the den seemed to shrink even more around me. All I could see were his boots in front of me. I couldn't raise my head, *physically* couldn't raise it. My whole claustrophobic world had narrowed down even further: two steps to the left, two steps to the right. Sealed pinewood floor. Plain brown boots. I realized, belatedly, that my reaction up at the cemetery hadn't just been because Felix had let his dominance out in full force. Alex and me submitting to him in the barn hadn't been just an act. Handing over dominance was a real, physical process, the same for the Were and the Athanate. I'd handed my puppet strings to Felix and he was jerking them now.

Dammit, I hadn't signed up for this.

The anger helped clear my mind. I *could* lift my head.

I ignored the trembling, the feeling in my throat that I wanted to whine, the stomach-turning desire to do anything to stop him from being angry with me.

I got one foot underneath me and started to rise, wobbling with effort.

Hands gripped my arms and lifted me. I panicked. But all he did was place me back in my chair, gently as a precious vase. The feeling of being crushed loosened a little.

Alex had told me how some alphas behaved—the sexual domination over all the female wolves that they enjoyed. He'd said Felix was different.

Is he?

"I apologize." His voice was even gruffer than usual. "You caught me off guard there."

His hand tilted my chin up, making me look at him again.

My eyes didn't burn out.

He looked even more tired—as tired as I felt. The dominance wasn't entirely gone, but it wasn't suffocating like it had been.

"It's not just you and your damned knot of problems. It's that arrogant, scheming bastard at Haven. I know all about Naryn from when he was Diakon before. I can smell his devious hands all over this."

"I…" my voice wouldn't cooperate. Felix picked my tumbler up off the floor and refilled it, giving me time to gather myself again.

"He knows you'll try and work around his orders. So he's using me to reinforce them. He's right; the bastard knows there's no way I can let you go to New Mexico. The packs there are *not* welcoming. You'd be dead in a day, if the Basilikos didn't get you first."

He took a swallow of his bourbon before continuing, his voice bitter.

"On top of that, he's offloaded the problem he can't deal with. He has no idea what to do about your crusis, so he throws the problem at me. If I succeed in keeping you sane, he'll say it was his idea. If I fail, well, what can you expect from an animal."

Anger let the dominance seep out again. I stiffened. I would not cringe.

"I won't try and avoid the responsibility for you, but I'm not going to have you sitting at Coykuti. That's only going to cause resentment in the pack. I need something for you to do."

He went back to pacing, a subliminal growl making the air throb in the den.

"You're looking to prove that the Adepts have some kind of ritual that would help a Were change. Noble certainly found some rituals that affected the way he changed." When he said that name, the anger in his voice was like blades running down my flesh.

"Go to the Adepts. You have better contacts with them than any of the pack or Altau. Find out what you can about rituals." He paused, brooding. "You know Olivia's likely to be next?"

I nodded. The grip on my tumbler helped hide the tremors in my hand, and I raised it for a sip, concentrating on the fiery taste and not how Felix's eyes seemed to stab into my head.

"If you can do something for her..." he murmured, looking away thoughtfully. "*If* you can, that might change the balance. It *might*. You'd still need to get rid of Gray and this Basilikos-Carpathian spy."

"I can't." The demon in my throat slipped that out while I was distracted. I tried to explain. "I can't send them away without cause. Athanate law. I've accepted them into my House."

"Renounce the Athanate—"

"I can't do that any more than you can decide not to be Were."

"Maybe leaving Denver is the only way, then."

His power built up again and flowed over me. I could barely keep my head up. It was a victory to stay sitting in the chair.

"I can't abandon Olivia either," I said, forcing each word out. "Or Alex."

"Or Ursula?"

"No," I whispered.

"I can understand Alexander, of course," he said. There was pain in his words. I wanted to make that pain stop. I wanted to say that I would turn Ursula away, but I couldn't. I couldn't. I bit my cheek to stop myself from speaking and tasted blood in my mouth.

"I can understand Olivia, if indeed you can offer her something I cannot. Because of Olivia, Ricky is torn. I can understand that, too. But Ursula? She's doing what I tell her, but I can feel her drifting away, more and more every day." He spoke quietly, almost softly. "What have you done? How have you seduced her away from me?"

I was panting with effort, sweat beading on my brow. There'd been no words, but I had promised Ursula. A promise that I wouldn't break.

"I. Won't. Say."

It was painful. Painful to remain sitting, painful not to tell him, painful not to throw myself at his feet and ask forgiveness.

The old-fashioned telephone on his desk rang.

For a second he let it ring. I knew the exact moment his attention turned away from me; the gorilla got off my chest.

"What?" he snarled.

He hadn't been expecting a call, clearly.

"I'll be outside," I said, my voice wavering.

I staggered on legs that felt like I'd run a marathon. At the door, I managed to glance back. His brow was furrowed and his fist gripped the phone tightly. He ignored me and I slipped out.

Chapter 15

I didn't want to eavesdrop on his call. It was polite for me to take myself out of the room.

I could tell myself those lies all afternoon.

The fight had gone out of me.

I made it to the porch and collapsed on the steps like a broken doll.

I was so tired. Not just from struggling with Felix's dominance, or the constant stress of keeping my Were and Athanate under control. I couldn't sleep without my personal nightmares exploding out of my head, and hadn't been able to do better than doze for a week now. I was working purely by being hyped up, and when the adrenaline ran out, so did all my strength.

I'd fought against becoming Athanate before I'd met the Altau. But difficult though that meeting with Skylur had been, it'd given me a glimpse of hope and purpose to my life. The physical advantages, the heightened senses, the sheer possibilities had swept doubts away, even when everything had become so much harder and darker.

And now I was doubting my decision again.

Every turn seemed like a trap, every decision wrong, and more than wrong. Every decision had the potential for fatal consequences, not just for me, but for all those I cared about as well.

Skylur out of contact. Diana missing. Naryn unheeding. Bian mistaken about Jaworski. Things going on that I had no knowledge of, which affected what decisions I could make.

And hanging over all of it, the lowering clouds of Emergence. The whole world could get torn apart in a struggle between paranormals and humanity, Athanate and Were, Basilikos and Panethus, if a single misstep was made.

I was nothing. I had no great power to influence the way Emergence went in any positive direction. Unfortunately, I could sure turn it negative.

I was just a pawn between Skylur and Felix, both so much more powerful than I that I could barely hold myself together in their presence unless they were being kind to me.

Skylur wasn't around. So the siren call in my head was to go back inside and throw myself at Felix's feet. Beg for his dominance, beg him on my knees, let his dominance roll over me and take all those decisions away. Give him all my problems and I would be free. And a slave too, of course.

A slave. But if I couldn't make a decision, then I couldn't make a wrong decision, could I?

Something whispered in my ear that complete surrender would also be the safe route to take against going rogue. I frowned. Was that right? Struggling to be me was the weakness that the disease of insanity would exploit?

If it was, then mindless obedience would be better than rogue, wouldn't it?

I wrapped my arms around my knees and dropped my head onto them, a fog of despair welling up inside me.

It'd been a long time since I'd felt this kind of bleakness.

Ops 4-10 had taught me to trust my training and my instincts when there wasn't time to think my way around a problem. Top had taught me one more important guide I could use: my sense of morals.

But I didn't have the information and the clear brain I needed to think my way around paranormal problems. Not all the instincts that the army had taught me were the right instincts to deal with Athanate, Were and Adept. And as for my moral compass—well, things seemed right to me now that wouldn't have back then. How could I trust myself?

Skylur and Naryn thought Diana might still be on a mission.

My instincts said she wasn't, and Bian agreed with me.

What was I basing it on? That she'd seemed reluctant to go? That I felt she'd be in touch as soon as she could? If not with me, then with Bian. But how could I trust my instincts after knowing her such a short time?

I couldn't change my mind about Naryn. He was wrong about Diana. I didn't care that he and Skylur had worked together for hundreds of years. He was a good Diakon, but that didn't mean he was a good leader.

In the meantime, Felix didn't want me to go, but he wasn't my immediate alpha. Could I argue that? Were didn't like those sort of quibbles.

If I went and brought Diana back, it would be worth it. I'd handle all the fallout.

If I was wrong or I failed in any way, I would make things worse. Hundreds of things could go wrong. Bian would be in more trouble. I might sabotage Diana's effort to get Romero back into the Panethus camp. Or New Mexico was full of hostile Were and Basilikos Athanate and I could start an all-out war, causing the discovery of the paranormal and the resultant apocalypse.

I couldn't move in any direction. It was like being hog-tied.

A familiar engine noise caught my attention and I looked up. David wasn't here, and there was no sign of the pink Merc, Ursula's van, or Evans' truck. The whole ranch felt empty again. Duane and Martha were probably busy with the dead man up on the hill.

I wondered idly if they'd bury him where he fell, or take his body down to the fertilizer factories they ran for just that purpose.

A vehicle came into sight. The engine I'd heard belonged to the Hill Bitch, the monstrous Jeep I'd borrowed from Altau, and Tullah drove it right up to the porch.

She opened the door and leaped out.

What's the rush? No point in any of it.

She hadn't gotten that message. "Come on," she said. She grabbed me by the arm and hauled me to my feet.

"What?"

"No time," she snapped and started to pull me to the car.

Her eyes were red. She'd been crying.

Problems with her boyfriend, Matt?

More shit I can't deal with.

I loathed myself as soon as I thought that.

I pulled back and pointed vaguely at the ranch. "Felix," I said. I couldn't seem to string a sentence together. Everything was catching up to me, and I couldn't think. How could I handle everything coming at me, if I couldn't think? In Ops training, we'd learned techniques for coping with compromised cognitive abilities from torture, sleep deprivation or drugs. Somehow, none of those techniques were working for me.

"Felix is being handled," Tullah said. "Come on."

The car door was open and she was pushing me into the passenger seat.

"Got to talk to Felix," I insisted. "He wants me to go talk to Mary. Rituals. I should be in New Mexico, but I can't go. Everyone says so."

"Yes, Boss," she said in the tone you use to placate children, as she fastened my seat belt.

She slammed the door and ran back to the driver's side.

There was my Mossberg shotgun mounted on the rack at the back of the cab. I didn't remember putting that there. Now I was losing track of my weapons. Not good. Something was stacked in the flatbed under a polythene sheet. There were bags on the back seat.

"What's happening?" The adrenaline started to clear the fog in my brain. The Hill Bitch growled back down the slope and through the gate. "What the hell's going on?"

Tullah bit her lip and gunned the engine. The Hill Bitch fishtailed on the gravel, shook herself like a gun dog, and took off down the road. To the right.

"Wrong way," I said, and pointed back to Denver.

She shook her head, turning to look at me. "I'm sorry, Boss," she whispered. "I'm sorry."

I tried to struggle back to full alertness, but it was too late. I realized Kaothos had already snuck up on me and the bitch had her claws deep in my head.

The lights went out.

Chapter 16

The late afternoon sun warmed my face.

I couldn't say it woke me, because I hadn't been asleep so much as unconscious.

I could hear children playing nearby, which reassured me. I sensed Tullah close to me, and Mary. And Kaothos, lurking. They knew I was conscious; one of the problems of being kidnapped by paranormals.

"I hope the three of you understand I'm really pissed," I said without opening my eyes. For some reason I was wearing someone's sunglasses and a Stetson. And my patched-up stockman's coat with the collar turned up, as if to keep the wind off my neck. I had to look like a convalescent cowgirl just out of the hospital.

"You needed a rest." Tullah's voice was defensive.

"A rest? You can call it arrest, but you're not police, so it's abduction."

It felt *good* to indulge my petulant inner child.

Somewhere in my head, there was a hissing, like rain on fresh, smoking tarmac. Dragon laughter. One of these days I was going to find some sneaky power that I could use to creep up on Kaothos and knock her out. See how she liked it.

Sweet of her to get my jokes, though.

"If you're quite finished, do you want to talk now, or should Kaothos just knock you out again?" Mary had her no-nonsense voice going today.

I opened my eyes.

No nonsense, and layers of underlying tension, even fear. Jokes aside, there was something very wrong for them to behave like this.

My senses automatically expanded, searching for threats. I sneezed. There was a bouquet of flowering plants on the park bench next to me—a mix of purple and blue: wisteria, fireweed and hyacinth. The blended smells sent my nose into overdrive—honey, burnt cork, berry and lemon. Mary had been smoking, too; there was a tang of tobacco lingering.

But, apart from the assault on my wolfy nose, there was nothing to concern us.

We were in a city park. Groups of children and parents played snowball games or chased each other across the white fields. Traffic passed on a highway not far away.

It wasn't a Denver park. A glance at the sun and I figured I'd been out for less than an hour.

"So what are we doing in Colorado Springs?"

Tullah gave a little smile. Mary snorted.

"Breaking up *your* logjam," Mary said, staring at me with her head back in an almost arrogant pose. Her hair was caught up in a headscarf and she was hiding behind huge Jackie O sunglasses.

Tullah glared at her. "It's *not* that, Ma. We don't have time to argue."

I cleared my throat. "Any time now. In little words, and plain sentences, so I can understand."

It wasn't Mary who started.

"You remember Ken Weaver?" Tullah asked.

He'd really done something to upset her; Tullah's anger was boiling out of her.

Ken Weaver was an Adept in the Denver community, quite senior as far as I knew. I'd met him when I visited Mary and Liu at the Kwan. It was a big step for an Adept like Weaver to make. Adepts regarded all Athanate as evil, only allowing that they might not start off that way. Older Athanate and Basilikos? The spawn of hell. No exceptions. Only Mary and Liu had accepted I might not be completely evil.

Weaver had taken one look at me and declared me Basilikos.

The problem was that, in curing Jen after she'd endured a day of torture and rape, I'd tried to fix too much. Unsure of my Athanate powers, I'd gone past the bodily injuries and pulled all the emotions of the day out of her head. That meant they ended up in mine.

I wasn't sorry. It might even have been the element of healing that was necessary for Jen.

Unfortunately, it was a disaster for me. Quite apart from blowing my own mental fuses, it was making me more likely to go rogue through either the Were or Athanate side. And Weaver had been right in a way; it did make me look more like Basilikos—as if I'd been feeding on fear.

Had it given me a taste for it? I suppressed a nervous shudder.

"Yeah. I remember him," I said.

"He's taken over as head of the community."

"And this is not good news?" I was getting antsy. I really didn't want to get involved in Adept politics and I didn't see why I'd needed to be kidnapped to be told this.

"Not for us and not for you," Mary snapped.

I'd never seen her quite like this. Angry, but not necessarily at me. More the sort of unfocused anger of a proud woman forced to act. I knew Mary had been the head of the community and had lost that position for daring to be associated with me as an Athanate. 'Cos of the 'all Athanate are evil' thing.

Again, it was Tullah who took over.

"Amber, we have to be back on the road in ten minutes. Just listen, please."

I caught the demon as it was about to point out I was listening, but all I'd heard was them dancing around something they didn't want to say.

"Weaver's used his position as the community head to start an investigation on Ma and Pa and me."

"What for?" I couldn't help interrupting.

"Those ex-special forces guys, what do you call them, Nagas? When they attacked the Kwan, Ma and Pa killed them."

No complaints from me.

"Weaver's within his rights. Any lethal use of the energy by Adepts has to be sanctioned. Of course there wasn't time, and under normal circumstances the council would just retrospectively agree. The problem is the way he's acting before calling the council to debate it. We think—"

"Hold on a second," I interrupted. "What about Longmont? Kaothos and you blew up a whole factory full of Matlal and ZK."

Mary and Tullah looked at each other.

"Longmont's being blamed on the Athanate," Tullah said. "Everyone felt it, but no one recognized the signature of the working and they all made assumptions about Alice Emerson. We haven't set them straight, but we're pretty sure Weaver knows the truth because..."

Her voice died away and Mary took over again.

"Because he did call a council, but that was to have them put a lock on Tullah. The excuse he used was that she is coming under proscribed influences. They never liked the idea of Adepts like Emerson working with the Athanate, and now they have 'proof' that Emerson uses lethal and indiscriminate force."

A lock. That meant a working of the energy on Tullah to prevent her from using her own power. No wonder she was so upset.

I got up and gave her a hug, scant comfort though it was.

"I'm sorry, Tullah," I said.

"They can't find out about Kaothos yet," Tullah said, blinking back tears, "so I couldn't fight it. They wouldn't understand her."

"I'm sure Weaver knows, and he understands perfectly well," Mary said. "One aspect anyway. He wants to get Kaothos' power under his control. To do that he'll make up anything about you, Amber, as an Athanate, and link it all in with Noble and Gray."

"We killed Noble," I pointed out. "But you've got a problem with Nick?"

"I didn't have a particular problem with Gray, certainly not once I met him," Mary said. "But again, Weaver is technically correct. Skinwalkers are proscribed because of their use of energy."

"But he's just another Were. All Were use the energy to change."

"The Were use it in a minor, fixed way. It's purely instinctive. A skinwalker uses energy consciously and has to grow his capacity and knowledge with each new shape he chooses. If there's an Adept law greater than the one about not using the energy to kill, it's the one stating that only Adepts trained by a community and working within a community can use major workings of the energy."

That sounded like legal bullshit to me, but I kept my mouth shut.

Tullah sighed. "The council have issued an order that Emerson, you and Nick all need to be brought before them. Teams of Adepts are out looking now."

"We need to warn—" I started, but Tullah grabbed my arm.

"All done, Amber. We got the whole House together while you were busy. Nick's gone back to ground. Everyone is aware. We even sent messages to Naryn and Felix about what was happening. Alice has been sent to New York by Naryn. She called in while she was on her way to the airport. David made sure she got on her flight."

My head was spinning.

"Felix…he wanted me to go to the Adepts and learn about any ritual that could help the pack. That's not going to happen…" I stopped, and thought a step beyond that. How would Skylur or Felix react if the Adepts imprisoned me? "Hold on, Weaver's practically declaring war on the Athanate and Were! He's insane."

"You're getting the picture," Mary said. "Weaver doesn't think it'll come to that. He's stupid but he's sly. He's got the council so worked up about everything, they're actually not thinking any of it through. We need time for them to come back to their senses, or something dramatic to happen—short of declaring war—to wake them up."

"We can't let them get hold of you, Amber," Tullah said. "They know about the hybrid Athanate and Were, which is bad enough. We can't let them know you're also an Adept."

"Until we're ready and can show you're trained," Mary said. "And they can't get hold of Tullah and give her a good examination either, because of Kaothos."

"Until we're ready, again," Tullah said. "So your House has come up with a plan. We need to go away and find Diana."

"My House—" They ignored me and kept speaking.

"And train you in safe use of the energy."

"And find out about rituals to help the Were change."

"And form a community."

My head was going back and forth like I was watching a tennis match.

"Jen and Alex said they'll have to stay in Denver," Tullah said. "It'd be too obvious if they left. So, you'll be away from some of the temptations of biting. If you need it, Jen will organize transfusions at a private clinic in New Mexico. Alice told us transfusions can work for a while to delay the need for Blood. We've all agreed this is the best plan."

My House is railroading me. In a good way, I guess.

But going into New Mexico with only Tullah as backup, and her unable to use Kaothos?

Then again, maybe the low profile would actually work in my favor…

Or had my House caught my erratic decision-making from me?

"There's another thing," Tullah said. "Bian sent us a message through Alice."

"Naryn will think you're at Coykuti. Felix will think you're at Haven or at the Kwan."

"Kaothos will be there to help you. Nothing major, but sleep and so on."

Knocking me out would be more accurate.

"Victor's taking over the PI business temporarily, and Jofranka will just work the front office while we're away."

"Stop," I said. "Stop. Look, some great ideas here, but there are a whole bunch of things you haven't thought through. *I* need to go down to New Mexico, yes, but both Naryn and Felix have told me just today how dangerous it is, and forbidden me to go anywhere near New Mexico. They're serious about the danger; Tullah coming along is not an option."

Mary stood up. "We don't have time to argue, Amber. Weaver will be alert. Whatever I do, I can't completely mask my signature in the energy, so if we stay here any longer, someone may turn up. I'm in enough trouble as it is. Now, you need Tullah to help find out about the rituals, and you need Kaothos because otherwise you can't rest. Can't have one without the other. And you and Tullah searching for Diana will be better than you alone. It'll be less dangerous for both of you than staying in Denver."

Tullah pulled me up with her and started dragging me back to the car.

"I'll explain more later," she said. "But we're only doing what you've taught me. When it's impossible to do everything, we should do the things we can that make the most difference. Find Diana. Get Larry's kin to safety. Find out if there is anything in the Spirit Dance rituals we've heard about that will help the Were. And so on."

"What exactly have you heard about rituals?"

"There's an old Adept in New Mexico, Chatima, one of the last shaman-Adepts, like your great-grandmother. She lives down near Albuquerque and we've passed a couple of messages back and forth with her about the Spirit Dance. We think she'll help."

"Keep away from the other Adepts in New Mexico," Mary said. "I don't like the sound of them. There's a...brazenness about them that isn't healthy. Tullah will need to explain about shaman-Adepts, too."

Mary had brought the pungent bouquet from the bench and she pinned it on me, then passed her fingers through the flowers.

My skin prickled; she was doing a working.

"That will work for a couple of days. They'll help confuse the Weres' sense of smell. The Athanate will still feel your marque," she tapped the side of my head, "but that's not so directional. *Don't* try channeling any energy. Adepts will spot that right away."

My head was still spinning. I was going to have to trust them on the planning for this.

I got worried when I planned something this complex, so having to trust others so completely didn't come naturally.

But among all the distractions, I realized that I had Mary right here, and a question for her that had been worming around in my brain the whole day. A question that was important, even if I had no idea why.

"Mary, can I ask something that's not related to any of this immediate stuff?"

"One question." Mary was looking around nervously now. We were nearly back at the Hill Bitch and Mary's car.

"The temple we found out at Bow Creek, the children, the ritual...is all that a working of some kind? The construction itself, it felt like it was crawling with energy."

Mary shuddered. "It probably was, but it's nothing in the temple or the rituals themselves. Inert objects can only receive workings from us. A dagger is a dagger, a temple is a temple. We can imbue them with workings. We can store workings and energy in them, but the shapes of the temple or the dagger don't make any difference. We could imbue a garden shed and an old trowel with the same energy."

She went quiet and I thought I'd gotten as much as I was going to get from her this time, but she spoke again as we got to the cars.

"You wonder why the Adepts are so concerned about Were and Athanate using the energy consciously, without training. This is an example. It may be they started forming this ritual with good intentions: to help them shorten crusis; to reduce the need for Blood; to hide from humans. I don't know, but whatever it was originally, from the description it seems like the ritual has gotten away from them." She grimaced. "It's difficult to explain this in a few words. Tullah will have more time to talk to you about it."

She took my hand and squeezed. "The ritual and the energy have no intelligence, no direction, but the power that it gathers is corrosive over time. A little step is taken, everyone can see it's a necessary step, hardly a concern, but it leads to another and another, and suddenly they are trapped. The steps above are too high to climb back out. They reach the major rituals. Progress requires pain, then blood, then death. First an animal, then a human." She shook her head. "Then a child."

"Understand me, Amber. The energy doesn't just come from the sacrifice. The child dies, and that's the awful end for him or her. But as much energy comes from the damage it does to the person who conducts the ritual, the focus of energy through that person, the creation of a channel for that energy. A channel that needs that energy, makes the user desire it, makes them want more and more. I've said to you before, there's no such thing as a demon. You can't summon one. But the power raised in a ritual like this feeds into the basest human desires. You might as well say it creates a demon of the person who performs the ritual."

Her brown eyes were staring into mine, as if from the bottom of a well. She scared me.

"The energy can do so much. It sits there and tempts us to use it. The greater the Adept, the less they use it. What if I told you we could make a ritual to help a werewolf change, but it would require the sacrifice of a rabbit? You might say: *What harm?* It's only a rabbit. The wolf would go and kill rabbits anyway. It wouldn't make any difference to the rabbit." She shook her head again. "That's a trap."

Mary stopped talking suddenly and gave both of us a hug.

"I'm putting my trust in you that you'll see the traps and avoid them. Spirit guide you," she whispered, eyes red, and then she turned and hurried to her car.

We got into the Hill Bitch.

"Are we going to be a good girl, Boss, and go quietly to sleep?" Tullah said sweetly.

I glared at her, but I pocketed the sunglasses, settled back in the seat and tilted the Stetson down over my eyes. Like a good girl.

"Wait, Kaothos," I thought. *"I have a couple of questions."*

"Yes, Amber Farrell?"

"This lock they put on Tullah."

"Yes."

"Don't bullshit me, lizard. You can break it."

"Yes."

"Tullah doesn't know?"

"No."

"And because Tullah doesn't know, Mary doesn't know. That's why Tullah doesn't know yet, because you don't want Mary or anyone else to suspect how powerful you are."

The lizard went silent. There was a quiet hiss, like a radio station that had gone off the air.

"Yes. They will react in fear if they know," she said eventually.

"But lies with good reasons and lies by omission are still lies. You can't lie to your community. And you really can't lie to Tullah. And if you're lying to Tullah, why should I trust what you say to me?"

More silence.

"You are right. We will speak with Tullah tonight. For the others, when we are ready, I will need to reveal my power."

"That's too slippery. We'll talk with Tullah tonight about a schedule for telling everyone in our community."

Again the silence: not yes, not no, exactly.

I went on. *"And at the same time, we are going to explain that while there are perfectly good reasons for me to be off on a trip with Tullah, I haven't forgotten that you want me to bite her. And that decision is going to remain hers to make."*

Any Athanate would want an Adept bound to their House. I could feel it like a constant little tugging in my head. I'd have to be careful to keep my guard up. And it was hard to second-guess a spirit dragon's motivation, but I could smell sneaky. Kaothos confirmed it by her argument.

"The benefits—"

"I don't care if there will be benefits. I don't care that you think if I partly infuse her she will be able to channel more energy. All I care about is that she is the one who will make the decision when she's ready. And if you keep trying to manipulate and maneuver her, I warn you, Tullah will start to hate you."

Silence again—a long, thoughtful silence.

"One more thing, lizard. Tullah can't hear me now."

"No."

"But I can tell you something and you can tell her?"

"Yes."

"Tell her I say her butt's getting bigger—she needs to spend more time down at the Kwan."

"Amber!" Tullah squawked.

I tilted the Stetson up and allowed myself a small snicker. "So, apprentice, we can speak telepathically so long as the lizard acts like a telephone exchange. Might come in handy."

I dropped the Stetson back down.

"Amber Farrell?"

"Yeah, hit me already, lizard."

"I will not lie to you, even by omission, so one last matter. I said I could break the lock on Tullah. I can, but..."

"But?"

"Other than small workings, like this talking with you, or helping you rest, my use of the energy is limited. For bigger workings, I need to channel through Tullah, but as with the explosion at Longmont, I cannot channel as much as I need to through her. And in fact, I cannot channel any major working through her while she is locked. I need to channel through you to break the lock, and I will need to channel through you if we try something major."

After Mary's little talk about the lure of channeling energy, that made me shiver. And channeling Kaothos through me had cost something last time. It'd hurt my spirit guide in some way and blown a few fuses in my head. But if we needed to, we needed to. At least Kaothos was getting the message about being open.

"Thank you. I understand."

A flicker of panic went through me as I felt Kaothos' grip in my head. What if I remembered none of this conversation when I woke? What if Kaothos could control me...

Those were my last thoughts before I sank into the darkness.

Chapter 17

I floated up. It was night and we were just pulling off an interstate. I guessed this had to be I-25, and that would make this the outskirts of Albuquerque.

I wasn't about to tell the lizard, but I did feel much better.

"What're we doing?" I said.

"Finding dinner," Tullah replied, as if that explained everything. "I hear a dog calling me."

She frowned as she said it.

"That's—"

"Yeah. Weird," she said.

"Just a craving?" I asked.

Was she catching my paranoia?

"Dunno."

Visible from the interstate was a fairground with rides, sideshows and craft stalls. And enough flashing lights to power all of the city's discos. It was almost 10 p.m., closing time, as we parked. Kids were being hauled back to cars and the rows of food stands were getting a late evening surge on the way.

Just because Jen had me eating gourmet didn't mean I couldn't appreciate carnival food. From time to time, anyway.

There was nothing obviously dangerous in the scene. Other than being in New Mexico, home to a possible traitorous Athanate House and packs of psychopathic werewolves.

I guess carrying the Mossberg wouldn't give the right impression, but Tullah had remembered to pack my HK Mk23.

We parked and wandered down the likeliest looking row, noses locking onto the best-smelling hot dog stand where we picked up a couple of the most popular offerings.

"Hmm. Some dog with your chili?"

Tullah tried to swallow before laughing. I looked around for anyplace willing to sell me a beer, but there wasn't one in this row. I had a look at the next row and was about to motion Tullah to follow.

When I looked, she wasn't chomping. Instead, she was turning slowly in a circle, peering into the thinning crowds.

We were surrounded by fast food stands and booths selling cheap souvenirs. There really wasn't that much to look at.

"What's up?" I said.

"Dunno, Boss. Itchy feeling. Something not right."

I laughed as if she'd said something funny and nudged us closer to one of the quieter booths.

Ostentatiously looking around for a trash can for my wrapper, I gave everything a once-over. Twice.

Performers were starting to drift in, some of them still in their costumes. A tired cowboy in a buckskin jacket and a sad-faced clown a couple of booths along were eyeing us as they ate their burgers. A spaceman and a five-foot rabbit walked by, laughing over something.

Nothing obvious, but I didn't know what I was looking for.

"Any idea what or where?" I asked quietly.

"No," Tullah said. "Boss…neither of us likes hot dogs and, okay, this is only a couple of minutes from the road, but still, why are we here?"

A little chill went down my spine.

"Hey," a voice said from way below my line of sight.

"Well, hello there." I bent my knees until she could look me in the face without getting a cricked neck. Given my luck with kids recently, I might have kept a little tension in my legs and a bit more distance than usual.

She was about eight, with dark eyes, wild hair like Jofranka's, and the most solemn little face I'd seen outside of church. Her blue dress had been pretty once, about a hundred washes ago. She wore no shoes, but silver bangles tinkled on her wrist as she pushed her hair back out of her face.

"What's your name?" I said, trying not to be obvious about scanning the crowd behind her. I didn't think she'd been set up as a distraction, but most of the people who were after us wouldn't bother about that. They'd take advantage of anything that distracted me.

"Tansy."

"That's a pretty name."

Tansy gave me the look that the comment deserved. "I'll get a better name when I'm older," she said.

"What would a better name be like?"

"Whatever I'm good at." She'd clearly had enough of the dumb grown-up questions. "Grandma says to come with me."

"Uh huh. And where would you take us?"

She had to have learned that exasperated look from the TV. "The booth, of course."

I cleared my throat. This was a new marketing ploy for me, and I was more than a little pissed at Grandma, sending an eight-year-old out to hustle for business.

"Actually, we're just here for the hotdogs—" I started.

"Amber, no." Tullah knelt beside me, looking intently at the girl. "Your grandma is Chatima, isn't she."

"Shhh." Tansy put her finger to her lips. "We shouldn't say her name where other people can hear."

"Okay. We'll come with you," Tullah said. She was frowning again as she leaned in to me and whispered: "Chatima means Caller. I guess that's one of her talents."

I wasn't happy, but Tullah was my expert on anything to do with Adepts, and thinking it through, it seemed unlikely that Athanate or Were could have had enough time to find out we were here, let alone set up an ambush.

We licked our fingers, ditched the wrappings and followed the strange little girl through the food area and out towards the craft booths. All the bright arc lights had been turned off here, though a few trails of flashing bulbs still pulsed away in the night. Booths with generators had small spotlights making bright pools around them.

I checked the HK in my shoulder holster as we walked.

The bad part was that the area was full of shadows. I could have hidden a couple of platoons of Nagas here. The good part; it was empty of innocent families. There were no buyers left, just vendors busy packing their goods away.

Except at the booth where Tansy led us.

It was an old, dusty, brown van with a hinged panel side that lowered to form a counter. One of the supports was missing. It had been replaced by a stack of fruit boxes and the counter sloped down on that side, sagging under the weight of beaded jewelry and blue stone trinkets, Navajo blankets and wooden ornaments.

There was a woman on a chair beside the van. She was snoring. It might have had nothing to do with the half-empty bottle of rye next to her.

"Grandma doesn't look like she's asking anyone to come to the booth," I said.

I got the look again from Tansy. "That's Louise. She's only here to watch."

Watch. Hmm. I bit my tongue.

Tansy's task of delivering us to the booth completed, she proceeded to ignore us and began to load their goods into the back of the van.

"Come," a voice said from the dark inside the van.

Tullah started to move forward and I held her arm.

A dry laugh. "Sometimes too cautious, other times not cautious at all. Don't be scared of me and my gifts."

"Who are you?" I said.

"I'm Chatima, shaman-Adept, and a friend to Mary."

Mary had vouched for her, and maybe she'd be able to tell me something about the Were ritual. *That* had to be worth some risk. I followed Tullah into the back of the van. The side panel was still open, letting in what little light there was outside, but the corners of the van were dark and full of shapes.

"Greetings, Mother," Tullah said as she sat.

"Welcome, Tullah."

"Greetings," I mumbled. It wasn't that I was deliberately being less polite than Tullah, but I was still trying to rein in the paranoia. A working, like the Weres' Call, but focused on us, calling us here to meet this woman. That was some serious talent.

"Welcome, daughters of Speaks-to-Wolves."

Daughters.

Chills ran down my back.

One of the shapes moved and there was the scratch of a lighter.

The candle was tiny—the light didn't even reach the sides of the van—but the flame painted Chatima's face in the soft red and yellow of fresh river earth, hiding her eyes and making a net of the wrinkles on her face, like a tracing of every path she'd ever followed.

The side panel was closed with a screech of hinges and a bang. Maybe Louise had woken up, or maybe Tansy was stronger than she looked.

"Sunstone and Sky-fallen," Chatima said, peering at me. I was as poorly lit as she was, but she seemed to see more of me than I could of her.

Sunstone meant Amber, I knew that. Sky-fallen I hadn't heard before. My wolf spirit guide's name was Hana, which meant Sky in Arapaho.

"Is Sky-fallen your name for my wolf spirit guide?"

She smiled. "No, not Hana. Sky-fallen is Tara."

My mouth fell open, and she laughed. "Oh, I can see her there beside you, but I won't tease you that I'm talking to her or I can read her name from your mind. No, Mary told me about Tara. New-fashioned messages rather than old-fashioned magic."

She reached to one side and brought out three small beakers and a bottle.

"Just water," she said. "The rye seems to have gone missing."

I snorted.

"Tara means Sky-fallen. A name from the old stories," she said, and waved us closer. "Come. No time for old stories tonight. We haven't got long and I have a gift for you."

We shuffled closer around the candle. I sipped the water carefully.

"Mary has told me what was lost," Chatima said, shaking her head. "Speaks-to-Wolves was caught, like you are caught, between one world and another. Between the old ways and the new. A hundred years ago, the working would have been passed from one hand to the next."

"You mean the necklace?" I asked.

She sighed. "The necklace is a part. The working is the whole: the token, the person, the place and the ritual."

"Then we can't help the Were unless we find the necklace first?"

"So rushed, but maybe tonight that's for the best." Her hands moved restlessly in her lap. It looked like she was pouring beads from one hand to the other. "The necklace is the easiest part to replace. The person, that's not so easy."

"What about the ritual? Can I learn it? Would that make me able to help the Were?"

She grimaced. "You might be able to learn, but who would teach you? This is Speaks-to-Wolves' ritual, not mine or Mary's. Not today's need."

"The ritual's lost, then? There's no point to the necklace?" My heart was doing a rollercoaster that would have worked for the fairground outside. One moment, I thought we had it, the next it was all a waste of time.

"No and no." Chatima leaned back. "I needed to see you to be sure, and I'm still not sure. Workings like this aren't lost, but they must be rediscovered."

She rocked where she sat for a moment, as if comforting herself. "It's a heavy burden you're so willing to take up. All of you. You must work together to do this." She looked to Tullah. "Your mother has turned away from the old ways, but did she teach you the steps?"

Tullah nodded, wide eyed.

"Teach them in turn to Sunstone and Sky-fallen. Then together, you will find a spirit place and one who needs your help. You may rediscover what was never quite lost. Make anew."

Tansy had been placing loads quietly into the back of the van. Now the van dipped as someone heavy stepped up.

I spun around in a crouch, the HK in my hand.

It was Louise.

She stopped where she was, looking at the gun with a hard, unhappy glare before turning her eyes to the old woman.

"You're casting, Chatima," she said. "They're looking for us again. I can feel them. Time to go."

I put the gun away, feeling stupid. Either Louise had been on watch in her own way, just as Tansy had said, or...I couldn't tell what was happening in the Adept world. Or both. All the things my everyday experience and instincts told me weren't necessarily so.

"Yes. Time to go, for all of us," Chatima said, and caught my hand. She drew it down near the candle's flame and held hers above it.

Suddenly, I remembered something Mary had said to me. In the deep, dark night, the energy was more powerful. I felt it now, hanging above me, like the promise of thunderstorms.

"So many of life's patterns dance in the candle," Chatima murmured. "Look at it, be part of it."

It was quiet, except for the beating of hearts and the rush of breath. It didn't feel like we were in the back of a van. There was only us, the vastness of night and the tiny flame.

That flame seemed to grow and pass through our hands like cool yellow smoke, soft as a feather. And beads flowed out of hers and pooled in mine, taking a shape and weight as they fell.

It was a necklace, made the same way as my bracelet, warm and strangely heavy in my hand. It had no wolf's eye, but strange patterns seemed to ripple across it.

The candle flickered and dimmed until all I could see were Chatima's eyes looking at me.

Shadows and embers. A figure swayed in the darkness. Fragrant smoke coiled in the air.

"Cursed and blessed," she whispers. *"You tread a difficult path, Amber, where every way bears death and sorrow and pain and loss. You are none of the things they will think you are. In the end, you will have no guides but yourself."*

Her hands press around mine.

"This is a token, a holder of knowledge, a helper to seekers, and it is more. It bears three truths for your spirit quest, three patterns written on it. That much I can do. The dark pattern others have written on you, that I cannot touch."

It got even darker. I blinked to try and clear my sight. She'd said some things that Speaks-to-Wolves had said to me; things I'd never told anyone. *How...*

"You have a thousand questions with no right answers," Chatima said briskly. "Trust yourself—all of you. You will find the way. Now go."

Louise turned on a flashlight.

Chatima snuffed out the candle and urged us out of the back with hurried farewells.

The candle and flashlight seemed to have destroyed my night vision. I couldn't see their faces. I couldn't see anything clearly.

And even as I was saying thank you, I was wondering how the hell I was supposed to figure this out. Tullah could teach me some basic shamanic workings from the sound of it, but there had to be a huge leap between that and a ritual to change a Were. Three patterns? Dark patterns?

Tullah led me away. She seemed completely in awe of Chatima, and she didn't seem to want to question a single thing.

It wasn't till we'd gotten all the way back to the Hill Bitch and I was wearing the necklace, running my hands over the beads, thinking about Olivia, that the sheer enormity of the task overcame me.

"She can call us from ten miles away, she's the last of the shaman-Adepts and she can't give us even a pointer to what we need to do? I'm going back," I said. The afterimage of the candle wasn't so bright in my eyes now that I couldn't make out the way we'd just come.

"Amber, no," Tullah called.

But I was already moving. "If she knows this much she can just tell us what to do, instead of us blundering around in the dark."

I ran back into the fairground, Tullah following with protests.

It had gotten darker where the booths had been. The lights from the food booths seemed to hinder rather than help.

I trotted into the area where the old van had stood. The space was empty, of course. There was one vendor left thirty yards further on. He was finishing up the last of his loading using a tiny LED flashlight mounted on his hat. I ran over to him.

"Say, you know the brown van that was over there?" I asked. "Couple of women run it and there's a young girl, about eight, who scouts for them."

"Oh, I know the one ya mean. Little girl, bangles, cute as a button. Doesn't take no prisoners."

"Yeah. Them. Where'd they go?"

He shrugged. "They gone's all I can say. Dunno where. See 'em at fairs, time to time. They come, they go. More way of life for them than a way to sell stuff, y'know."

"Any idea which way they went?"

He grunted and picked up another box. "Too busy packing to watch 'em, lady."

I got the hint.

Chapter 18

"Where are we going?" Tullah said half an hour later. I was driving now.

"I feel mysteriously called," I replied, getting her back for the whole Chatima thing. "We're going to see someone I know who has a business around here. I've forgotten the exact address, but I'll know it when I see it."

I'd gotten off the interstate again and I was following San Mateo Boulevard south, through a district full of chain restaurants and auto sales. I was still wearing the necklace. It felt oddly heavy around my neck.

"Shouldn't we check into a motel somewhere first?"

"No, I want to get a feel for this place before we do that."

I took a right and followed the road down the side of a shopping mall, then right again onto a wide street with grass verges and trees, bicycle paths and a couple more small restaurants. It was close to the interstate, but discreet. There was a self-storage warehouse across the way, a dog-grooming boutique, an ocean of parking spaces, and one tan brick building illuminated by spotlights pointed up its walls. I knew I'd found it.

About fifty cars were clustered around that building, so I guessed business was reasonable.

There were few windows; if you were inside and looking out then something was going badly wrong with the club. Instead, to break up the blankness of the walls, an artistic design of intertwined brown and white lizards had been painted, circling the building at the height of about ten feet. It was cleverly done; in the uplighting, you lost a little of the detail and it made you think of naked bodies writhing together. In the daytime, hey, it was just art.

"Amber, this looks like a strip club," Tullah said as we walked across the drop-off area and up to the front doors.

"Oh, at the very least," I said.

The glass doors opened and a doorman with the sort of shoulders that made any jacket look too small ushered us into a plain lobby. I couldn't say it was a warm welcome. He probably thought we didn't look like the types to spend money inside, and he was right. I guessed that was better than being taken for working girls.

"Hi," I said brightly. "My name's Amber. I'm here to see Dominé."

He blinked at the name. It looked like Dominé had kept her previous operating style; her name hadn't been well known to patrons when she was based in Denver. Still, knowing the owner's name wasn't a magic way to get in. The bouncer pressed his earpiece once, nodded silently and stood in front of the inner doors with his hands held loosely at his side. His nose twitched. I was still wearing Mary's bouquet and I must have smelled like a major disaster in a perfume factory.

Above his right shoulder a spy cam swiveled and focused its cold eye on us.

Dominé ran sex clubs. Back when I'd been released from the army, Colonel Laine had me scouring the fringes of the social scene in Denver hunting for vampires, as we thought of them then. Dominé's Club Agonia had been flagged as a possible place they might use, and the colonel had gotten me to visit the club on their vampire-themed night.

Dominé herself had nothing to do with them, but three Matlal Athanate had visited the club. Unfortunately, the three had tipped over into rogue behavior. I'd done what I could, which ended up with my killing all three, but not before Dominé had lost two of her staff. Despite that, when she'd left, she sent me a message to contact her if I was ever down in Albuquerque. And here I was, not exactly sure of my welcome. But Dominé was sensitive to the paranormal, and I was eager to know anything she could tell me about the city.

Behind the doorman, locks clicked open.

He moved smartly to one side.

"Welcome to Club Vasana, ladies. Dante will escort you to see Dominé," he said, opening the door for us and actually managing a smile. "I trust you'll have a memorable evening."

"Brace yourself," I muttered to Tullah.

Dante was waiting for us in the indigo-carpeted hallway.

Dominé designed the most outrageous uniforms for her staff. Last time I visited her old club in Denver, the general staff, who worked the doors and the bars, had been dressed as romantic highwaymen, with black Zorro masks, velvety jackets, puffy lace cuffs and silken ruffs. The wait staff had been nearly naked in a take on BDSM cowboy porn.

Dante was positively subdued in comparison to that. She wore an Al Capone suit, chalk stripe, with big shoulders and narrow hips, complete with black silk shirt and thin white tie, though big Al wouldn't have been able to teeter along on the pin-sharp pumps she wore. Her blue-black hair was cut short as a boy's, and teased into an old-fashioned wave curling over her forehead.

For a moment, I wasn't entirely sure whether Dante was he or she. The face was exquisite but androgynous. No makeup and pale, the lips unfashionably thin and the jaw strong. Something in the glossy onyx eyes made me decide to stay with *she*.

The voice was low but feminine. "Please," she said quietly, "follow me."

The main club was in the middle of the building, separated from the curving corridor by a wall of dark glass. Sounds of good dance music came through, but it all seemed a lot tamer than Club Agonia had been.

Dante turned and led us down a set of painfully white marble stairs.

A matching pair of doormen stood at the bottom, male and female, their suits the same as Dante's. They were guarding a double set of smoked glass doors.

Dante exchanged nods with them and pushed through.

We were in the VIP section of the club, and we got the first glimpse of Club Vasana's wait staff uniforms. They were dressed as police to complement the mobsters, naturally. That is, if police uniforms comprised mainly the peaked hat and handcuffs. Pants had shrunk till they weren't even as much as a hand's width top to bottom. Shirts were a white collar attached to a strip two inches wide down their fronts, with a nipple-height bar of the same size going around the back. The guys had nightsticks hidden down their pants. Maybe. And those boots; well, I didn't know much about Albuquerque, but they were definitely not compliant with Denver PD standards.

"Oh, my God," Tullah muttered.

The room was soundproofed from the main club, and the VIP room music was being provided live. A shock-haired redhead in a split dress the same color as her hair was performing a slow motion belly dance while laying down dreamy, smoking vocals to an old disco number. Snakes of dry ice fog floated down from the ceiling and caressed her body. She sounded like she was about to reach orgasm at any moment.

On either side of her, wait staff couples, stripped down to thongs, danced on podiums. Or rather, they were using their bodies to apply baby oil to each other in time with the music. The podiums were harshly lit from below, giving the illusion the couples were trapped in glass cylinders.

The clientele were draped over low couches in the shadows at the sides, or dancing under the laser-slim spotlights.

We passed close by one of those dancers. She was still half-dressed in a business suit, with a pink silk blouse hanging untucked over a pencil skirt bunched up almost to her waist. This morning's elegant hairdo was now unraveling over her shoulders.

She was firmly locked between two of the male wait staff, all oiled, gleaming muscles and slow churning hips.

From the ecstatic look on her face, I guessed she would still think it was worth it, even when she found out later that there was no way of getting the baby oil stains out of those expensive clothes of hers.

Probably just another night at Club Vasana.

And then, like a snake sliding through the layered sensations, through the hot oil and dry ice and the floral shield of Mary's bouquet, through the adrenaline buzz of the club: another scent and presence.

"Were," I mouthed at Tullah, as we descended a last set of steps into Dominé's private area.

Dominé wasn't a paranormal, but she sensed the true desires and needs of all people, paranormals included. What if she'd followed that thread down the rabbit hole? What if Club Vasana was the favored nightspot for local Were?

Just how good an idea was this?

Chapter 19

Dante knocked on an oak door at the end of a short corridor.

"*Entrez.*"

Dante waved us in, remaining outside to shut the door quietly behind us.

Dominé sat at her desk in a black tux and bow tie, which contrasted sharply with her thick white hair, worn loose and flowing over her shoulders. A single red rose was pinned on her lapel.

She came around the table to greet me like an old friend.

"Amber, what a wonderful surprise." She kissed me on both cheeks and held me by the arms as she looked me over, head to toe. Her eyes still had that depthless feel I remembered. It made their gray seem almost transparent.

"Well, well, well," she murmured, and turned. "And this is?"

"Tullah," I said, with a little smile. "My apprentice."

"*Très intéressant.* Delighted, Tullah." They shook hands, and we sat down around her desk. The chairs were big and soft, the frames made from an unfamiliar bronze wood, and padded with leather the color of old blood.

She'd already had a bottle of champagne delivered in a bucket of ice. She popped the cork and poured three narrow glasses.

I took the opportunity to scan the area while she was distracted with the drinks. My ability to sense paranormals had expanded enormously since I'd last met her a year ago. I sniffed with my wolf nose. I reached carefully with eukori.

She felt...different. But there was no sense of Athanate or Were or Adept about her, and nothing to indicate there'd ever been Were in this office. I relaxed. A little. If I could hide my Were scent, I'd assume others could.

"Is it only a year?" Dominé said as she handed us our glasses. "You should have called. As it is, you're lucky to have caught me. There's not enough for me to do here. Club Vasana runs itself." She waved a hand dismissively to indicate all the floors above us. "Next week I will be back at my new club in Los Angeles."

"Sounds as if things are going well," I said. "I got the meaning of Club Agonia. What's Vasana mean?"

She laughed. "That which your subconscious desires. Or maybe you could think of it as an imprint on the soul which disposes you to certain actions. For my members, I would like it to mean the habit of pleasure."

That tickled me, so I held my glass up and proposed a toast: "The habit of pleasure."

We touched glasses and sipped. The champagne tasted exquisite, and I purred a little appreciation of it, which made her smile.

"But you aren't here on vacation, are you?" she said. "Not even a study trip. You're not looking for the pleasures my little club provides."

"Hmm, no."

Diana had left Denver without her kin. She'd visited Canada to finalize the Canadian Houses becoming associates of Altau. Then she'd come here, to Albuquerque, and the trail stopped. From what I understood of Athanate society, in Canada, they would have offered her their own kin. But here, where did she go for Blood? Not House Romero until she was sure of them. I doubted it was Club Vasana, but stranger things had happened to me.

Tullah had prepared a standard missing persons packet before leaving Denver. She pulled a photo of Diana out of her pocket and handed it across to Dominé.

"Our friend came to New Mexico, and now she's missing," I said. "There's a small chance she might have come to a club like this."

Dominé held the photo tilted, to catch the subdued light.

"This one I would have remembered," she said. "And sadly, I do not."

She handed it back and sipped her drink. "If she were merely seeking a companion, I don't think she would have needed to put herself to the effort of visiting a club."

It was a question, delicately phrased. I understood, if I wanted any more, I would have to be more open. My Athanate instincts were to tell her nothing, but she already knew the background from our last meeting a year ago, when I'd been a policewoman hunting the rogues in my spare time.

"She has a need for Blood," I said, "and she might have come looking for those who provide it."

"Ah. The secret people. And you, Amber." She leaned forward, chin resting on her hand. "You hunted them. To protect those who could not protect themselves, you stared into the abyss. Yet you call this woman *friend*. I think, as the philosopher would have said, the abyss has stared back at you. You have become what you hunted."

"I have." I could see Tullah twitching at how open I was being with Dominé. "It turns out that the secret world is more complex than I thought." I took another chance. "I think that's not news to you at all. You have some unusual guests tonight, for instance."

"Not guests at all." She sat back, a little frown mark appearing. "Let me be completely open. I wanted to take no sides in these disputes. To protect myself and my staff, I had to."

"You've made a deal with the local pack? They're providing bodyguards?"

She appeared genuinely uncertain.

"We're not here to take sides either, Dominé. We just want to find some friends and go back to Denver."

She came to a decision as she poured us more champagne.

"Naturally, I'm not supposed to speak about it. Yes, I have an arrangement with the werewolves. They protect me from the vampires and the witches. I'm wondering about how useful it is now." She made a gesture at us. "No one has come to warn me about you."

"We're unusual, we're not local and I have this to confuse them." I touched the little bouquet pinned to my jacket. "And we'd like to leave without disturbing anyone or attracting any attention to you. We've no interest in meeting the Were. Quite the opposite."

She nodded, relieved.

"Are you sure about this arrangement you have with them?" I asked. The Were that Larimer had told me about didn't sound like the kind of people Dominé should be doing business with.

"One doesn't enjoy paying protection," her mouth twisted in that French way that said *what can you do about it*, "but it's been satisfactory."

She opened a drawer on her desk and brought out a tourist map and marker pens. Motioning us forward, she started to color blocks of the map in green. "These streets here, there are many clubs and pubs your friend might have been advised to visit. Places one might go to meet other people without commitment."

She changed to red. "And here," she marked a location with a red circle, "this club is where the pack meets. I understand you want to avoid them?"

"Yes. Thanks." I looked at the red-circled club and grinned. *Bot Wobbly*, it said. Not a name that reached out to me. But Dominé marking it was really useful. I didn't want to trust to Mary's bouquet too much.

"Last thing." I dived into my pocket for the crumpled piece of paper that Larry had given me just before he'd been captured at Cheesman Park.

"Do you have any idea what this is? I think it's supposed to tell me where to find some other friends I'm also looking for."

It was a mass of strange, illegible squiggles and lines on both sides. I passed it over to Dominé.

She took it, squinted, and clicked her tongue in impatience. She pulled the lamp on her table closer. It was an old-fashioned banker's lamp, with a steel cylindrical shell directing the bright light downward.

She held the paper under the lamp and turned it around and around.

"I can see nothing that makes any sense," she said and shrugged expressively.

"May I?" Tullah reached out and took the paper.

Under the lamp, the markings on both sides were clearly visible. While we watched, Tullah tentatively folded it, pulling the paper one way, then the other. Straightened it back out. One fold, then two.

On the third attempt at a multiple fold, she stopped. What had been random lines on both sides while the paper was unfolded now joined up, as long as the light was shining through it.

"Ah," Dominé said. "A trick. So clever."

Unfortunately, that didn't get us very far.

"Is that a river?" I asked. It looked like a stylized image of two large rivers being joined by a few tributaries.

"There's a word here," Tullah said. "VAN."

"A particular type of van? A place name? A person's name? Van something?" I sighed. "Good job working out the trick, but I think we should send this back for David to look at. It's the kind of puzzle he likes."

Holding it up against the light, Tullah photographed it with her cellphone.

"I'll log in to send it," she said, meaning when we had access to some internet and could use Matt's untraceable email system.

I finished my champagne.

"Of course, you must stay in the guest rooms," Dominé said. "Behind the shop on the opposite side of the road. Not for club members, naturally—for staff and friends."

Tullah was trying to shake her head without Dominé seeing it.

"Thanks. That would be great," I said. "Just for one night. We'll find our way around tomorrow."

"Dante will take you over. Maybe we will have dinner to celebrate finding your friends. There are some wonderful places to eat if you know where."

We left it like that, and Dante took us out of an emergency exit and across the street.

Chapter 20

"You sure about this, Boss?" Tullah said after she'd finished sweeping the room for bugs.

I sighed. I'd showered quickly while she'd searched, and I was toweling my hair.

The room was small and neat, with two double beds. It could have been any small hotel, but the huge advantage was we were untraceable. Just so long as Dominé was trustworthy.

"Yeah," I said finally. Like any hotel or motel room, this place would be a nightmare to try and defend from a serious attack. The front door was off a passage with a single entry and exit point. The windows overlooked a flat roof and a tiny courtyard, currently full of the Hill Bitch. Having our car close at hand was good, but the roof was easy access for someone to get to us.

My initial thought had been to go to sleep fully dressed and ready to run, but I decided I trusted Dominé enough to wear some sweats that Jen had packed for me when my House decided to send me off to New Mexico.

Which thoughts brought me to how to call home.

Tullah had brought a couple of new encrypting phones that her boyfriend Matt had set up to connect securely with the phones at home or the Kingslund Group, but I used her laptop and the room's internet connection instead.

I found Tullah had installed new levels of security which prevented me from using the webcam, so it was voice only, but I got through immediately. Despite the hour, they must have been waiting by the computer.

"Honey—"

"Amber—"

Alex and Jen spoke over each other.

"Are you okay?"

Having just their voices to listen to didn't stop my heart from aching when I heard them.

"I'm fine," I managed without tearing up. Been away a day and it was like I'd had bits of me forcibly torn out. *Man up, Farrell.* "What about you?"

"We're fine," Jen said. "We're here surrounded by guards, in a safe place, not alone in the middle of enemy territory."

"I'm not alone, but I would have been if I'd planned it."

"Ah. Yes—" Jen started, but Alex overrode her. "Had to do it this way."

I let it pass. I wasn't going to spend time arguing with them. "Yelena?" I should have been there. I shouldn't have dropped this problem on them. What if she'd—

Jen laughed, a lovely rich sound, even on the laptop speakers. "Well, no complaints from Gary and Leon. She'll be upset she missed you, but she was dead on her feet. I sent her to bed. I think one of the twins might have snuck in with her."

I sighed. That sounded as if it'd gone better than it might have.

"Alex?" I wanted his opinion as well.

"I only saw her very briefly at dinner, but she wants it to work, and I like her." He growled a little. "It'll be better when her marque's changed."

"Does Pia think—"

"She's just come in now."

"Hi, Amber," Pia said quietly. "If you're asking whether we'll be successful changing her marque, then yes, of course. It'll be even easier when you're biting, but David and I have started already."

Manassah had been Bite Central today, by the sound of it.

"That's good, but I guess what I was really asking is, will she really be part of our House? She's Carpathian and she's been acting the part of a Basilikos. We're Panethus."

Pia hummed a bit before answering carefully. "Well...I can't give you a definitive yes or no. The Carpathians wouldn't have sent her out to live like she did if they hadn't conditioned her to be able to handle it. But that would mean she could default back to Carpathian behavior, and we know next to nothing about that, without access to Skylur or Diana. She says she will tell us everything, but she wants to talk to you first. And that should be face to face, I think."

"And Nick? I think I'm hearing Yelena and the twins didn't stop at Blood. I understand he's in hiding somewhere, but do we know what he's feeling about this?"

"Not at the moment," Pia said.

She seemed to have more to say.

"What is it?"

"We're growing House Farrell, but not to a plan. We need three or four kin for every Athanate." She frowned. "It's a problem, and it will get worse quickly."

Everything seemed to be a problem.

Jen spoke again. "Honey, Bian's going to be coming over soon. I know what she told you to do, but I don't want her to have proof of the fact that you're in Albuquerque, so we need to finish this quickly."

I understood. Bian was in a difficult position. Some things, like actually hearing evidence that I was in New Mexico, would have to be reported to Naryn, and I wanted him on my case like I wanted hives. Of course, if Naryn actually questioned Bian, he'd find out what she'd told me to do anyway, but hopefully, he was too busy.

The trouble was, there was so much to organize with my House.

"Okay, I hear you, Pia. Let's talk alternatives next time I call. Meanwhile, I'm emailing David an image which we think is a map of some kind—something here in Albuquerque. Please get him to look at it for me."

If anyone could solve Larry's puzzle, it was David.

"Will do," Alex said. "And you need to call Agent Ingram. He's been trying to find you."

"Yeah." That, I'd expected. "And what about Keith?"

"He's calmed down some. Julie's okay, but Keith not so much. I guess we need to be able to show him he and Julie are safe," Jen said. "Oh, yes. Our lawyers have had Noble's court order thrown out."

I'd forgotten all about that. Noble's scheme had involved getting me institutionalized in his care, and that needed a court order declaring me mentally incapable.

"Thanks—"

"De nada. We're doing everything to back you up. Alex has sent you an email with what we know about the New Mexico Were," Jen said, "and Pia's put in everything about House Romero."

"Which isn't much," Pia said. "Bian's at the gate now. We have to finish this."

"Last thing," Jen said. "Alice Emerson was pretty clear she wants you to hold off from both your Were and Athanate sides for the moment. No changing, no biting. I've put what she said in the email as well."

"Wait. Wait," I said. "Bian's there now? This is about Naryn wanting kin—"

"Trust us," Jen said. "Alex, stall Bian for a second, please. Honey, I'm sorry, I know this is going to freak you out. I'm going to Haven."

"Jen! No!"

"Listen to me. Because Alex and I are your kin, we're head of the House kin as well. We've both agreed, we're not sending anyone else there until we know we can trust Naryn. We're discussing it with Bian tonight. The point is, I'm a prominent citizen. Naryn won't dare do anything bad to me."

I tried to interrupt again, but she rolled on.

"You've got to put this aside and concentrate on your job, which is to get Diana back. That's for your own health as well as stopping Naryn from pulling this kind of shit." She raced on. "Gotta go. Talk again tomorrow. I love you, honey, I love you. *We* love you."

Her voice had gotten scratchy. She shut off the connection and it felt like she'd cut a physical link between us.

Tullah emerged from the shower, hair wrapped in a towel like an Indian princess.

"All okay?" she asked.

I nodded. No, it wasn't, not by miles, but I had to admit, this was what we had to be doing. Jen's decision was only what I should have expected of her if I'd thought about it instead of reacting with my gut.

It sucked. It all sucked.

"So...time for school then," Tullah said. "Magic 101."

"Uh, no." I gave myself a shake. "Advanced Dragon first. You there, lizard?"

The room got fuzzy. The dragon's body seemed to emerge from the walls. Next to the door, the small desk and flat screen TV disappeared, to be replaced by Kaothos' head and unblinking eyes.

"Isn't someone going to feel that, or whatever it is that Adepts do when they sense someone using the energy?" I spoke out loud; it was more natural than *thinking* words at Kaothos.

Dragon laughter.

"If I did manifest, yes, they certainly would. It would also be uncomfortable for me to manifest in a wall. Untidy, too, as far as the wall is concerned."

"So you're just messing with my head again."

Kaothos blinked.

Tullah looked back and forth suspiciously.

"You two were talking in the car? You've been planning something?"

"We were talking and we planned this discussion. I have lied to you, Tullah. I am sorry. I was trying to protect us, but it was wrong."

Tullah had gone pale and tight-lipped.

Okay, maybe that could have been introduced better.

"There is good news," I said, and Tullah glared at me.

"This isn't a joke—"

"No, it isn't. What Kaothos lied about, by not telling you, is that we can remove the lock on your powers."

"But..." She stopped and her face went blank. After a while, a little frown line appeared between her eyebrows. "This isn't about me knowing, it's about Ma knowing?"

I nodded.

Normally, it was Tullah who'd tell me that she wished she could do what I did and put everything else aside and focus like that. Now I was thinking the same thing about her. At least one of us was working efficiently.

We sat silently for a minute, Tullah's face turned toward Kaothos, and I guessed they were in conversation. The frown line disappeared briefly and then came back worse than before.

"No!" Tullah said. "Amber, it might damage you again if we use you as a sink for the lock's working."

"Okay...I don't know what you two are saying to each other, but what are the alternatives? Would the Denver community *ever* unlock you once they find out about Kaothos?"

"Ma could break the lock."

"Would she? Go against the whole community? I know she's going against Weaver at the moment, but I get the feeling that none of the community would trust you and Kaothos. Am I right?"

"Amber is correct," Kaothos said.

"But what if we kill Hana?" Tullah said. "We hurt her so badly before, she's barely able to talk to you."

It was true, Hana hadn't developed into the sort of talkative spirit guide that I'd expected when I'd first become aware of her.

"I think some of that is because she's helping with the Were side of me," I said. "She helped me fight Noble. She helped me be a wolf."

"Possibly," Kaothos said. *"Sit back for a moment."*

I slid up the bed until I was leaning back against the headboard.

Hana appeared on my lap—a warm, sleeping bundle curled up nose to tail, bigger than she had been before.

Kaothos was just a visual illusion. Hana was warm and heavy. I could feel her fur. I scratched behind her ears gently and she stirred without waking.

"She's still a pup," I said, even though she'd grown much more than an ordinary wolf would have in the few weeks since I'd known she was there.

"A spirit guide's appearance changes with the growth of the bond between you."

"We *think* the damage isn't permanent," Tullah said, glancing aside at Kaothos. "She's just recovering. The sleep is like her representation of the state you two are in. Helping you with your wolf instincts is something else entirely."

"Is there a difference for Hana between channeling your energy through me, like I did for the explosion at Longmont, and this acting as a sink that you're talking about?"

"It *is* different, but it's still channeling energy."

"It's important," I said. "We have to get your capabilities back."

"Why? I can't use them. If I do, I'm going to light up the town with an Adept signature that will have every one of them hunting me down. Even when we go back to Denver, I'll have to spend all my time *not* using it. The community will completely freak out when they discover Kaothos. If they find out by Kaothos blowing up another building…"

"Okay. Okay. We have to do it sometime and we have to reveal Kaothos as a well-behaved little dragon, maybe with the help of the Adepts from the Empire of Heaven."

"If I came up with that, Boss, you'd have said it wasn't so much a plan as a handful of straws to grasp."

I had to laugh. I'd taught her too well.

"How strong are you exactly, lizard?"

"Stronger than any of them." I could hear the pride in her words. *"I will grow stronger than the whole community together."*

"Yeah, and I can see why that might worry them."

"But to do that, I will need Tullah able to channel more energy and that—"

"Yeah, I remember, she needs to be infused with Athanate prions. You want me to bite her. Not happening at the moment."

"I understand."

"Make sure you do." Tullah and I spoke together.

"Not that it's going to be a problem," Tullah said hesitantly, looking away, "when you're sure you're okay."

My Athanate flexed in pleasurable anticipation.

Hana vanished. I took a break in the bathroom to calm down. Not what I needed at the moment—my Athanate getting hot to bite again.

I came back and climbed into bed. Kaothos had vanished too, and I found I wasn't in the mood for Magic 101.

Tullah didn't take the hint.

She sat in the lotus position on the edge of her bed and clapped her hands together, smiling like a primary school teacher.

"Now class, pay attention."

"Do we have to?" I whined, laying it on. Couldn't give my apprentice an easy time.

"Yup. The sooner we start, the sooner we'll be finished."

"Mary said we shouldn't do any channeling."

"Everyone can channel a tiny bit. That creates enough background noise that what we do won't register at all." She clapped her hands again. "No more excuses. Now, there are reasons Adepts don't explain about the energy, and one of them is it's very difficult. If you're teaching someone something physical, or scientific, you can show them. You can go through the working from the first principles. There are rules. It works every time, or there are reasons why it doesn't. There are words for everything that people agree on, more or less." She hugged a pillow to herself. "The energy isn't like that. Every interaction is personal. I can't really tell you what it will feel like for you. I can't tell you how to do something. I don't have the words to best capture what you need. I can't give you a book of rules. I won't be able to explain why it doesn't work sometimes. All I can do is guide your learning, but that's a long process."

"Wow, I feel better already."

There was a sizzling laugh in the darkness. She was still here, of course.

"Attend to your lesson, pupil."

"Go lie on a hot rock, lizard."

"Hold on. Can I block Kaothos?" I asked. "Prevent her from knocking me out?"

Tullah nodded. "Just the same as you prevented Matlal from attacking you by making a mental barrier, you can do the same for Kaothos."

There was an unspoken *at the moment* behind her words which gave me a shiver.

"Diana taught me to fuel that with anger. Does that mean if I lose the anger, I lose the ability?"

"No. Once you've done something like that it becomes easier to do it again, and then it starts being something you want to do. Like Dominé was saying about *vasana*. That's why we have to be so careful with the energy."

This was making me feel so much happier. Not.

"Chatima said there was a difference between shamanic and, what was it, 'new ways?' What's that about?"

"As good a place to start as any," Tullah said. "Modern Adepts regard shamanic workings about the same as completely untrained workings."

She scratched her head. "The modern way is to work everything from first principles. All very formal. You don't learn to set something on fire, you learn to vary its temperature until it reaches the point it catches fire. That kinda thing."

"Shamanic works much more on intuition and feel. Visualization and ritual. Your spirit guide helps. They're like a reservoir of instinct about what will work. And of course, they're a better channel to the energy."

"Does that mean I'm wasting my time until Hana starts talking to me?"

"No, we can get you doing some small workings, in preparation for when she recovers. And the necklace probably doesn't need Hana."

"Okay. I guess it's shamanic." I rubbed the beads between my fingers. I liked the smoothness, the warmth they seemed to hold.

"Yeah. The working certainly isn't a step by step. Ma might be able to understand it, but most Adepts would just get confused." She clapped her hands. "Let's try lesson 101. It's common to shamanic and modern. Close your eyes."

When I'd obeyed, she went on. "As you know from Ma, magic isn't the word we use. We just call it energy. We don't know where it comes from or where it goes to, but I want you to visualize it flowing through you. Try to think of it like air, or pure, pure water, welling up inside you and flowing out in every direction."

I focused on my breathing. Something I couldn't see or feel that came from somewhere I didn't know, flowing through me to somewhere else I didn't know.

Yeah. But the breathing helped.

"Everyone has it and everyone touches it a little. What Adepts do is consciously weave and sense the energy. Power is how much you can change the flow and how far or how long you can do it."

I remembered lying on the sofa at Manassah, half-dreaming, my eukori reaching out and touching the sleeping minds of my House. And the Call of the pack.

So maybe I could think of eukori and the Call as touching and sensing this energy. That made it more real for me.

"One reason we don't like to call it magic, is that magic is supposed to do completely impossible things. You can't turn time backwards. You can't turn a car into a cow. The energy does real things, and to use it consciously, you have to visualize what you want it to do in a consistent way. But we're not going to do that yet. I just want you to keep your eyes closed and try and visualize the energy flowing through you."

My usual meditation method was visualizing my movements through the martial arts forms taught to me by Liu, so I had practice in these sort of mind exercises. It felt odd to sit and visualize my body being still and something else moving. I tried thinking of wind blowing in my face, or water flowing down my body.

From inside, Tullah had said.

How could I imagine the feeling of something flowing out of me, like I was leaking? Those images weren't helpful. It wasn't working.

I was about to open my eyes again when I thought of sand.

Mom and Dad are laughing. I'm sitting on the sand in the Great Dunes Park down in southern Colorado. Desert sand with the mountains as a backdrop. Big blue sky above. I'm holding up handfuls and letting it trickle out between my fingers. It's so fine, it's like holding water in your hand. The wind catches it and makes fantails down the side of the dune.

I'm fascinated by it. I try counting seconds—one thousand, two thousand, three... How long does it take for a handful to escape? How many grains of sand in a handful? How many in a dune?

As I stopped looking for it, I felt the energy flowing through me, like a million tiny particles blowing away in the wind.

My eyes were still shut but I could feel the room around me.

"Sand," I said. But not like sand. Falling away in every direction, even upward. And falling out of Tullah, and some of what fell out of Tullah fell into me, and the other way around as well. "Cool."

Then I noticed the flickering darkness around Tullah and, without thinking, I stretched out my real hand toward her.

I got a zap like an electric shock.

"Oww!" I jerked upright in bed. "That freaking hurt."

Tullah looked at me in amazement. "Kaothos? You didn't—"

"No. Amber did it herself. She acted as a natural sink for a tiny bit of the working of the lock."

"But I didn't get a shock when I touched her before."

"As you visualized the energy, you were channeling it. That's what connected with the lock." Tullah was still sitting, but she was practically bouncing on her bed. "Let's try something."

The reawakened enthusiasm in her was wonderful to see. She'd brightened my life all those long days when all I'd had to worry about was where the next paycheck was coming from and what the Colonel might want me to do. And whether I was turning into a vampire. It felt good to see it again. But…

"You're sure this isn't this going to register with the local Adepts?"

"You won't be able to do anything that strong."

Famous last words, I thought.

Tullah ignored my caution. "Come on, lie back and think of sand."

I did, but for all the excitement of the first step, the second step died of boredom a half hour later. However she had me try to envision it, I couldn't make the flow of sand vary. She wanted me to make it spin, like an eddy in a stream, or ripple. I couldn't.

Tullah tried to pass it off as unimportant. "First attempt. It's nothing." But she was disappointed, and I guessed I was too.

Was it my fault? Or was it because Kaothos had burned out Hana? Or was it that I didn't really have any capability, other than as a sort of sink for other people's workings?

In the end, we turned out the lights and lay down.

"What about the stuff Chatima said about patterns in the necklace?" I said.

"Huh? What're you talking about?"

"Nothing."

As I'd half suspected, part of Chatima's message had been for my ears alone. Which meant I would have to work it all out alone. Wonderful.

Tullah's thoughts were elsewhere.

"Y'know the wait staff in the club," she said. "The boys. Were those nightsticks down their pants, or, I mean are they like, for real?"

"Ohhh, you noticed," I said. "Only one way you ever gonna find out, girl."

Which meant I was laughing as the reptile struck again and I went out like a snuffed candle.

Chapter 21

FRIDAY

The next morning, the search started off every bit as grindingly dull and unfruitful as I'd promised Tullah and Jofranka that PI work could be. I liked that it was a salutary lesson—not so much that I was participating in it.

After breakfast, we started with reception desks at downtown hotels and worked outwards in a spiral. We took in car rental companies and cab stands. Bars and clubs would have to wait for later in the day. We showed Diana's photo, checked them off the list and moved on. Of course, the staff at many of the places we visited worked shifts, so we'd need to visit them again.

Pia had found the names of a couple of hotels that Diana had used before. There, I left a copy of her photo and a burn phone cell number to contact me.

Around mid-morning, I walked in and then straight back out of a hotel, pushing Tullah in front of me. There were werewolves in the hotel.

A tense few minutes followed, but Mary's bouquet seemed to have worked; no one came out looking for us.

We took the opportunity to sit in the Hill Bitch for a while, drinking takeout coffee and watching to see if there was anyone obviously sniffing our trail.

Nothing.

I couldn't put Agent Ingram off any longer. Tullah set up the laptop and latched onto a couple of unsecured WiFi connections. Matt's program, still using the tap-dancing octopus animation, made a secure connection with a remote server on the other side of the world and then opened a telephone line for me.

"Now I'm a-guessing I know who this is," Ingram drawled when he picked up. He had tracers on his phones and was always mildly upset when Matt's software defeated them.

"Howdy," my demon answered before I could stop it.

Agent Ingram ran an FBI project called Anthracite, their continuing mission to seek out strange new organizations hidden in the USA, because they were out there somewhere. I didn't believe there was even a suggestion of X-Files in their brief, but Ingram himself was both mentally flexible and dogged in pursuit. If it was out there, he'd find the truth. The paranormal world was running out of shadow to hide in.

He'd been distracted by unraveling Ops 4-16, but he wouldn't forget there was something else out there. My task was to introduce him to Diana and see if we could use Project Anthracite to help manage the process of Emergence without the catastrophic effects that would result from premature discovery of the paranormal world.

Yeah, Ingram was important, but my demon didn't care. Luckily, neither did Ingram.

"Howdy right back at you, Ms. Farrell. Now, would you be available to come talk today?"

"Unfortunately not, and the people I want you to meet are all unavailable. I'm working to fix things right now."

"And *where* would you be working to fix things, if I may ask?"

Damn.

"Ah. That's kinda operationally sensitive."

"I did say, Ms. Farrell, that whatever patience Job has seen fit to pass to me personally, the FBI cannot wait. I do recall, I did also ask that you not wander away."

"I know. I'm sorry, but it's unavoidable. I'm doing everything I can. Give me a couple of days. Please."

A couple of days could mean three, right? In a few days, maybe I could squeeze a couple more. How long was it going to take? The longer it took, the more difficult that meeting was going to be.

"Hmm. I *am* busy with the documentation your Colonel Laine has provided to me. Handy, since those Naga folk did such a good job of destroying everything on your old base."

Thank you, Colonel.

"Can I ask how it's going?" I said.

He snorted. "More tangled than a backwoods family tree." He sighed, and I imagined him lifting his boots onto his desk. "That up-front committee, with the fancy acronym, JF-CoStPROE, they were in cahoots with Petersen and his bosses, whoever *they* may be. There were five of them on the committee. Three dead and two left the country, far as we can tell."

"Dead? Killed?"

"Officially a suicide, a car accident and a mugging gone wrong." I could tell what he thought of those. "And those Nagas, most of them left in planes that flew over Mexico and out into the Pacific till their tanks ran dry. No flight plan, no communication with ATC."

"Parachuted somewhere quiet," I said. A whole battalion, probably gone over to Basilikos.

"We figured." He was quiet for a moment. "Lots missing from those records, Ms. Farrell. Got holes like a back road speed sign in Henderson County. Nothing on the colonel's last job, for instance."

He was referring to Obs, the Ops 4 medical research department. The department which would have records of me and the whole story of prions and Athanate and Were.

When I didn't respond, he went on: "The people who worked there seem to have disappeared, and your former colleagues have been unwilling to speculate on what went on in the research area. Or what it meant with respect to you."

"I guess we'll have a lot of explaining to do."

"You surely will. A week and no more. I thank you, and good day to you, Ms. Farrell."

I turned the laptop off. He'd seen through my ruse of asking for a little and a little more. When he said a week, he meant it.

"Come on, time to get back on the trail," I said to Tullah, and we set off on a second round of door to door.

It was as fruitless as the first.

The highlight of the morning came from a small independent car rental company. The owner had a Weimaraner, a big dog with the blue-gray hair and the mad yellow eyes they sometimes have. He also had an irate customer on the phone, and he wasn't paying attention. The hound had picked up on the emotions and decided we might be partly to blame. He escaped from behind the desk, knocking his human over in his frenzy.

The owner was scrabbling on the floor, trying to get back up, swearing at the dog, apologizing to his customer (who thought he was being sworn at) and trying to shout warnings to us, all at the same time.

The mutt, meanwhile, had taken one sniff of me from close up and sunk down with his jaw on my boots and that *I didn't mean it, please love me* look in his eyes.

"Hey, look out!" The owner crawled through the desk gap after his hound. "He'll have your arm off, soon as look at you. Duke! Duke! Here boy, here."

"Yeah." Tullah and I were kneeling down, patting him. "Who's a good boy, Dukey."

I couldn't adopt him into my pack, so poor Duke got left behind with his puzzled owner, who hadn't seen Diana.

∞ ∞ ∞ ∞ ∞

"See anything suspicious?" Tullah said as we finished our coffees on our second break, sitting in the Hill Bitch and watching the street.

I shook my head.

I was itchy with apprehension. That could be anything. My training said I'd stuck my head above the parapet in enemy territory and there was a limit to how long we could do this before someone did come sniffing.

My head told me that this was safer than the alternatives.

The burn cell trembled silently in my pocket.

"Rock and roll," I said.

It was a text: *Abt yr frnd. CTN. Lobo campus @1pm. Duck pond. I'll find u.*

CTN: can't talk now, as Tullah had to explain.

Why not? I wondered.

Lobo was the nickname of the University of New Mexico, a couple of blocks from where we were parked. Of course, it also meant wolf. I could so do without the eerie coincidences.

Tullah had her laptop sucking on some unsecured internet connections and showing the street map of the university area. The Duck Pond was right in the middle of the campus, in a park area. She pulled up a couple of pictures of it.

She wasn't looking happy. "Trap?"

"Not an obvious place for it. Lots of people around." I shrugged. "We can't ignore it. Let's see if we can turn it on its head, though."

I looked through the gear Tullah had packed for us in the back. The fright wig was likely to draw attention to me rather than the reverse, so I ignored that. I tied my hair in a quick bun on top of my head and covered it with the Stetson. Slipped on sunglasses. Running shoes. Tullah had a man's linen jacket which was a bit small for me, but I put it on over the HK shoulder holster and pushed the sleeves up. I hid Mary's bouquet in the pocket. Either it was losing its potency or I was getting used to the smell, but I wasn't sneezing now.

Tullah had gone into a store nearby and bought a bright red UNM hoodie with a stylized wolf on the back. She tied her hair in a ponytail, flipped the hood up and wore sunglasses. She put her Sig in a belt clip holster hidden beneath the sweatshirt and spent a minute figuring out how to get it clear for a draw.

"Okay?"

She nodded. We had fifteen minutes.

"You walk about thirty yards behind me…what?"

She was shaking her head. "I'm the one who looks more like a student, Boss. You look different than you looked earlier, but we can't do anything about your height. If I'm in front, we have a better chance of spotting someone before we're seen. And Kaothos will be able to tell me if someone we met this morning gets close to me."

It would give me a better view of what was happening. I had to concede.

If there was nothing that alarmed us after a circuit of the pond, and we found someone we'd talked to in the morning, one of us would approach him or her. Otherwise, we'd pull back and send a text to try and set up a meeting somewhere of our choosing.

Tullah started walking toward the university and I started talking to Kaothos. We found we could still communicate at twenty paces, but not at thirty, so I stayed twenty paces behind her.

"Tullah, what's with the sacks of fertilizer in the back of the Hill Bitch?"

"Cover. Gives us an excuse to drive around and ask for addresses, for instance. Y'know, pretending to be delivering the stuff."

"Way complex, 'prentice. You didn't have to pay for them, did you?" The fertilizer was from Larimer Agricultural Fertilizers, the Denver Weres' factory that they used to get rid of bodies. That gave me a little shudder. The processed remains of the Nagas killed on Coykuti might be included in those bags.

"Nah. Those were just some Alex had in his shed."

Kaothos made Tullah's voice sound like hers. It felt odd, and we had to carefully mentally speak the words we wanted Kaothos to transmit, but it might be useful. Kaothos assured me that it was undetectable, and we had one of the small intercom systems as backup if we needed it.

"Noticed anything surprising this morning?" I asked as we crossed Central Avenue, the old Route 66.

"Yeah. No Athanate."

I'd wondered if she'd noticed the absence of Athanate marque.

As for the local pack, there was the one hotel that had Were inside. But out on the streets, there'd been traces of Were marque everywhere. And even keeping my Were to myself, I could feel the Call from the locals. I was in another pack's territory. It made my wolf anxious; not a big thing, just a constant awareness of her watchfulness.

Of course, I was also in another Athanate House's mantle. I should really have been as concerned about that as I was at being in another pack's territory.

We arrived at the Duck Pond and I followed Tullah around it, falling further back. I was the ambler, walking slowly and talking on my cell. Tullah was the busy student on her lunch break, mixing up walking with some general loosening exercises.

Anyone we'd met this morning could have been in disguise, just like we were, but there was no one who looked familiar. The meeting time came, and we made one more circuit. My paranoia started to blossom: the jock in the jacket that looked too warm for the weather; the group that stood to one side arguing with lowered voices; the old woman clutching her bulging grocery bag. And was that my bracelet starting to itch? Could I trust it if it did? Or didn't?

The sun was bright and the park was getting busier as more people came out for their lunch breaks.

Then I was alongside Tullah, taking her by the elbow and pulling her along. "We need to move."

She was getting very good; she didn't immediately look to see what it was. When we passed a trash bin, she half turned, pretending to throw some litter in. She saw what had made me make a move.

"You have a phobia about clowns, don't you?" she said. "Was this a childhood trauma? Did the nasty clown make you cry at your fifth birthday party?"

"Very funny. Keep walking."

I'd been spooked by clowns once before when I was out with Tullah, and it'd been a false alarm. It wasn't this time. The clowns moved differently as soon we started walking away. How they hell had they made us?

"There are several advantages to the clown disguise," I said, quoting the Ops 4-10 manual. "The appearance is disarming for most people; no one automatically suspects a children's entertainer. Afterwards, the incongruity of it makes people suspect their recall is faulty. The disguise can be complete; the makeup or mask is part of the uniform and makes the person unrecognizable, even with facial recognition software. The clothes are traditionally loose-fitting, allowing space to hide weapons and a different set of clothes—"

"What about those flipper shoes? They're not going to run in them."

"Velcro straps. Running shoes underneath. Get ready to run."

One of the clowns thumped a drum. Loud enough to muffle the sound of a small pistol. This might be a classic, by-the-book attempt at a hit. How long had they had to put it together? Would they have managed to coordinate backup? What would their plan be once they decided we'd spotted them?

They were good. One of them played a flute and was leading them like a piper. All part of the performance. They'd probably keep it up as long as they couldn't be sure we'd spotted them. Then the piper started to dance a jig that was as good as a trot, and he was *definitely* leading them our way.

I pushed us toward a library that had the look of an old adobe fort in a Western. That was leading us away from the students; I didn't want any innocents caught up in this. Unfortunately, it was also making it more dangerous for us. I had no idea what the layout was at the far end of the park and we had no time to research it.

With a couple of half-glances, I timed it. The clowns moved clear of the last clump of students. Their faces all turned toward us, like eerie mechanical dolls. We were out of time.

"Run," I said.

Chapter 22

We skidded around corners of surreal buildings designed by a giant using melted Lego building blocks. Every color from plum to sand and pink.

The clowns had stripped off their flipper shoes and they were quick. A gang of running clowns? Yes, they were attracting attention, naturally, and just as naturally, people were laughing, assuming it was a student prank.

Tullah and I sprinted past a large police administration building. Tempting, but we couldn't afford the attention.

Straight ahead was the sort of building we needed.

We crossed the double lanes of Lomas Boulevard, ignoring the blaring horns and cursing drivers, and into the University of New Mexico Hospital. Through the emergency entrance, where the ambulances pulled up. Well, it was an emergency.

And we got lucky. There must have been an accident and the place was full of police and firemen.

A security guard emerged as we ran in. I pointed back at the clowns just entering the building.

"They've got guns!" I yelled.

I was gambling on the clowns not wanting to start shooting at bystanders.

There was a horrible moment when I wondered if I'd miscalculated.

Too late now. We were on the stairs when the clowns collided with security and police. People started shouting.

We dropped our pace and marched through the building.

"Slow down." I grabbed Tullah's arm before we emerged into the main entrance area.

Too late.

Not all our pursuers had piled into the hospital behind us. A guy came trotting in the front doors. He was carrying a backpack, plenty big enough for a clown suit. He was also trying for casual, talking on his cell, but his head jerked a little and our eyes met.

Damn clumsy, but he knew I'd made him.

There were emergency stairs right by us. We ran up.

Any hospital is a maze, but the key to getting away from someone was knowing your way around. We didn't. We couldn't rely on all his friends being caught up with security. Everything pointed to this being a professional job, and that meant there would be one or maybe two small teams close by as backup.

In a couple of minutes he might have friends spread through the building.

Time for desperate tactics. There was no one else on the emergency stairs at the moment. That was as much as I could wish for.

"Keep running up the stairs—as much noise as you can make."

"Okay, Boss," came back through Kaothos.

I flattened myself against a wall on one of the landings.

He came running up them, focused on chasing the noise in the stairwell. Straight into my roundhouse. I wasn't holding back; I couldn't afford that luxury. Unlucky clown. The kick launched him backwards.

"Come back down now," I called up after Tullah, and trotted down to see how badly he was hurt.

I'd broken his breastbone and ribcage. As he'd fallen, he'd smashed his head on the steps, but Athanate were tough and I could feel a pulse.

Tullah came up as I stripped his jacket off.

I took mine off and gave it to Tullah.

"Swap with your hoodie. Hair inside and collar up. Sunglasses back on. Go find the courtesy wheelchair in the lobby and bring it to the foot of the stairs. *Go!"*

A last, queasy look at the man and she obeyed, bundling the sweatshirt inside its hood so it looked like a bag. We couldn't leave him here. I wasn't sure how thoroughly the medical staff might check him before his friends came and took him away, but I didn't want to be the person blamed for letting the rest of the world know about the Athanate before we were ready.

I put the guy's jacket on and ran through his pockets and backpack.

Comm system, wallet, cellphone, sunglasses, key ring. Black ski mask and gloves. The clown disguise. And a freaking taser.

Crap. Snatch job rather than a hit.

Tullah came back with the wheelchair. I carried the guy down and arranged him in the chair with his sunglasses on and the ski mask folded back like a hat, hiding the blood on his head.

Then we wheeled him through the lobby and outside, as slowly and innocently as we could manage.

We left him looking as if he was snoozing in the sun, his cell turned on in his pocket. His friends would find him in minutes. It had slowed us down a little, but both sides of the Athanate struggle agreed on one thing: humans finding out about us accidentally did no one any good.

Tullah and I took the first cab that pulled up.

Our pictures were on the hospital security cameras. That couldn't be helped. But other than running through the security, we hadn't actually done anything wrong in the main areas. The section of stairwell where I'd kicked the guy didn't have cameras, and he wasn't going to press charges when he recovered.

When the cabbie turned into Lomas a minute later, I had him pull over.

"Sorry, changed our minds," I said and handed him a twenty.

With Tullah nervously looking around, I led her through the campus toward the Duck Pond.

Athanate marques were formed of two elements: the scent and the telergy. Running away from the clowns, there'd been no chance to smell anything. The telergy part was never more than a sensation of presence, and between my paranoia and the tingle from Mary's bracelet, I wasn't sure what I'd felt.

I could hardly believe what my nose had been telling me about the guy I'd knocked out. I needed confirmation.

I was glad I hadn't killed him, for Tullah's sake. It wouldn't have been the first time she'd seen dead bodies up close; her parents had killed a platoon of Nagas who'd attacked the Kwan. And she'd been the one to choose to come on this road trip with me, but I had a horrible premonition she'd have her fill of dead bodies soon. I was a magnet for conflict.

I was listening to their comm system, and I heard when they found the guy in the wheelchair and realized their comms were compromised. Someone said a code and they switched frequencies. I tossed the system in the trash.

As we were walking back across the park, I let my wolf nose inhale the rich broth of smells. They'd found some way, like we had, of reducing the Athanate scent, but not eliminating it. And it told me I'd been right in the stairwell; I knew the marque from before.

But it wasn't House Romero, or Matlal, or any Basilikos.

It was the Warders.

Chapter 23

The voice that answered David's phone was very definitely not David. It was female, smooth, and *ever so* polite.

"Umm. Could I speak to David…or Pia, please?" I mumbled, trying to catch up. Had David suddenly got hold of a girlfriend? Damn. What if he was trying to find someone to become kin and I'd just gotten him in trouble?

"I can certainly see if Mr. Thaler or Ms. Shirazi is available. Who should I say is calling, please?"

Ah, yes. He was at the Kingslund Group, working in the office. I guessed some of us had to.

"It's Amber Farrell."

"Oh, Ms. Farrell, I'm so sorry, I didn't realize. You're on the list, of course. I'll put you right through. I do believe Mr. Thaler and Ms. Shirazi are in a meeting together."

David must have put the fear of God into the staff; she actually sounded nervous that she hadn't known it was me. How would she? Did he play them recordings of me yelling at people?

"Amber?"

"Mr. Thaler." I laughed.

"Don't start on that. Are you all right?"

"Yeah. I don't only call you when the sky's falling on my head."

"Hmm. Hold on." There were some clicks and the echoey sound of being put on speaker. "Right. That's got the encryption running and we're on conference now. Pia's here too. Any news on Diana? Can we do anything?"

"Nothing on Diana yet. And yes, you can. Tell me, what's the story on the Warders?"

"Skylur expelled them from Panethus territory and revoked their status as a non-aligned House," Pia said. "The New York headquarters has been closed and Alice is there taking oaths from those that wanted to apply to join Altau. I guess the remainder can apply to Basilikos Houses or try and find some free territory elsewhere in the world and hold it."

"Okay. In the Assembly, there was something about the Warders building new laboratory facilities in New Mexico, wasn't there?"

"Yes," Pia said doubtfully. "I didn't think those facilities were ready, and with the House expelled and Matlal's funding exposed, I can't imagine the project is still running."

"Maybe. Thing is, there are Warders here in Albuquerque. We haven't had the slightest sniff of Romero, but half a dozen Warders just tried to snatch us. They have to have been well embedded to pick up that we were searching for Diana."

They went quiet on their end for a couple of seconds.

"This should be passed on to Naryn," Pia said finally.

"I know. Let's hold it for a day and see what happens. As soon as we tell Naryn, he'll start trying to get me back. I can't dodge another direct order for long."

They had me give a brief description of what had happened. That darkened the mood all around. I went through the guy's wallet and gave them his name and address in New York according to the ID. If it wasn't fake, maybe Bian could deduce something from that.

The cash I would send as an anonymous donation to the VA Medical Center out near the Albuquerque airport.

"You're too exposed, Amber." David was sounding worried. "We were expecting Romero, and for them to be disorganized. This is way too prepared. What if they'd used a sniper instead of a snatch squad?"

I couldn't think of any arguments. It'd always been a gamble coming down here and looking for a clue that the pair of us could usefully pursue. This mission needed more. It needed a force big enough to track down Romero and confront them, and big enough to fight off Warders at the same time.

The fact that I needed Diana back for my own reasons didn't change the facts.

"I worked out that puzzle, though," David said.

"Huh?"

"The picture you sent me. Just emailed it back to you. Looks like a river system? It's a partial street map of an area of Albuquerque called the Sandia Peak Enclave. It's right at the eastern edge, up against the slopes of Sandia Mountain. Don't have a house number, but I'm guessing you go to the end of the road where it's marked VAN."

"Thanks, David. That's something I guess we can do."

"Let's do it now," Tullah suggested. "It'll get us away from any Warders who are out looking for us in the center of town."

"Yeah." I felt depressed. Ending the conversation with David and Pia by trying to sound cheerful only made me feel worse.

It wasn't just the adrenaline rush leaving me. We were sitting here in Albuquerque unable to do one of the main things we'd come down for. I hated that. We had a necklace that was supposed to be helping with Olivia, but which had us both baffled. Now we had an address to find Larry's kin, and that was something. But while we were doing that, Jen would be getting ready to go out to Haven, where Naryn waited, and there was nothing I could do about it, no comfort I could give her, none of the protection that she deserved.

I had to stop this brooding and focus on the next task, or risk screwing that up as well.

I let Tullah drive, and soon we were heading east on Central Avenue.

Larry's kin had been a faceless mass in my mind, and that might change this afternoon. I didn't know their names; I didn't even know how many of them there were. All I had was a bone-deep sense of Athanate obligation, through Larry, to them. I had to start thinking of them as people and individuals right now. They probably wouldn't know what had happened to Larry, so my first task was going to be the painful one of telling them he was dead.

What then?

They might not want to be part of House Farrell. They might not want to move to Denver. And if they did move, what would they do? I couldn't support them all. What skills did they have? Would they still want to be kin, and if they did, would my House want them as kin?

I didn't even know if they'd all be in one place.

Tullah turned north and we started to skirt the border between the city and the Sandia foothills.

Another day. One more day to contact Larry's kin, sort out what they wanted to do, and then I'd have to call Naryn and explain that Albuquerque had been taken by the Warders.

He'd call me back to Denver. I'd have to leave it to Altau to find Diana when they could.

Meanwhile, my Athanate side would start to demand Blood. Without Diana, they'd have to lock me up for everyone's safety. I especially wouldn't be trusted with my kin.

Maybe Kaothos could knock me out long-term and they'd put me on some kind of IV drip until other people sorted it all out.

It was no comfort that this expedition hadn't gone as badly as it might have. We'd managed to get in and out without screwing with the Were, or getting tangled with the Adepts.

But no Diana.

Can't get any worse, I thought.

Chapter 24

The road became uneven as it started to climb the foothills. There was almost no traffic.

The houses were more spaced out, half-hidden in gullies or dips in the ground, shaded by piñon and other small pine, surrounded by dry yards and yellowing grass. All the houses looked like little pink and brown forts, as if made from pastel-colored modeling clay and weathered by the sun and rain.

We reached the point on the map. Smoketree Drive, number 117.

It was a split level, with the twin doors of a wide garage facing the drive and the house itself above them, nestled between blue-green shoulders of scrub oak and mountain juniper. Two panoramic windows looked blankly over our heads.

We parked and got out.

It was silent, except for the wind whistling. No one came to see what we wanted. The house looked empty, but my gut said it wasn't.

Tullah looked in the mailbox, flipped quickly through a dozen letters and replaced them.

"Savannah Copeland," she said. "Van for short, I guess."

I walked up the steps at the side of the house. Slit windows allowed me to see down into the garage. There was no car. I'd left Mary's bouquet in the car and I sniffed to try and tell if this was Larry's house. There was no Athanate scent I could find, just a gentle floral trace from the spiky blue fountains of oat grass by the path. He wouldn't have been here in a couple of weeks or more, so it wasn't much of a test.

There was no response to a knock on the front door, and walking around to the back revealed only empty rooms. Nothing was open.

I could break in easily enough, but it turned out my apprentice had been studying some useful PI skills that I should have had. It took her ten minutes and a little set of metal picks that she swore she'd gotten from the internet, and we were in.

A short hall led to a bright, airy living room. The floor was tiled in warm ochre except for the center, where there was a cream carpet. Comfortable sofas and chairs surrounded a low coffee table with a tiled top. There was an enclosed fireplace, a flat TV against a pale wall, a music center, an original painting of the trickster coyote trotting jauntily across a wide desert canvas. A sandstone patterned lamp stood to one side, and tiny spotlights were attached to the exposed beams.

Everything was placed just so, everything clean. No photos, no magazine tossed to one side, no sign of being lived in, but it had been. It wasn't like a show home. There was wear on the seats and a chip missing from the edge of the painting. This was a house that had been used and loved.

"Savannah?" I called out. "Van?"

Silence.

There was a small den with a high-end computer sitting on the desk.

I touched the back, where the power supply would stay warm for fifteen minutes or so. It was cold. The room had a trace of Larry's marque.

The kitchen was all handmade wooden cabinets and stainless steel appliances. Everything was unplugged and the fridge door slightly open.

At the back of the house, there were two bedrooms up a short flight of stairs. Clothes in the closets: male and female all mixed, at least three or four people. Beds made. No dirty laundry. Bathrooms clean and polished—no toothbrushes or half-used soap bars.

Everything said empty house. Why did my gut say otherwise? Something was very wrong here.

"Empty?" I thought at Kaothos.

Tullah shook her head.

The last door led down to the garage by a narrow set of steps.

The light switch wasn't working, but my eyes could see well enough. We walked down, Tullah brushing the wall with her hand.

Most of the space was taken up by bulk-buy house supplies, power tools, a workbench with plastic sheets covering it, and a lime-green Kawasaki off-road motorbike propped on its kickstand. There was nowhere to hide.

The door at the top of the stairs closed.

The click that followed wasn't the lock. It was the slide action of a large caliber automatic. I didn't get to see what type because I was blinded by a powerful flashlight.

"Hold it right there."

Suckered. A hiding space behind the door. Impossible to see with the door open.

"We're holding," I said, and spread my arms wide, with the hands open.

I figured if we were going to be shot, it would have been while we were looking the other way. It takes something else to shoot someone who's looking at you, and I didn't think Savannah Copeland had reached that point quite yet. If I could keep my throat demon under control, maybe she wouldn't get there while she was pointing a gun at us. I could hope.

"Who are you?"

"I'm Amber Farrell, House Farrell," I said quietly. "And this is Tullah. I came here because Larry asked me to come."

My wolf ears could pick out the little intake of breath at his name.

"I don't know you. Why should I believe you? Why hasn't he called?"

Tears weren't far away.

"You know, don't you?" It was as gentle as I could make it.

The flashlight trembled.

"He's dead, isn't he?"

"I'm sorry. Yes, he is."

"Did you kill him?"

I could feel the blind anger lashing out in the words, and I could almost feel the pressure growing on the trigger.

"No. Van, he was betrayed by House Romero and sent to Denver. I did what I could. I offered to take him into House Farrell, and he agreed, but before we could—"

"Why should I believe you?" she shouted.

"I don't know how I can prove it, Van, but I have the directions he drew. He wanted us to come and help you, so he gave me the directions. May I take it out of my pocket?"

"You've got a gun. I know you have. Don't try anything or I'll kill you."

"Amber, it's in the other jacket," Tullah said.

Shit. She was right. I was still wearing the jacket I'd taken from the Warder.

"I can describe it," Tullah said. "Larry drew a map that you could only see if you folded the paper top left to bottom right and then fold the sides in so it looks a bit like a maple leaf. Then you had to shine a light through it and the lines all matched up."

The sound of harsh breathing came from the darkness at the top of the stairs.

We'd done almost as much as we could in the short time we'd had.

"We have to pass control back to her now," I said through Kaothos. *"And just wait."*

The next thing she said or did was critical.

A round through my head would be very critical.

"Why didn't you come sooner?" The flashlight was starting to wobble. Even if you lift weights, a big automatic is heavy to hold straight out like she was. But I could feel the pressure ease off the trigger, even if she wasn't aware of it.

"We came as soon as we understood the puzzle," I said.

She wasn't listening. "If you'd come sooner, they wouldn't be dead," she sobbed. "Sal and Rob, and now Claude. They wouldn't be dead."

A sudden anger exploded in my gut, catching me off balance. *My House.* Larry's kin had names now, and they'd been snatched away from me.

I had to take deep breaths until my heart stopped racing. Now, my hands were trembling too.

"Tell us what happened, please." My voice sounded strained.

"When...when Larry disappeared and we couldn't get through to the Diakon, and then we couldn't get through to any others, I got the four of us to hide here. I'm supposed to be the head of his kin." She was crying freely now, the flashlight and gun sinking down. I could make out her shadowy figure behind them.

"But I didn't have everything ready. There's just the security room. There wasn't enough food. We ran out of cash and we didn't want to use the cards until we knew what was happening. It was my responsibility and I failed. Rob and Sal took the car to go back to the town house. There was stuff there they were going to bring back."

She sank back onto the steps, sobs racking her body. I wanted to do something, but the gun was still waving around and she was hardly aware of it.

"They never came back," she said. "Why didn't I tell them not to go?"

Hindsight was wonderful. I wasn't going to second-guess her, and I needed her to move on.

"What about the other guy, Claude?"

I was pretty sure that the gun was now only accidentally pointed at me, but I'd rather be deliberately killed than accidentally killed, so I stayed at the bottom of the steps.

"Claude wanted to go down and talk to the wolves." She hiccupped. "Even though they scare the shit out of us. He said they'd tell us what had happened."

I could hear the pride fighting with all the other emotions in there.

"I told him he couldn't. It was too dangerous. We'd have to wait for Larry. And I couldn't even stay awake. Now he's gone."

I could imagine it. Living in the tiny security room most of the time, creeping out to use the house and then scrubbing it clean so it looked as if they weren't there, and creeping back. The shame of not being ready for this. The food running out. The pressure to make decisions. The pressure when decisions went wrong. The self-doubt. The exhaustion. It was amazing she had lasted this long.

"Claude is kin?" I asked.

"Yes."

Lie.

"He's not, is he, Van?"

"Brother," she whispered. "My little brother. I was supposed to protect him."

And there was a sound, a heavy truck stopping right outside.

Tullah and I looked at each other.

"Van, I'm worried about that truck. It's not garbage collection or deliveries, is it?"

"No. It's just a coincidence. Claude would never betray me."

"I'm not saying that," I said.

Even if that was the most likely thing—that Claude had been caught and tortured into revealing this location. The *why*, we'd have to deal with later.

"Look, I'm trained to deal with this, but you've got to let me do it. You stay down here."

The truck engine was still running. It made a lot of noise, probably enough to mask the sound of small arms gunfire. Cab doors slammed. Someone was coming up the drive.

Savannah slid off the steps and dropped down to the floor of the garage.

Without the flashlight in my eyes I saw a woman barely older than Tullah, slight but stringy-tough, Native American totem tattoos snaking down her arms, platinum blonde hair cropped close to the scalp and eyes that were close to despair. She was looking blankly at the automatic in her hand as if she'd forgotten she'd been holding it.

"Just wait here. You'll be okay now," I whispered, pulling the Browning .45 gently out of her grasp. Then I ran up the stairs with Tullah close behind.

Chapter 25

There were two men in courier delivery uniforms coming up the drive. Their van was blocking any view from the road. The first guy was carrying a clipboard and a red document zip bag, while the second was struggling alone with a large box. He put it down in front of the garage, while Mr. Clipboard gave the house and the Hill Bitch a once-over. They were professional, trained for a job that had nothing to do with deliveries.

"Stall him at the door," I said to Tullah. "Whatever you do, don't put any part of your body in front of the door. Gun in hand, safety off, finger on the guard, 'prentice. If he comes through that door, kill him."

I looked into her eyes. No one is ever ready. I wondered what I'd looked like when Top had stared into my eyes like that. If I could, I would take the action away from her, but if I couldn't, I thought she'd handle it.

I ran up into the bedrooms and checked that there wasn't anyone coming up behind the house. No—they weren't expecting any serious resistance. Behind me I heard the doorbell.

Eight seconds, said the little timer in my head.

Mr. Clipboard had a pistol in that zip bag. Mr. Box had ten gallons of gasoline and a lighter. And I'd bet there was a third guy in the van.

Six seconds. I let myself out of the window and landed quietly on the ground.

"Who is it?" Tullah called out, her voice shaky.

"Haul 'Em Parcels, ma'am. Delivery for...ah...Copeland." He had the bored tone down pat. "That you?"

Four seconds.

"I'll need to see some ID."

Oh, good call, Tullah.

I crept up to the corner and checked the HK.

"I can't see it from there." I heard Tullah's voice. "Hold it up to the peephole."

"Tell Tullah: DON'T get in front of the door," I said to Kaothos urgently, hoping I was in range.

Two seconds.

"Can you see that now, ma'am?"

"Yes—"

He shot right through the door. Four shots. With the silencer it was no more than a pop-pop-pop-pop.

I came around the corner in a crouch, double-handed grip on the HK pointed at him.

He'd dropped the clipboard. His gun, clumsy with the silencer attached, was out of the bag. He had his weight back, about to shoulder charge the door, when he saw me and started to swing his gun at me.

Tap, tap. Tap.

And I was already pointing at Mr. Box.

He scrabbled for a gun he had in a belt clip in the small of his back. Lousy place for a draw.

Tap, tap. Tap.

Two down.

"TULLAH!"

"I'm fine."

There was a whir from the front of the house and the high-pitched snarl of an engine.

What the hell?

I ran down the steps, just in time to see Savannah thread the Kawasaki through the gap left by the van and go screaming down the road, front wheel lifting off the tarmac as she whipped it through the gears.

And the driver came sprinting around the side of the van, gun already leveled at me.

Tullah fired at the same time as I did, so for her first, she got one of those where you can say to yourself that no one could be sure you actually killed the guy.

She was still staring at him down the barrel of her Sig when I came up and put the safety on. I got in front of her.

"Go inside," I said.

She turned wide eyes to me. "What...Savannah...where?"

"I think I know what happened." I took Tullah's Sig and snugged it back into her holster. "When I said Claude wasn't kin, she thought it meant I didn't care what had happened to her little brother. Then, in her eyes, we practically accused him of telling these guys where she was."

"She's gone to find him?"

"Yup. She's gone to get her little brother back."

"But where?"

"No. *Were.* W-e-r-e. He went to talk to the werewolves," I said, turning her towards the open garage and giving her a push. Keeping her busy would keep her mind off what she'd done. "Now, I'm betting that Savannah had some bulk purchases of cleaning stuff in the house. Go grab us some bleach."

I pulled the plastic sheeting off the workbenches, tore it into sections and started to roll the bodies.

It took us twenty minutes, but we got the bodies wrapped in plastic and in the back of the van. The steps and drive we cleaned down with bleach and power-sprayed it all away.

I found some sealant and duct tape. Using them, I patched together a temporary repair of the front door.

None of it would fool the police for more than a minute if they decided to look, but who was going to report it? Not the Warders. I didn't want a genuine delivery man to turn up and find bullet holes.

We left a note for Savannah giving one of our burn phone numbers, just in case, and locked up behind ourselves. Then I drove the delivery van down to a truck stop diner and left it. The dead guys hadn't had a real comms system, just cell phones. I left one of the cells in the cab, switched on. The Warders would zero in on it and then they could clean up their own mess.

All the rest of their small gear I stored in the zip bag and slung that into the back of the Hill Bitch. Cell phones were off and SIM cards taken out. This hit team had been working to a protocol; the calls and data had been erased, but Matt might still be able to dig something out of them. Even better, they'd used GPS to find Smoketree Drive, and the route hadn't been erased.

I climbed back into the cab of the Hill Bitch.

"Let's go find a motel," I said. "I need a shower."

Tullah drove without speaking. Every now and then she took a breath as if she were going to say something.

I could guess what it was.

"No," I said. "It doesn't get better. It shouldn't get easier. If it does, that's the time to worry."

She nodded and turned onto Route 66.

Chapter 26

After our showers we went back out and found a diner, where we ordered a late lunch.

"What now?" Tullah asked when our spice-rubbed steaks arrived.

"We work on our one and only lead in this town: Savannah."

"I don't follow."

"What happened downtown?" I said.

"We got chased by a group of Warders."

"Think that through."

She chewed on her chili with steak garnish.

"The Warders didn't just stumble across us. They were warned."

"What does that tell you?"

"They set something up to watch for someone like us." She thought some more. "That takes time and local contacts. House Romero has to have been cooperating with them. Doesn't that prove Romero has gone over to Basilikos and Diana's been captured?"

I grimaced. "Not enough for me to go back to Naryn."

"Warders running around Albuquerque and hunting down kin is 'not enough'? What will it take?"

"I just need a bit more," I said. "Bian and Naryn think it's Jaworski or Romero himself."

"You're not sure?"

"Diana didn't think Jaworski had gone over. But he's the Diakon for the Santa Fe Romero. Charles Romero has another guy who's Diakon here in Albuquerque: Jiaro Amaral. Savannah's got to have some idea about what's going on and whether it involves all Romero, or just some of them. She might also have heard something about Diana. There had to be a reason that she was being hunted."

"Okay, but how are we going to find her?"

"Maybe she went to the Were club that Dominé warned us about. Or maybe they'd have an idea where she went."

"Amber, I thought you wanted to keep away from the Were."

"I do. But Savannah is part of my House now. I have to talk to them."

"These are the rabid, kill-'em-first, ask-questions-later wolves. Can't wait. That'll be so much fun. How do you manage to talk without getting your face eaten off?"

"We have a friend who can give us an introduction. I'm going to ask Dominé if she can call ahead and tell them why I'm coming in."

"That's not the same as an invitation, is it?"

"No." I had to admit it wasn't.

"Permission to speak my mind, Boss."

Meaning she was asking to say something that would otherwise have got her head bitten off. I eyed her. She didn't pull that sort of thing often with me. She didn't need to.

"Yeah?"

"You're making decisions and then making up justifications for them. You want to go after Savannah because you feel she's your House. It's, whatever you call it, the Athanate imperative."

I gritted my teeth. I couldn't argue against her assessment. "I can do this, Tullah. I can pull it off."

Tullah sighed. She could see I was going to do it no matter how much she objected. "I hope so," she said.

"Amber, this is not safe." Dominé shared Tullah's view of my idea, her voice crackling on the speakerphone when we called from the motel. "I'm not their friend, I'm just a client they protect for money."

"I know," I said. "But these guys have to have the same concerns the rest of the paranormal world has. Whatever their reputation, they can't go killing people randomly. That means they have some restraint. I'm not threatening them, and they shouldn't have any interest in my friends. Why would they want to keep them?"

"But if they are keeping them, for whatever reason, why should they treat us any differently?" Tullah said. "Maybe they're pissed off with Athanate. Maybe they're the reason there are Warders downtown. If they've got them, they're risking a confrontation by taking Romero kin, so why would House Altau mean any more to them?"

They were both right. I was rocking back and forth, busting my brain to come up with an argument that they'd missed.

I couldn't.

But I couldn't just turn around and leave. I was an Athanate, the leader of a House, and Savannah was part of that House. The thought of abandoning her felt like breaking my leg and grinding the shattered edges together. As nothing but a human, maybe I'd be able to walk away. Maybe.

"Hélas," Dominé said. "I see it is not a matter for rational thought. Very well, I will take you there."

"No. Dominé, just tell me where, give me a name and number. You can't come."

"Why, because it is too dangerous? Why is that a reason for one and not the other? Besides, I am safest of all of us. They have an income from me, and that is something they *are* rational about."

You hope.

"Ah. No. Safest is my apprentice. She doesn't come in with us. If something goes wrong, she has to be able to do something."

"Like what?"

Thank goodness, Tullah wasn't arguing with me.

"Improvise." I snorted. "I'm joking. This isn't a bad TV movie. Tull, if we don't come out and call you, you point the truck north and you don't stop till you get to Denver."

Chapter 27

It took me an hour to get to my meet with Dominé downtown.

I saw her waiting outside the station and came quietly alongside. She jumped when I spoke.

"You sure about this?" I asked.

"I am not sure about it, as you put it, but I am sure about what will happen if you go alone. I have called. They are expecting us and we will not be welcome, but they will at least listen. Come."

Clubs were scattered in the area on either side of Central Avenue, but she led us a block south.

I remembered the name of the club she'd mentioned, the Bot Wobbly. Tullah and I had given it a wide berth while we were doing our door-to-door, but without knowing it was there, we could easily have walked past it without noticing.

That was, except for the scent of Were. Not the pine woods and mountain marque of the Denver pack; a drier, dustier scent. Not unpleasant, just not *home*. And not welcoming.

I slowed Dominé down inside, letting my eyes adjust.

There was no one on the desk and the place was silent—still too early for business. A long, dim passage sloped down into the basement where the main club was. We walked down through a brash gallery of overlaid posters advertising club events dating back years.

The inner door to the club was guarded by the creature that gave the place its name: a 1950s Sci-Fi robot hanging from the ceiling, made from old trash barrels, dented cans, random scrap metal and a deep-sea diving helmet. Brushing past made it clatter softly like a beat-up wind chime.

Center stage in front of us was a sunken circular dance floor, softly lit from below and ringed above by a sculptured metal gantry like a Hollywood spaceship, with clusters of spotlights hanging down from it. Curving stairs led up from the dance floor to the bar on the far wall. To the left of the bar, a series of round platforms like huge steps rose higher as they progressed along the entire perimeter of the club, ending in one ten feet above the bar. I could make out the bulky shapes of DJ and lighting control equipment up there, harshly backlit.

Cool air was blowing down from vents behind us, and I'd left Mary's bouquet behind.

I'd just announced to the Were at the bar that a strange wolf was in their territory. In their club.

A group of them sat there. One slipped off his stool, but other than that, they just watched us walking toward them.

Dominé held her head high under that gaze. *Don't doubt,* she'd said; *they can smell it.* And she was right.

A shape detached itself from the equipment on the platform above the bar. There was the metallic sound of tools landing back in a box and a mild oath. A female voice. The backlighting made the form strangely distorted as she stood looking down. Without warning, she launched herself into the air.

My hand closed on a gun that wasn't there. She landed lightly, halfway between us and the bar.

"Good afternoon, Rita," Dominé said, as if this was normal. Maybe it was, for this Rita.

"Dominé." Rita's voice was light as an evening breeze. Her tawny hair was pulled back into a ponytail and fixed with a leather tie. Her face was an expressionless oval and her hard eyes didn't flicker from Dominé until they snapped over to me. "Stranger," she said.

"Amber Farrell," I said automatically. "House Farrell and Pack Deauville."

Her nose flared and she took one step closer.

"Stranger," she said again.

Yeah, she had it. Stranger and stranger; and not just me. Rita was Were and her scent marque said Albuquerque pack. But the other part of her marque—the faint mental signature that Athanate were better at picking up—that felt different, nothing like any of the werewolves I had met. Nothing like the guys at the bar.

It was crazy, but I was sure she wasn't wolf.

"Come. Both of you," she said, spinning on her foot and walking—no, *slinking*—past the Were at the bar.

I didn't like both of us being taken somewhere. Dominé was just here to introduce me. I'd wanted her to leave immediately. Would arguing reveal weakness? I didn't know, and Dominé was already walking.

There was one of those subliminal Were snarls from the bar as we followed Rita.

"Don't mind them," she said. "Their bite is for when they're given cause, isn't it, boys?"

Behind the bar, she led us into a storeroom, turning on the light and then leaping up onto a stack of crated beer that put her about five feet off the ground. She folded her legs gracefully into a half lotus.

At Rita's gesture, I closed the door behind us. Dominé's face was pale and she was working hard to hide her fear.

I was tempted to match Rita and leap up somewhere, but I was here to ask for things. I leaned against a stack of barrels and waited.

"Dominé says you've lost someone, Stranger."

"Someones," I said.

Three of them, to be exact.

"Why are you looking for them?"

My Athanate wanted to say *mine*, at least about Savannah. I settled for, "My need and duty."

"Not *yours*." The emphasis was neatly put. If they had Savannah and Claude, they'd know they weren't my House.

This...*cat* was too quick to let anything past her. Yeah. Cat. Cougar. Were-cougar maybe. Cool, really cool, but I had a job and neither of us were here to make nice. And I had a feeling Rita didn't make nice so much as toy with prey.

"Not officially mine, no."

"Unofficially? Explain."

I glanced at Dominé. Athanate rules dictated that what happened in our world wasn't shared with humans, but Dominé clearly knew about Were and Athanate. Putting the right names to them was a risk, but less than the risk of Rita misunderstanding something I said if I talked around it.

"The need part: my Athanate Mentor, Diana Ionache, came down to meet House Romero. She's missing, and I need to get her back safely," I said. "The duty part: an Athanate of House Romero called Larry Dixon was taken from Albuquerque and compelled to assist in an attack in Denver. I was working to help him escape and adopt him into my House when he was killed by Matlal."

Rita's unblinking stare gave nothing away.

"By adopting him, I adopted his kin as well. His last request of me was to find them and get them to safety, if I could. I gave him my word. His kin are in danger; two of them are dead. I saved the third, Savannah, from an attack, but she left to try and find her brother, Claude." Still nothing from Rita. "I understood he'd come to you. I'm here to get them back, if you've got them."

"For what, exactly?"

"To take them somewhere safer."

I hated being in this position, but I had no choice. Rita had all the aces in this conversation.

"We have them: your stray, *not-yours* kin, these *Romero* kin," she confirmed. The way she said Romero made it sound like a curse. "I'm not sure that giving them to you would make them safer, unless House Farrell is bigger than we've heard. Or maybe Pack Deauville, whatever that is, has hidden numbers of themselves in Albuquerque the way you seemed to have. Maybe with help from our *friend*."

Her eyes went to Dominé and back. She blinked, once. Other than that, she hadn't moved.

I swallowed. "House Farrell is small, and I've brought no Were into New Mexico. There are only two of us here. We did stay with Dominé, but the trick we used to remain hidden today is an Adept working. Nothing to do with Dominé."

"A Were-Athanate hybrid, and a friend of Adepts. You *are* strange, Stranger, and you weren't invited into our territory."

"I apologize," I said.

I was here on *Athanate* business. Best to keep the legal arguments for later, I thought.

"Seeking forgiveness rather than asking permission." Rita sprang lightly off the crates, making my heart jump. "Not always the quickest way or the best result."

She crowded Dominé, who was doing excellently at hiding her fear, for a human. The effort was wasted on Rita. She knew exactly the effect she was having.

"Dominé, we have had a good working relationship. Treat it very carefully. I look forward to seeing you in LA."

She stepped back and I let the tension go. I had no idea how fast Rita was and whether I could have stopped her from hurting Dominé if she'd wanted to. It was a horrible choice to be faced with: react too late and have Dominé injured, too early and mess up the great 'relationship' we were building with Rita.

Now it was my turn. I don't scare easily, and I'd gotten used to having dangerous people glaring at me from very close. I met her green eyes and tried to keep everything calm and cool. Not pushing, but not being pushed either.

"Luckily for Dominé, you interest us, Stranger—Athanate and Were and Adept. But these *Romero* you want, even just kin, they have uses. They have value," she said.

I opened my mouth to protest, but she went on.

"We're in the middle of an Athanate battle that affects us all and is no choice of ours. And the *Romero* have Were blood on their hands. That comes at a cost. These strays are important enough that someone is trying to kill them. Why? What secrets do they have?"

"I don't know."

Romero had Were blood on their hands?

She made a sound deep in her throat. "Come and see the alpha if you want to get your strays back. Bring the Adept working that hid you from us. You should think hard about how you will pay us. Think very hard. If you make it worth our while, we might even know something of your Mentor."

Might, she said. It wasn't a promise. It was an indicator of how badly the search was going, that it was the best thing I'd heard. If the alpha really could tell me something definite about Diana, I'd take all the crap he could dish out and kiss him on both cheeks.

"Thank you," I said, working hard to be polite. "When and where?"

"Ten tonight, alone. Look for the Calle del Bosque down in Barelas. If you can't find him, you aren't supposed to be there." She blinked again. "Now go."

I got Dominé back onto the street and made a call to Tullah. She picked us up outside the station, and drove us toward where Dominé's car was parked.

Dominé hands were still shaking. Tullah had gotten us take-out coffee, and Dominé had to leave the lid on to stop hers from spilling.

I took Tullah through what had happened.

"Rita can be like that sometimes." Dominé spoke calmly enough.

Her eyes went from me to Tullah and back. For a human she knew far too much about the paranormal world, and both my Athanate and Were were uneasy with that.

"You were good in the club," Dominé went on as we stopped by her car. "With Rita, you must meet her toe to toe. You cannot be prey and expect to have any standing with them. You must be a predator. You must have a threat and something to bargain with."

We got out and she pulled me aside, not trembling any more, but nervous in a way that seemed unlike her. She fiddled with her car keys, her fingers kept touching her jacket, and she didn't meet my gaze.

"What is it?" I asked.

"This meeting tonight. If you must do it, *helas,* you must do it. I think I shouldn't be telling you any more."

"But?"

"There is one more thing you should know about," she said. "The alpha, Zane."

My skin prickled. Felix's words about the New Mexico packs came to mind: *You'd be dead in a day.*

"What about him?"

"You know something of the Were? The way some packs work? The way their alphas behave?" She waited till I nodded. I was no expert, but Alex had described how different packs worked. "Then you know an alpha can demand rights with every female in the pack. Even outside the pack, what he wants, he takes. I think Zane is like that."

"He's violent?" I frowned. He couldn't get away with that for long, surely. "You know this?"

"Not violent. Not when I've seen him at the club, anyway." She laced her fingers together to still them. "I've seen him only twice. Both times there was this aura around him. Very dangerous. Very attractive. Both times he saw a woman he wanted, and he had her that night. I don't know him well enough to know if he has a type, but I have this feeling you'll intrigue him."

This aspect of dominance, Alex had told me about. Not many alphas used it, as far as he knew. As an Athanate, I could hardly criticize; we used the same kind of attraction on humans. But it was useful to know I might be on the receiving end.

"Thanks for the warning."

She looked at me, looked away. "It's not *precisely* a warning."

"Ah."

That chilled me in the pit of my stomach.

I could see what she meant. If I went to the meeting tonight I had a choice.

I might be able to use his desire to get what I wanted from him—to get Savannah and her brother freed.

What had Yelena said about the choices she'd had to make? *They got what they wanted; I got what I needed.*

I'd been more comfortable about that when it hadn't been me faced with it.

Or I could go in straight. Rita had implied he wanted something from me, and I didn't think that was sex. We could negotiate about whatever it was.

Then if he made a move on me and I refused, where would that leave me?

It wasn't something Dominé could help me with.

"Thanks," I said again, and we hugged. "I promise I'll come look you up in LA if there's an opportunity."

There wasn't much chance of that, the way my life was going.

She left and Tullah drove us down near the airport. We checked into one of the high turnover hotels, paying with cash.

I hit the gym to burn off the tension and chew through how bad it looked.

It was crazy bad.

First off, I was disobeying Naryn and Felix by being here, and both of them had legitimate authority over me. I was sort of on the run from the Adepts, and if I didn't get back to Denver soon, with Diana, and some explanations for Agent Ingram, I would be on the run from the FBI too. Clean sweep—Athanate, Were, Adept and human.

Given that I *was* here, I was discovering things that I should be reporting back. Naryn should know about the Warders and Amaral. Felix should know that the Albuquerque pack looked to include Were-cougars. Oh, and I should be reporting Dominé to both of them, probably.

My best argument against calling Naryn and Felix was that I hadn't actually nailed anything down. The Were might know something about Diana; presumably I'd find out tonight. I wasn't completely sure that Amaral was a traitor, or whether it was Charles Romero himself who'd brought in the Warders. And I wasn't *sure* that Rita was a Were-cougar— I'd never met one.

All of which felt like rationalizing to support what I was doing, which was to follow my instincts. The same instincts I'd decided were very dubious and not to be relied on in the paranormal world.

Whatever I did, I knew the next step was the big one.

So far, all I'd done was kill and injure some Warders, who shouldn't have been here in the first place and were, in any event, trying to kill Athanate kin to whom I had a legitimate connection. Nothing there that was going to make the situation for Panethus any worse, or directly affect Altau.

As long as I wasn't captured by Basilikos. I shouldn't forget that, ever.

I switched from the treadmill to weights and started to pump.

On the Were side, I was trespassing. I didn't think Rita's invitation was permission to be in Albuquerque—more an invitation to hand myself over for judgment.

They might kill me. They would be within their rights, by Were law. Felix might decide to declare war over my death, but he wouldn't be under any obligation to do it. Nor would the pack pressure him to avenge a stupid bitch who'd ignored his direct command.

Rationally, the worst thing I could do was fight back. If I killed a Were down here, that would give Zane legitimate reason to attack Felix, *and* the Albuquerque pack would pressure him to do it. All of which was the last thing either of them wanted, with the Confederation looming over both of them. I might end up responsible for Colorado and New Mexico falling to the Confederation.

The Were instinct was to not go. If I went, I knew the Were instinct would be to fight like a cornered wolf. Could I hold back?

And yet, despite all of that, the Athanate side of me was demanding that I go. The possibility of getting Savannah back and finding a clue about Diana was too strong.

There had never really been any doubt.

I had to go in alone and I couldn't expect any backup: even if we removed the lock on Tullah, we couldn't use Kaothos' power without alerting the Adept communities and causing huge problems on that side.

Back in Ops 4-10, part of our training had been how to continue a mission when we were compromised: by exhaustion, wounds or the enemy drugging us.

A phantom Ben Haim floated up behind me to whisper in my ear like he used to.

It's vital to go into a mission with your key objectives burned into your brain. If you're compromised, if you can't trust your decisions at any point, you have to trust those you made beforehand.

Objectives: Find out where Diana was and what was happening to her; rescue Savannah and her brother; get out alive.

Nothing they could say or do to me should get in the way of those. Nothing.

I would wear my HK. Dominé had said not to look like prey.

But if it came down to it, I couldn't fight back without risking much more than my life.

I could try to surrender. I might not survive, but I wouldn't be the cause of a war.

I burned that into my brain and hoped my instincts wouldn't override it at a critical moment.

When my arms began to shake and I was getting worried looks from the other gym users, I went to cool off in the showers.

The women's changing room was empty.

I leaned on the basins and stared at my reflection.

"What was it Top used to say? *Just when you think you have nothing left, you have yourself.*"

Tara stirred behind my eyes.

And that's not nothing, she said. *Besides, remember the movie? "Sometimes nothing can be a real cool hand."*

Tullah waited with me in the lobby.

She had one more go at me.

"You're thinking with your gut," she said.

She was right. But was it my human-trained instincts, or my Athanate instincts? And if they were Athanate instincts, then they had to be the best indicator I had of what another Athanate might do in my place.

In the end, I silenced her by taking off the necklace and handing it to her.

It would be up to her to try and find how it worked if something happened to me. And it would be up to her to communicate with Naryn and Felix and my House. She knew I'd loaded it all on her. It was a testament to our friendship—and her courage—that she accepted it.

I gave her a hug.

"So. How do I look?" I asked.

"Tough hombre." She tried to smile.

I was in white T, jeans and cowboy boots. Under that, well, I'd found Jen's sense of humor included packing me only racy black underwear. Still, it wasn't as if anyone else was supposed to see it, and I felt her sense of humor like a light in a dark tunnel.

Over the T, I wore my shoulder holster, battered stockman's coat, and the Stetson.

In my mind, tumbleweed blew across the scene and I could almost hear the Spanish guitar music in the background. All I needed was to switch my shoulder holster to the hip. Oh, and a little black cheroot to chew on.

But that wasn't guitar music. It was the cabby leaning on his horn.

I doused the smile. It was time for the game face.

My gut tightened like a spring.

Chapter 28

The cabby dropped me on 8th Street, at the entrance to the Calle del Bosque. He said something about not being able to take me all the way there because it was too narrow to turn around. He wouldn't meet my eyes, and as soon as the fare hit his hand, he was pulling away.

Great vote for the area.

This was Barelas, the oldest part of Albuquerque, whatever the tourist literature said about Old Town. It lay right up against Highway 314, the traffic a constant hum in the background. Somewhere behind me was the distant clatter and squeal of slow-rolling stock cars going into the main railroad yards.

I was looking down into what might be the poorest, most derelict street in town. Lighting didn't seem to be a big priority.

There was a shed on the left; peyote graffiti crawled up the walls like psychedelic snakes.

Loud music came from one of the houses down the Calle. One block away, someone was slamming a door over and over again. A black cat slunk around the corner, turning bright eyes to look at me, as if to ask what the hell I thought I was doing here. A slight breeze in my face brought me the smell of damp earth from the Rio Grande. And Were. Lots of them. Their Call seethed in the night; a song whose words I couldn't quite make out.

Dead End, said the sign in front of me.

No shit.

I didn't know which house it was down here, but '*if you can't find it, you aren't supposed to*'.

They were all about cojones, these Albuquerque Were. If you can't handle it, don't come.

I started walking slowly, not trying to hide the sound of my footsteps.

The cabby was right about the width of the street. It was narrow—an easy place to get trapped in a vehicle. The first houses I passed were all dark. No streetlights. Not a single porch light showing. I walked in the center of the street, scanning for threats with all my senses. The wind had thrown streamers of sand and dust across the tarmac, and it crunched under my heels.

Every door and window on the Calle was barred. On the houses near the entrance, the bars had been white and ornate, almost delicate, as if lace had been drawn across every opening to the buildings. The next houses didn't bother to disguise the function of the bars—thick square grilles or prison-cell poles. They claimed their yards with heavy chain-link fences, protecting decaying trailers which looked as if they were slowly sinking into piles of litter; sheds made of fiberboard and plastic sheeting; dusty, broken furniture; rusty trucks.

There *was* space for turning a car about halfway down; a small area of churned earth on my left. But a group of men stood in the middle of it, smoking and watching me, not looking as if they'd have moved out the way.

Were.

Murmurs of their conversation reached me, mostly unintelligible, full of street slang and quicksilver Spanish.

"Hey, *Marimacha*," one called out. "Wrong 'hood."

That part I got. Been there, heard that before.

"Wrong *town*," one of the others snickered. "So fucking lost."

"So fucking *dead*."

I didn't ignore them, but they weren't moving and I didn't think they could insult me to death, so I rated them as low threat for now. Not worth giving individual target designations to. Team Yak would do for the whole bunch.

There would be worse ahead.

The houses here were ugly cinder block, squat and square. Walls had been painted; it was difficult to tell, but pink or yellow seemed popular. It had been a long time ago; dirt stains crept upward from the ground, reaching the bottoms of the windows in some cases. Roofs had growths of small vents and satellite dishes sticking out of them. One house had abandoned toys scattered in the yard and an empty bird cage leaning against the fence.

Behind me, Team Yak was standing in the road now, blocking my retreat. They'd shut up, so it wasn't all bad.

They were a problem I'd need to deal with when I came out.

When.

I got to the dead end; a stop sign and a chain link fence. Beyond that, there was a dusty path and scrub. I could smell the Rio Grande in the darkness.

A way out if things went bad?

The last house on the right was different.

It was much bigger than any of the others, though still squat and ugly, and it was surrounded by walls rather than a wire fence. There were trees in the yard and slatted shutters on the windows. The only way in was through a huge double gate of ornate metalwork. This was the house where the music was coming from.

And the Were scent. A lot of Were scent.

It pressed on me. It wasn't my pack's scent. I wasn't welcome here.

I shook that feeling off. True, but not useful.

The gate was unguarded. It was the same message as the rest of the Calle: *Come on in, if you're man enough.*

That raised the smallest of smiles.

The gates opened to my tentative pull. I'd half-expected a screech of juddering hinges, like in a horror movie, but the mechanism was oiled and smooth. I walked into the yard and pulled the gate closed behind me. There was a snap of bolts, making me jump.

The gate was locked.

My decision to come. The alpha's decision if I got to leave.

The yard was too dark for human eyes. I could make out the bulky shapes of SUVs and a score of motorcycles parked randomly, some of the engines still warm. The sounds of the world outside were muted. Nothing moved in the yard except me.

One of the trucks had an air scoop that looked horribly familiar.

I walked across to check it.

My night had just gotten even better. Lance Evans, the ringleader of the Boneheads that had harassed Olivia, had made it as far as Albuquerque.

Shit. What was he here for?

Felix had said he would head south, but to the border packs: Gold Hill or Ute Mountain. Had he gone straight past them and come here? Was he in trouble, and if he was, did I owe him anything?

No. Felix exiled him. If Evans was in trouble, that was his lookout. Not on my list of objectives.

The front door was open and I walked in.

The house layout was odd. I'd walked into a room which ran the width of the building. It was like a hell-raising bikers' club house. Badly lit. Music blaring. Battered sofas around the edges, takeout boxes and six-packs of beer stacked on the floor. Pool table pushed against the far wall. Shotguns close to hand. There was a swamp-odor of motor oil, pizza, dope and pent-up aggression.

And like a river in the night, under it all, the smell of blood.

The reception committee were all Were. All hulking brutes. We were supposed to have developed past the caveman stage, but I was looking at a dozen guys and gals who'd missed that bus. They stood watching me. No one said anything.

They had to be Team Troll.

I had no doubts they could collectively tear me apart. Most of them looked as if they wanted to. But if they'd intended to kill me, a single shot from the shadows outside would have done it.

The Albuquerque pack wanted me to come in.

I'd see about getting out when the time came.

But all this couldn't be just for me. Team Yak were out there as an early warning system. Maybe a visible deterrent for casual passers-by. Team Troll were here as guards.

No, not all of that for me. So, what the hell had I landed in now?

A man and a woman came in through one of the internal doors and walked over to me, shouldering their way through the Trolls.

She was my size, five-ten. He was over six feet. Both had long blue-black hair held back from hawk-proud faces with scarlet bandanas. Eyes hidden in shadow. They could have been brother and sister. He was dressed in work boots, heavy jeans and a tan T with a flaming skull image. She was all in black leather: boots, low-rise pants that fit like a paint job and a vest with the same skull icon.

I stood still and waited. They circled around me.

"Smells like snake, Bode," said the woman. Her voice was surprisingly light, but smoky.

"Sure slithered a long way from home," he grunted back.

She stopped in front of me, her weight shifting like a boxer's. "Snakes fuck wolves in Denver?"

One way of looking at it.

But tonight wasn't about how physically tough I could be.

All I wanted was to get past them and find Savannah, but as Dominé had warned me, I knew that how I got past was important too.

I let my mouth twist and looked right through her, as if I was bored with it all.

"Stupid for Larimer's half-breed fuck-bitch to come to Albuquerque," Bode said. He'd gotten close enough behind me to hiss it right into my ear. "Even more stupid to come here, to the Calle."

The woman leaned closer, snuffling. Maybe she was trying to figure out how no one had been able to smell me in Albuquerque, or maybe she was just memorizing my marque. Whichever, she was more nervous this close to me than she was letting on.

I had to show I was predator, not prey. Standing silent might look too much like prey to them.

Time to bite back.

I flared my nose and sniffed back at her.

"That smells tasty," I growled quietly, and drew back my lips as if my fangs were going to manifest.

She flinched. She tried to hide it, but she couldn't. *Ooh. Fang-phobic.*

Bode knew I'd seen it and he didn't like it at all. He was about to spout some more crap when I stopped him.

"Look, this is fun and all that," I said, as if I couldn't care less, "but I'm here to see the alpha, not the guard dogs."

Bode edged the woman out of the way and got in my face.

"What you want, half-breed?" he said.

"You've got some friends of mine. I want them back."

However well I'd kept it down so far, the adrenaline storm was starting. The Athanate equivalent—the elethesine hormone—was right there with it, and I could *feel* everything start to go super-focused and timeless. My eyes would be going starless, sucking in the dim light. Fangs weren't far behind.

Right on cue, I felt the scratching inside. My wolf wanted some of this.

Shit. Shit. Close it down.

Savannah's life might depend on me.

I didn't know what the alpha wanted with me, or what he thought I might offer in return for Savannah and her brother.

I was sure he knew exactly how I was being provoked. He couldn't just want me to lash out and get killed—there wouldn't be any point.

So I couldn't. I had to stop myself.

The ability to not hit someone is the true art. This anger must come out, but this is not the way, the time or the place. Strive only for peace and control.

My Shi Fu, Tullah's father, Master Leung. That advice was never intended for this situation, but it'd do.

The ability to not hit someone is the true art.

Keep focusing on that.

I shuddered and let my breath trickle back out.

As my heart rate dropped, my eukori snuck out and tried for a flank attack, but Bode's aura was hard as a tortoise's shell. I finally let everything relax.

Bode backed up and held out a hand, palm up.

"Some kind of secret handshake, *Bode*?" Barely a wobble in my voice.

"Give me your weapons," he said.

"What kind of alpha is worried about a handgun?" my demon snarked before I could stop it.

Crap.

"Haz?" Bode said, and the woman nodded warily.

Maybe this had been discussed before—*let the half-breed in with her weapons if she wants, see if she dares try something.*

Haz, if that was her name, had gotten herself under control again, and her voice was steady as she told me to walk, pushing me toward the door they'd come in.

Bode stepped up on the other side.

With my senses stretched to their ultimate by the effects of the elethesine, I could sense and smell the room I was about to enter.

Humans. A sense of fear like razors cutting into flesh.

Different marques. Were. Athanate.

The alpha, whose half-shielded dominance made the room pulse like a beating heart.

Lots of blood.

And death.

Chapter 29

Through the door was a smaller, bleaker room. It was empty of furniture.

A couple more Trolls stood by the far wall, one of them with bloodstains splattered across his chest. Beside him was Rita from the bar this afternoon, neatly dressed, arms crossed and stony faced. On my right, there was a group of Were, including Evans. Savannah was trembling in a corner behind them, her arms around a young guy I assumed was Claude. I'd thought he'd be about eighteen, but he looked sixteen and terrified. Savannah's face lightened with a sliver of hope as she saw me.

Too early for that.

There were two male bodies on the floor: Were—not from Albuquerque—blood congealing in pools around them. One alive, one not.

A woman slumped against the left wall, wrists fastened behind her, clothes torn and blood-soaked. She'd obviously been tortured. She was alive, but only just.

Oh, God, no.

She was Athanate. Athanate from House Romero.

Finally, in the middle of the room, commanding the space, the man who could only be the alpha, Zane. He turned and glared at me. His eyes were different colors: brown and green. Any shielding he'd had up to then dropped away, and dominance flowed off him like a sandstorm in the desert—stinging and crackling with energy.

It made my skin crawl and set my pulse racing.

I'd expected him to be a huge version of Bode, and he wasn't that. He was big enough, but more contained—wiry strength rather than rolling muscle. His face read like a map of the secret history of New Mexico: dark, proud and fierce; red and brown, black and white, all rolled together. His pants and button-down shirt were loose and casual, hiding his strength rather than advertising it. His hair was tightly coiled rings, dark as wet otter and springing up from his head.

"The last of our uninvited guests."

His voice was rich and full after the hoarseness of Bode and Haz. It was the sound of a leading man in an old Hollywood film, but more careful, as if it was something learned later in life. And completely at odds with the staring eyes.

Don't be prey.

"I'm in New Mexico on Athanate business. I needed no invitation from you for that."

His pack stirred and their anger seethed through the room.

My wolf wanted to react. I wanted to snarl back.

Push that thought down.

"And as for being here, in the Calle, I did receive an invitation." My eyes went to the injured woman and my mouth ground on. I couldn't stop it. "I didn't realize it was to witness torture."

"Torture? You're too late for that," he said.

He looked at the woman and back at me.

"Do you have a problem with that?" He shrugged and opened his arms, indicating the woman on his right and the group with Evans on his left. "Are you with her? Or with them?"

My heartbeat thudded in my head. Did he just mean Athanate or Were? It couldn't be that simple. This was one of those questions there was no right answer to.

Ignoring the threatening rumble of his pack, I stepped closer to the alpha.

"Neither. I'm a hybrid. I don't fit into your groups."

I looked at the woman and swallowed dryly. What outcome rested on this? "I don't believe there are affiliations between my House and Romero any longer."

My Athanate hardwiring agreed with that.

I looked at the other group. I recognized Iversen and pointed. "I'm certainly not with him or the Confederation." I pointed at Evans. "Or him."

Being pointed out challenged Iversen. He found his balls and stepped forward.

"I know it's not formally an invitation, but I'm an accredited representative of the Confederation—"

"Your *accreditation* is something you can wave in front of packs that acknowledge the Confederation," the alpha snarled at him. Iversen put his hands up and stepped back. Reluctantly. He didn't want to be grouped with Evans and the other Were either.

"Bode," the alpha said, and jerked his head at the bound woman.

It was so sudden, it caught me off balance. Bode crossed the space with three strides. His head distorted, stretching into gray fur and fangs. His hands wrenched the Romero's head back and before she had time to realize what was happening, he'd bitten right through her throat. Arterial blood sprayed over him.

Shit!

Savannah screamed.

I took a step and stopped.

The woman was already dead. There was a growl from the Albuquerque pack that reached into my chest, and told me in no uncertain terms they'd wanted her dead.

The alpha was watching me, waiting.

There was nothing I could do for her. And I knew little about what had really just happened. I had other responsibilities, however sick to my stomach I felt.

Not on my list.

I had to put it behind me.

Concentrate. Information on Diana. Savannah and Claude. Me.

It was getting harder to not respond. The smell of blood in the room, every new shock—it was all loosening my hold on both my wolf and my Athanate. I closed my eyes and thought about running through a sun-dappled forest, breathing cool mountain air, a carpet of fallen pine needles springy beneath my bare feet. Anything but the hot stench of blood in this claustrophobic room.

Whatever it was he was expecting from me, the alpha seemed satisfied by what he sensed.

"Get this cleaned up," he said to the Trolls. He turned and walked towards a double door next to where Rita stood. "Bring that one." He pointed down at the Were lying unconscious on the floor.

"The rest of you, follow me." He waved to include all of his 'guests'.

I let the Were go ahead and went over to Savannah, blocking her view of the rest of the room.

"You two okay?" I whispered, even though the whole room would be able to hear.

She managed a nod, her eyes still shocked and unbelieving.

Both of them were crying. Claude jammed the heels of his hands against his eyes, tried to wipe them and sit straighter. He'd been knocked around. There was bruising on his jaw and cuts on his forehead, but nothing like the beating the others had taken. Savannah hadn't been injured, from what I could see.

My gut clenched.

"I'm sorry," Savannah mouthed at me, her eyes flicking over my shoulder to the Were, spilling more tears.

I shook my head. No time for that now. No time to question what had happened to Claude to cause those injuries. I knew there'd be a limit to this alpha's patience.

"Come on," I said.

I put the Stetson on Savannah's head and draped the stockman's coat around both her and Claude. It wasn't cold, but they were in shock. A little warmth would help. And I knew they'd also feel better with the illusion of a barrier between them and the Were, however flimsy.

And as far as the Albuquerque pack were concerned, their scent would mingle with mine. It marked them.

I hoped that was going to be a benefit.

We walked together into the next room. It wasn't so bare. There was a tiled floor of polished stone, heavy wooden furniture, light from wall lamps, windows with curtains. In comparison to the last room, it was luxurious.

The other Were guests were already sitting at a table in the middle of the room. There was a sofa against the wall. I guided Savannah and Claude there before joining the rest.

I had to walk around the unconscious Were.

The alpha watched me as I pulled up a straight-backed chair.

Good. Attention on me, not on Savannah and Claude.

We were sitting around an ancient oriental dining table—heavy, circular, with carved legs like elephant trunks and the top tightly covered in dark green baize, like a card table.

The alpha was opposite me. Iversen was sitting to the alpha's right. The Were whose marque I didn't recognize was to my left and Evans was sitting to my right. Evans still had the bruises and black eye from our last meeting, and hate flared in the expression he cast my way.

He and Iversen were silent: apprehensive and angry. They hadn't expected the killing, and the suddenness—the casual brutality of it—had shocked all of us. From their reactions, they hadn't been in that room much longer than I had. I didn't think they'd seen the Romero woman tortured.

The last Were, the one to my left—he was different, less shocked. More...I drew in the scents in the room, letting their messages flow down into the wolf...more excited.

He'd *enjoyed* seeing the woman killed. He'd have enjoyed being there earlier.

My stomach threatened to heave again, and I concentrated on the alpha.

His elbow was on the armrest of his chair, his hand held up and Haz touching it. I thought for a second that it was an odd gesture of affection, but Haz's fingers were pressing patterns in his palm. It seemed the Albuquerque Were had a variation of sign language for speaking when there were other werewolves around.

Handy.

She was looking at me as she signed, and I could imagine what she was telling him about me.

After a minute, he nodded. "Thank you, Haseya," he murmured.

She joined Rita and Bode against the wall behind the alpha. Rita's face still showed no emotion. Bode and Haz glowered at the rest of the room. Not just me on their shit list, then.

The alpha nodded at the Trolls and they left, pulling the door closed behind them.

Then he focused back on me.

"I'm Zane," he said.

"Yeah, the alpha of Albuquerque," I replied, anger bubbling up again. I struggled to keep my voice level and reasonable. "You know who I am and why I'm here."

"Yes. Rita has explained. Including your claim that these two," he indicated Savannah and Claude, "are Farrell kin. I find that interesting. The boy's not any Athanate's kin, and the girl doesn't have your marque."

He held up his hand to stop me from speaking. "I've heard your explanation." His eyes wandered arrogantly over me, lingering, full of sexual heat.

With the coat off, the HK was in full sight, tucked into the holster under my arm.

"A Mark 23, by the look of it," he said, and extended his hand across the table.

Crap.

Nothing I could do about it. My mouth dry, I pulled the HK from the holster, rechecked the safety and handed it over, butt first.

I didn't *think* he was going to shoot me, but then I hadn't thought he was going to kill a Romero Athanate in front of me either.

His eyes held mine while he ejected the magazine, cleared the chamber, worked the slide and dry-fired.

"Well kept, well used," he murmured.

He pushed the release pin and the gun came apart in his hands. He held the components to the light, ran his fingers down the metal and rubbed them together, gauging the amount of oil I used. Then his fingers danced like brown spiders over the gun, slotting it back together in seconds.

Only I was allowed to show off like that, and I'd earned the right with years of teaching recruits in 4-10 until they could do it like me, in the dark and behind their backs, upside down and underwater.

He checked the safety and placed it carefully on the table beside him.

Ask for it back, his expression dared me.

I wasn't going to give him any indication of how much I wanted it. I kept my face calm, and the tension around the table eased off a fraction. The sense of violence that had been pouring out of Zane had ebbed while he played with my gun.

Suddenly he became a host. The change was as unnerving as the killing of the Romero had been.

"You know Mr. Evans and Mr. Iversen," he said, waving at them.

I nodded. Neither of them liked me, but they liked each other even less, from the looks that passed across the table.

"And this is Mr. Fuller of Gold Hill, who arrived accompanied by Mr. Evans."

Evans had joined Gold Hill, then. But why come down here?

"They're all claiming to be envoys," Zane said, his voice neutral. "Are you an envoy too, Ms. Farrell?"

"Amber," I said automatically. "And no, I'm not an envoy. I came down here on Athanate business. These two kin have done you no harm. I just want to take them and be on my way."

The mismatched eyes glowed and the wolf showed through again.

"*On your way*," he repeated. "But rescuing these humans wouldn't conclude your business in New Mexico, would it?"

"No." I glanced around the table. Maybe it hadn't been a good idea to be open with Rita about searching for Diana. I certainly didn't want to talk Athanate problems in front of others.

Zane pursed his mouth. "So you're claiming more Athanate business. Our worlds overlap in New Mexico, and you are Were as well as Athanate. What might Larimer be interested in, down in Albuquerque, I wonder?"

Iversen stirred as if to interrupt, and Zane stared him into silence.

"I have no idea what information Felix might be interested in," I said. "I'm not here officially."

"Unofficially?" His voice went smooth. "Both Athanate and Were?"

Was that good or bad? If I wasn't on Felix's business, then any mistakes I made didn't affect the Denver pack? Or he felt he could do what he wanted with me without Felix being forced to respond?

I didn't want to try lying. Felix thought he could tell. I wasn't sure about Zane's ability.

I nodded.

Iversen ran his hand across his mouth, his eyes narrowed thoughtfully.

Fuller frowned and squinted at me. I got the idea that unofficial in his mind clearly meant I had no protection. His look was sexual as well, but he had nothing of the heat of Zane's eyes. Fuller's eyes spoke of rape.

"Reckless," Zane said.

Had I miscalculated here? Rita had implied he wanted something from me. Now it looked like I'd landed in some bullshit involving the Confederation, a rogue pack and a lethal dispute between Romero and the Albuquerque Were.

Concentrate. Diana, Savannah, Claude, me. Nothing else matters at the moment.

"A gambler," Zane went on. "Do you play poker, Amber?"

Not the question I was expecting. What the hell was the alpha's grand plan behind this meeting? Or didn't he have one?

But poker? When we were back on base with Ops 4-10, the troops had split into two groups—those that were playing poker and those who couldn't play poker because they'd gotten stuck with some official duty that required both hands, both eyes and both sides of the brain.

"Yeah, I play poker."

Never played with Were before. How did everyone bluff when they knew how fast hearts were beating and how much adrenaline was being pumped?

Haz brought a new pack of cards from a cupboard, tore the wrapping off and put the pack in his hand.

He tossed the jokers aside and began to shuffle, his fingers showing the same dexterity as he had with the gun.

"It's Friday," he said. "Friday is poker night, a tradition in my pack."

He paused in the shuffle to sign a message *flick-flick-flick* with his fingers at Haz. Apparently, they didn't need to touch to sign.

"Athanate betrayals and uninvited guests have caused me to lose my partners temporarily, but I don't see why the tradition should stop for that."

Betrayal? Had they had some kind of deal with Romero?

Rita had said that there was Were blood on Romero hands.

Fuller and Iversen didn't react to the words; it seemed they didn't have any more idea than I had what might be going on in Albuquerque.

While I was searching for reactions from around the table, Haz had taken tumblers and a bottle from a cupboard. I looked sideways as she placed a tumbler in front of me and poured. I couldn't see the label. It was some kind of brandy and the logo was a buffalo's head in flames. It was probably a clue as to what my head would feel like, if my Athanate metabolism didn't beat the brandy into submission. It smelled foul.

Iversen was angry. "I didn't come here to watch you play card games. I—"

"Not watching." Zane's gaze fastened on Iversen. "You want to negotiate, Iversen, you'll need to win concessions from me. Play cards."

"What? You mean you'll make an agreement on the outcome of a card game? Is that what the stakes are?" Iversen couldn't believe it. "With Gold Hill as well? Are you out of your fucking—"

"No!" Zane snapped, his wolf flaring in his face, his shock of hair shaking with the vehemence of his words. "The stakes you're playing for are *lives*."

He leaned forward. I'd thought he let his dominance out before, but I'd been wrong. It lashed out over the table now.

"Lives that my pack has lost today, caught up in a fucking Athanate war, with Romero changing sides and betraying us. With the Confederation stalled at the Colorado border and trying to get an agreement to sneak in the back way. With the border packs killing each other to offer themselves as an association to anyone who'll shake their hands."

He stood, resting his fists on the table, and his head swung from one to the other of us. His wolf boiled inside him, just beneath the surface, leaking out of his eyes, making his voice harsh.

"You," his eyes stabbed at Fuller, "you bring me a wolf from Ute Mountain, as a *gift*, who dies on my floor. And a stray Cimarron cub from Kansas, who you've beaten senseless and who is likely to die as well. Which brain cell was firing when you thought it'd be a good idea to get me involved in your dispute with Cimarron?"

"You two," he glared at me and Evans. "Denver pack, one turning up claiming to be part of Gold Hill and the other claiming to be Athanate, only interested in Romero kin and a companion who's fallen into Romero's clutches. Do you think I'm a fool?"

"What's at stake? All our lives, mine included, if this clusterfuck grows. So, tonight, here," he rapped the table, "where I make the rules, we play for lives so you, each of you, understand."

He settled slowly back into his chair, his dominance folding into him with the same elegant motion.

My skin felt too small. My wolf wanted out with an urgency that made my whole body throb. I had to force her back down. This wasn't her battle, however infectious the anger was.

I had to distance myself from Gold Hill as well, but my mouth wouldn't work.

With my wolf gone, the Athanate had come out instead.

Shit.

Iversen and Fuller were alphas—not the alphas of their packs, but lieutenants. They weren't in Zane's league. Evans hadn't had any rank in the Denver pack. The three of them were scared of Zane. I was an alpha, but bringing my wolf out here would be a challenge.

Meanwhile, my Athanate was sitting there, enjoying the fear. It wasn't the same as Rahaimon, feeding on emotion, but it felt close.

And so what? Poker was a game of instinct and reasoning. Reasoning was the Athanate strong suit. The Athanate would be good at this. The wolf wouldn't.

And it was important. I had no illusions—Zane meant what he said literally. I couldn't separate the crazy from the cunning, but the man was dangerous and on a knife edge of anger at something.

However the mechanics of it went down, there was death in this room. One or more of us were going to end up like the Romero woman. I had a strong feeling that losing at this poker game would be fatal. And *none* of us would get out alive if we didn't humor him.

Strangely, with the growing threat of death, the game got simpler for me.

I was good at poker, but there wasn't the slightest chance I was going to play fair. I would use every advantage I had over the rest of the table.

I relaxed, for the first time since walking down the Calle. My body felt loose, like I was going into a fight. Sweaty. Sharp. Focused.

First things first: there wasn't enough attention on me.

I took my shoulder holster off as if I were finding it uncomfortable, making sure to stretch and arch my back while I did. Not a lot to show off, but you work with what you've got.

With the holster slung over the back of the chair, I ran my fingers casually through my hair, fixing my eyes on Zane.

Where the hell was this coming from?

"If we're going to play a few rounds, Zane," I said, "we can't bet with lives every round. And I didn't come with any money."

I managed not to call him 'honey'. That would have been too freaky.

And redundant. Everyone sensed the change.

I ignored the glares from either side. This was as much about pissing them off as it was about diverting blood supply from the alpha's brain, but Zane was the key. I concentrated on him.

His expression was closed. Maybe he saw what I was trying, but he wasn't going to give me any advantage by showing a reaction to it.

"From what you say, you're a sub-House of Altau and a sub-pack to Larimer," he said. "You're good for it. I'll take your marker."

"Well, I'm not here officially, so I'm not sure they'd honor my debts."

"Then you'd have to find some other way to work them off," he snarled.

He made a sign for Haz. She brought out a briefcase from a cupboard and opened it on the table. It was full of banker's straps of Franklins. The base was all neatly sorted, but thrown on top were rolls of bills with elastic bands around them.

"Mr. Iversen arrived with $10,000," Zane said, holding up the rolls. "I think that amount sounds like someone who's serious."

Haz took the rolls and laid them next to Iversen.

"That money wasn't for gambling," Iversen said. "It's for my expenses on this trip."

Zane smiled at him without humor.

Haz took a couple straps out of the case. One she put next to me, one next to Zane. I glanced down at the mustard yellow strap. One hundred bills of a hundred dollars each. I just taken on a debt to the Albuquerque pack of $10,000.

Crap.

Iversen looked furious, but he didn't argue anymore. He nervously snapped the elastic off his rolls and laid the bills flat.

Zane looked at Fuller.

"Ahh...we didn't bring that kind of money, either," he said, ducking his head slightly. "We're just here to get recognition of our status."

"Gold Hill's not the kind of pack with a balance in the bank," Zane said, not indicating whether that counted against their pack status or if it was just a comment about whether he'd take their marker.

"No," Fuller admitted. If it was about status, he'd missed it. He shifted on his seat. "There's a truck outside."

Evans looked as if he'd been gut-punched, but he held his tongue.

"Don't need a truck." Zane shook his head. "But you have a cabin and land up the top of Hollenbeck Creek. I'll take a marker against that for both your stakes."

"That's pack property. Not really my authority." Fuller cleared his throat and fidgeted some more.

"Are you an envoy or not?" Zane asked him, voice barely above a growl.

Whatever Fuller had been expecting, it wasn't this. Being honest with myself, I hadn't expected it either.

Behind that question was a second one, full of threat: if Fuller wasn't an envoy, what the hell was he doing in Albuquerque?

Finally, Fuller nodded, and Haz gave him and Evans each $10,000.

"Five card draw," Zane said.

Five card draw is simple enough; even idiots can play it. And idiots with pay in their pockets had been warmly welcomed in 4-10, because it was still poker, where someone could win the shirt off your back with frightening speed.

Zane tapped the deck on the baize. "Ante, Mr. Evans," he said.

I had a moment to wonder what Evans was doing here. Fuller didn't need a driver, and Evans was brand new to his pack. All he'd achieved so far was to put his new pack an extra $10,000 in debt.

Evans peeled off a hundred.

We matched it around the table till it reached Zane. With a flicker of impatience, he put in a thousand.

Hmm. I like. Even if I'm not sure I like that I like.

Cool it down. I could do this without my pants catching fire.

The rest took a breath and we all matched.

Zane dealt.

"So, uh, okay. The money is like a marker," Fuller said. "And we're supposed to be staking our lives. But no way you're staking yours. I mean, your pack wouldn't let you, wouldn't let us. So what're we playing for? Just the deals we came to talk?"

"If that's not enough, why did you come?" Zane said. "Did you think there wasn't any risk to what you did?"

"What if *you* lose?" I said to the alpha.

"You want me to put in something you can focus on?" He stared at me, then nodded at the sofa. "Those two. It's your call, Mr. Evans."

My heart skipped a beat.

Evans bet cautiously: a couple of hundred.

"What if I win? What value are they to me?" Iversen said.

I raised Evans by a hundred.

"House Romero has apparently contracted Athanate mercenaries to hunt them down," Zane said. "They're turning Albuquerque on its ear to find them. That tells me they have value to the right person."

Fuller matched me. His attention wasn't on the cards. He licked his lips, his eyes darting across at Savannah.

Sick shit.

Iverson matched.

"They're mine," I said, my voice coming out low.

"Everything that comes to the Calle is mine," Zane said.

He doubled the bet, sent it around the table again.

Match or fold, he was saying.

His fingers flicked a message over his shoulder.

Haz went and dragged Savannah and her brother off the sofa. She made them kneel beside Zane's chair.

Savannah clamped her jaws shut to stop any sound from escaping. She wrapped her trembling arms around Claude and pulled him against her as if she could protect him with her own flesh.

I felt the sweat break out on my brow. My vision went gray and narrow. *Mine!*

Diana. Savannah. Claude. Me. Whatever it takes to get out of here. No kneejerk reactions.

"They're mine," I said again, more growl than words.

"I've lost pack to their Athanate House," Zane said. "Our healer. Our young. Bode's own cousin. Why not give them to him? Why should your claim be better than his?"

We all matched the new bet.

I was working on automatic, all my attention locked on the alpha.

"You want them so bad?" he said, eyes trailing over me. "What are you offering?"

When I didn't reply, Fuller snorted. "She's all show and no touch, like some stuck-up bitch finds herself having to work in a fucking strip club." He rolled his shoulders and his voice took on a 'we're guys together' tone. "Not like yours," he said, his eyes passing over Haz and Rita.

Zane didn't blink, didn't acknowledge Fuller, but his eyes shaded golden.

Was he angry at me, or Fuller?

There was no time to think about it.

"What are you offering?" he snarled at me again.

My wolf came back and a growl built up inside. Breath was coming shorter. I had to find a way. Appease the wolf. Get momentum behind me again.

I took a swig of my drink. It was every bit as bad as it looked and smelled. It gave me no pain to turn my head and spit it as far as I could across the room.

"Shit, a bottle with a neck that narrow," I gasped, not acting at all, "what I want to know is, how'd you get the buffalo to piss in it?"

Bode had come up onto the balls of his feet as soon as I'd spat.

There was absolute silence in the room. I was focused on Zane, but he was as tight as a metal drum.

Still, I could feel Haz, and she'd bitten her lip to stop herself from laughing. If she was going to laugh at my jokes, I'd have to adopt her, and to hell with Zane and Bode. I let my eyes linger on her neck. My jaw pulsed pleasantly.

She'll learn to like it.

I felt queasy when I had that thought.

Zane lifted a commanding finger, breaking the moment. Haz turned back to the cupboard.

Now she held a tall glass jar, a damned pickle jar with an aluminum screw top. The sort of jar 'billies used for keeping their 'shine in the ramshackle shed way up on the hill where the po-lice didn't go.

That's what she'd been laughing about. Not my joke. I was about to get a good reminder of what's outside of the frying pan.

Haz casually tossed my buffalo piss onto the floor and poured me a slug of 'shine, with only a slight tremble in her hands.

I sipped. It was strong all right, eye-squeezing strong, but helluva smooth and—what was the word Jen used for a well-made drink?— *assured*. Orange rind and pinewood campfire.

"Thank you," I whispered hoarsely. "That'll do just fine." Haz ignored me and repeated the service with Zane's glass.

The others kept their buffalo piss.

Evans looked like he'd swallowed broken glass. I blew him a kiss.

Damn. I'd just won the first round.

No, said Tara. *That's what a hustler always lets you think.*

Chapter 30

We were several hands into the game.

It'd gotten quiet. Despite the stakes, the game had developed a rhythm around the playing styles.

Iversen was a percentages man. He knew the odds and worked them, but he had no feel, no presence at the table. He wouldn't lose much, but he wouldn't win.

Evans had gut cunning, but he had a tell and no balls to speak of.

Fuller took dumb-ass risks. He'd made a comment about Rita joining the game so he could win the shirt off her back. Rita's eyes passed over him like an undertaker gauging dimensions.

But none of the others at the table were important.

The alpha opposite me was like death at a banquet, which in a manner of speaking, he was. He and I were still circling each other, looking for weaknesses.

We'd taken small wins. Neither up nor down.

Whenever I felt his eyes on me, I'd lick my lips or tilt my head and watch him right back.

He'd respond, trying to unnerve me by staring fixedly at my breasts.

Iversen and Evans were furious at the byplay.

Fuller alternated between looking at me and Savannah.

Good. I was distracting all of them.

That gave me time to think.

What the hell was Zane getting from this? As he'd forcefully pointed out to me, he held everything and everyone here.

If he didn't want a deal with the Confederation, maybe he wanted information from Iversen. Could I use that?

New hand. I had a pair of tens.

"Tell me, Iversen," I said as he picked up his cards, "since the Confederation claims to work on consensus and benefits all, why did you use the Medicine Bow pack to subdue the Cheyenne pack?"

That was information I'd picked up from Alex's files. I hoped it was good.

"That's a lie!" he snapped.

"That so?" I said. "Strange. No one remembers them having any quarrel before Medicine Bow joined you."

Evans bet five hundred and I matched him. Fuller followed, but I could tell he didn't want to.

Iversen looked at his cards again, frowning.

"That'd have been right after the Rock Springs alpha challenged Medicine Bow," I said. "Not the old alpha. The new one that you installed."

Evans tapped his fingers on the table. It was his tell. He wanted to push this hand.

"Why don't you come clean about it?" I went on. "The Confederation is nothing more than the founders trying to extend their territories by bullshitting or beating other packs."

"Just shut up." Iversen said. He was from Wind River. The other two founder packs were Bozeman and Bighorn.

"And Colorado's a big problem, because either you keep growing, or all the packs you've tricked and beaten will start tearing you apart from the inside."

"Shut up!" he said again.

He folded his hand. Sweat sprang up on his forehead. His reactions were giving him away and he knew it.

The Central Mountain Confederation were stuck. They'd gone as far north along the Rockies as they could; at Fort St. John up in Canadian British Columbia, they'd run out of sizeable packs. And southward, they'd been stopped at Colorado by Felix. If New Mexico refused to deal, they'd have to expand sideways, away from the Rockies. Those packs were smaller, more widely spaced. Everything would become more difficult to control. *Much* more difficult.

Crunch time, and Iversen knew it. They had to take Colorado.

Had I just handed a negotiating lever to Zane?

He wasn't looking at Iversen. He was looking at me.

I shifted in my seat and ran my tongue slowly over my upper lip.

Evans drew two cards. I took three and ended up holding three tens. Not bad.

Fuller drew five. Plain dumb, with the size of the pot relative to his pile.

Zane took a single card.

"And what's the reason Denver doesn't want to be part of the Confederation?" Zane said.

"Larimer doesn't do deals," Fuller said.

I couldn't remember if Alex's files said he'd tried to approach Felix, but no way would Felix deal with Gold Hill.

"Not true." I said. "I'm Pack Deauville. We're a sub-pack of Pack Larimer."

"That hasn't been settled," Evans said.

"If you don't like that, then try this. The Denver pack has a deal with Altau. That's nationwide, in case you missed the news."

The betting went around and I just knew I had Evans. Fuller folded. That left me and Zane staring at each other over the biggest pot of the evening so far.

"You're full of shit," Iversen said. "That deal is worth nothing. Altau is overextended."

"Busy at the moment, I'll give you that," I said. "But that's not going to last forever, and then the Confederation is up against all of North America." I leaned forward on the table and smiled at him. "Bigger bet than you're used to, boy. Think you can sit at that table?"

I raised.

Zane matched.

Evans' heartrate spiked.

"What's the reason Albuquerque doesn't want to be part of the Confederation?" I asked Zane, trying to rattle him.

"We came to ask Albuquerque *and* Santa Fe," Iversen spoke over the alpha. "Maybe I'd have been better off going straight to the top."

Oh, hell. Albuquerque was a sub-pack of Santa Fe? There was another alpha in New Mexico that was senior to Zane? Someone crazier than him?

How the hell did we not know, right next door in Denver?

Was this a Felix problem?

There was a knock on the door. Haz went over and opened it. Someone handed her a piece of paper. She read it and handed it back. She returned to stand behind Zane's chair.

His attention broken, Zane folded and held up his hand for Haz to press out a message.

We hadn't made any rule on escalating. With Zane out, Evans put in only a hundred.

Pussy, but I'd already beaten him. I matched and we showed.

My tens beat his eights.

That put me ahead of everyone, but the game hadn't shaped up yet.

"Straight to the top? Not your style, going straight anywhere, Iversen," I said, keeping my voice sweet. "That's why you ended up talking to a bunch of Matlal renegades to try and con your way into a justification for moving on Denver. Gonna try that with Gold Hill down here?"

Iversen's face went pale.

"I'm not listening to any more of this." He leaped to his feet, and all of us instinctively jumped up. Bode surged forward.

"*Sit down!*" Zane's voice lashed out.

Iversen and the others crumpled back into their chairs, faces sagging in shock.

My knees went like jelly, but my wolf was damned if any Were other than Alex or Felix was ever going to pull that dominance crap on me.

My skin was itching to let her free. Only the sight of Savannah cowering on the floor beside Zane held me back. So I growled and stayed put. I'd ride it out. I could do it. I could do it.

And if this all went to hell in the next few seconds, my HK was just across the table. It would be easier to go for it from a standing start.

Zane ignored the rest of the room.

His eyes bored into mine and he spoke again, quietly. "Sit down." His dominance washed across the room again, more controlled this time, more like a tide coming in.

I braced myself and stared back.

Haz reached for my gun, her eyes narrowed, but Zane's hand came out and stopped her.

Then, I sat down. Slowly.

Every heart, mine included, was sprinting. We were all on a hair trigger for fight or flight. Except Rita. She hadn't twitched. She leaned against the wall, watching.

The silence stretched, until Zane broke it. "You're done, Mr. Iversen."

"What do you mean? We've spent all our time on this game. We haven't even talked yet."

Zane stood and leaned over the table.

"We've talked enough." He scooped up the remainder of Iversen's pile and threw it into the center of the table. "You won't be needing any 'living expenses' because you're getting on a plane back to Bozeman tonight. One of Bode's team will escort you to the airport."

"You can't just ignore the Confederation. I'm the accredited representative—"

"That has no sway except where packs have submitted to you. New Mexico is not open to the deal you're offering. Not Albuquerque, not Santa Fe, not anywhere in New Mexico." Zane's voice rose, became harder with each word he ground out. "You and the Confederation will not set foot here again."

Zane's dominance and anger seemed to feed each other. He wasn't my alpha, and I still felt I should be making myself small.

Iversen got to his feet slowly, still pale, his hands still adrenaline-shaky. He was smart enough—and a diplomat enough—to wipe any expression off his face. The Confederation might want to try again, whatever Zane said, so it was his job to back out without burning those bridges.

He was getting out, and I imagined he was secretly relieved.

"One last thing, Mr. Iversen."

Iversen turned.

"Those teams you had in the state." Iversen started to deny it, but Zane talked right over him. "The one just out of town here, and the one that hid out in Los Alamos, ready to sneak off into the Carson Park or meet you in Santa Fe. Don't wait for them at the airport."

Iversen dropped the pretense. "You'll send them back a different way?" he said.

"No," Zane said. "We'll bury them. You get to go home, Iversen, because I need one person to take my message back."

Chapter 31

Fuller dealt the next hand.

I barely looked at my cards, my mind working furiously. If Zane was going after Iversen's companions, was he after mine too? Rita knew I wasn't here alone. Had she told Zane? Were his people hunting Tullah right now? What would they do if they found her?

Rita's face gave nothing away. She might as well have been a statue.

What could I offer Zane, to prevent him from harming her?

Would saying anything only bring his attention to her?

Say nothing. Stay focused. Diana, Savannah, Claude, me. That's what I was here for.

The less attention I brought to Tullah, the safer she was.

At least I hadn't mentioned to Rita what Tullah was. They might think Tullah was Athanate, which meant they would be searching for a marque.

I had to concentrate.

"You sure twisted his tail," Fuller was saying to Zane.

Groveling little creep.

The alpha didn't reply. With the remains of Iversen's money already in the pot, and a large ante, he opened the betting big.

"So, you're claiming to be Gold Hill?" Zane said to Evans. "Nothing to do with Denver?"

Evans nodded, his expression guarded. He matched the bet.

"Since when?"

"Since he got kicked out for convincing his friend to challenge Felix," I said.

Evans glared at me, but held his tongue.

I matched the bet. Fuller and Zane followed.

"Not long ago, from the look of it," Zane said, "if that's when you got those bruises."

I laughed. "No. Not long, but he got those from me." I leaned across the table. "Want to tell them what happened, Bonehead?"

"Shut the fuck up," Evans yelled, getting half out of his chair before a growl from Bode sent him back down.

"Recently arrived at Gold Hill, then," Zane said, drawing two cards.

Something clicked in my head, and as Fuller drew three cards, I realized what he had brought Evans here for.

It was the old joke about how fast you had to run to get away from a tiger: not faster than the tiger, just faster than the guy next to you.

Fuller couldn't have known beforehand what was going to happen to Iversen's teams, but some animal cunning made him realize he'd be safer if he had another pack member with him. A throwaway.

Whatever story he'd spun Evans, the man hadn't seen it, and he wouldn't see it now. Although he'd sat down at Bode's threat, his face was red with anger. He wouldn't be thinking straight for a long time. Probably right up until it hit the fan.

That was his problem, though. Not mine.

I glanced down at my cards. I had nothing in my hand, and the stakes were high.

It's not the hand, it's the way you play it, Top whispered in my ear.

It wasn't just the biggest pot of the night, it was the breaker, the pot you get to when the true shape of the game emerges. The point where the losers know they're going to lose, if they've got any sense. The point where winners think they could win it all.

Pull out. Athanate.

No. Take them. You can do it. Wolf.

I stretched slowly and ran hands through my hair again.

I thought of Diana in Romero's hands.

Savannah, walking into the Were club to find her brother.

Tullah, Olivia, Alex, Jen. Waiting on me.

My heart on fire, I matched the bet.

"How many you want?" Fuller said, his hands nervous on the deck.

"None."

Both Fuller and Evans twitched. My asking for none had them mentally running around in circles: exactly what I wanted them to do.

Zane didn't twitch. He wasn't that kind of player; he went very still.

Fuller matched as well. He was way down on his stake, to the point where even he had to realize there was no way back for him.

Zane started the final round of bets. Again, he went high. His face said calm, but his pulse didn't.

He'd sensed it too. We'd reached the endgame. There was blood in the water.

What kind of hand has he got?

"You say there's no deal between Larimer and Gold Hill?" Zane said to Evans.

Evans shook his head, his eyes staring at the back of his cards as if he could magic a royal flush out of them.

"And Pack Deauville is sharing territory?"

"Yes," I said, before Evans could speak. "Bet or fold, Bonehead."

Evans folded, seething with an ugly hate directed at me.

My turn.

This was a *real* cool hand.

They knew my heart rate had been all over the place. I let it ramp back up at the thought of the gamble, and then I focused on Rita.

Reached out. All the way across the room. Synced with her heart. Everything calm.

She frowned, sensing something.

"All in," I said, and shoveled everything into the center.

This is insane!

"I can't match that," Fuller's voice rasped.

I just ignored him. I wasn't hunting him.

Zane took a swallow of his 'shine, leaned back in his chair and stared at me.

My bet was more than he had left on the table.

"I'll take your marker, Zane. A big, bad boy like you, I bet you're good for it. Or you could work it off." I dipped a finger in my drink and licked it. "Or you could give me back my kin and answer a few questions. Help me out a little."

Shit, I'm crazier than he is.

Bode and Haz were back alongside his chair. Between them, they'd worked up one of those subliminal growls that I could feel vibrating in my chest.

I let it go. I'd been growled at by the entire Denver pack before. These two were nothing compared to that.

Instead of fear, I let the deep fire in my belly come welling out, lighting up my face. Let Zane look at that. Let him want me.

The first chink of hesitation showed in his mismatched eyes.

The moment stretched—and stretched. Evans and Fuller forgot to hate me and waited with everyone else. No one breathed.

I sucked the last of the 'shine from my finger and smiled.

Zane folded.

Game over.

.

Chapter 32

Fuller reached for my cards and I slammed my hand down on his, claws emerging from my fingers.

"You don't get to look for free, and you have *nothing* I want," I snarled at him.

He started to get up and my wolf came out.

Stop!

I could feel my face stretch into a fanged nightmare and the howl building up in me.

No! Diana, Savannah, Claude, me. Stop it!

I stopped.

It felt like an express train had gone past my shoulder at full speed, leaving me shaken and startled in its wake.

Hate this room. Hate these people. Hate. Bite them. Rip them.

Mountains. Cool air. Running.

My wolf subsided.

Calm.

Fuller was twitching in his chair, blood leaking from the back of his hand.

Zane gathered the cards. It was quiet except for the purr of the shuffle in his quick fingers.

He rapped the deck on its end and set it down.

The look he gave Fuller and Evans wasn't pleasant. Evans certainly realized it, and it was just about penetrating Fuller's head that they'd made a bigger mistake than he'd realized.

"I have no intention of recognizing Gold Hill and Ute Mountain," Zane said flatly. "The territories are too small, too close. The way they're run is backward and constitutes a danger for all of us."

Fuller tried to speak, and Zane's eyes narrowed. Fuller shut up.

"I'm speaking for all the New Mexico Were," Zane said. "There's one territory there, for one, well-run pack. You have a chance, one chance, to go back and tell them that."

All the New Mexico Were. Shit.

They had a sort of Confederation down here already? Nothing I'd been told hinted at that. To outsiders, New Mexico was simply lethal, keep-out territory.

Which is how they could set up something like that with no one the wiser.

"Make a deal with the Confederation, and it's a declaration of war," Zane finished. "Am I clear?"

"Sir," Fuller stuttered and blushed.

"Should we go?" Evans asked.

Fuller shifted in his seat. Sweat stood out on his brow. He and Evans had gambled away a cabin that probably didn't belong to them. They had nothing to show for it, but he wanted out of here more than he wanted that cabin back.

"You understand and remember everything I've said about Gold Hill and Ute Mountain, Mr. Evans?" Zane said.

"Yes," Evans said, and then added "sir."

"Well, I suggest you take your truck, drive straight back up to the border and tell them, then."

Evans got to his feet slowly, waiting for Zane to dismiss Fuller.

He didn't.

His fingers flicked at Bode and Haz.

Bode escorted Evans out.

Haz moved to take Savannah and Claude.

Before I knew what I was doing, I was blocking the way.

Mine. You will not take them away from me.

Haz froze in position. Savannah and her brother pulled free from her, but there was nowhere to go.

"They are guarantees against your good behavior," Zane said from far away. "They won't be harmed, unless you give us reason."

I could feel some of the Troll Team gathering behind me.

I couldn't fight all of them.

Diana. Savannah. Claude. Me. Nothing else matters.

"See that they aren't," I said to Haz.

I touched them gently on their arms as they were taken past me, trying to reassure them that I would get them out.

Then I walked back to my chair, every step painful.

Fuller and I were alone with Rita and Zane. And an unconscious Were from Cimarron on the floor.

"And now?" Fuller said, his voice strained. He raised his trembling hands in question and glanced sideways at me.

The ceaseless pressure of Zane's domination was like being scrubbed with sand, but he was fixed on Fuller now and wasn't sparing me so much as a glance.

"I've had enough," Zane said. "You made some statements earlier, Mr. Fuller. Were you insulting these women specifically, or do you have an issue with female Were and Athanate generally?"

He held his hand up and flicked his fingers.

Rita nudged herself upright off the wall. She'd been standing there without even shifting her weight for the entire time. The whole room felt different with her moving, like a big ornament had been misplaced. Was there something she was broadcasting? Did were-cougars have the equivalent of the Call?

Fuller raised his hands again. "No offense intended to you and yours." His face was slick with sweat, and his eyes darted around the room as if looking for another way out.

"I didn't take any offense," Zane said.

Liar.

I doubted Zane would be upset at the comments directed at me. But comments at his pack? Fuller had misjudged badly. *Really* badly. He was beginning to see that.

Zane's fingers moved again.

Rita stood at the end of the table, opposite Fuller. He didn't seem to have noticed, but her eyes had shifted to cat. The green got colder and the pupils split vertically. The stare never left his face.

She was wearing a tan leather jacket, neatly tailored. Her fingers undid the buttons and she slipped it off her shoulders, letting it fall to the floor. Pulled the zippers down on her boots and twisted her feet out.

"Hey," Fuller said. He laughed nervously and shifted his weight back in his chair, wiping his hands down his jeans.

She undid her shirt buttons, one by one.

The music from Team Troll outside had gotten low and soulful. Rita moved with it, not swaying or dancing, but every motion measured and graceful. Another time, and in another place, Fuller might have found it erotic. Maybe with another woman, one without that intense, expressionless stare. He wasn't dumb enough to think it was intended to be erotic tonight. He knew this was all bad, and it was focused on him.

The shirt joined the jacket on the floor. She wore no bra. Didn't wear a top to sunbathe either.

Were get naked. They lose the sensitivity to baring their skin. That wasn't the same as not being aware. Alex was aware when he was naked in front of me—unconcerned but very aware. Rita didn't care. It made no difference to her.

The rasp of the zipper was loud. She eased her velvety pants over her slim hips and let them drop.

She didn't have the sort of mobile body that I guess would be regarded as the ideal stripper. She had the taut, rippling body of an athlete and the movements of a ballet dancer. But her body wasn't tuned for athletics or ballet; its business was death.

She pushed her lace underwear down and she was naked.

She didn't wear *anything* for sunbathing.

Her nose flared. She leaned on the table, eyes pinning Fuller to his seat. Leaned more, her fingers hooked into claws, one knee coming up—and suddenly there was that visual distortion, like light had bent around her, and the cougar's back legs landed on the tabletop.

The eyes hadn't moved from her target, not even to blink.

"Fuck!" Fuller said.

As a human, Rita was about five-six and a hundred and thirty pounds. As a cougar, she was seven feet long and three-six high. She looked magnificent, but I was glad I wasn't in front of her.

The cougar took a leisurely step, a rolling of shoulders and hips, the soft placing of a paw. Under the tawny hide, the muscles moved exactly as Rita's had.

Another step.

"Hold on now. What the hell is this?" Fuller said.

Zane's arm reached up, and Rita stopped. Not just stopped; became completely motionless.

"I needed one of you to go back and tell Gold Hill I'm not interested," Zane said. "That was Mr. Evans. He's on his way now. You trespassed on my territory."

"But I'm an envoy," Fuller said.

"An envoy of nothing. I don't recognize Gold Hill as a pack. You are a stain on the earth, and a blight on the land. We will cleanse you all, dig you out of the hills until the soil no longer remembers you and the rain washes the last of your stench away."

"I brought these for safe passage...the Ute Mountain guy and..." Fuller indicated the Were on the floor.

"Which only serves to remind me how sick you are," Zane said. "But I'll give you a choice."

Fuller looked eagerly at him, but I could hear nothing in Zane's voice to justify hope.

"You can have a clean death; Ms. Farrell will put a bullet through your head before you blink." He picked up my HK and gave it to me. "Or you can chose to fight Rita, and if you win, you go free."

I swallowed.

Crap.

I didn't like being put in this position, doing Zane's dirty work for him.

Fuller was nothing to me. I'd seen the way he looked at Savannah. He was sick and, if I heard right about Gold Hill, he was near rogue, but for me to just shoot him while he was unarmed?

Zane wasn't finished playing games.

But I still had to get out to take Savannah and Claude away. Their lives against Fuller's? I flicked the HK's safety and rested the barrel on the table.

Fuller scrambled to his feet, angry and scared.

He was big, not like Bode, but he was bigger than Rita. His wolf would be bigger, too.

He narrowed his eyes, estimating.

I'd made my calculation when I saw Rita change. The cougar that stood motionless in the middle of the table was a killing machine—cold and deadly. Fuller had no chance.

He fumbled with his clothes, shedding them quickly and changing to wolf.

His wolf was heavier, deeper in the chest than the cougar. Those jaws were stronger than a cougar's. If he could get a grip on her neck…

He snarled and Zane's hand dropped.

Rita was off the table in a blur. Fuller backed up, trying to make room, and lost it right there. Moving forward, his weight might have counteracted against hers. As it was, she hit him squarely, knocking him over, and her jaws snapped onto his throat while her claws ripped his body away.

He struggled, choking in his own blood, paws scrabbling at her, and then he was changing again—back to human, in flickering starts, his limbs juddering.

Rita's head jerked forward, the teeth biting deeper. The grip muffled her scream of victory. She shook him once, hard, and I knew he was dead.

Her paws pressed down and she heaved away, tearing his throat out and coughing it onto the floor. Blood pumped feebly. The body twitched one last time and everything went still.

Zane stood beside her. He rested his hand on her head and she turned cat-like into the touch, closing her eyes and seeking the contact. Then she shuddered and changed back to human.

She drew her legs up under her and leaned against Zane, looking at Fuller's body.

Chapter 33

Everything felt disconnected, like I'd walked into a movie halfway through and couldn't quite follow what was happening. I could put Fuller out of my mind. I hadn't had to kill him and I wasn't going to shed any tears for him. In a strange way, I was more concerned about Rita. There was something almost broken about her.

On the surface, Fuller had managed to scratch her face and blood was trickling down her cheek.

I put my gun back on the table and took Fuller's shirt. I got the bottle of buffalo piss from the side and soaked the shirt in the liquor.

"Let me clean your face," I said, kneeling in front of her.

"Thanks." Her voice was quiet. She watched me silently, all the blazing intensity gone from those green eyes, which still flickered unsettlingly between human and cougar. I wiped the blood from her face. Some of the arterial spray had gone over her shoulders and neck, but the brandy cleaned it easily away.

"You want me to help heal that?" I asked, pointing at her wound, which was still bleeding. Her face was about to get bloody again.

Her eyes went over my shoulder to Zane before she nodded. "Please."

I pulled her head forward, tasting the unripe berry flavors of aniatropics in my mouth.

This had better gain me goodwill from the Albuquerque pack.

I closed my eyes and licked the wound. I was afraid that the taste of Blood would set the Were or Athanate off, or my face was going to scrunch up in revulsion, but it didn't feel odd at all.

On the other hand, my jaws began to throb lightly, and I finished up as quickly as I could.

"Thanks," she said again. The wound had stopped bleeding.

Zane brought her clothes from the other side of the table and I helped her away from the spreading pool of blood. She still seemed a little dazed, willing to let me dress her. I had the feeling that if I stopped dressing her, she would just stand there until this blankness passed.

I pulled her pants up, easing them over her hips. The zipper caught. I had to slip my hand in against her taut belly to free it.

She made a little sound in the back of her throat.

Damn.

It was too warm and my jaws began to pulse again.

I'd been pushing out the Athanate sex pheromones all evening. Now I was wondering what Were-cougar Blood tasted like.

Stop. Don't piss away any goodwill by biting one of Zane's lieutenants.

I helped her into her shirt and we did the buttons up together.

Her face was losing its strange blankness. The eyes finally turned human again and stayed that way.

That close to her, I got another shock. Just visible on her neck were fading Athanate bite marks.

I couldn't help it. I leaned forward and sniffed.

Unlike Haz, Rita didn't mind at all.

It wasn't recent. I didn't think she was kin, but from the slightest trace I thought I could detect Romero.

What had Zane called the situation down here? A clusterfuck. That just about summed it up. The Were in New Mexico were united into some kind of a super-pack. That group having a deal with House Romero which might have included one of Zane's lieutenants being a bite babe for some Athanate. And then a betrayal. Deaths on both sides. An understandable suspicion of other Athanate.

The only thing left to wonder was, where did that leave me?

A couple of the Trolls came in. Working silently, they wrapped Fuller's body in a plastic sheet with a practiced familiarity and took it out.

Zane paused in his task of picking up the scattered bills, and his fingers flicked a message at Rita.

"I hope we meet again," she murmured to me, and walked out.

The bills neatly sorted into piles of bloody and clean, Zane frowned as he ran his hand over rips that Rita's claws had made in the baize of the tabletop.

"So, *Amber.*" His voice pressed down on his first use of my name. "You're asking for kin's lives and Athanate information and a free pass out of my territory. What else? Romero heads?"

I shivered. He might mean that literally.

"Just what I came for."

"Not interested in what's been happening down here generally?"

Diana. Savannah. Claude. Me. Take it and go.

"Of course I am, but I'm worried that I'm running out of time."

"You might be right about that," he said, and I shivered again. I'd meant Diana was running out of time. I wasn't sure what he'd meant.

Still, the HK was back in my holster, slung over the chair. Half a second away.

He waved me back to my seat and we sat down again, facing each other across the damaged table.

"What kind of people are you in Denver?" He tilted his head to one side, crazy eyes roving over my body again. "If this Athanate information you want is something we got from that Romero woman, does that offend your delicate sensibilities?"

I took a steadying breath.

Concentrate. Ignore everything else. Don't set him off.

"I can't afford to let it. But we're not like Basilikos. We're Panethus—"

"That's what the Romero Diakon said, too," Zane interrupted me. "In fact, to listen to Charles Romero, they are the true soul of Panethus, and Altau is just a power-hungry bastard who's to blame for endangering all of us with his scheme for Emergence. A scheme that profoundly affects the Were, and yet which we haven't been asked about. Not that we haven't learned over time that Athanate aren't willing to share."

"I understand. I do. And I believe things are changing. And Skylur isn't a power-hungry—"

"Really? Claiming all of North America as his domain doesn't show a taste for it?" He leaned forward angrily. "What are we getting into, without so much as a vote?"

"Shut up and listen to me," I snapped. "If there was a body that represented the Were, Skylur would probably talk to it. In the meantime, it's not a matter of deciding to reveal ourselves to humans or not, it's a matter of controlling the reaction when they do—"

The doors banged opened and Haz came in, carrying a bundle of clothes which she dumped on the table.

She glared at me and left, slamming the doors again behind her.

"If you want to discuss this in depth," I said more quietly, "you need to talk to Skylur or his Diakon. I can arrange that."

He grunted and leaned all the way back in his chair.

Something subtle changed in his face.

"Your colleague, Diana Ionache, came to Albuquerque and met with Charles Romero and his Albuquerque Diakon, Jiaro Amaral," he said. "She was very confident, and very foolish. She's now a prisoner."

Relief and alarm clashed with each other in my head.

Relief that Zane had made some kind of positive decision about me, and alarm that Diana was in danger.

And how was she taken prisoner? Diana was one of the most powerful of Athanate, and the most respected.

"House Romero, as you will already realize, has broken away from any association with Altau. Not to join Basilikos, but to form a new, pure Panethus." His mouth twisted. "Unfortunately, there's trouble already."

"What sort of trouble?"

"Charles Romero actually believes that bullshit about saving Panethus. Amaral doesn't, whatever he says. He's been making deals behind Romero's back: with Matlal's Diakon, Vega Martine, the Taos Adepts and the Warders. Who knows who else."

A cold anger formed in my chest. Amaral would have been the one to betray Larry, handing him over to Vega Martine to compel, and causing his eventual death. And Amaral would have been responsible for the Warders hunting and killing Larry's kin, on the chance that they knew anything about what had happened to Larry.

Amaral was a dead man.

"We tried to warn Romero, and Amaral sprang a trap to divert us," Zane went on. "Bode's cousin and our healer were guarding some new Were. They were lured to a farm by the Romero woman we killed. All of them were slaughtered."

His fists flexed unconsciously.

"You know what Amaral tried to claim?" he said. "That Rita had gone berserk. That she was responsible for the recent disappearances from House Romero. People like your friend, Larry Dixon."

The alpha's dominance was whipped up into a storm by his anger and it lashed out over me.

I bowed my head. This wasn't aimed at me.

Behind me, the door opened briefly and was closed again. Haz checking everything was okay; his own pack were worried about the alpha's state of mind.

Zane ran a hand across his face.

"Charles Romero was suspicious. He left town earlier with some of the remaining Albuquerque Athanate, and your colleague Diana. Amaral is still somewhere here with the ones who support him, and with the Warders. We're trying to track down where they're hiding."

"Where has Romero gone?" I asked "Do you know?"

"Santa Fe would be very dangerous for them," he spoke with certainty. I could tell he *wanted* them to try and hide in Santa Fe. Then he shrugged. "Romero's Santa Fe Diakon has a place somewhere out on Highway 14. They probably think they're safe, but Amaral has spies in Romero's camp. Your friend will be in the crossfire."

"Thank you," I said quietly. I had to wrap this up quickly and get out there after Diana, wherever she was. "You know, this has nothing to do with Savannah and her brother. All that talk of value or revenge was crap."

"I still want something in exchange for them."

I steeled myself. "What?"

"Association."

My stomach flipped. I couldn't. Naryn was still ready to kill me for hitching Altau with the Denver pack.

"I don't have the authority. You need to talk to Altau directly."

"Not with Altau. Not yet anyway."

No better. With Felix already under pressure for his decision over me, I couldn't make a promise about a deal between the Denver pack and crazies from New Mexico.

Even if I was starting to suspect they weren't as crazy as they made out.

"I can't speak for the Denver pack—"

I stopped when he raised his eyes to the ceiling.

"An association between Albuquerque and Pack Deauville," he said.

"I…"

"You *are* a pack, aren't you? You were claiming it not an hour ago at this table."

"Yes."

"And you are an alpha of the alpha pair?"

I nodded. But I didn't know if I needed Alex's permission. Or Felix's. We shared territory in Denver, and how did association impact that? What if the Denver pack decided we couldn't share territory?

"You've just suggested I talk to Altau about Emergence," he broke across my chain of thought. "How am I supposed to do that? Either I turn up on Denver territory, or you bring him down here and turn up on my territory. If we don't have some kind of arrangement, your offer is worthless."

Not crazy at all.

Put aside the eyes and the voice. The foaming-at-the-mouth threats. The swinging between moods like a bipolar lunatic on anabolic steroids.

He'd had us all here around this table. He'd found out Iversen knew about the association of packs in New Mexico. He'd seen how Iversen reacted to the threat of Altau and the thought of associating with Gold Hill. He'd killed one of the Gold Hill lieutenants, and sent Evans back there with a clear message that would have Gold Hill attacking Ute Mountain—doing half the job he intended to do anyway. And he'd maneuvered me into a position over an association with Albuquerque where I could hardly refuse.

What else had he found out about me and Denver? What had I given away without thinking?

Was his aim to get Colorado and New Mexico to take a stand together against the Confederation?

And make a deal with Altau?

Not crazy. Not crazy at all.

Just a great front to keep other packs out.

"Well?" he barked.

I opened my mouth to agree and suddenly, there was a hesitant touch on my boot. I froze. I didn't dare look down and draw attention to it.

The Cimarron wolf, the guy who'd been beaten so badly by Fuller and Evans, was awake.

He was young. I wasn't good with Were ages, but I thought he was a new wolf. A cub, Zane had called him.

What the hell was he doing?

And what the hell was I going to do about it?

I cleared my throat. "What's the story on the Cimarron?"

Zane shrugged, frowning at the change of subject. "Apparently, he was attempting to come down here and visit me when Fuller and Evans found him. I wouldn't be surprised if the rogue packs have been scouting out the Cimarron's territory. He probably wanted to check that they weren't friends of ours before responding."

"He had permission from you to come here?"

"No."

The Cimarron knew I was aware of him. He dragged himself forward and pressed his head on my boot.

Oh, my God. He was pleading with me. Were-style submission. *Protect me.*

I felt the hair on the back of my head stir like hackles. He was getting straight through to my wolf.

And now Zane was aware the Cimarron was conscious again. Just as he was aware the wolf was begging for my help, and I was responding.

I couldn't leave him here.

Oh, shit. Diana, Savannah, Claude, me.

My training said he wasn't my concern. With the seesaw of Were and Athanate tonight, my head was completely screwed.

When in doubt, stick to your objectives.

I had two strays to take home; I couldn't jeopardize them for a Were I'd never met.

My gut refused to agree.

Zane was watching me with the sort of unblinking stare that Rita used.

"He's just a cub," I said.

"Who may have heard things said this evening. I'm trusting to your discretion, and Larimer's. Why should I trust his? Will you vouch for him?"

I couldn't. That would mean adopting him.

Would that start a war with the Cimarron pack? I didn't know.

"Please," the cub whispered.

"What if I send him to Denver?" I asked.

I didn't know enough about the Were in general and this one in particular. He could be a criminal cast out of Cimarron. Or an envoy. For that matter, he might be here trying to make an alliance with Albuquerque against Denver.

But I could send him to Felix, who'd said that the Cimarron pack was okay in his eyes. Then it'd be Felix's problem and decision. If Felix didn't like him, he wasn't in any worse position than he'd be down here.

That didn't mean Felix would like *me*. He'd see it as me getting him caught up in more Were politics.

Zane nodded agreement.

Shit. Shit. Shit.

Chapter 34

Bode and Haz both came in when Zane called out.

"Clean him up and find him some replacement clothes, Bode," Zane said.

Bode lifted the cub to his feet and helped him out the door.

Haz had another report to make. She took Zane's hand again and started pressing her quick-fire patterns into his palm.

She reached the end of her report and he brought her hand to his lips, pressed a kiss on the back.

"Thank you, Haseya," he said.

Haz's face didn't twitch, but I could sense her body respond to the kiss like a flower in the sun.

Yeah, one of those alphas.

She left. I didn't think she wanted to.

"Well, two strays, and now a third," Zane said.

He retrieved his glass from the floor and poured himself another slug from the moonshine jar, before strolling around the table to offer me some. I shook my head.

Close up, the alpha seemed to take up a lot of the room.

He leaned his butt against the table. "Strip," he said.

"What?"

"You can't walk through Albuquerque like that." He had a point. There were patches of blood soaked through my jeans where I'd knelt on the floor, from the knees right down to the ankles. Some arterial spray from Fuller ran across my T as well. He waved a hand at the clothes Haz had brought in earlier. "Haseya is close enough in size to lend you these."

He was challenging me again.

Damn him.

I wasn't body shy. The army had taken care of that. But this was not-so-subtly different.

I wasn't going to squirm like prey. I wasn't going to ask him to leave.

I peeled off the T.

Oh, God. The underwear. Jen's lacy black underwear.

I sat and pulled my boots off.

"I like the underwear, by the way," Zane said.

"Thanks." Voice level. Go me. I was *so* not going to say *it likes you back.*

I unzipped my bloody jeans and wriggled out of them.

It was as bad to turn away as it was to stay put. There wasn't a lot of my butt that was covered by the material.

The bastard was enjoying it.

"*Three* strays," he said. "What's that worth?"

I hadn't even heard him move and he was suddenly right in front of me, hot and hungry, putting out his sexy alpha song. The Were laugh at the Athanate for getting sex and Blood all mixed up. Well, the Were did exactly the same thing with their dominance games.

My pulse pounded in my throat.

Savannah and Claude. Whatever it takes. Forget about the cub. Concentrate on the kin.

I put my hands on my hips.

I wasn't going to keep playing dumb, and I wasn't going to go in blind.

"Let's get this straight. You want sex in exchange for giving the three of them to me?"

He pressed in on me.

"I didn't say that," he murmured.

There wasn't anywhere else to go. My butt was up against the table.

He had no idea what he was doing to my body.

"Didn't we reach an agreement on an association in exchange for your kin?"

"Okay," I managed to say. "I mean, yes. Association. Kin."

His hands slipped onto my waist, and I gasped. Goosebumps rippled across my belly and down my arms. The scent of Albuquerque wolf filled my nose like the whisper of nighttime wind through a dry arroyo.

"So," I said. "So. Sex for the cub."

"I didn't say that either," he whispered right into my ear. His body pushed against me.

I lost my balance and grabbed hold of his arms.

He was strong. He had a lean powerful body, a good core. I knew he'd have great abs. *Good thrusters*, we used to call guys with a well-defined six-pack in 4-10.

His knee worked its way between my legs, nudged them apart.

"Stop," I said.

"Don't tell me you don't want it." He kissed my forehead, his hands kneading my back. "You got the cub. No price. This is just us."

"You're a fool, Zane." It was so difficult to speak. I had to force each word out. I didn't want to speak anymore. The air felt so thin.

"I don't think so," he whispered, his head turning, kisses marching down my cheek to my throat. "I can hear your wolf. She wants me. I'm no fool."

"You are." I breathed it into his ear.

The asshole wasn't listening.

His body was molded against mine. My heart was going like a trip-hammer, but the rest of me had gone all liquid, as slow as honey.

"Why?" He sounded genuinely puzzled. His lips pressed against my neck. He leaned away just enough to slip a hand between us. His fingers traced the contour of the lacy bra over the swell of my breast, slipped the strap.

"Because you're not talking to my wolf," I ground out as he bent his head. "She's got what she needs at home."

His head bent as his lips flirted, teasing, slipping slowly down. And that made his neck into a graceful arch, right in front of me, just under my mouth.

I could feel the hot pulse of Blood beneath the dark skin, pounding its seductive message. Luring me out.

I couldn't speak another word. The air seemed to squeeze from my lungs and my fangs manifested, already aching to plunge into his dark skin.

What was it Pia had said? *The harder the loving, the sweeter the feeding.*

My fingers dug into him and my eukori began to snake into his head.

I thirst. Submit to me, wolf. I will drink from you.

And the nightmares started to ooze out of my strongbox.

"No." I groaned with the effort of *not* biting.

"What?" He blinked and finally looked up. "Shit!" he yelled.

And he fell onto his ass.

This time it was Bode, Haz *and* Rita bursting in to see what the hell was happening to their alpha.

If it had been just Haz, I might have been in trouble, but it was Rita in front of me.

Zane choked out something in slang and waved Haz and Bode away as he got back to his feet, angry and confused.

Had I just screwed our deal?

Rita must have caught some of that on my face.

She gave a tiny shake of her head and distracted me by grabbing the clothes from the table. She helped me to dress, as I'd helped her.

"Great underwear," she muttered, and bit her lip.

Haz's spare clothes turned out to be a pair of her skin-tight leather pants, a T with the flaming head logo, and a motorcycle jacket. My holster went neatly under the jacket.

As soon as I was dressed, she ushered me out. Savannah, Claude and the Cimarron were waiting.

Claude and I took the groggy Cimarron between us.

The two guys had been given sweats. The pack had found some more biker clothes for Savannah.

"You stepped on his ego; he's not going to die from it," Rita said in answer to my question. "And yeah, in case you're wondering, we knew he was going to hit on you. It's something male and female alphas do, sorta sizing each other up. Haz doesn't like it, but she's not as mad at you as it looks."

She snickered. "He sure as hell wouldn't have been expecting fangs."

I believed her as far as it went.

But Zane was nowhere near as crazy and impulsive as everyone made out, and he'd spent a lot of time watching my reaction to his dominance displays. Just how much had he found out this evening, and why did he think it was so important?

Was he really aiming for an association with Felix? Or a challenge?

Did how I responded to him give him information about Felix?

My paranoia had been squashed beneath my wolf and Athanate battling. It came out again now with a vengeance.

The gate swung open silently. The Calle was black and empty before us.

"Stop!"

My heart stuttered and the wolf came back with a snarl.

Zane was striding down from the house.

I squared up, standing in front of the others.

Mine.

He ignored that. He had a fat envelope in his hand.

"Your winnings, and my cell number," he said. He put his arms around me and slid the envelope into my pocket. Not my jacket pocket, the butt pocket on my borrowed leather pants. Which was very tight.

I let it pass.

"Let's try that again," he whispered. "But a bit more slowly, next time."

I chuckled.

I didn't even bite his head off when he slapped my ass to send us on our way.

Chapter 35

The Cimarron cub's name was Benjamin. "Just Ben," he slurred.

Haz had washed and sealed his wounds. With Ben's Were constitution he should be fine in a couple of days. Right now, he looked like a war casualty. I was worried whether we'd be able to get him on a Greyhound looking like he did.

We'd walked out of the Calle and across the road, down toward the railroad yards. No one seemed to be following. I called Tullah and asked her to pick us up, far out of sight of the Calle. Paranoid maybe, but I didn't want the Albuquerque Were to know what transportation we were using if I could help it.

I contemplated trying some Athanate healing on Ben, but I was still on edge from Zane. I was worried that anything like that would tip me over into fangs or fur.

Meanwhile, he seemed to be getting sleepy, which wasn't a good sign.

"Talk to me, Ben," I said. "What happened to you?"

"Came to see Albuquerque alpha," he mumbled around his battered lips. "Was just following my nose downtown. Didn't expect to get jumped by Gold Hill."

"Why come down here? You've heard what the New Mexico packs are like?"

"Uh. Had to talk to someone," he said. "The alpha, he had it right. Gold Hill are fixing to move east."

"Grabbing territory?"

"That's part of it." He stumbled, then winced as Claude tightened his grip. "Cimarron has a lot of territory. All strung out along the old Cimarron Trail and Route 56. We run the Kiowa Grasslands and the Rita Blanca as well as the Cimarron Grasslands."

Pack pride shone through his voice.

Tullah pulled up and Ben was silent as we eased him into the back of the truck.

"Greyhound station," I said to Tullah.

As we moved off, Ben went on quietly: "There are small packs in Mills and Clayton, between us and Gold Hill. We work with them."

"You share territory?" I couldn't help the disbelief in my voice.

He tried to smile. "Long as you don't call it that. We 'coordinate' so we don't run into each other. Kinda time-share. Anyhow, Gold Hill are trying to take over the Mills pack. Want their name and their territory. We don't want that. We don't have an association, but we'll fight alongside Mills. *Unless* Gold Hill has backing from Albuquerque or Santa Fe. That'd mean us going up against the New Mexico packs. Don't want to do that."

"Okay, so you had to find out."

He nodded. The Hill Bitch wasn't designed to be comfortable, but we'd propped him against our bags and his body was sagging from the effort he'd put into walking.

"Put your mind at rest," I said. "In case you didn't overhear this part while you were lying on the floor, Albuquerque will cheer you on against Gold Hill."

"Got to call my..." he stopped, squinting at me in the darkness and rubbing his head, "my alpha, got to tell him that. Please."

"Yeah, I understand." That was a problem. Zane didn't want anything from our conversation getting back to Cimarron. And I had made an agreement with Zane to send Ben to Denver.

"Why the Albuquerque pack?" I asked, playing for time. "Why not Santa Fe? That's closer."

He shuddered and slipped lower in the seat. "Yeah. Santa Fe's the boss pack. Everything you've heard about the Albuquerque pack? Santa Fe's ten times worse." His eyes closed and he frowned. "Worse. Worst."

"Stay with me, Ben."

"Half-head," he murmured. "You could take Albuquerque, Ms. Farrell. Could take Zane. I felt it. You're Coyote smart. Not Half-head in Santa Fe. Don't go up against him. Please."

"You had your head rattled, Ben. You're not making sense. I don't want to fight anyone."

Savannah had been silent all this time. Now she spoke. "He has a concussion. We can't put him on a bus tonight."

We had no option. I had a possible lead on Diana and a promise to Zane.

"You could help him heal with aniatropics," Savannah said, as if it was obvious what I should do. And it was, if you didn't take my problems into account. If I didn't get all fangy.

Tullah's eyes met mine in the rearview mirror.

"You'll ride shotgun?" I asked.

She nodded.

"Okay. Pull over. Let's give it a try."

Savannah was kin and Claude obviously knew all about what Larry had been. Officially, since he wasn't kin, Claude shouldn't have been here to watch this, but if any Athanate House had license to bend the Athanate security rules, it had to be House Farrell. I almost grinned.

Kaothos edged into the back of my mind.

Any sign of losing control, fangs or fur, and you knock me out, okay?

I will, Amber Farrell.

Kaothos was being a very serious dragon tonight. Good.

Savannah realized something was odd. Her gaze went back and forth, but she didn't say anything. I was impressed with how resilient both she and Claude had been, given how their lives had been over the last couple of weeks, let alone the last couple of hours.

I loomed over Ben, looking down at his sleeping face.

Cute. Not Alex, and nothing like Zane back in the Calle. It was only a kiss; a healing. No more than I'd done for Rita. I didn't need to rattle the strongbox.

I let my eukori loose, imagining it drifting down on him like a net of spider silk.

His eukori was spiky and half-formed, as if he really wasn't sure what he wanted to be like. That was fine by me. I wasn't here for his spiritual development.

I felt his heart and matched it with mine, beat for beat. I tentatively stretched my senses inside him, feeling out the damage.

The taste of aniatropics flooded my mouth and I kissed his unresponsive lips.

There was a flash of memory: doing this for Jen in Bian's van, bringing her back from the brink. My heart did a double beat and I had to wait until it was running smoothly again.

If I could heal Jen, I could do this for Ben.

Without being able to visualize it clearly, I felt the damage in his head: the blood leaks; the pooling fluids; the pressure.

There was another moment of panic. What should I do?

Step by step.

Aniatropics would help the wounds heal and stop the blood loss. That's what they had evolved for. I could feel his body's defenses. I knew where they needed to be and what they needed to do.

Or I knew what they needed to do in my body.

I panicked again and nearly stopped. Tullah could feel the connection waver through Kaothos. She reached over from the front and squeezed my arm.

Step by step.

Slowly, his veins and arteries repaired. His blood flowed freely through his system again. Shivers ran down my body. His blood, not his *Blood*, not something I craved. Kaothos' claws pinched little warnings inside my head.

I felt his body restore itself. Fluids drained from the pressure points. Breathing got easier. His eukori became more settled.

It seemed to take forever. My time sense was warped.

At some stage I must have sat back. I wasn't sleeping, but I was only vaguely aware of Savannah checking Ben's pulse. She woke him and started checking his eye movement and asking him questions.

My House, I thought lazily. I was pleased she had some medical knowledge and the confidence to use it.

My House.

My jaw started to pulse.

Kaothos pinched me again and I clambered stiffly out of the truck to suck some cold air into my lungs.

"We haven't got an option," I said to Tullah when she joined me. "We have to put him on the bus. We can't take him with us."

"We could send them all together."

I shook my head. "I need Savannah. She knows House Romero. If Charles Romero really thinks he's still Panethus I may be able to talk to him about Diana, but I need Savannah to give me a way in."

"Send Claude along with Ben?"

"Maybe, if he and Savannah are okay with that. They've had a bad time. I don't want to add to it."

Savannah stepped out of the truck, leaving Claude talking to Ben. She'd pushed the sleeves up on her borrowed biker jacket. Tattoos spiraled down her arms, making them totem poles and ending with the raven just above her wrist.

Raven. The mystery bird, I seemed to recall from something Alex had said.

It was the first chance we'd had to really talk since we'd rescued her, and she didn't want to meet my eyes. Seeing where I was looking, she pulled the jacket sleeves down and hugged herself in the chill night air.

"I messed up, big time," she said.

"Yeah." I wasn't going to gloss over it. It'd worked out okay, but that wasn't her doing.

"Why did you follow me?" she said. "You risked yourself."

"I made a commitment to Larry."

"Is that it?" Her face flushed, and she mumbled an awkward apology.

"No, that's not it." I said, irritation trickling into me. "I couldn't ignore what I'd heard about the Were. I had to do something. But you're right about the main reason. Larry was my House and you were his kin. That makes you part of my House and that means you're my responsibility."

"We're not property," she said. "Claude isn't even kin, anyway."

Ungrateful little idiot. My vision locked down. I grabbed her and shoved her against the Hill Bitch, anger suddenly flooding through my veins.

"You made a choice for yourself. You made a choice for Claude too, when you included him in the Athanate world. Once you make that commitment, you have to stick with it. You don't have options anymore."

Kaothos was scrabbling against my mind, but my anger had built a wall she couldn't breach.

I didn't need restraining; Savannah needed to be aware of the realities of her situation.

My jaw pulsed and my fangs came out, aching.

She twisted to get away and I grabbed her hair, pulled her head back to expose her throat.

Fear surged out of her and I tasted it, hungered for it. And for her Blood.

"Amber!" Tullah fought her way between us. "Stop!"

Claude was tugging at my wrists to loosen my grip.

I was stronger than both of them.

"*Mine,*" I said, my voice dark with need.

"Not like this." Tullah was in the way now, preventing me from biting Savannah.

I couldn't bite Tullah. I'd promised I wouldn't. I'd given my word. That had to mean something.

And I'd given my word that I wouldn't bite *anyone*.

What would Diana think of me acting like this?

I let them go and we staggered apart.

Tullah pushed Claude and Savannah back into the truck.

I felt sick.

"I can't handle it," I muttered. "I've run out of time."

I leaned on the back of the Hill Bitch and rested my head on my arms. I was strung-out, tired from adrenaline overload, constant pressure and not enough rest over the last few weeks. The nights of unconsciousness that Kaothos produced just weren't as good as sleep.

If Tullah hadn't been there, I'd have bitten Savannah.

Maybe my bite would kill her, maybe not. But I'd been enjoying her fear.

I was standing at an Athanate crossroads. In Ops 4-10, Top had drilled us so that our training became hardwired into us, became instincts that could be trusted under life-and-death stress. He'd told me that in every moment, I was the sum of all I had been and done. As an Athanate, what I would become was dictated by the road I traveled now. Every step.

Dominé had it right—*vasana*—the experience that created a desire for more of the same. If I fed off fear now, that's who I would become. I would have no desire for anything else. I would be Basilikos.

"You can, Boss. You can do it."

Tullah tugged me around and, ignoring my protests, hugged me tightly to her.

I stiffened.

"Don't," I said. "Stop. I don't know if I can control myself."

"If you can't, you can't, and I'll know no one could have tried harder," she said.

My jaw was throbbing again.

"Please," I whispered. But my arms moved on their own, circling her body and hugging her back.

"Boss, you can bite me. I give you permission. You're not putting out your gimme-your-neck vibes, you're not influencing me in any way. Just the opposite."

"This is Kaothos making you," I said.

"No," she replied.

No, Amber Farrell. I have promised, hissed the lizard.

Tullah turned her head. Her neck was an inch from my fangs. All I had to do was sink down and my Athanate instincts would do the rest.

"Better to bite me," she said. "I'm not scared. I'm not feeding any monsters."

"But it could kill you."

"Maybe. Still better to bite me than Van. Kaothos could keep me alive, Van hasn't got anything like that, *and* she has Claude to look after." She sighed. "And all this stuff about how dangerous your bite might be…the Athanate have no idea. Not really. You're the first hybrid."

"And look how well I'm doing," snarked the little demon that lives in my throat.

That glimmer of humor made me snort. The fangs went away.

I bent my head and kissed her neck, just where I would have bitten.

She jumped at the touch and then laughed, realizing I was teasing.

"Thank you," I said and let her go.

We got back in the truck.

"I'm sorry, Van," I said. "That was shit you didn't need from me."

Savannah nodded jerkily, still trembling. Great. Now, along with Keith, I was somehow going to have to convince Savannah to trust me. If I survived—and managed to get Diana back—I was going to have a lot of fences to mend.

"Here's the thing," I went on. "Ben, I have to put you on a bus to Denver. I've done what I can for you, and I think you'll be fine with a couple of days' rest. I'm not sure whether they'd let me put you on the Greyhound unless someone goes with you."

"I need to call—"

"I hear you. Listen, I'm going to have to call Felix tonight. You give me a contact number. I'll get him to call your alpha. Felix can judge what to share. I'm guessing that'll carry more weight."

He nodded reluctantly. Tullah gave him a pen and paper.

"Now, I've given a commitment to Zane, so what you heard in that room stays with you until I say otherwise. I'm not sure why Zane's so touchy about it, but that's not for you to be wondering about."

I let a little of my alpha wolf bubble up. The guy had submitted to me. That didn't make me his alpha, but it gave me some hold over him.

"You got the right, ma'am." He ducked his head.

"Amber," I said.

He managed a smile, but I thought it'd be a while before I got an Amber out of him.

I turned to Claude.

"Will you go with him, please, Claude?"

Savannah started to protest, and he looked nervously from me to her.

"What about Van?" he said.

"I need her as an introduction, if we can catch up with Romero and it turns out he hasn't gone Basilikos as well."

"Um. Boss." Ben tried the name carefully. Of course his wolf ears had heard what Tullah called me. "I can make it to Denver okay on my own. If you've got a ski cap or something I can pull down, no one's going to notice. It's going to be the late bus. You wouldn't believe the state of some people on those buses."

I laughed.

"We're running out of time." Tullah checked her watch.

"Okay, okay," I conceded. "*If* we can get you on alone."

Ben was right. The man in the ticket booth barely glanced at him, and the driver was busy helping people load suitcases. Ten minutes later we waved Ben goodbye.

As we drew away from the station, I had Tullah stop and I got out.

All my earlier efforts to prevent the Albuquerque Were from seeing the Hill Bitch had failed.

The Troll who'd been trying to watch without us knowing looked embarrassed I'd made him, but he had the balls not to bolt. I gave him the GPS I'd taken from the Warders who'd come to kill Savannah.

"The routes logged in here might show you where the Warders are hiding in Albuquerque," I said.

His eyes went wide and he stuttered thanks before leaping onto a Harley and smoking tires back to the Calle.

I grinned to myself. He was probably supposed to wait until he saw us leaving, but then maybe the GPS information would be more important. I hoped so.

Tullah turned the Hill Bitch east to leave Albuquerque for the Turquoise Trail.

Chapter 36

Tullah drove and I worked the cellphone. Claude fell asleep leaning on his sister, but Savannah looked like she was pinching herself to stay awake. And watching me.

I called home first. There wasn't time to cruise the streets and leech off unprotected internet signals, so I used one of the encrypting phones Tullah had brought. I was calling Manassah, so the phone system there would cooperate to make this a secure line.

Despite how late it was, Alex answered immediately. David and Pia were in the background.

"Jen?" I asked immediately.

"Nothing yet." His voice was quiet in a way that told me he was barely controlling his emotions. He wasn't a happy wolf. Pack and House had blurred together, so as alpha, I guessed Jen's safety was his responsibility too.

Frustration soured my mind. There was nothing I could do about the situation in Denver from here. There might be nothing I could ever do. This was the Athanate world, the one I'd just been telling Savannah to accept. I'd made a decision. Jen had made a decision. Suck it up.

Instead, I told him what had happened earlier.

Whatever other problems Alex had were driven out by his reactions to the danger I'd put myself in and what I'd found out at the Calle. It took a while to persuade him to stay in Denver. It helped that I was already on the road out of Albuquerque. It didn't help that I was heading into Santa Fe territory.

"Hopefully, I won't need to go into Santa Fe itself at all," I said. "I keep thinking, if Zane isn't so crazy, then maybe the Santa Fe alpha isn't either."

"That reputation for violence? That's not just rumor, Amber." Anger was seeping into his voice.

I had to push onward. We were both angry and it wasn't achieving anything.

"Yeah. But why do you think they put such an effort into it?" I said. "And why're they so sensitive about secrecy?"

He grunted. "I don't know. I've heard of packs that were weak and tried to hide behind a reputation for violence. Packs that form associations can be defensive about it, because it might look as if they're weak."

"Confederation doesn't have that problem."

"I'm not saying it's reasonable." Alex snapped.

I couldn't put into words the difference between the image everyone had of the Albuquerque Were, and the *feeling* I had from meeting them. Zane and Team Troll could tear you apart; Rita *would* tear you apart, and she'd do it with that dreamy, detached look on her face—but they wouldn't do it indiscriminately.

Once I'd gotten past the rabid, psychopathic front, I decided I liked the Albuquerque Were. That was probably not a sane thing for a werewolf to admit. How was I going to explain it to Alex? Let alone Felix.

Long before that, I had more immediate explaining to do.

"So, in the end, I had to agree to a limited association with Albuquerque. We can visit them and they can visit us. And part of that bargain is for Felix to look after Ben, who's on his way by Greyhound." I paused.

I'd messed Alex around. I'd left him in Denver waiting by the telephone while things happened around him and there were dangers to pack and House. That wasn't a good place for a werewolf, much less an alpha.

"Can you pick the cub up from the station and take him out to Coykuti?" I tried one last request, meekly.

"No," Alex said. "I can't, and I can't wait for Jen to come home." His voice sounded choked and I could almost feel the grip of his hand crushing the telephone. "Amber, I've got to go out there now."

"Alex, what's happening?" I said, and before he answered I knew.

"Olivia. Ricky's taken her out there to Felix. It's getting close, Amber."

The sudden silence on the line was shocking.

Why take Olivia to Felix? Because I'd let her down. Alex and I were her alphas, but I was away chasing other problems and I'd landed Alex in the middle of those problems as well. Olivia had joined our pack from Felix's and now we'd failed her. Her only option was to go back.

I felt sick.

"Alex?"

"I'm going now, Amber. I've got to," he said. "Call Coykuti as soon as you have a secure line."

There was a muffled noise and then David spoke. "Hi, Amber."

"Alex has gone?"

"Yeah. Look, I don't really know all the background, but Olivia going out to Coykuti isn't just about you not being here."

David always saw things others wouldn't. He knew me, and that meant he knew how bad I was feeling.

"Felix is hoping that having her around will send a message to the rest of the pack that he's okay with her being in a sub-pack," David went on, and slowed. "And I guess he's also saying that getting her through her first change is more important than exactly where she is in the pack structure. He's doing what he can. There's a little time."

"Thanks," I said.

It was up to me to do the rest, if I could, in whatever the 'little time' turned out to be.

"I have something on Jaworski's hideout," he said.

I sighed. Just what I'd taught him to do: he was getting me to focus on what I could achieve now.

"You found it?"

"Maybe. It's my best guess, anyway. I'll send you an email with the details. Hold on. Just downloading some more satellite photos."

There was a pause.

"Yeah. This feels right. Reasonably big place, all by itself, long way from anywhere else," he said. "You'll be able to get our email?"

"We'll find a motel with a connection, or I'll go hunting with Matt's octopus. Thanks, David."

"No problem. I'll pick up Ben and take him out to Coykuti, too."

I thanked him again, and we signed off.

Felix's telephone system didn't have Matt's security modification, so I was forced to hold off talking to him for a while.

I spent the time with my fingers running over the necklace, wondering how on earth I was supposed to help Olivia with it, and then slowly falling back into the puzzling tangle of Were politics.

How had the Confederation and the New Mexico packs managed to overcome the perception that association between packs was a sign of weakness? The Confederation wouldn't be considered weak now; it had sucked in all the Rocky Mountain packs between Cheyenne and Calgary. But it had started with three packs.

How many had the New Mexico packs kicked off with? Who'd made the first move? Zane? Didn't feel right. If Half-head was the big boss, did that mean he'd started the association? How?

If the image Zane projected wasn't the real wolf, what about Half-head? What was he like?

Where had he gotten the nickname?

I shuddered.

Tullah found us a motel, and twenty minutes later we were inside setting up Matt's secure connection through the WiFi. There was only one internet signal, rather than the half-dozen his system usually used to chop the communications into bits, but Tullah assured me that this was a redundant level of security.

There are no redundant levels of security in the zone.

That had been instructor Ben-Haim, back in my Ops 4-10 days. I'd learned all my paranoia from him. In the paranoia stakes, I was not worthy to secure his sandals.

We sent Savannah and Claude to use the bathroom first while Tullah downloaded David's email and I called Felix's number.

He picked up immediately.

"This had better be good, or bad," he growled.

Bad, I guess.

"Felix, this is Amber. How's Olivia?"

"Not good," he said abruptly. "I'm hoping you're with the Adepts and calling because you've discovered the way to help Olivia."

Oh, God. Straight in.

"No. Not yet. I'm sorry." I squeezed my eyes shut for a moment. Olivia. My pack. Her eagerness, her sharp sense of humor and the trust in her eyes when she looked at me. I'd promised her I would find a way, and here I was, on a mission to save someone else. And myself. Nothing for Olivia except a necklace and some cryptic comments I hadn't begun to understand.

I took a deep breath and tried to focus. "There's a problem with the Denver Adept community," I said. "The leadership has changed and I'm not welcome. In fact, I think I'm going to have a serious problem with them."

"Are you safe? Where are you?"

Whether he intended it or not, the fact that he was immediately concerned that I was safe made me feel better about this conversation.

"I'm safe at the moment. As to where I am, well, I was able to find a shaman-Adept, and she gave me a replacement token. A necklace like the one Speaks-to-Wolves used. The problem is, no one seems to know exactly how it works. I haven't figured that part out yet."

"That's something. Why am I hearing in your voice that there's a problem? Why not bring it here?"

"I can't just yet," I said. "The thing is, following that trail has taken me to New Mexico."

There was a brief silence.

"Well, you're calling me. Either you've managed to evade the New Mexico Were, or you're going to tell me you've started a war."

In a way, I'd have preferred to have him shout at me. The joking covered real, deep problems, and his voice sounded so tired. Even though Olivia had switched packs, I didn't think that had changed his feeling of protectiveness for her. He'd lost a pack member like this last week. Another so soon would be devastating.

"Uh. No and no," I answered his questions. "It's complicated."

"I'm listening."

"I didn't come here just to find the necklace. I have Athanate obligations as well."

"Naryn knows this, and he refused you."

"Yeah."

I could hear him summing up all of it to himself. Disobeying my alpha. Disobeying Naryn. Problems with Adepts. Worst of all, not there when my pack needed me. He really didn't need a loose cannon like me.

"I needed to rescue some kin," I went on, "and it turned out that meant I had to go visit the Albuquerque alpha."

"You met Zane, and you're telling me you just walked away."

His tone was surprised, shocked even, but he let me take him through what'd happened. What I had to say was more important than whether I'd disobeyed him. He was smart enough to prioritize—the strategic overview came first. Tactical stuff like chewing me out could wait. I just hoped that the chewing wasn't going to be literal.

I had to do the same with my worries for Olivia, put them on the back burner, however much it hurt.

The bare bones of what had happened didn't take long.

I needed to convince Felix that Zane was an acceptable neighbor and not a rabid alpha. Even if Felix didn't want to form an association with the New Mexico packs, it made sense for us to be allied against the Confederation. More than sense; maybe it was the only way we'd all survive. When the Confederation heard that their plan to go around Colorado by making a deal with the New Mexico packs had failed, they'd turn their attention back to us in Denver. They'd tried the careful approach last time, sneaking in by allying themselves with outcast Were. This time, their desperation might lead to something much more direct.

And if Felix was having problems, some of them caused by me and Alex, he might be vulnerable.

Could I fix everything in one shot?

No matter how important I thought it was, I had to persuade Felix first. It was like pushing water uphill.

"No, Felix, Zane's not crazy. Think about the way he handled the border packs," I said. "He has no intention of making any deals with them. Those packs are a problem, you said so yourself. So he sent Evans back with the idea that maybe Gold Hill would be acceptable if they took out Ute Mountain. From what he said to Fuller afterwards, what he's done is chop the problem in half. Gold Hill will take out Ute Mountain, and then at some stage he's going to get rid of Gold Hill."

Felix flat-out didn't like it. "That's Athanate-style politics," he said.

I guessed I'd convinced him that the Albuquerque Were weren't rabid, but at the expense of suggesting to him they weren't good Were.

Crap.

"And it's the same thing for this Cimarron cub," Felix went on. "I'll take him, and I'll make the phone call to his alpha about Gold Hill. I have no real problem with that, but this is exactly Naryn's style of dealing with things. Zane's trying to get Denver tangled up in a territory dispute, and using us and Cimarron against Gold Hill, so he has less to do at the end. We take damage and he's stronger."

And I could see the logic. Face to face, maybe I could convince him that wasn't what Zane was doing. Over the phone, I was limited.

Felix didn't want to hear much about the Albuquerque alpha that was good. The news that I'd had to agree to a limited association to free Savannah and Claude only added fuel to the fire.

The thought of Zane in Denver as my guest and possibly talking to Altau had him pacing restlessly. I could hear the pad of his bare feet against the wooden floors.

He went back through what had happened, concentrating on Zane's efforts to dominate.

"He was trying to gauge my strength by testing himself against you," Felix said. "Why would he do that, unless he was thinking about a challenge or encroaching on Denver territory?"

"I don't think—"

"After all, he's confined to Albuquerque and its surroundings," he talked over me. "He'll be looking over the border and seeing the Denver pack sprawling across all of Colorado. Like every other pack in the area, he'll be wondering how hard it would be to take a slice of our territory."

"But how could he run two territories, with Santa Fe and Cimarron in between?"

Felix didn't have an answer to that. He changed tack instead.

"How screwed are you with Altau?" he said.

"I don't know, Felix. I haven't made the call," I replied. "If I have something solid to report about Diana, that might buy me a little forgiveness, so I'm holding off until tomorrow."

He was silent for a moment.

"What about forgiveness from the pack?" I asked quietly.

As strong an alpha as Felix was, the Denver pack was too big and powerful for him to simply command them on matters like this. I'd already been an issue with them, now I'd added to the problems. I hadn't even convinced Felix I'd done the right things down here. Convincing the pack would be much harder.

He snorted.

"Understand, I'm trying to deal with this the way it is, not how I want it to be. So, I'm not going to try giving you orders I know you won't obey. And personally, I hope you find Diana and she helps you past your crusis problems." He sighed. "I value you and Alexander, your Athanate House and the tremendous things your kin can do for us, but from the pack's immediate point of view, the key fact is that you've made a deal with Albuquerque for you and Alexander, one that's a potentially huge security problem for us."

I tried to argue, but he overrode me.

"That's the way they'll see it, until you can prove otherwise, which is going to be too late," he said. "The fix is easy. The pack will say that you and Alexander cannot share our territory. I'm pretty sure we could argue a border territory for you. Alamosa down south for instance, or somewhere out in the San Juan."

Exiled.

Thinking of the similarity to Gold Hill and Ute Mountain made that really hurt.

"What else would fix it? I mean fix it so we could stay in Denver. If I worked out the ritual to help Were change?"

No response. There was background noise on the line. Someone crying. And I heard Martha's voice, speaking soothingly.

"Felix? Felix! What's happening?"

Oh, God. Olivia.

He came back on the line.

"It's started," he said, his voice bleak. "Olivia's just had the first of the attacks."

He was silent for such a long time I thought he'd put the phone down again. Then: "If you have a ritual that works, I'd like to believe it'll change the pack's attitude, but that's not the point really. Time's run out for Olivia. You've got a couple of days, no more."

Chapter 37

By the time Felix and I finished talking, everyone else had been through the bathroom.

They were all sitting there, watching me struggle to overcome my reaction to the news about Olivia.

We'd gotten a family room with two double beds, so close together there was barely room to get between them. We split up naturally, with Savannah and Claude in one, Tullah and me in the other. Claude was already asleep when I came out of the shower. Savannah was sitting on the edge of the bed, nervously watching me. She'd borrowed a pair of shorts and a T from Tullah to sleep in. Her heart rate was inching back up.

I guess I'd given her cause. I'd nearly attacked her, and by the end of my conversation with Felix there wasn't anyone in the room who doubted how close to the edge I was.

But Savannah's worry wasn't for her personal safety. As I moved around the room drying my hair, she shifted slightly so she was shielding Claude from me. I didn't think she was even aware of it.

I sat on the bed facing her. The gap was so narrow, our knees touched.

Tullah gave me a frown.

No one appreciated how much effort I was putting into *not* biting.

Maybe if I hadn't been *not* biting when Olivia offered it, she'd have more time now.

Focus on the here and now.

I studied Savannah, which made her drop her eyes.

How do I start building bridges?

"I'm sorry about earlier," she said suddenly, looking down at where her fingers worried the edge of the blanket. She spoke quietly to avoid disturbing her brother. "I'm not good at talking. Y'know. At expressing myself."

She'd caught me off guard. I was supposed to be the one apologizing.

"That's fine. I'm sorry too, for the way I behaved."

Savannah's eyes flicked across to Tullah. "You're having problems with Blood. I understand. I should have thanked you for saving us right away, and not...." she faltered.

"And not challenged me."

"Yeah. And you're right. We made choices. I mean, we can't go back. We're kin."

I gave a little hum of sort-of agreement and she was silent for a while.

"Pretty tats." I reached out to run a finger down the spiraling design on her arm.

I was trying to shift her onto some other topic and let her calm down. People who put that amount of effort into getting themselves inked are usually happy to talk about it. Her tattoos were a blend of Native American totems and Celtic spirals that I thought were lovely.

"They're beautiful, actually," I said. "Who came up with the idea?"

"They're my design," she said. There was pride in her voice, but instead of calming her, my attention was having the opposite effect.

She swallowed, her heartrate edging up.

"I...I just want to ask, Mistress—"

"Amber," I interrupted.

She nodded jerkily and went on. "I wanted to ask you to give Claude some time before you...."

She slipped her T off and moved across to sit beside me, putting one trembling hand on my leg.

"Please, feed from me instead. I'm...well, I haven't..."

"I wasn't planning to bite him tonight, Van," I said. "Or you."

"Oh."

It wasn't what Savannah wanted right then, but I slid an arm around her and hugged her slight body to me.

I felt her willing herself to relax.

I sighed. The right thing to do was to send her off into her own bed at once.

Despite everything, my Athanate was enjoying this too much. I wasn't about to bite her. And this girl had spent half the evening crouched down on Zane's floor, with a dead body and an unconscious Were for company. Was I worse than that?

Amber. Tullah's voice inside my head. *See yourself as she sees you.*

My eyes went blurry and I felt dizzy. Kaothos was messing with my head.

She sent me a glimpse of myself from Savannah's perspective.

Frowning. Strong. Overwhelming. Strange. Scary.

I blinked and eased up on the hug.

She saw me like that. How did I see her?

Savannah was a contradiction. On the surface there were the tattoos, the punky hair and the awkward speech. Nothing extreme, but not mainstream either. She was also Athanate kin and that was hardly 'normal'. But beneath that level was a woman, barely more than a girl really, who craved normal. I'd seen inside her house in Albuquerque. Apart from the hiding space, the place defined normalcy. For Albuquerque at any rate. She'd been the one who'd created that feeling.

And she was the same girl who'd beat up on herself for not being able to do more for Larry's other kin. Who'd risked her life without hesitation to rescue her brother.

The sort of person I hoped would be at home in House Farrell.

But also the person who, if I was reading the signals right, wasn't at all comfortable with the idea of me biting her. Or anything else I might do to her. It made me wonder about her arrangements with Larry.

And again, she'd put all those fears aside when she'd thought I might be wanting to bite Claude. *Bite me instead…*

Overactive hero complex. Who does that remind me of? Tara snarked.

Shut up, smartass.

I planted a kiss on the top of Savannah's head and willed my body to put out some of the pacific pheromones instead of the Athanate sex appeal that I'd been pumping out at the Calle.

"Go on, into bed," I said to her, and pulled her T back over her head. "Careful not to wake Claude."

I swiveled and slipped into the sheets as Tullah got in the other side.

"Thank you, Amber," Savannah whispered.

"What kind of work do you do, Van?" Tullah asked to lighten the atmosphere a touch.

"I'm a biologist. I was working towards getting a research position." She sighed. "I guess that's gone now."

"You'll find something new," I said. "What about Claude?"

"School." Her voice was getting fainter. A couple of questions later she slipped off.

Tullah took my arm and wedged it under her pillow.

"I'm not going to go sleepwalking," I complained. "Or sleep biting."

"Course you aren't," she replied. "Not now, anyway."

"Am I really that bad?" I murmured, thinking of the image that Savannah had had of me.

"Sometimes," Tullah said, yawning. "You're kinda wobbling. One minute, it's you, and the next it's the monster."

"Thanks for the vote of confidence. David's email come through okay?"

"Yup. Sycamore Ranch, not far from here. Something about the ownership flagged it, and he also found that Jaworski is from the Polish for sycamore."

"Hmm. Okay, we look tomorrow." I switched the lights out, but I wasn't finished.

"So," I said, dragging the sound out. "I have some questions for you."

Tullah was suddenly nervous. With my behavior over the last day, I guessed I couldn't blame her.

"You know when you turned up in the Hill Bitch and kidnapped me, Felix had just gotten a call. You wouldn't know anything about that, would you?"

Tullah cleared her throat. "I can tell you it was Alex and Jen. All I know is they had some plan that would divert him."

Interesting.

What the hell had they cooked up? Felix had said something about my kin doing 'tremendous' things for him. I should have questioned him about it.

Were my kin really working together? And what did it mean for them—a temporary truce? I'd have to ask them at the next opportunity.

"Okay. One more little puzzle," I said. "When I woke up after the kidnapping, we were in Colorado Springs, in a park."

Tullah nodded. She seemed to be finding the pattern of the blanket fascinating, tracing it with her fingers in the dark.

"In the *middle* of a park. A couple of minutes' walk from the car."

"Uh. Yeah."

"So how did I get there? Did you carry me?"

No way they carried me. I'm five-ten and one-forty plus.

"No." She ran her hand across the blanket one last time and then looked at me. "We did a zombie on you."

"A *what*?"

"It's sort of..." She paused. "Look, zombies don't exist like the stories. You can't take a body and just give it some instructions and then let it go running off to kill people and eat their brains or whatever."

"But..."

"Well, you can pilot somebody. It's not really very useful in most situations. You can't just jack in and control something as complex as a human body. Gross motor function only, and not much of that—"

"So, I'm getting a picture here...stumbling, slobbering, swaying..."

Tullah blushed. "No, we walked on either side. You probably just looked as if you were feeling sick. The kids in the park didn't even notice."

"So much better." I had to work to sound grumpy.

"We should have a quick lesson on using the energy," she changed the subject hurriedly, "and then you need some rest."

"Yeah. Tell me, first, are we being dumb? Why don't we break the lock on you and just rely on the lizard and your workings to achieve what we need?"

She snorted softly.

"Kaothos and I aren't that strong yet, whatever she says. And her signature in the energy is distinctive. We couldn't be sure we'd be strong enough for whatever we wanted to do, and from what we saw with the Denver community, we'd have every Adept in the land united against us."

"Okay."

"Your signature, on the other hand, is hidden," Tullah said thoughtfully. "You seem to have this ability to channel other workings, but without Hana it's almost as if…"

"As if I can't use the energy at all."

"No." She scratched her head. "I'm not really a shamanic Adept; I mean, I know the basic training, but I'm trained more in the standard stuff. If I didn't know you and someone asked me, I'd say you have a little latent ability and nothing more. But Chatima knew you had much more ability—enough that she gave you the necklace. Anyway…tonight's Adept exercises…"

We were both tired. Tullah kept going, but it wasn't long before I was sliding toward sleep and the nightmares began to stir.

Then Kaothos came out and claimed me again.

Chapter 38

SATURDAY

Sycamore Ranch lay about halfway down the side of the hill, in a small, steep-sided canyon formed around a lazy creek. The main compound was four pink-roofed buildings in a square around a shady courtyard. A couple of SUVs were parked neatly in front. To the right of the ranch house, there were wooden barns and outbuildings.

A hundred yards beyond the ranch, the small arroyo meandered down the bottom of the valley. There was flowing water in it now, but the ground told me that this place got dry.

Regardless of that, between me and the ranch there was an orchard, laid out on terraces stepping down the hill; I could see lemon and cherry, fig, orange and lime. I was peering through the leaves of a creosote bush, so any citrus smell or anything else that might have drifted up was masked by the acrid resin. There was a white-painted water tower about two hundred yards to my left on the ridge line. I guessed that served the orchard.

There were no corrals, no sign of herd animals and no obvious farm machinery. It was no working business; apart from the fruit trees, this was just a house.

A cool wind blew and the sun shone.

Peaceful. Still.

Except for the vultures. The early arrivals were fighting over a body in the courtyard.

We'd approached the ranch by a dirt road that dog-legged this hill. I'd had Tullah stop when I spotted the vultures circling lazily, and I'd climbed up to check before we drove around the hill.

Tullah slipped in beside me, keeping behind the bush. It was easy to forget sometimes that she was still learning.

Savannah and Claude were waiting in the Hill Bitch. That wasn't good, exposing them like that, but we'd run out of options.

What had happened?

Was Diana in the ranch?

I lifted the binoculars and began slow sweeps of the buildings, looking for anything out of place, any hint of someone waiting. I wanted to run down there. I wanted to scream. The thought of getting so close, beating all the odds of finding Diana, and then being too late was like ice in my heart.

But a little closed canyon, one road in and out, no one around for miles. It was shouting 'trap' at me.

That cold feeling spread to my spine and lifted hairs on my arms. I swung the glasses up to have a look at the water tower.

It was too perfectly placed. It had line of sight on the road as it curved around the hill, it overlooked the whole hilltop, the orchard, the house, the stream and the hill on the opposite side of the stream. A perfect place for a sniper.

In the shadows beneath the cylindrical body of the water tank, there was a second platform, almost invisible until you really looked. Just enough space for a couple of people to lie down and maintain a great 360 degree lookout.

It had been built for the purpose, and I was right; it would have been a great place to post a sniper. All of us would have been dead, but it was empty today.

Okay. Missed it on the first pass. Not at your best. Put it behind you.

I couldn't make any more mistakes like that.

So why might someone spring a trap without posting a guy with a rifle in the water tower?

What if they hadn't had time? They were still in the ranch?

I turned my attention back to the valley below.

The courtyard door to the main house was open, shifting with the breeze.

There was something wrong about the scene, something beyond the ugly contrast of peacefulness and death, unused sniper posts and open doors, but I couldn't put my finger on it.

"Anything you can do to tell me if there's anyone alive down there?"

Tullah shook her head. "What about your bracelet?"

"Nothing at the moment, but I always worry about how it works."

She smiled.

"I'm going down," I said finally. "I need you to watch from here. Keep an eye on the road as well." I handed her the binoculars and checked my cell. One bar of signal.

Damn.

Amateur hour. We needed tactical headsets, and full assault gear. And while I was at it, a squad of Ops 4-10 and one of those silent recon drones. I had a shotgun and a cellphone.

Suck it up.

I made sure Tullah knew which cell I was using.

"Call me if anything changes," I said.

"Be careful." She was worried, but she took the glasses without arguing and copied my slow sweep over the ranch and the outbuildings.

I hefted the shotgun and slunk over the ridge, staying low and moving quickly. The orchard beckoned; it would give me some good cover as I approached the house.

It was where I would have set a trap. Then again, I'd have had a sniper in the water tower.

Unless, maybe, I wanted to lure someone down into the ranch and capture them.

I slithered down into the cover of the trees and checked all around me.

There was nothing there, other than relief from the smell of creosote bushes.

I slipped through the trees and down the hill. My view of the ranch was obscured, and I had to trust Tullah to see what I couldn't, ahead of me.

Crouched at the lower edge of the orchard, I still had another twenty yards to the corner of the first building. And now the smell of the orchard and the creosote plants on the hillside couldn't mask the insidious smell of death.

It wouldn't have been there yet for a human, but I was relying on my wolf senses.

I tried to block out the death and focus on the rest.

The marque was House Romero; we'd found Oscar Jaworski's House. But it was just the scent. The marque's other component, the *feeling* of a presence, simply wasn't there.

Didn't mean there wasn't anyone else here.

Pressure was growing on me to act.

I sprinted across to the closest part of the building and trotted down the side, glancing in windows as I went past.

Stopped. About halfway down I could make out one body in a room. Two in the next. Still silent. And still no other scents or marques.

I went on. Down at the end, I tried a door. It was unlocked.

Booby-trapped? Someone waiting?

Got to keep moving.

Pressing myself against the wall, I pushed the door open.

Nothing. No explosions, no reactions, no movement at all apart from the vultures.

This was starting to stretch my nerves like violin strings. I'd have almost welcomed an attack.

Stupid thought.

I went in and began to work my way through, room by room, sprinting down corridors where I had no cover, whipping myself around corners and into rooms.

The buildings all connected, all the way around the courtyard. The bedrooms were luxurious, the living rooms wide and airy, storerooms neat. The kitchen could have catered for a small army. The dining room would have seated thirty.

The only sound came from my footsteps and my pounding heart.

I could barely breathe. Any second I knew I'd find Diana.

Room after room.

Five bedrooms had bodies in the beds. Some of them had been shot while sleeping. Others had leaped up when someone came in. There was no difference in the end result. Athanate and kin, male and female, dead and tangled in bedclothes.

Whoever had done this had struck last night, probably in the early hours of this morning, in almost complete silence.

This was Jaworski's secret retreat. Why no bodies outside, apart from the one in the courtyard? Had he felt so secure, he'd posted no guards? Or had they betrayed him?

Either way, he'd made a huge miscalculation and it had cost him everything.

He was there, the only one I recognized, in the huge living room—surrounded by bodies, dried blood splatter, the smell of death and violence. And flies.

There was no one alive in the ranch.

And no Diana.

There was no cellphone signal either.

I needed the exercise to clear the images out from behind my eyes and the smell from my nose. I ran up the hill back to Tullah, picking out the rocky parts where I got good traction.

"No one alive down there," I panted when I reached the top. "I want Claude on that platform underneath the water tower, watching the road. If he sees anything, he runs as fast as he can down to the ranch. You and Savannah come around in the car. I need both of you."

Back in the building, I paced through the main rooms again. Clouds of flies swirled up as I passed. It was worse, going back in.

And I found one I'd missed before. Unlike the others, the woman had realized what was happening. She'd tried to hide underneath a solid desk in a study. They'd found her, and shot her where she'd knelt, curled up in a ball.

I took pictures of every body with the cellphone. All of them were Romero Athanate or Romero kin. All killed with gunshots.

Some of them had been killed by being shot in the head as they lay wounded.

I went into a bathroom and closed the door.

The water was cold on my face, shockingly cold.

I stayed bent over the sink. I didn't want to look in the mirror.

In Ops 4-10, I'd had to deal with death on every mission. Ours. Theirs. Some I remembered; I made myself remember them. The others had begun to blur into a mass. I stopped seeing them. When I left the army and set up as a PI, I'd decided to make a rule: no killing unless completely unavoidable. It had worked for a while. It had brought me back to a place where lives mattered.

Now I was feeling the blindness coming back. I'd killed Nagas on Coykuti Mountain and Warders in Albuquerque. I could argue I had no options, but I'd felt nothing. Today, I'd just walked through a building full of dead bodies and all I could feel was relief that Diana wasn't one of them.

The rest hadn't meant anything to me until I found the woman in the study.

Was this normal? What did *normal* mean for me?

I splashed more water on my face, and after that, I took towels and scented gels, creating a mask to breathe through. I opened every window and door as I went back out. As soon as we left, the vultures and smaller scavengers would come in.

I cleaned everywhere I'd touched.

Then I went out to where Tullah and Savannah waited with the truck.

"They're all House Romero, and they're dead," I said to Savannah. "You don't want to go inside, but I need to know some names, or if you recognize faces."

I held up the cellphone. She didn't want to look at it.

"It might help us figure out who did this and why. Think you can handle it?"

Her face was pale and her mouth pressed into a thin line. She nodded jerkily.

I gave her the cellphone and she started to go through the pictures.

"I've seen him before," she said on the fifth picture. "I'm not sure of his name."

Then she went on to a couple more. Tears sprang up in her eyes.

I looked at the picture. The woman who had died in the study.

"Sienna," Savannah said, the tears sliding out the sides of her eyes. "Sienna kin-Romero. She was kind to me."

Romero's own kin.

She wiped her face angrily and went on. She didn't know any of the dead in the other side rooms.

The main cluster of bodies was in the central living room, a huge, glass-fronted space that projected out onto a stone patio.

She knew more of them.

Lying beside Oscar Jaworski was Charles Romero himself, the leader of House Romero, former Panethus Athanate House of New Mexico.

Now, the leadership of House Romero had been eradicated. The last man standing was Amaral and he didn't look to be keeping the name Romero.

When Savannah finished her task, she staggered away to lose her breakfast.

Tullah looked as pale as Savannah.

"I'm sorry," I said. I fastened the towel mask over her nose to cut down the nauseating smell. "I need you to see something."

"I know," she said. "I can feel it, too."

"Close your eyes. You don't need to see the rest."

She obeyed and I guided her back through the horrors of the massacre, into the main living room and then down a short side passage to another room.

Just outside the door to the room, a Romero Athanate lay face down. He had a 9mm Sig automatic, still neatly holstered on his waistband. He'd been shot twice in the back.

I maneuvered Tullah past the body and into the room.

It was the center of that feeling of wrongness I'd felt, even up on the top of the hill. A feeling like the Aztec temple in the barn out at Bow Creek ranch. An evil feeling.

The room itself was a large guest bedroom overlooking the patio. It had views down to the creek. There were closets and a bathroom on one side. There were no bodies here. A vase of sweet-scented jasmine and lilies stood on the side of a vanity table, fighting the smell from the rest of the house. There were chairs around a coffee table and unfinished soft drinks for a small group. The bed was made. The only other sign of occupancy was a small rolling suitcase beside the bed.

Standing in the room itself was like listening to nails dragging down a blackboard.

This was the one place in the house where a hint of different marques lingered.

Tullah stood inside and opened her eyes.

"There was a working in here. A binding." She closed her eyes again. "Like the lock they put on me, but much more focused. It's strange."

"There were Warders here," I said.

She shook her head. "This working was Adepts. Strong ones. Did you find any..."

"There aren't any dead Adepts or Warders in the house."

She walked to the window. It had been open when I first came to the room.

"Read the scene," I said.

"The Warders came in here." She indicated the window. "They were let in by the Adepts, who were inside, restraining someone with a working. Someone powerful."

She walked back to the door.

"The Warders started killing here," she pointed. "Silenced gun, maybe. The dead man was guarding the door. I can't say whether he was keeping people in or out. Probably out. They weren't really expecting anything— only one guard armed with a handgun."

She'd done the job I'd brought her in for; to read the working in the room. But she wasn't finished. Her face pale and determined, she walked back to the living room and looked at the group of bodies that included Jaworski and Romero.

There were six bodies.

"Each of them..." she stopped and turned away to look at a wall. After a couple of deep breaths, she managed to go on. "Each of them has multiple wounds."

"And the shot pattern?" I pressed her.

"Minimum two to the body, one to the head." Her eyes flicked at me over her towel mask. "Like you were taught in special forces."

The Warders had been well trained, or they'd been accompanied by Nagas who didn't have a marque and didn't leave a smell I could detect in this slaughterhouse.

There was more, but she'd had enough; I let her escape.

After the Romero Athanate had been killed in the living room and side passages, there were no more armed people except the intruders. The rest of the building was a butchery. They'd used silencers and most of the dead had died without fighting. The direction of the bodies and shots all pointed to the threat coming from inside the building.

Tullah's analysis had been right, as far as she went.

A small group of Adepts had been in the bedroom suite. House Romero had left them with a guard on the door. They'd let in someone through the window; there had been no struggle in the bedroom. The intruders had killed the guard, then they'd killed everyone in the living room and worked their way through the remainder of the buildings.

They were trained professionals. They worked efficiently, they used silenced guns and their shot grouping was excellent, even in the dark.

They included someone who knew the layout of the house. Someone who knew who was in the house. Someone who was trusted. Charles Romero had betrayed Skylur and Panethus, and he'd been betrayed in turn.

There was one other thing, and I went back to the bedroom to double-check.

Underneath everything else, it still held a scent of her marque.

The rolling suitcase: the last time I'd seen it, Diana had been pulling it behind her as she went to catch a plane at Denver airport.

Chapter 39

I joined Savannah and Tullah outside.

The smell in the courtyard was bad, but nothing compared to inside.

The trees that provided the shade were sycamore. They were mature trees that looked as if they'd been well tended.

I hadn't liked Jaworski, but somehow I hoped the thought of him visiting the ranch and checking on his namesake trees would be the memory that I took away with me.

We walked away from the house and stood next to the truck.

"Diana was in that room with the Adepts," I said to Tullah.

"She's part of this?" Tullah frowned.

I shook my head, my mind working to put this all together. "Weaver got the Denver community to put a lock on your abilities. What does it do, exactly?"

"It prevents me from manipulating the energy, except for trivial amounts."

"If you did the same thing to a Were, what would it do?"

"They wouldn't be able to change."

"And an Athanate?"

Tullah was still frowning. "Well, it would stop them from manifesting fangs, I guess. I don't know for sure."

"What about a much, much stronger lock? The sort of thing you sensed inside."

"Everything would be blocked eventually. All telergic abilities, like eukori and compulsion. But at that level, you start turning off things that sustain the Athanate. You'd kill them."

"Okay." I chewed on that and an idea came to me. "What about your zombie working? That allows you to move someone. Would it allow you to reach in and turn some abilities back on?"

"That's complex. Really, really complex." She scrubbed at her face with her hands. "I'm not sure, Boss." It took her a second or two, but she caught on quicker than I thought she would. She gasped. "You're thinking that's what they did to Diana?"

I nodded. Diana was a very old, very powerful Athanate, with abilities I probably couldn't even dream of. The main sticking point as far as anyone capturing her — and keeping her — was how? This could be the answer.

The idea of adepts manipulating Diana like a doll gave me chills. If they could do that...

Tullah was still turning it over in her mind.

"We have to get somewhere where we can call Ma on a secure line," she said.

"Okay."

But her guesses were enough for me. I didn't have a choice about my next step anymore: I had to speak to Naryn about what I'd found.

I turned back to the ranch. Was there anything more I could do here?

The Hidden Path, the historic guiding principles of all Athanate behavior, said that the results of Athanate battles should not be left for humans to find. But we couldn't spare the time to bury bodies, and setting fire to the ranch would probably bring emergency services here faster than if we left it alone. Normally, Athanate Houses had a disposal crew who could be called out, but obviously, there was no way I was calling any Athanate in New Mexico and telling them where I was. Opening the windows and leaving vultures and insects should do a disguising job. That was the best I could do in the circumstances.

The police would still know there'd been a gunfight and a lot of people killed.

The point was troubling me: why had the scene been left the way it was?

"Amber!"

Claude's voice drifted down the hillside.

He was running; running too fast. He slipped and tumbled down the steep slope from the water tower, sprang back up and kept going. He was waving back over the hill, where the road came in. Someone was coming.

Shit!

The shock cleared my mind, letting me see the dullness that had crept in. I'd been creeping around, worried about Diana, worried about my becoming Basilikos. All the time, the biggest, most obvious threat had been right in front of me. The one I'd thought of first and dismissed.

A freaking trap. Not a sniper on the tower; not an ambush in the orchard. Something to keep us here awhile. A house full of dead bodies. And a single way in and out.

I looked around.

The building was designed to be defended, but not by four people. Make that two people, really.

That was the second trap, to retreat into the ranch house.

Not going to happen.

I needed to take control right now.

"Get in the car," I said.

Who was it coming down the road? Nagas? These Warders with special forces training? Whatever remained of House Romero that had gone over to Basilikos with Amaral?

Savannah tried to run towards Claude, who was doing great getting here on his own. Tullah bundled her into the car.

"Are we going to have to fight our way out?" Tullah called through the window.

That's what my wolf wanted to do. I could her snarling in eagerness, but the abrupt clarity in my feel for our position helped restrain her.

I shook my head. "Hold the shotgun and have your pistol handy."

Claude stumbled the last few steps and leaped aboard.

"Nice work," I said to him and started the engine.

Two SUVs came around the hill.

One immediately stopped across the road where it was narrow, blocking it, and the other bore down on us.

"Shit!" Tullah swore. "We can't get out."

The wolf snarled again. *Just watch me.*

Had I said that out loud?

I fought her back down. I needed to focus.

"Buckle up tight, Tullah," I said. "Van, you and Claude, down into the footwell. Stay there."

"What..." Tullah began.

Too late.

The wolf wasn't done. I felt her bleed into me. I was going to show them.

Eyes sharper. Teeth bared.

I dropped the clutch and we shot forward, spraying dirt from the drive.

The second SUV skidded to a stop and turned side on, eighty yards away, confident that was all they needed to do. That told me they weren't Nagas.

Armed guys in tactical vests spilled out. One of them had a bullhorn. As if all he had to do to stop me was ask nicely. *Idiot.*

I fired the Mk23 one-handed through the open window, just to see what they would do. They ducked. Yup. Not Nagas.

I laughed and shoved the Mk23 back in the holster.

Forty yards and closing fast. Pedal down. Engine screaming. Tires roaring. Aimed right at the nearer SUV. Guys backpedaled away from it, falling over themselves to get clear.

I pounded on the steering wheel. Faster. Faster. "Yeah! Run, you chicken-shit bastards," I screamed at them.

"Boss?" Tullah yelled. "Boss, what…"

"There's a reason she's called the Hill Bitch." I spun the wheel and pointed her nose uphill.

As Claude had found on his way down, a lot of the hillside was slippery with loose dirt, but underneath was good, solid rock. The engine snarled as the tires bit in.

We rocketed up the first part to the orchard. It had been terraced, but there was a path that rose through it. Taking that put the orchard between us and the SUVs.

The Hill Bitch began to buck like a rodeo steer as I drove over the uneven surface, but she didn't miss a beat.

At the top of the orchard, the path stopped and we hit a section where the underlying rock was laid bare.

"What's happening below?" I shouted, over the roar of the engine.

"Some of them are firing," Tullah said, her voice choppy from riding the bumps. "Not all. Looks like an argument. Neither SUV moving yet."

"Don't know whether to kill or capture," I said. *Amateurs.* "Going to end up with neither."

They would never hit us now.

The nose veered off to the left as the tires lost purchase on loose stones. The whole car swayed and tilted, the slope on my side looking like a sheer drop.

There were screams from the back seat. Tullah gasped and grabbed the chicken handle.

I laughed again.

Fun!

The tires regained their grip and I pulled the nose back up.

A shot ricocheted off the side of the hood, leaving an ugly scar six inches long.

Seemed like the kill faction had won the argument.

Let them try.

We needed to be over that hill quickly.

I dropped a gear and let the engine race. Rows of creosote bushes went down under the nose. Tires roared and clouds of dirt billowed out around us.

Another shot hit us somewhere on the roof, punching through.

Savannah screamed.

I could feel the movement behind me.

"Keep your heads *down!*" I shouted.

Come on, come on, come on!

Yes!

One more burst of acceleration and the car heaved up. The ground in front of us disappeared completely. Almost vertical. Nothing but sky beyond the windshield.

Freaking A!

"Yeaaaah!" I punched the roof with a fist.

The Hill Bitch bounded over the lip of the hill and the nose came crashing down.

Nothing but hillside beyond the windshield now.

We slithered down towards the road, more than a hundred yards below us. The traction was even worse on this side. The backside fishtailed and the bushes thumped and screeched as we tore around them, through them, over them.

Tullah's knuckles were white from her grip on the chicken handle, but she still had hold of the shotgun.

I whooped and hollered, wrestling the wheel.

"Erosion ditches!" Tullah yelled.

Rain had cut deep channels on either side of the road below us. Hit those and we'd be stuck.

The Romero SUVs would be back in a couple of minutes. We couldn't afford even a small delay.

"Got it. Got it."

The Hill Bitch slithered sideways, jinked, lurched. The tires bit and spun and bit again.

Then we were racing straight, on rocks, parallel to the road, ten yards above it.

Now Tullah's side looked like we were about to roll over.

Instead of looking down, she twisted around and checked behind us.

Two hundred yards ahead the drainage leveled out. I laughed manically, pounding the wheel again.

No problem. We'd join the road there.

We hit a large rock and the front reared.

"One SUV just came around the corner," Tullah grunted as the Jeep plunged, banging against the limits of the suspension.

We skidded and swerved. I was losing height too quickly. The erosion ditch seemed to be calling us down the hill. Closer and closer. Quicker and quicker.

It was dustier too. The tires lost more grip. The view behind us disappeared.

We sideswiped one last bush, and the nose of the Hill Bitch twitched upward as we hit some firmer ground.

Closer. Two yards. One.

And the front tires hit the level section.

"*Yeaaaah!*" I whooped.

The Hill Bitch shook herself like a dog and we were hurtling down the dirt road, raising a huge dust cloud behind us.

The adrenaline high buzzed through me.

Calm it down! I needed to stay focused.

Sweet truck that she was, the Hill Bitch wasn't going to outrun a couple of SUVs on the open road. And they'd have friends out there somewhere.

I couldn't see a thing behind us. They were somewhere in that cloud.

About three hundred yards ahead, there was a junction. Left took us back down to Highway 14.

It all came together in my mind.

I turned right at the junction and hauled the emergency brake on, skidding us around in a circle. I opened my harness and lifted the shotgun out of Tullah's hands at the same time.

"Get in the driver's seat and be ready," I yelled as I leaped out.

I ran screaming into the dust cloud, shotgun at my shoulder.

The pursuing SUV emerged suddenly.

The guy saw me. His best option was to run me down. But he wasn't a Naga. He saw the shotgun and the flash as I fired and his nerve broke. He instinctively swerved away—and his instincts got him killed. I pumped two more through the windshield and side windows before the SUV hit the bank opposite the junction at full speed.

I ignored them. There was a remote chance that there were survivors in the car, but it was just that—remote.

I was panting. My mouth pulled back in a snarl. My fingers halfway to wolf claws. I nearly fumbled the reload. The dust cloud was drifting away. Not good. Not good. I needed cover, surprise. They had to see me late. The last thing they'd see.

Tullah raced the Hill Bitch past the junction. Was she abandoning me? Athanate and wolf rose and howled in fury.

No. She stopped at the roadside, in the dusty run-off.

Then she gunned the engine and dropped the clutch.

The wheels spun and kicked up more dust over the junction. Enough to blind the driver of the second SUV, foot on the gas, engine racing as he struggled to catch up.

They shot out of the dust, saw the crashed SUV, me and the shotgun, all at the same time.

The driver hit the brakes hard. Anti-skid locked in, sounding like a machine gun going off, but it was too little, too late. I had time to fire one shot through the side window into the cab and then the second SUV hammered into the back of the first.

It struck at an angle, flipping itself over onto its back.

I didn't wait and I didn't waste any more shells. They weren't chasing us anymore, and that was good enough for me. I was back in the Hill Bitch and away before the second SUV had stopped rocking.

Heart thudding, lungs struggling. Everything seemed so clear and yet far away at the same time.

My hands were automatically fumbling with the seat belt. Buckle up. Be safe.

I started laughing. *Be safe.*

Tullah's worried look was like having cold water thrown over me.

Shit, shit, shit. Get it back together.

I closed my eyes and waited till the heartrate fell to a more normal range.

Haul it back. Haul it back. Forget buckling the seatbelt.

Now to act normally.

I turned in the seat and leaned over the back, forced myself to speak calmly. "You can come out. Are you okay?"

Savannah and Claude crawled out of the footwells, trembling and pale as ghosts.

Savannah had busted her lip on the seat when she'd stuck her head up.

She put her arms around Claude and they huddled on the back seat, not looking at me.

Any bridges I'd built last night hadn't survived.

Tullah drove on a little, then took a couple of turns and pulled off the road to park by a stand of trees that gave us good cover.

"Boss," she said, her voice strained, "we need to talk."

We got out.

The sun shone, but there was a chill wind out of the north. We walked a few paces, out of earshot.

"What the hell was that?" she said in a low voice.

I blinked.

I'd saved us, hadn't I?

Kaothos seeped into my mind.

Look, Amber Farrell, she said.

She unraveled the view from Tullah and Savannah. I didn't recognize the woman laughing and screaming and throwing the Hill Bitch around. The woman running at an SUV armed with a shotgun and a bucket of crazy.

She scared *me*. God knows what the others had felt.

I was completely losing it. The worst part was it hadn't *seemed* that crazy while it was happening. How long before I didn't come back from an episode like this?

"It's crusis mania, isn't it?" Tullah said. "Bian warned me it might get this bad. One minute you're worried and second guessing yourself, the next you think you're invincible."

I took some slow, deep breaths.

She was right.

I guessed, I *hoped*, I had time still. Just. I could find Diana. I could. As long as it was in the next day or so. If not, Kaothos would have to knock me out and keep me that way.

We returned to the Hill Bitch.

"I'm gonna get you guys out of here," I said to Savannah and Claude. Their relief was obvious.

I called Pia on the encrypting cellphone. She understood what we needed immediately.

"We're all ready," she said. "I'm sending coordinates back in a text. Meet us there."

"Okay." My House seemed to be on top of this. Maybe Victor was coming down in a helicopter. That'd be great. Savannah and her brother could be safe in Denver in a few hours.

"Do we have a direct number for Skylur?" I asked. I couldn't put off reporting what had happened now. But anything to not have to speak to Naryn.

"No. Amber, don't call anyone until we get there. I'm getting us underway now. I'll give an ETA by text."

The connection went dead.

She'd cut it off without giving me time for any news. Nothing about Jen.

A cold feeling settled in my stomach and the last of the adrenaline high leaked away like air from a punctured balloon.

Chapter 40

The coordinates Pia had sent led us to a private airfield on somebody's ranch. Another old friend of Victor Gayle's, I guessed. The place was empty; just a half mile of packed dirt strip, a tired windsock and a barn.

Even in my post-mania brain fog, I knew the ETA they'd given us was too short—just ninety minutes after we'd spoken. The distance to Denver was around 300 miles. Even the best army helicopters couldn't fly that quickly. So, either a mistake—which was unlikely—or it wasn't Victor flying them down in a helicopter. This wasn't an airfield with facilities; I hoped whoever was flying knew what they were doing.

I alternated between worrying about that, about Jen, and about my latest manic episode. And despairing that I hadn't been a few hours earlier at Sycamore Ranch.

I'd gotten out of the Hill Bitch and I was fretching. That's what Mom had always called it when Kath did it. Fretching was fretting and twitching rolled into one. I'd never done it as a child or teen, but I was sure fretching now.

Where had they taken Diana?

Could I have rescued her, if we hadn't stopped to get some sleep?

And if the mania got so bad that Kaothos knocked me out now, or Naryn ordered me back to Denver, who was there to help Diana?

I had 'proof' that Diana was a captive—Tullah's analysis of the working at the ranch. Would House Altau believe an Adept about that? If they did, would they take over the mission? Would that be better for Diana's chances than me and my team, or worse?

And in the same way Athanate could help a human heal, would an Athanate be able to help Olivia survive? Would Bian do it for me? Could Pia or Yelena?

The cellphone beeped at me—a caller I didn't recognize.

This couldn't be good. Other than my House, only Dominé had this number.

It turned out she'd given it to Zane. This *really* couldn't be good.

"You have a problem," he said without preamble.

No kidding.

"Yeah, like Amaral's people wiping out House Romero and leaving them for the vultures?" I said.

"Yes."

"Then trying to come back and catch us at Jaworski's ranch." *Oh, my God. Zane sent us there. He can see where this cell is. What if he…*

No. No. I couldn't have misread his hatred of all House Romero, Amaral included. I fought my paranoia to focus on what he was saying.

"I guess that didn't turn out the way they expected," he said. "Look, I'm sorry we didn't pick up on that. We're only tapping into their comms here in Albuquerque. We're not getting the whole—"

"My colleague, Diana, was there before the attack," I cut him off. Too bad if he was offended, but I was still riding a shitstorm of conflicting emotions from my wolf and Athanate. "You have any news on her?"

"That's why I'm calling," he said.

He *was* offended. I could almost feel him try to squeeze his dominance down the connection.

Suck it up, Zane. I'm not your bitch.

"Turns out Amaral pulled out of Albuquerque completely last night," he went on. "Seems like he diverted to kill Romero and collect your friend."

So Amaral did have Diana. What the hell did he want with her?

"So where's he gone? Santa Fe?"

"No. He wouldn't dare."

Ah, yes. With the association between the Albuquerque and Santa Fe Were, Amaral wouldn't risk going anywhere near there.

"Well, where else would he go? Another city? You knew Jaworski had a secret hideout—what about Amaral?"

"I'm giving you what I've got, Farrell." Now he was really starting to get annoyed with me. "All I know is he headed north. I don't know what his alternatives are up there. It's not my territory."

"It's this guy Half-head's territory?"

His grunt confirmed it.

Great. A whole new Were to deal with, and with me firing on half my cylinders.

"That's the other thing," he said. "You need to go in to meet the alpha in Santa Fe."

I didn't like the sound of that. "Half-head, you mean? If Amaral's not there, why would I want to go into Santa Fe territory?"

"You're already in their territory."

Damn. I hadn't even thought about that when Pia was picking out landing places. Were territory. Athanate territory. It was impossible to keep it all straight.

"So, my 'needing' to go—is that an invitation?"

"For now," Zane said.

I didn't have time to mess around with alpha games. "To do what?" I asked, exasperated. "He wants to grab a coffee and exchange life stories? Or he has information for me?"

Zane snorted. "I *strongly* recommend accepting, while it's still an invitation. Anyway, the Santa Fe Were will know where Amaral is heading."

I had no other leads, but I was getting wary of sticking my head on the block.

"An invitation means safe passage?"

"Take no violence into Santa Fe and you should be safe," Zane said. "At least, until you open your mouth." *Funny guy.* "There's an art gallery in the Railyard Park; be there alone at 4 p.m. No cellphone, no electronics. Someone will contact you with instructions. And for your information, the name's Cameron, not Half-head."

"Should I wear a pink carnation?" my throat demon said, but the line had gone dead.

Tullah looked at me questioningly.

"We have a lead on Diana. Maybe. The problem is, to get it, I gotta go see the Santa Fe alpha."

"Both of us?" Tullah said, and I shook my head.

"You need me," she said. "And Kaothos. You're barely holding it together."

"I'm fine," I said, though we both knew I wasn't. "Anyway, he was very clear. Can't risk ignoring his instructions."

Tullah pressed her lips together. She wasn't happy, but there was nothing either of us could do.

I ran a hand across my face. "We also have a problem with the Hill Bitch. We have to assume Amaral now knows what she looks like. From what Zane was saying, we'll be safe enough in Santa Fe, but afterwards we'll need to head wherever Diana has been taken."

"We could rent a car."

"No. We'd need a license and credit card for that. Someone could be watching. Unless you have a good set of fakes."

Tullah frowned in thought. "Victor has contacts down here who may be able to help. I'll call."

She took her cellphone out and started scrolling through her lists.

My wolf ears caught the sound of an incoming aircraft and I tensed. It was just a dot in the sky, and it *should* be our side. But using the cell *could* have given our position away to Amaral.

Trust no one, hissed Ben-Haim in my head.

My cell rang again. Pia. Short and tense. "We're on the approach. Is it all clear?"

"Yup," I said. "Keep a lookout as you come in, though; you have a wider view from up there."

I turned to face north. I could see it more clearly now: a long-nosed turbo-prop. The sort of plane that could make the trip from Denver in an hour.

As it swooped closer, I recognized the type—a Pilatus. I'd only ever seen them at a distance; it was the kind of plane you saw at small airports being chartered by millionaires. No way I could afford this, so it had to be something that Jen had set up.

It was going to look like a Ferrari in a farmyard out here.

Whoever was flying it knew his business. There was a smoothness about the approach that told me the pilot was probably ex-forces, with thousands of flying hours behind him.

A rock-steady descent ended with the main wheels touching right at the start of the landing strip. This might be the first time this plane had ever landed on dirt instead of tarmac, but the pilot made everything look routine. He used about three quarters of the strip and then backtracked to park in the open area next to the barn.

The pilot went through shutdown procedures, and finally the door cracked open.

I was already trotting toward it.

Jen was the first one out.

My heart lurched.

She'd had her hair done, and she was wearing a suit like she was going to an important meeting. She'd once said to me it was like putting on armor before a battle—a way to hide your vulnerabilities. She'd gone for the whole thing—the clothes, makeup, sunglasses. A scarf. I missed a step and almost stumbled.

A damned scarf to hide the marks on her neck.

Naryn. The bastard. I was going to kill him.

I sprinted up to her and grabbed her in a hug. "I'm sorry," I whispered. This was all my fault. If I hadn't left her to come down here, I'd have found a way to prevent this.

She kissed me and immediately pulled back.

"Honey, what's wrong?"

She's trying to be cool about it for my sake.

"Naryn. I'll kill him," I said through clenched teeth.

"What? Oh, God, I'm an idiot. I'm sorry. I'm so sorry. This scarf isn't hiding anything." She yanked it off. "Look, no bites."

"I thought…the clothes…the scarf."

She shook her head and buried her face against my neck.

"I'm sorry. I'm an idiot," she said again, the words muffled. "I just wanted to look good for you."

Pia and Nick had come down the steps, and I could feel that Pia was unhappy. Worse than that: she was tense as a bowstring.

"Take a minute," she said, attempting a smile. "Then we need to talk urgently." She looked over at Tullah and the others. "I'll go greet our refugees."

She walked off. Nick gave my shoulder an awkward pat and followed her.

"What the hell?" I frowned and then shook it off. "First things first. What happened to you?"

"Bian worked it all out with Vera," Jen said.

"Huh?" I said. The relief was obviously making me good with words.

"Naryn asked for kin from House Farrell." Jen raised her head. "Vera said she should be the one. She was due for an Athanate health checkup anyway, and as far as she was concerned, if Naryn wanted Blood in exchange, she thought it was a good deal."

I made a mental note to thank Vera.

Then the truth dawned on me.

"So, it was Bian—"

"Bian nothing, honey." Jen kissed me lightly. "Yes, I got to see the leopard's den, with the bed the size of a football field and the infamous black silk sheets."

Despite everything, I couldn't help a faint grin at that picture.

Jen continued: "Bian gave me a hug and told me to take a nap for a couple of hours while she was working on finding out how much damage Marlon did to their security files."

"If it wasn't you telling me, I wouldn't believe it."

"I know," she said. "That's why I had to come down here."

"What about Blood for Bian?"

Jen laughed.

"She has contacts with the fake vampire groups in Denver. They're so into it, they've persuaded themselves they need blood. They always have supplies—bags of blood."

It would have been nice if Bian had told me that before I left.

"That works?"

"Only if it's fresh—a couple of days," she said. "She did tell me the sensation—you know, the cold blood going through the channels—she said that was awful, but she'd be okay for another week. Normally, I guess Altau would have their own backup supplies, but this emergency has caught everyone by surprise."

I was almost sagging with relief. "And Vera?" I asked.

"Yeah, she's fine," Jen said. "Naryn's a jerk, not a monster. He wasn't out to get us."

I'd reserve judgment on that.

Maybe I'd completely overreacted, and maybe being in Denver myself would have made it worse.

"Pia said he was emphasizing the Athanate obligations of Farrell to Altau," Jen said. "Apparently, that's normal."

Yeah.

I squashed that.

"You're all amazing," I said. One load put aside. "Any news of Olivia?"

"No change," Jen sighed. "Okay at the moment."

Yelena stepped down from the plane, and I knew she was the last person out.

Ahh. So my House has a hotshot Carpathian pilot.

My Athanate purred with pleasure.

Yelena joined Jen and me in the hug. We did the Athanate neck kiss and I felt a second thrill: Yelena's marque was almost perfectly House Farrell.

"Mistress," she murmured. Her eukori seemed to show contentment, but tinged with a nervousness toward me. At least she wasn't upset like Pia.

What had happened to upset Pia so much? Was Yelena the source of the problem?

"Dancing Girl," I teased her.

Yelena laughed and turned to join the other group.

Jen kissed my neck, obviously feeling left out of the Athanate greeting rituals.

Suddenly, I felt warm. And my jaw pulsed, catching me off guard.

"Did you charter the plane?" I asked, to cover it.

"Hell, no. It used to belong to Matlal." Jen grinned and threaded an arm through mine before leading me on a circuit of the pretty aircraft. "Yelena flew it for House Matlal and knew it was kept at Centennial Airport. My lawyers have claimed it in recompense for breach of contract by Matlal on part of Jack Tucker's business that we bought."

Neat.

I let out a whoop of laughter and kissed her just below her ear.

She swung around to face me, putting her hands on my shoulders.

"How are you, really?" Jen said, frowning. "You still look tired. Is Kaothos helping you sleep?"

I huffed. "It's not sleep so much as knocking me unconscious. So, you planned that as well?"

"As well as what, honey?" Her blue eyes looked so innocently up at me.

"Everything else. Getting me abducted. Packing suitcases with special underwear for me."

She smiled and squeezed my arm, eyes still worried.

"We're all doing what we can," she said. "That's what the House is for. And just look at you." She ran her hands over my leather-clad hips. "Nice pants. *Very* nice."

I faked a scowl. "A loan when my jeans got dirty. Don't change the subject. Did your planning happen to include a mysterious phone call to Felix, which just happened to coincide with Tullah showing up? Don't give me the innocent look. What on earth did you say to him that distracted him so easily?"

She cleared her throat.

"Alex and I decided that Bitter Hooks should be established as the heart of a new reserve for wildlife. We want Felix to set up a committee to oversee that and plan for expansion."

Alex and Jen? Agreeing on something?

Jen waved a hand. "It'll be something to get the green groups off my back. I'm sorry, I should have discussed it with you as well. Of course, the pack will be able to use it, and it might just make some of them pause and think more positively about a second pack sharing the area."

"But the cost…" I said. And why should she need to discuss it with me? Had Felix been hinting about this during our last conversation? Why not come out and say something?

"I told you I didn't want to build a resort out there anyway," Jen went on. "I always wanted to keep it wild, and this just makes that official. We'll still be able to visit whenever we want."

"Mmm. Thank you, anyway. Did I mention you're amazing? And beautiful?"

She shrugged, caught between dismissing it and being pleased.

She didn't want to talk about it.

Intriguing.

There was no time to follow up.

Pia returned and herded everyone into the back of the plane.

"Sorry, Boss," she said. "Direct orders from Skylur."

Oh, shit. This isn't good.

Chapter 41

At the back of the passenger area was a space intended for storage of luggage. It had been converted into a state-of-the-art mobile communications center with three large screens.

Savannah and Claude got ushered into the pilot and navigator seats at the front of the plane. The rest of us sat with our chairs swiveled to face the comms.

Pia glanced at her watch.

"We have less than ten minutes before Skylur's conference call," she said without preamble as she switched on the screens. "It would be easiest if I just start by showing you this. It was broadcast to all Panethus Houses on the dark net early this morning. The man speaking is Jiaro Amaral, former Diakon of Albuquerque for House Romero."

She pressed a couple of buttons and the left-hand screen showed a somber-faced man with a high, wide forehead and dark hair, partway through a speech.

"…and it is therefore my sad duty to inform you that, at some time in the early hours of this morning, Charles Romero, House Romero, and Oscar Jaworski, Diakon of Santa Fe, House Romero, along with a number of their House, including kin, were killed by assassins."

My mouth dropped open. He was announcing what he'd done? Why?

I found out with the bastard's next words.

"This attack was carried out, or led, by a person you will be familiar with from the last Athanate Assembly. Her name is Amber Farrell, House Farrell, and she is a fully associated sub-House of Altau, bound by oaths as witnessed at the Assembly."

Tullah gasped.

Amaral was publicly accusing me of the slaughter at Sycamore Ranch. Of taking out most of House Romero. The enormity of the lie stunned me; blood pounded in my temples.

Amaral spoke his lies ponderously, as if they'd gain believability from being delivered slowly. "There can be no dispute that this is just one thread in the Altau plot that was initiated by their incredible attempt to subvert the whole Panethus creed and claim the entire continent of North America…"

Pia shut it off.

"He goes on at length," she said. "He claims Diana's support in declaring himself House Amaral, at the same time asserting his domain's independence from any Altau claims. He's called for Skylur to refute the charges against him by handing you over for trial."

"It's lies from beginning to end," I said, shaking with anger. "What's he trying to achieve?"

"Leadership," Pia replied simply.

"But the leadership of Panethus was settled at the Assembly, wasn't it?"

"No. The Assembly's not concerned with internal politics of the two creeds. That's why it was immaterial that Basilikos changed leadership in the middle of it, from Matlal to Correia." She sighed and ran fingers through her hair. "The leadership of Panethus is formally decided by a meeting called a Convocation. Amaral isn't in a position to call one yet, so he's too smart to do that. What he's trying to do instead is set up a power base, founded on two weaknesses."

"What are they?"

"A lot of Panethus are conservative by nature. They're very wary about Emergence, and it wouldn't take much to get them to vote against it. His first step, though, is the dozen Houses in the USA which are not directly associated with Altau."

At the Assembly, Skylur had sprung a few surprises. Diana had negotiated with the entire group of Canadian Houses, previously part of the Midnight Empire, to join Panethus as sub-Houses of Altau. Then Skylur had revealed that Altau had been setting up secret sub-Houses throughout the US. The endpoint of that was Skylur declaring all of North America as his domain. Any House which didn't want to swear an oath to him and become a sub-House of Altau had to leave.

At the time, I hadn't really thought about it. I had no real knowledge of these other Houses, and if I had, I'd have probably thought it was no big deal. They were already sworn to Altau as leader of Panethus. Was it such a big thing to become a sub-House of Altau?

Apparently, it was.

"The negotiation process to get those Houses to accept Altau is ongoing," Pia said. "It's reached a highly sensitive stage. Romero was always seen as an unofficial leader of the unincorporated Houses. That's why Diana went to Romero directly, despite the danger. Now that Romero's dead, Amaral is portraying this as the threat from Altau—bow down or get killed."

Naryn's voice joined in. "And if he succeeds in gathering some of those dozen behind him, then he is well placed to lead a vote against Skylur at a Convocation." His face had come up on the right-hand screen, with Bian sitting next to him. "Emergence is a divisive issue, all through the Panethus ranks. We can't afford this."

He frowned at the screen. "I can see you're in an aircraft. I suppose it's too much to hope for, that you can easily prove you weren't in New Mexico?"

Skylur had appeared on the middle screen as Naryn spoke.

I took a deep breath.

"No. I've disobeyed you, and I'm down near Santa Fe. Worse, I was at Jaworski's ranch, but I was only there after Romero and Jaworski had been killed."

"Diana?" Skylur's face was devoid of emotion, but that one word carried a weight of dread.

"It appears she was there at the time of the attack, but I saw no evidence she was hurt," I said. "I've received further intel that indicates she's with Amaral, and that they're heading north to an as-yet unknown location."

"She's part of this?" Pia looked shocked.

I shook my head. "Tullah and I believe Amaral is holding her by force."

Skylur stopped me. "From the beginning," he said.

I took it from the point where I'd left Haven. Just talking it through helped me calm down a little. While I talked, I watched their faces. Naryn would take a long time to forgive me. Skylur was unreadable.

When I finished, there was a long silence.

Finally Skylur spoke. He sounded cool and contained, but I wondered what he was really feeling. From what I'd seen, he and Diana were extremely close. "This crisis doesn't exist in isolation. We have four major points of opportunity and vulnerability." He counted them off on his fingers. "One: Los Angeles. Correia has claimed this city for Basilikos. If she wins it, she will strengthen her grip on Basilikos and destroy Altau's credibility in Panethus. If she loses, she's vulnerable to Basilikos infighting."

I'd known whatever Skylur was doing in LA was important, but I hadn't realized how big it really was.

"Two: Amaral splits Panethus into pro- and anti-Emergence groups. Neither would be strong enough to resist Basilikos alone, and worse, with Basilikos rebranding themselves as the party of the Hidden Path, we would almost certainly lose the anti-Emergence group to them."

Did Amaral see that?

Was he genuinely just trying to take over Panethus, or was he another strand of Basilikos strategy?

Had he handed Larry over to Matlal directly, in which case the bastard was pure Basilikos already, or had he been duped, maybe in the same way Bian's second-in-command had?

Did he really think the Warders were still neutral?

"Three: Haven itself," Skylur said. "In the same way losing Los Angeles would destroy Altau credibility, so might losing our home."

"Four: Diana." He paused and gathered his thoughts. "I accept your analysis that Diana could have been captured and constrained by Adepts working for Amaral. In fact, it's the only possibility that make sense; I can think of no way that she would credibly support him, by force or otherwise. However, that leaves us with a dilemma. In order to refute Amaral's claim to Diana's support, we would have to publicize our belief that he has been successfully holding her captive. The problem is that his mere ability to hold and manipulate an Athanate of Diana's power and abilities increases his credibility and damages ours. That alone could swing a vote against us at a Convocation at the moment, with Emergence issues splitting Panethus."

"Also," Bian said. "If we reach a stalemate on the other points, or even resolve them, and leave Amaral in New Mexico, that will also destroy Altau credibility. Like losing LA. You claimed the whole country. You can't let him walk away with a state."

Skylur nodded.

"But if Amaral were to capture Amber as well," Naryn said, "he might exploit the continuing uncertainty and interest in the effects of her Blood to influence key votes."

By that, he meant that although Skylur had cleverly dampened the main interest in my Blood by demonstrating I was a hybrid, there might still be some who would want to 'experiment'.

I shuddered.

"Regardless of that," Naryn went on, now speaking directly to me, "Amaral's principal use for you—or your dead body—would be proof that you were in New Mexico, lending credence to the claim you killed Romero."

For once, Naryn was on the side of keeping me alive and unharmed. I guessed that was a plus.

There were a lot of possibilities on Skylur's list, and he hadn't even included minor ones.

We couldn't cover everything, and Skylur had to make the decision about what to do. He was the one with the broadest view of the situation. And I knew I had to do what he said, whether or not I agreed. I'd handed over that level of control with my acceptance of becoming Athanate and my oath in the Assembly.

I felt it in my Blood, as strongly as I felt submitting to Felix.

What if they demanded different things from me?

"I have to stay here," Skylur said eventually. "If we lose Haven, we lose Haven. Naryn, you're responsible for getting Diana back. You're going to have to choose sub-Houses to abandon. Every single House in America is a target, but Basilikos can't go after all of them, and minor ones we can win back if we have to. Form a group large enough to attack Amaral, given he has Warders and Adepts assisting him. Amber, you assist Naryn by remaining alone in New Mexico and finding out where Diana is being held."

"We don't need to abandon Haven," I said. "We could get an ally to help."

They all knew what I was suggesting. Allies from other countries wouldn't have the time to get here, but the Denver pack…

"The Denver pack needs *our* help because they're trying to hold all of Colorado against the Confederation," Skylur said. "*And* Larimer hasn't convinced the pack he's doing the right thing in having a sub-pack. He can't loan us any significant number of people, unless you think you've got something to offer him."

"Nothing new, but exactly what I implied might happen when I threatened the Confederation."

There was a slight pause. "Explain," Skylur said.

"The closest, least well-held Confederation territory is Wyoming," I said. "Rather than abandoning our House in Cheyenne, for example, to prop up Denver, why not attack the Confederation in Wyoming in exchange for Larimer's help at Haven?"

"House Thompson would be happier staying in Cheyenne," Bian supported me. "They may even have informal links with the Cheyenne pack; the old members before the Confederation took over. And there are also the Colonel's recruits on hand in Wyoming."

Alex's files had told me that the Confederation had taken over the Wyoming packs one by one, by supplanting alphas through carefully selected challenges: first Rock Springs, then Medicine Bow, then Cheyenne. I took a moment to brief the others on that.

"They've managed to keep a lid on it so far, but I'm sure the Wyoming packs aren't happy they were used in that way," I said. "So, apart from killing the Confederation alphas that were planted in those packs, this operation might even be bloodless, and it could set off a ripple through the Confederation that goes all the way back to their center."

"Hold on. That may be fine for the Were, but the Colonel is still in the recruitment phase," Naryn said. "He doesn't have an operational force yet. This action, whoever does it in our name, brings us into direct conflict with the Confederation. We also have to consider the ramifications of how this would look to Panethus."

Skylur held up a hand, as all of us wanted to get back in with points. I remembered Bian's comment that Naryn and Skylur went back a long way together. However good the arguments Bian and I were making, Skylur was much more likely to side with the man he'd built up so much trust with.

"Amber?" Skylur said.

Being first up wasn't necessarily the best in a time-sensitive argument. I had to make it good.

"Naryn and Bian are much better placed than me to say how the association with Were will play out across Panethus as a whole. My only personal experience is that I heard House Passau from Germany express a great deal of interest in how to structure alliances with the Were. But more important than that, isn't it something that's completely necessary for Emergence? Are we really going to come out into the daylight and leave the Were and Adepts to find their own way? Would that even be possible?"

No one interrupted me, so I kept going.

"One way or another, we're already in conflict with the Confederation. My apologies, I caused that at a bad time, but no one has told me what I could have done instead that wouldn't have been worse." Still quiet, so I continued. "Regardless of that, from the position we're in now, my strategy would be for every House in the US and Canada to immediately make contact with the local pack with a view to an alliance, at whatever level that House is comfortable with. Apart from some local problems, that doesn't increase our commitment by much and yet, from the Confederation side, it's freaking huge. Suddenly, they're getting reports that Altau is linking up with every other major pack in North America. Without warning, they're surrounded. If nothing else, it will stop them in their tracks while they figure out what it means for them. Felix would understand. He'd work with us in exchange for that."

I hoped.

Still no one complaining. It seemed I was on a roll, so I turned to the question of the Colonel and the new Ops 4-10 recruits.

"And Naryn, the Colonel isn't recruiting raw troops. He's recruiting wholesale from an elite unit that was active just weeks ago. An operation like this wouldn't need many of 4-10 to make an impact, and the Colonel would probably even use it as a recruiting aid, to show them the kind of work they'd be involved in."

I paused, and Skylur raised an *are-you-quite-finished* eyebrow. I took a deep breath and tried to calm my heart. This was the tricky part.

"Lastly, again my apologies that my *unauthorized* and *independent* actions in New Mexico have caused trouble for Altau. But given where we are, I have a solution that works with that."

I could feel Jen and Pia on either side of me, picking up on my fear.

"You publicly disown my actions, regardless of whether they're truthfully reported or not."

Pia immediately understood the implications. "Amber, no!" she said.

I placed my hand on her knee, silencing her.

"I will operate down here entirely for my own benefit, which might or might not be to Altau's benefit as well. Any risks I take are my own."

If I didn't tell them explicitly what I intended, they could deny knowledge in front of a Truth Sensor.

What happened down here in New Mexico was key.

It definitely was for me personally. My paranormally-fueled emotional swings were getting out of control. I didn't think I was going to make it without Diana to help me.

I also didn't think Emergence would survive if Amaral split the Panethus party. And if Emergence went down, so would Altau. The whole Athanate structure of the USA and Canada would implode. It said something about the level of the danger that, in my opinion, the least damaging outcome would be that Basilikos would win, because worse than that would be the conflict revealing the paranormal world at the worst possible time—not just disunited, but weakened by fighting. The allied governments of the world could take us out, if they chose to. And they probably would.

And for me, going on alone made a crazy kind of sense.

Amaral would be expecting a reaction from Altau—diplomatic or in force. What he might not be expecting was exactly what he claimed I was. A lone assassin.

Acting without instructions from Skylur, I'd do my best to kill Amaral and rescue Diana.

If everything went well, I'd have Diana as proof of Amaral's lies.

If not, Altau could claim I'd gone rogue. Then, whatever else happened, at least I wouldn't have taken the whole structure down with me.

Chapter 42

There was a long silence.

Naryn had become thoughtful. He looked as if he had plenty he wanted to say, but he was waiting for Skylur.

Naryn might be able to read him, but I couldn't. It's difficult to tell in a conference call, but I felt Skylur was staring directly at my image on his screen. His face was often unreadable, but now it had gone completely blank, almost cold. For a moment, I wondered if I'd insulted him.

His eyes moved.

Was he looking at Naryn, now?

There was a nod, almost imperceptible.

Then his screen flicked off.

"Clear the plane," Naryn said at once. "Except for you, Amber."

Without Skylur there, he was the one in authority. We had to do what he ordered.

I nodded to my House. Yelena looked angry, Nick and Jen confused. Pia scooped up my hand in hers and raised it to her lips. Her eyes shone with unshed tears as she turned to go.

That was unnerving.

What had I done?

The door closed behind them, leaving me and Naryn staring at each other's images.

He looked even more tired.

"I am taking full control of Altau operations outside of Los Angeles," he said. "Our secure communications with Skylur have just gone down, almost certainly as a result of Basilikos actions in the area. We are working to repair the connections, but until such time, I will act with the entire authority of House Altau in all matters. Do you understand?"

Pure bullshit. But why?

To do the same as me. To match my bid.

My mouth worked, but I couldn't form the words as the realization bit deep into me.

If this went wrong, Skylur would find himself in front of the Assembly or a Convocation of Panethus Houses. In the same way he needed to be able to disown me, he might need to disown the actions of his House while he was 'out of communication'.

Naryn was about to put his head on the block right next to mine. Probably the last thing he had ever imagined himself doing. I had to feel a grudging respect for the man.

But Skylur and Naryn hadn't had time to discuss what to do. There'd been no more than a glance between them. Could I simply trust that Naryn was going to do what Skylur would want? Or would he take his chance to sacrifice me?

"I can't hear you, Amber," he said.

"Yes," I managed to say. "I understand."

"I do not accept your attempt to disassociate yourself from House Altau. Your orders are to remain in New Mexico and you will make all attempts to connect with the Altau operation to rescue Diana. We will be there in forty-eight hours. You will not communicate with your House during this operation, other than through me. In fact, you will pass control of your House to me until this is concluded. Do you understand?"

No! Mine!

My vision went gray. I could feel claws begin to break through my fingers and dig into the armrest of the seat.

Shit.

He was talking double-speak. Triple-speak. I had to understand what he was saying, what he wasn't saying, but wanted me to understand, and what he didn't want me to do. I needed to be in control of myself. And parse that through my paranoia that he wasn't doing what Skylur wanted him to do.

I needed to think clearly.

Calm.

Tara in my ear: *How can we trust him?*

He'd matched me. He'd put his neck on the block. That much I could believe.

What was important? Getting Diana back. Keeping Altau safe. Emergence. He'd said he was taking Diana's situation seriously. He'd bring Altau down here for a rescue in two days.

My House and my Pack had to step back for the moment.

No!

Yes!

I had to do this. I had to.

Think, and stop reacting.

Tears beaded in my eyes, and anger swept through me. I would *not* cry in front of Naryn.

"Yes," I said through my teeth.

"Good." The word was soft, as if he was afraid a louder sound would tip me over the edge.

I'd stay down here. That part he'd ordered me to do. I'd do my best to kill Amaral and rescue Diana. That was what I thought he wanted me to try, but which he could deny he'd ordered.

Failing that, I'd find out exactly where she was being held—Naryn would need that if I didn't succeed.

And if I failed and Naryn succeeded, I'd be dead, but my House would be safe, isolated from me by Naryn. That's why he'd ordered me to hand over control.

If we both failed, maybe Skylur would be able to retrieve the situation by denying us.

Then, my House *might* be safe from retribution, from what I understood of Athanate law.

If all three of us failed, none of it would matter anyway.

"You will ensure that you retain permission from the Weres for your presence, so that there is no way they can claim Altau caused their rights to be infringed."

I nodded.

"You could request their assistance. Nothing you might agree to with them can be in conflict with House Altau's association with Larimer. Nothing you discuss is binding on either side, until ratified."

Is he saying what I think he is?

An alliance or association? With the New Mexico Were? Anything as long as it doesn't step on Felix's toes?

We couldn't discuss it in plain language. He couldn't be seen to pass me an authority that linked directly back to Skylur.

On the other hand, I couldn't deliver a done deal.

I could dangle a promise in front of Cameron that Naryn might renege on, and damage Athanate-Were relations for years to come.

How much did I trust him?

"Yes," was all I could say.

"If Panethus consider Amaral's establishment of himself as a House legitimate, he will still need four other Houses to join him in a demand for a Convocation, and that demand has to be made from Altau's domain. That's going to be a logistical problem for him to do safely."

He paused before he spoke again, turning his face and speaking even more quietly, as if he were talking to someone else—an aside that I wasn't supposed to hear.

"Diana would prefer to die than be responsible for the failure of Emergence and the victory of Basilikos."

My gut twisted.

What the hell was I supposed to make of that? If Amaral managed to maneuver into a position where he could use Diana that way, I was supposed to kill her if the opportunity presented itself?

Of course, killing her would be signing my own death certificate as well.

"I'll talk to Larimer, the Colonel, and House Thompson in Cheyenne," he was saying. "And others."

My plan and Skylur's plan. With his twist on it, maybe.

"Inform Pia of the transfer of authority and tell her to call me as soon as she gets back. Good luck," he said. The screen cleared abruptly.

I sat looking numbly at it for a full minute before I could get my brain working again.

I had to tell my House that I was passing control to Naryn for the moment. I couldn't tell them the real reason behind it, in case they found themselves in front of Truth Sensors.

That didn't go over well.

Tullah wouldn't talk about leaving me, and just tapped her watch to tell me we were running out of time if we were going to do something about the Hill Bitch and still get to the meeting in Santa Fe.

"Naryn doesn't think I'm part of your House anyway," she said. "He didn't mean me."

She was right about the Athanate viewpoint. And Kaothos...maybe there was a wild card there I could use.

Everyone else had to go.

It wasn't fair, but the world didn't owe us fair.

I hugged Jen to me, trying not to think that this might be the last time. How much would be left unsaid, undone, if it was.

"I love you," I said to her. "Both you and Alex. Tell him for me."

"I promise," she said.

She glanced to see how far away Pia was.

"Next time," she whispered into my ear, "you have to bite me."

"Jen—"

"I'm not afraid. The Athanate don't know what's going on inside you. I can feel it. I know how much it's hurting you. Your need is greater than the danger."

Pia was coming closer.

Jen kissed me. Too quickly: a brush of lips and she was gone. And I was aching with the emptiness she'd left behind.

Pia didn't speak as we kissed necks.

She was near tears. I didn't think my careful evasions in describing my conversation with Naryn had fooled her.

And she'd spoken quietly and urgently to Tullah while I was with Jen.

She ushered Savannah and Claude into the plane and followed them.

Which left me with Yelena and Nick.

"They're leaving you without backup," Nick complained. Whether he still had doubts or not about being House Farrell, he was too closely linked through Yelena. I couldn't let him stay.

"Yeah. But they're giving me enough rope," I said with a smile and a clap on his shoulder to offset the words.

"We have a saying," Yelena said. "Give two women enough rope. One will hang herself, but the other will climb the mountain."

I laughed. She'd totally made that up, but I appreciated it.

"So tell me, Dancing Girl, is there anything in my Carpathian Blood that's going to help me with my mission down here? Invisibility? The ability to turn into a bat and fly away?"

I hadn't said what that mission was. The Assembly might or might not still be operating, but there was nothing to say that Panethus wouldn't use Truth Sensors to figure out what had happened when I 'went rogue'.

"Sorry, no invisibility spell." Yelena ignored my Dracula references. She was getting used to me already. "Your reach with eukori will be far greater than other Athanate of your age, and touching the eukori of one paranormal will boost your range even further. Carpathians use eukori much more. It is part of our rites. Lesser Communion we call it when we touch another's eukori." She looked thoughtful. "That might give you a way to attack that they will not suspect. Amaral himself will be strong, though."

"Amber beat Matlal," Nick said.

Yelena shrugged again. "Matlal without his Diakon, Vega Martine, was not strong."

There was something about the way she said that. Something about the *feel* of Vega Martine's eukori that last time I'd seen her, at the Assembly. And all the talk afterwards that she had to have been able to change her marque and disguise herself as Altau to get out past the Lyssae. Suddenly, my mind was racing.

"Is Vega Martine another Carpathian spy?" I said.

Yelena jerked in surprise. "Yes. A different Carpathian House: Lazar. One of the old ones."

"How did you—" Both Yelena and Nick started to ask.

"No time," I stopped them. "Yelena, you have to tell Naryn about this. Is there anything else you know about her?"

"She's *old*," Yelena said, in that Athanate way that means many hundreds of years. "Powerful. But her mission? No. I don't know."

We had a lot to talk about, but I was short of time.

"Nick, give me a minute with Yelena, please."

"Okay, but one last thing." Nick frowned and looked away to where Tullah was climbing into the Hill Bitch. "You remember, we spoke about the two wolves inside." He tapped his chest over his heart.

It seemed like another lifetime. Nick had told me a Chippewa story, how each of us has two wolves inside, one good and one bad. The practical Chippewa advice in response to the what-do-I-do question was: feed the one you want to grow.

"This is not feeding the right one," Nick said, glancing toward Tullah again.

"What do you mean?"

"Most folktales about the Thunderbird say how wise and kind it is. My people, the Chippewa, are different. We tell of the forming of the clans from the totem spirits that came to teach the first people their skills. There were seven totem spirits, and six made clans—the catfish, the crane, the duck, the bear, the marten and the moose. The seventh was the Thunderbird." He paused. "But it was too powerful. The people who tried to form a Thunderbird clan died out, until eventually the Thunderbird had to return to the great ocean."

That was like a cold hand running down my spine. "A dragon is a Thunderbird?"

He was still watching Tullah, still frowning. "Maybe," he said. Then he turned and climbed onboard the plane.

Alone with her, I crowded Yelena. Not my sergeant's in-your-face crowding, but enough to make most people uncomfortable. Time was running out, and there was more I needed to hear from her.

Her long, silver hair lay across her shoulder. I ran my fingers through it, enjoying the sensation.

"You like House Farrell? Being part of my House?" I said.

"Yes, Boss," she said easily, completely unfazed by having me in her face.

"Hmm." I let my eukori reach for her. As before, she put up no resistance—there wasn't the feeling that I got with Bian, whose eukori seemed to have depths that were blocked off.

I gave her hair a tiny pull and we were even closer.

She was relaxed. Maybe a little puzzled, but open to me.

"When I was in the army," I said, "I had an instructor called Ben-Haim. He was the guy who taught me most about clandestine operations. He had a phrase: *a spy can lie without breathing, but she cannot breathe without lying.*"

Yelena didn't flinch.

"He was right," she said. "When I was a spy, if I'd stopped lying, I would quickly have stopped breathing too. But I have not lied to you, Mistress. I am not a spy anymore."

From the feel of her eukori, she was telling the truth. Or Carpathian spies could lie with their eukori.

"No one, not even Vega Martine," she murmured, "can lie with their eukori open like this."

Truth or not? A classic unverifiable statement.

But I believed her.

"Then tell me—why did you appeal to me for asylum?"

"I have not lied to you," she said slowly, her accent coming back. "I did not lie to Nick. You gave Larry sanctuary, I knew that, and I was tired of the lying, tired of the fear."

"Fear of being found out?"

She shook her head. "Every day, what I was pretending to be, it was…seeping in, yes, like a stain in my head. I was afraid that one day I would not be able to see the stain."

That was so close to the way I felt about Basilikos, my paranoia twitched. Standard subversion tactic. Was she trying to gain my sympathy?

But her eukori settled down, welcoming me in.

"I have nothing to hide from you," she said.

My jaw throbbed and I had to close my eyes to concentrate.

Our eukori twisted together.

I'd had it nearly right when she'd climbed through that window behind me in Denver. I'd thought of her as a dark, poisonous orchid. That didn't feel right any more. Dark, yes, but powerful rather than poisonous. No sweet-faced singer in the choir, this one. Sharp. Deadly. Violence wound up like a spring. A thing of beauty and a lethal weapon.

Fine, so long as I kept control. So long as she was *mine*.

My Athanate purred with pleasure.

And this close, my nose was full of her marque—*my* marque. Not my marque without the wolf overtones, that David and Pia had—my complete marque.

"Nothing to hide?" I said. "Not even this trick with the marque?"

From what I understood about the Athanate marque, she shouldn't have developed my marque unless we'd exchanged Blood. But Carpathians didn't play by exactly the same rules.

"This marque is not a lie, Mistress," she said. "This Carpathian secret is something that can be used to lie, but my marque is telling you the truth. I want to be House Farrell; my marque becomes yours without exchange of Blood."

"And there are more secrets?"

"None that is as dangerous as this one. Mistress, all other Athanate fear this. You must be very certain of your safety when you reveal what you can do."

"*I* can do?"

"What you will be able to do," she said with quiet certainty.

One last little probe.

"This *desire* to be House Farrell; you really mean it?"

She nodded.

"So when did you decide you wanted so much to be part of my House?"

"Truthfully, it was as soon as you confirmed the oath, after Bian had told you it was the wrong oath, that you had made a mistake."

"Just that?"

She nodded again. "I have learned more about you over the last days: from Pia; from David; from Jen. Nothing that makes me change my mind."

Her eukori began to simmer again. There was more there, much more, when we had time.

I pulled her head down and kissed her forehead.

"I'm glad," I murmured. "Go. Fly safely."

I walked away to join Tullah, as satisfied as I could be with my House.

Chapter 43

"This is the place? You're sure?"

"Yup. This is where he said."

We'd made record time from the airfield. Tullah had asked Victor Gayle for any contacts he had in the area, and this was the one he'd come up with. A guy called Drake, on the outskirts of Santa Fe.

He'd described him as a friend from the service. Victor had been a helicopter pilot in the Cavalry. I was kinda expecting to be directed to another airfield to meet some aircraft mechanic.

Nope. We were south of I-25, with Santa Fe visible to the north across the highway. We were driving through a cluster of hardscrabble buildings and houses. A railroad wound lazily past. The only thing I could say in its favor was that it was poor enough that the Hill Bitch didn't look out of place.

"There." Tullah pointed, and I turned onto a dirt track.

At the end was a shed made of corrugated metal, with a sign hanging askew in front.

We pulled up in front and got out. At the top of the sign was a stylized eagle, poster red faded to pastel pink on a soft yellow background. Below it said: *Drake Auto Salvage – KEEP OUT*. There was a little skull and crossbones like an exclamation mark at the end.

"Lovely," I snarked.

"Kind of you to like it, Missy. You lost?" The guy had come around the side of the building. He wasn't far off fifty, dressed in old coveralls with an Arizona D-backs baseball cap pressed down on scraggly brown hair. He'd opened the top half of the coveralls and tied the arms around his waist, revealing skin so tanned and sweaty it looked like old polished wood. His pale-eyed squint passed over us to the truck and back.

"Victor said to come look you up," Tullah said.

The man blinked. "You Amber and Tullah? Why didn't you say, huh? Pull the heap around the other side."

I patted the Hill Bitch's hood as I walked back. Only I was allowed to make comments like that about her.

"Way Vic was spouting, I was 'specting a couple of hulking Amazons, with big hairy arms like a desert cactus," Drake said when I'd parked. "Y'all look sorta normal."

Tullah batted her eyelids at him, and I bit my lip. Nice to be called normal sometimes.

He got out some folding chairs and patted the dust off them before offering us beers. We sat in the shade of his shed and sipped ice-cold Santa Fe Pale Ale. However dilapidated Drake's shed looked from the road, his fridge worked well, and the equipment in his shop had the sheen of long use and good maintenance.

"Now y'all looks like you teach Sunday school, for sure," Drake said to Tullah after a couple of minutes of stories about Victor that I was *so* going to remember. "But I'm guessing if'n Vic sends me someone, they'll be up agin it. What can I do, huh?"

Tullah was handling it fine, so I took another swallow and made a mental note to get some of these beers to take home.

"Well, it's the heap," Tullah said, cocking her head at the Hill Bitch. "Kinda stands out, and we need to get past some folks without raising a ripple."

"Quiet like," he grunted, nodding and looking at my truck.

I'd parked her alongside his tow truck. My truck looked meaner than his truck. The golf ball dimple dents that covered every inch of her were the proud reminders of every hill she'd made her bitch, but they were…distinctive.

"And if you've got a working wreck of an old car we could rent for the day? Just need to get into town and back. Without raising that ripple."

"Maybe," he grunted again, eyeing us both. Then he launched into another story about Vic while we finished our beers. Tullah glanced at her watch. We weren't late. Yet.

Afterwards he looked the Hill Bitch over. We took everything out—our clothes, bags of fertilizer, shotgun—and stored everything we weren't wearing in a lockup cage in the corner of his shed.

When we'd finished that, we found him wheeling a street-legal off-road bike out into the front yard. It was a mean Kawasaki 650 in a sort of military color scheme: matte black for the engine, forks and swing arm, and a deep, matte green for the tank, exhaust cover and seat.

Yum.

"Now, this is what I put aside when Vic called, but I'm wondering if you ladies are all up to it."

There were a couple of full-face helmets dangling off the bars and I put one on. Very handy for hiding my face. Tullah tried the other on for size.

"I've ridden before," I said casually, with the visor tipped up.

"Recently?"

I shrugged. "Don't they say you never forget?"

"That's bicycles," he said. The little creases at the corners of his eyes deepened.

"Huh." I pulled out half my poker winnings and slapped the bills in his hand. "Whatever you can do for my little truck in a day. And her name's Hill Bitch, not Heap."

"Huh?"

I pressed the starter.

"You be holdin' on real tight, Tullah, babe," I drawled.

I felt her grip my waist. The engine snarled with an angry crackle that promised fun.

Drake started to say something. Too late.

I whipped the throttle, dropped the clutch and got the front wheel to leap off the ground. Tullah squealed and gripped harder. I balanced it down the short dirt track all the way back to the tarmac. There I slapped it back down, leaned over on one leg and cracked the throttle again. The back tire smoked and screamed as we swung around in a lazy circle.

Drake was doubled over laughing. I heard something that might have been a rebel yell, but I didn't wait to find out. When we were lined up the right way, I flicked the Kawasaki back up and we shot off to Santa Fe with the back tire still screaming.

Up to it? Yeah.

It remained to find out whether I was up to it with the alpha of the Santa Fe pack.

Half-head. Great name. Just great.

Chapter 44

I walked down the narrow streets of Santa Fe old town, squeezed between tan adobe walls on either side.

"Keep going straight," said the voice in my ear.

Thirty minutes ago, I'd followed Zane's instructions, leaving Tullah to lie low with the motorbike while I waited alone at the gallery in the park. A Were had come up and given me a tiny comms headset.

This was my second time around the old town, following the directions from the headset.

Walk. Turn left. Stand still.

I knew it was just to check that I had no one with me, but they were jumpy, and it was catching. I could feel it in their Call, like a wooden hinge squealing.

Into the camera shop.

It had a 'closed' sign on the door. I walked in and an anxious Were patted me down, then followed it with an electronic scanner. Nothing. I'd left my cellphones with Tullah.

"What's in the shoulder holster?"

"Heckler Koch, Mark 23."

"You copy that?" The Were spoke into a mike and listened to the reply.

"Go out and turn left," he said to me.

After the rush to make the meet, walking around the town gave me time to think about what I was doing.

I had a reason I wanted to see the alpha of Santa Fe—he was the only way I'd find out where Diana was.

But why did the alpha want to see me?

And why such an elaborate procedure?

Zane had said I would be safe. How much did I trust him?

Trust no one, whispered Ben-Haim.

I didn't want to, but I had no options. I shivered.

I reached a wider part of the street I was walking along. The walls fell back and were replaced by a gray stone building on the left and a restaurant on the right. There were empty tables in the sun, and parasols advertising beer cast long, deep shadows across them.

A waiter watched me from the gloom inside the restaurant's door. Spicy cooking smells drifted out.

"Across to the right," the voice said at the junction.

It was an old mission church, a simple box-shaped construction, even the bell tower. The walls were adobe orange, supported on the sides by angled stone buttresses. The adobe had softened in the weather until there were no sharp edges. A white cross was thrust up into the blue sky from the flat top of the tower.

Misión El Sagrado Corazón. Sacred Heart Mission, said the sign.

The door was old and heavy, layered with a pattern to look like a castle gate. It creaked as it opened and a priest stepped out. *Not* a Were, my nose told me, but someone who was around them a lot.

Interesting.

"Good afternoon, my child," he said.

He had a long face, saved from looking gloomy only by the sense of peace he projected. His pale green eyes were sharp.

"There will be no weapons in the house of God. I will keep your gun safe for you."

It was a neat trick to have your enemies disarm themselves voluntarily.

Paranoid? Not me.

And an alpha werewolf who was probably going to be six-six, two-fifty, incredibly strong, quick *and* crazy wasn't a weapon?

But I wouldn't be able to find Diana without the alpha's help.

I slipped the HK out of the holster, checked the safety and handed it over.

"Thank you," he said. He was holding a cloth over his hand. He took the gun and wrapped it up without touching the metal, then motioned me inside.

He locked the door behind me, leaving me alone and unarmed, while he was outside, with my gun. With my fingerprints all over it.

Not paranoid at all.

I stood still until my eyes adjusted.

There were lamps set in the wall, but they were off and I couldn't see any way of switching them on. The main light was from the sun spearing through the high, thin windows and turning strips of the church into molten bars that hurt to look at. A few votive candles flickered on a rack in front of the altar.

My nose flared. Wood, wax and candles; old, dry sweat and soft, heady incense. And finally a hint of Were, like the Albuquerque marque, but mingled with something I couldn't place.

I could see no one. Above my head was the wooden floor for the bell tower, with plenty of space for someone to be waiting up there. In front of me were pews, an organ, a pulpit and the altar itself.

I took a few more steps down the aisle. The floor was stone and I didn't try and muffle the sound of my boot heels.

Why was Half-head playing hide and seek?

Was all this security really necessary to meet the most powerful Were in New Mexico?

And where were we going to have a chat? Sitting in the pews?

"Wait inside the confessional," the voice in my ear said. "Close the door behind you."

Huh?

Then I saw it. What I'd thought was an organ was, in fact, an old confessional. Like the church, it oozed age. When it had been made, it had been simply a wooden cabinet with two doors. In parts, I could still see the rough cut of the original timber posts. Over the years it had been carefully and lovingly modified: ornamental panels of woven wood in the doors, a plaque inlaid with white crossed keys, a cross on the top. Climbing lizards had been carved all the way up the corner posts. The wood was dark with time and worn smooth with the passage of hands.

In front of it on a stand, a single, intensely aromatic candle burned. Closer, the scent was cloying, making me want to sneeze.

I guessed the alpha wanted me to sit in here, unable to see when he came in or how many he had with him. Standard tactics to unnerve me before he hauled me out for whatever interrogation he wanted.

I huffed and went in the door marked *Poenitentes*. It was cold and dark.

"Just wait. Do *not* open the door until you are told."

The connection cut.

I pulled the earpiece out and stuffed it in my pocket.

It was silent in the church. No noise reached in from the outside. Which meant that noises inside wouldn't get out either. I was isolated from the rest of Santa Fe.

I shivered again.

And I knew exactly when the alpha came in.

His aura of dominance pushed at me. I half expected to hear pews being shoved aside.

Even half-masked by the church's smells, the wolf scent thickened, making my stomach knot.

I heard footsteps outside the confessional: strangely light and measured. A sense, not just of dominance—more a radiation of *anger*, like standing too close to a fire. And a noise like a dying man's breathing.

What the hell?

How weird was this going to get?

I'd delivered myself, handed over my weapons, sat defenseless in a tiny box waiting for an alpha that the Cimarron Were believed was stone crazy and dangerous.

Crazy, weird or deadly. I was about to find out.

I braced myself for my door to open.

What I really wasn't expecting was for the other door to be opened and the confessional to creak as the alpha sat, separated from me by the thin wooden wall.

What was he doing?

Leaving someone waiting and unable to see was standard technique. But he'd gone and given up a double handful of advantages. By shutting himself in the confessional as well, he'd lost the ability to physically intimidate me and he'd lost any clues from my body language.

Which was scary. It meant he didn't need those advantages. Or he thought he didn't. He was going to rely on his paranormal capabilities. So I needed to exercise mine.

The anger I felt from him: it was reeled in. Underneath it, his marque felt complex. It was deep and strong. And strange. And...restrained. Prickly, defensive. A threat of violence barely held back. I felt his dominance pushing at me, probing and pressing behind my eyes. A bit like Felix, more like Zane, not exactly like either of them.

A little slot beside my arm slid open with a bang, making me jump.

"I guess *Father forgive me, I have sinned* is the way these conversations usually start," the demon in my throat slipped out.

My wolf was feeling prickly right back at Cameron, but why pick *this* alpha to needle?

There was a moment of beguiling calm. Then, without warning, his anger erupted.

"What the fuck are you doing here in New Mexico?" The force behind his words hit me like a punch. His voice was deep and buzzy. Not because he was sick or had a problem with his throat—he was using a voice distorter.

Why? Would I recognize the voice somehow?

"I explained to Zane—"

"I know what you said to him," Cameron cut across me. I could feel him stand and press hands against the panel between us as if he were about to break through. I braced myself, just in case.

"The idiot screwed it up," he shouted. "He screwed the whole fucking thing sideways to hell."

Shit. Even through the distorter, there was no disguising the fury.

Did he think I had something to do with Amaral killing Romero? No, he couldn't be that angry about the death of an Athanate who'd betrayed the Were.

The guy might be as unstable as the rumors said he was; he seemed like he was likely to go off at any moment. And I'd been trying to convince Felix the New Mexico Were weren't crazy.

Except...the elaborate setup and carefully planned meeting weren't the work of someone impulsive and unstable.

I tried to analyze the situation. The anger was real. Had I fallen into some New Mexico Were politics? Involving what? Something that happened at the Calle. To do with the Gold Hill pack? The Confederation?

There hadn't been a hint of it when Zane called me this morning.

So something must have happened during the course of the day. Or Zane had played me. Sent me to take the brunt of the alpha's anger.

The confessional didn't let air circulate. Sweat beaded on my brow.

I couldn't afford to get caught up in local problems. I didn't have time. Diana didn't have time.

Wolf didn't care if I was being played or not. Wolf wanted out. I dug fingers into my thighs and tried to keep my head clear.

"I don't know what you're talking about," I said. Calmly. "I'm only here to find my colleague, Diana. Zane suggested—"

Cameron steamrollered over me. "Larimer sent Evans down to infiltrate the Gold Hill pack, or make a deal with them."

"No!"

Shit! If they thought Evans and I were down here on pack business, they'd leap straight to the assumption I would have in their place—we were spying in preparation for an attack on them.

"Evans was expelled from the Denver pack," I said. "Felix suspected he might head to the border packs, but it's nothing to do with us where he chose to go."

"What deal did Larimer make with the Confederation?" he shouted. He was still up against the wall of the confessional. I could see it quivering.

"None!" My wolf growled, too angry to hide now. "We kicked them out and we'll fight them."

Cameron grunted. Hell, it was almost as if he liked me snarling back.

Was he testing me, like Zane? Or would he come through that panel and go for my throat if I said the wrong thing?

"And Altau and this new House, Amaral," he said. "What association do they have?"

"None. Romero broke the old association by kidnapping Diana. Now he's dead and Amaral has her. I have to get her back. It's urgent. I thought Zane understood that," I said, and swallowed. "What the hell has happened?"

"Why did Altau send you alone? Isn't Diana important?"

"We didn't *know* what had happened until today. Altau will be coming."

He grunted again. "They will indeed."

I wouldn't say he'd calmed down, but the ferocity of his aura was no longer pounding against me like storm surf.

My wolf lay back down, muttering unhappily. *Fight. Fight.* If he was trying to put me off balance, he was succeeding.

I closed my eyes and tried again. "What's happened?"

There was a creak as Cameron sat.

His voice was still distorted, but at least the level was normal. Now the anger was replaced by sarcasm: "This morning, 'acting in response to an appeal from their associates, Gold Hill', a team from the Confederation took out the Ute Mountain alpha and three of his lieutenants. The Ute Mountain pack is now part of Gold Hill."

Shit! And part of the Confederation.

"I need to call—" I was on my feet.

"Sit down. Larimer knows now, if he didn't know beforehand."

"He wouldn't have known beforehand," I sank back down onto the seat. "I've spoken to him about Gold Hill and he thinks they're scum. He won't talk to the Confederation."

"He didn't think badly enough of Gold Hill to clean them out."

"They're in New Mexico, not Colorado," the demon in my throat snapped. "Why haven't *you* dealt with them?"

I heard him come to his feet again.

Oh, shit. Shit. Shit.

In the quiet, I could hear our hearts beating rapidly. Had I just lost all chance of getting help from the Santa Fe Were?

"Something's wrong with this timeline," I said hurriedly, to cover it.

"What?"

"It makes no sense. There hasn't been enough time for Iversen to make a deal with Gold Hill," I said.

"Unless there was already a deal."

"No. At the Calle, Iversen didn't know about any deal with Gold Hill, and neither did Fuller."

"Or they fooled Zane while he was distracted." Cameron was shouting again.

Distracted by me. He suspected I was part of it—diverting Zane's attention at the critical time.

My wolf gathered herself like a coiled spring.

"No," I said. "Definitely Fuller didn't know, and anyway, Gold Hill can't be smart enough to manage something like that."

"So, you tell me, little alpha," he said. "You tell me how they made a deal and sent a team to gut Ute Mountain, in the time they had."

"Just wait a second," I said. My brain was racing to catch up. "Look, you found Confederation teams in place while Iversen was talking to Zane. One near Albuquerque, one near Santa Fe."

"Yes?"

"What if there were more you didn't find? And what if the Confederation hasn't really made a deal with Gold Hill, but—"

"They broadcast it, for fuck's sake."

My wolf came back out snarling and I leaped to my feet. "They're telling you what you're going to think anyway!" I yelled. "I say Amaral's the one who's making the deals. He organized this."

"Shit, you're crazier than me, bitch," Cameron yelled back.

We were both standing now, and shouting at each other through the thin wooden panel.

"Where's Amaral gone? Tell me," I said.

"Taos."

Seventy, eighty miles north. Zane had said Amaral wouldn't dare go to ground in Santa Fe's territory.

"So Taos is outside your territory?" I said.

The growl nearly broke the voice distorter. "No, but it was part of the deal with Romero that we kept clear of Taos. We have no one there yet."

We both shut up for a moment.

I was panting with the effort to keep my wolf harnessed.

Cameron's breath bubbled through the distorter.

"The Confederation has teams slipping into the state," he said finally. "We thought they were all heading for Gold Hill, but there's nothing up there but a few houses and cabins. They *could* be heading for Taos."

That was as close as I was going to get to a concession that I might have a point.

There was a murmur of voices in the church.

Someone ran across to the confessional and opened Cameron's door.

Silence. Another pack who used sign language.

The messenger left and Cameron spoke again: "Gold Hill has just broadcast, claiming a territory from Taos to Alamosa, north-south, and Clayton to Durango, east-west."

A large rectangular shape sprawling along the border between New Mexico and Colorado, overlapping by what, thirty miles to the north and forty south? Gold Hill and Ute Mountain were just a couple of drops in that sea.

A deliberate provocation?

"I know I'm right," I said. "Amaral's made a deal with the Confederation. Gold Hill's just doing what they're told in return for the territory."

"Maybe," he growled. "Or maybe this talk of plots and conspiracies is to distract me. Zane says I should believe what you say, but if he made a mistake reading Iversen, who's to say he didn't make a mistake about you? He thinks with his balls. Not something I've ever been accused of."

He beat his fists against the sides of the confessional, as if he was on the point of changing to wolf, and the pain would help him stave it off. Any harder and he'd splinter the wood.

The confessional groaned as he thrashed from side to side, fighting the change. If he shifted, he was going to explode through that panel in an avalanche of wolf—claws and fangs.

I put my hands on the wooden panel separating us. I could feel him, just on the other side of it, growing angrier and angrier. The shock of his blows quivered through my fingers.

And right along with the vibration and noise, his dominance flared through the partition, pressing on me until I wanted to squeeze myself against the far wall.

It ramped up and up, pushing, streaming through, battering down on me until it was a physical effort to keep my head up and my back straight. In the dark little cubicle, it felt like the wooden walls were bowing inwards to crush me. No light. No air. No space.

In Ops 4-10, I'd done the high-G training they use for fighter jocks. I'd been spun in a sadist's version of a fairground ride until my world collapsed into a narrow, gray tube of pain and I was grunting with the effort to keep conscious. This was just like that.

But I'd handed dominance over to Felix, and Alex was my alpha. Cameron could go screw himself if he thought he was the biggest bully on the block. Anger was my fuel, and there was a point where I was pressed back as far as I would go.

He had home turf advantage. I wasn't going to beat him, but I wasn't going to cower.

My senses went strange. Colors blurred. Sounds and smells came at me like a flood. A million separate things and one thing, one thing, one thing pounding in my head. I would not bow to him.

What I pushed back against seemed like a mirror image of myself, but bigger, distorted. Immensely strong.

I'd lost my voice and I snarled instead.

My body shook. Tears ran down my face and my knees wanted to buckle.

And suddenly, it stopped. There was nothing pushing me, nothing to push against.

I was standing with my hands still on the wood separating us, listening to my heart beating like a trip hammer. Hands. Not paws. My lungs were laboring and sweat ran down my face. My eyes blurred and I slowly, *slowly* focused on the fine grain of the wood right in front of me.

With the pressure released, I felt light-headed, as if I'd run a race at high altitude.

"Impressive, little alpha." The voice distorter rendered a shaky chuckle into the sound of a ripsaw cutting through old, dry board.

The little slot between cubicles slammed shut and I felt the confessional flex as Cameron stepped out.

He'd fought off his mania. His voice was suddenly steady again.

"I don't know where in Taos they're holding your friend. And I don't know much about Athanate politics, but I think you've got no more than a day to get her out. We're still monitoring some Amaral communications. He's called a meeting of Panethus Houses in the US that aren't yet associated with Altau."

"Thanks." My voice was level. Quiet but level. *A meeting. Not a Convocation.* "Will you help us? I mean Altau. It's very important to get Diana back. For everyone. Human, Adept, Were and Athanate."

The distorter bubbled quietly.

"We have our hands full with the Confederation. *If* you're right, that will mean we're helping you, by attacking Amaral's allies. And in exchange, I'll expect Altau and Larimer to allow me the right to visit Denver."

My mouth opened and closed a few times.

It was an argument as complex as a maze, the sort of thing I expected from Athanate, not Were.

If Amaral was supported by the Confederation, and Cameron's attack gave assistance to Altau…

If Gold Hill was supported by the Confederation…

I couldn't argue. It was help of a kind.

"Just call ahead," I said faintly. Naryn wouldn't care about a visit, but Felix was going to string me up and leave me for the crows.

"Good! Wait in there, please," he said, suddenly polite. It jarred. "Since I invited you into Santa Fe, your welfare is my responsibility while you're here," he went on. "There might be Confederation teams in the area. I've assigned you a bodyguard who'll stay with you until you leave the city. She'll come pick you up in a minute."

The floor creaked slightly and paused.

"You interest me," he said. "We'll speak again, but right now, I have a war to run."

His footsteps moved away surprisingly quietly.

I swayed and blew out an unsteady breath.

What the frigging hell was all that about?

Fine, Cameron was entitled to wonder if Zane hadn't been thinking clearly when he'd interrogated me. But the key questions about whether Felix was in any way involved with Gold Hill, or whether Skylur had a deal with Amaral had been asked and answered. Felix certainly thought he could catch me in a lie, so I assumed Cameron did, too.

So what was all the dominance-flexing about?

All that craziness?

He couldn't be as crazy as he made out he was and still run a pack, let alone a group of packs.

So why? To keep me off balance and more worried about setting him off than getting information from him?

Well, it worked, said Tara. *More or less.*

And why not let me see him? Why the voice disguise? Someone I might recognize? Was he an anchor on the news or something? A *politician*?

Jeez!

Rita had told me alphas try it out on each other. I hadn't believed it then, and I didn't now. Cameron had been testing me. Pack Deauville wasn't of interest to him. We were a side note. The only reason I could think of was Cameron might want to go up against Felix someday, and he thought he could estimate Felix's strength from mine.

You did take the challenge, Tara pointed out.

Clearly, attacking Felix was not something he was going to try in the near future, but the more I saw of the New Mexico Were, the more I understood the craziness hid a group with long-term plans that weren't at all crazy. And my gut was starting to tell me this alpha was probably the least crazy of them all. I'd have to warn Felix.

A bodyguard to escort me around the city, keep me safe?

Bullshit.

Cameron just didn't want me looking too closely at anything sensitive.

As if I had time.

Where the hell was this guard?

I needed to be on my way.

At least I had an indication of where Diana was. If Amaral was there and he was gathering his allies, it shouldn't be too difficult to find his headquarters.

I was beginning to see what I needed to do. Step by step.

The question was, could I do it?

Chapter 45

"Amber?" a familiar voice spoke. "Ready to go?"

Rita. My bodyguard was Zane's freaking Were-cougar lieutenant.

And his executioner.

No. They wouldn't need a cougar to come all the way to kill me sitting in a little wooden box.

I opened the door and came out.

She was dressed in anonymous work clothes—dull brown jacket, cargo pants and tough boots.

I snorted. "Cameron had you come up to Santa Fe for interrogation instead of Zane?"

She shrugged, not denying it. "Wanted a different perspective."

She meant Cameron wanted to hear from someone who I hadn't been seducing across the table while we would *both* have been better occupied interrogating Iversen.

I could see the point. The Confederation envoy might not have known everything, but he had to have some idea about what was poised to happen.

Gone. Get over it.

There was no sign of the priest outside. Rita gave me the HK back and we walked into the cool Santa Fe evening. She also handed Mary's bouquet to me, still sealed in the little zip bag I'd used when I went to the Calle.

"We never got around to talking about this, but you left it in your pants pocket."

"Thanks. Completely forgot."

"We understand the principle of it now," she said. "We're looking forward to speaking with your Adepts when we come to see you."

"They're not 'my' Adepts, and I can only ask them."

"Hmm."

"What about the GPS I gave to the young guy who was watching us at the bus station? It might have had some places the Warders were using. Was it any use?"

"It was." She smiled and got that dreamy look on her face again. "Oh, yes."

I didn't have time to dig any further. My brain was still going flat out. The shouting match with Cameron had done some good. My thinking felt clearer than it had in days. Nothing like someone crazier than you to make you feel sane. I had to suppress the giggle that threatened to surface. Rita probably thought I was crazy enough as it was.

"I need to buy some things," I said.

"Give me the list."

"Running clothes, shoes, backpack, ski hat, all dark, LED flashlight with head strap, water bottles, maps..." I ran through my list. "And I need to hurry. I have to get back to my friend."

Rita waved a cab down to take us to a mall near I-25. Inside, I borrowed her cell and called one of Tullah's burn phones.

"Mike Papa Two, in ninety," I said when she responded and I ended the call. She'd be at the second of our chosen meeting places in ninety minutes.

I handed the cell back to Rita, who smiled. "Someone just tossed a burn phone into the trash, somewhere in Santa Fe."

I smiled back and said nothing.

"You didn't need to do that," she said. "You have Cameron's authority to be here. We're not going to chase after your companion."

My expression didn't change. I liked Rita. But I didn't trust her, or any Were from New Mexico. Not yet.

"So," she said to fill the silence between us. "What's it like being hybrid? Two alphas pulling you two ways?"

I snorted. "Yeah." Skylur wasn't anything like an alpha, but I knew what she meant. I glanced at the cabbie, but he was singing along to the radio and I doubted he could hear us.

"You screwing both of them?" she said.

I coughed in surprise.

"I'm assuming Altau's already been there when he bit you," she went on. "And you and Larimer—an alpha pair? Gotta make sense."

Rita had the tact and diplomacy of a Mack truck.

"Ah...look, I've been bitten twice. Neither of them was Skylur, and neither of them involved sex."

"Oh." she thought that over. "And Larimer?"

"No."

"Why? He hasn't got an alpha mate at the moment, has he?"

"Because I have an alpha mate already. Why are you asking?"

"Just making conversation."

My impression was the Were-cougar made conversation for the same reason her cat sniffed trees—to gather information.

"So, Larimer still doesn't have a mate, then?"

I nodded. I didn't think that was a secret, or tactically threatening.

I was saved from more questions by our arrival at the mall.

Eighty-five minutes and one more mall later, the place which happened to be where I was due to meet Tullah, I had what I thought I needed and I tried to persuade Rita to leave me.

"I promise, I'm leaving Santa Fe immediately," I said.

"Cameron will have my hide," she replied. "Probably while I'm still alive."

I sighed. It was time for a little experiment.

I opened my eukori and touched Rita's.

She tensed. The Were don't use eukori like the Athanate do, but they're fully aware of what the Athanate might do through it and they can sense when it's used.

I wasn't trying to influence her or compel her directly. Yelena said I could boost my range with power drawn from another's eukori.

Are you there, lizard? I broadcast.

Yes. Why are you shouting, Amber Farrell? And Tullah is concerned by your companion.

Are you all right? came through in Tullah's voice, overlapping with Kaothos like a garbled echo. *I'm right here. I mean, I have you in sight.*

I tried to turn the volume down. *This is Rita, the Were-cougar that I told you about. Just being a guard to keep me safe, but...*

"What are you trying?" Rita said, frowning. I realized my lips were moving as I subvocalized to talk to Tullah through Kaothos. It probably looked like I was trying to cast a spell. Or just being crazy, talking to myself.

Which meant Rita was distracted long enough for Tullah to come up behind her.

"Should I kill her now?" Tullah said brightly.

Rita spun around.

Tullah stood with her hand very obviously holding something in her coat pocket that pressed against the material and was pointed at Rita's stomach.

I was glad Tullah hadn't tried putting the gun in Rita's back. I was still unsure how quick and dangerous Rita was. And I didn't want either of them hurt.

As it was, we'd given Rita enough of a shock, and a little message to take back to Cameron and Zane.

Push us around and we might bite back.

I shook my head at Tullah and she stepped back. I snaked a friendly arm around Rita. She wasn't someone to push around too much, but I couldn't resist teasing a little.

"Rita, kitten," I said, "I hope Zane brings you up to Denver when he comes to visit. I want to find out all about Were-cougars. But meanwhile, we have things to do in Taos."

"I have to come with you," Rita said. "Far as the city limits."

"Only room for two, unfortunately."

Tullah tossed me my helmet and we walked out of the mall to where she'd parked.

Rita followed, but only to watch us mount up.

If she'd been in her cougar form, I'd lay good odds that her tail would have been thrashing.

It was cute, from a distance.

Chapter 46

A little over an hour later, I turned off Highway 518 onto a dirt track and stopped out of sight of the road.

It was cold and dark. I killed the headlight and leaned the bike on its kickstand. Mixed pine covered the hills, painted silver and black in the moonlight. They whispered all around us.

Tullah shivered. "What's up?"

I hadn't been talkative while we'd been riding.

Tullah was too smart for me to lie, and part of the truth would have to be enough.

"You have to turn around here and leave me," I said.

"No! I won't. You need—"

I ignored her. "First, we break the lock on your powers."

She went quiet. Kaothos stirred at the edges of my mind, eager. Tullah was eager too, but she was scared as well.

"You don't know if you can," she said.

"Well, here's where we find out."

She stared at me. "Why? I mean why now? Why here?"

"The *here*, because I wanted to get close to Taos, but not too close. Not so close that the Adepts in Taos come looking to find what's happening. I'm worried they're working with Amaral. And close enough so I can run there using a back route into the town." I pointed with my chin down the dirt track. "That's the old Spanish Trail. I'm betting that Amaral will be watching the roads in, but I'm also betting he hasn't got anyone watching the trail."

I guided her over to some flat ground. We sat cross-legged on crunchy beds of old pine needles.

"The *now*, because there's a risk. And if I'm caught there are things I need you to do. Things only you and Kaothos might be able to do."

"Don't talk like that. Anyway, Kaothos and I aren't that strong."

"Maybe not yet. Maybe this is insurance for the future." I sighed and unfastened the necklace. I held it in my hand. It was warm and heavy. "Olivia will need help very soon. I know we haven't figured out the first thing about this ritual yet, but you and Mary have the best chance of doing it." I leaned forward and put the necklace on her. "Promise me you'll try."

She rested her hand on it.

"I won't need to. You'll make it and you'll know what to do when the time comes." She looked away. "But I promise."

"Thanks. And once we break the lock, never let them put it back on you. They'll want to. I've heard all Mary's tales about how terrible the dragon spirit can be." I laughed. "As bad as being Athanate, the way she tells it."

Tullah joined me, her laughter uncertain.

"I don't trust Weaver," I said. "I'm getting so I don't trust Adepts, apart from Mary and Liu. And Chatima. So, if things go wrong, I don't want you to go to the Adepts; I want you to meet with Naryn and Felix. Give them all the support you and Kaothos can, because if Amaral wins, Basilikos wins. And everything down that path is bad."

"You're right about *some* Adepts," Tullah said. "Weaver has still got them all dazzled in Denver. And news from home is they've heard that the Taos Adepts community are in with Amaral. Weaver has links with them."

"All the better for us to break the lock out here."

"And after?"

"After, you go return the bike and pick up the Hill Bitch. Load everything back in and pick these up." I handed over a sizeable cut of my poker winnings and a list of even more things we needed.

"Steel barrels, denatured alcohol, petroleum jelly, electronic circuits, welding kit? What the hell?" She frowned.

"Put together with good ammonium nitrate fertilizer, courtesy of Larimer Agricultural Fertilizers, which we have waiting back at Drake's Salvage?"

Tullah's eyes widened. "You're going to make bombs."

"Yeah. No doubt Naryn will bring firepower when he gets here, but maybe we'll need it earlier."

I wasn't exactly lying. But my real reason was I needed Tullah to be far away for a while. Let the Taos Adepts feel Kaothos near Santa Fe, concentrate on that, while I snuck in the back way.

Kaothos? Speak privately.

Yes, Amber Farrell? I could hear puzzlement in her voice.

I will free you if you promise me one thing.

What is this thing?

If Amaral wins, kill me and Diana and keep Tullah safe.

That's three things, Amber Farrell, and Tullah will not agree to the first.

Don't tell her.

There was a long silence. I covered by getting up and fussing with attaching the motorcycle helmet I no longer needed to the handgrip on the back of the Kawasaki.

But this is lying, Kaothos said. *You warned me—*

I know. I'm an Athanate, I'm evil. I grimaced. This wasn't how I wanted to say it. *I know,* I said again, *and I'm sorry, but it's important.*

Kaothos sank into unhappy murmurings.

Tullah and I sat again, closer so our knees were almost touching.

This wasn't a spirit place like Bitter Hooks or Coykuti Mountain, but the hush of the pines seemed to make it easier for me to fall into the trance-like feeling where I visualized the energy flowing through me as sand. In the forest of night, the energy came alive.

But it didn't feel right. I tried to ignore it and study the shape of the flickering darkness that wove in and out of Tullah.

The lock was like a Celtic knot, a pattern of threads turning and folding in on itself.

If there was just a loose end, I felt I could tug it and the knot would slip apart.

No such luck.

Leaning closer, I attracted some of the darkness itself, like the reverse of a candle flame swaying toward me.

The sensation of sand became uncomfortable, as if the grains were scratching underneath my skin.

It was wrong. The image of sand had been too easy. It was a wrong turn.

Your whole life has been a path leading to this one point.

I had no more than an hour or so training with Tullah. What else on my path had led me here?

Chatima.

She wouldn't have any trouble with this lock.

The silvered pines faded from view and instead I was back in the truck behind the fairground, sitting just like this, gathered around the single candle Chatima had lit. The touch of her hands, the way she'd cupped them, the sensation of the necklace gathering, all of it filled my mind.

Sunstone. Sky-fallen. *You* she'd said—not meaning me alone, meaning *both of you,* meaning me and Tara.

Life's patterns dance in the candle. Be part of it.

The candle. Flame, not sand.

The scratching stopped.

Flame passes through me. Not burning. More like yellow smoke.

I was dizzy. Kaothos was speaking. I couldn't hear. I was sweating.

I reached for Tullah. The sensation was like putting my hand into a bees' nest. Heat rippled down my arm.

We're not the flame. We're the wick. Tara/Sky-fallen. Bless her.

"Wait—" Tullah. Scared.

I plunged my hand into the dark knot of workings around her.

The shock passed through me in slow motion. I could feel it hit my heart, squeeze my lungs.

I got half-way up onto my feet. My heart had stopped. I was blind to the rest of the world. My whole vision was taken up with the intricate working that surrounded Tullah. So complex.

Kaothos roaring.

Then: *That strand. Weaker.*

The knot pulsed. I could feel the strand. But it was pulling energy from Tullah to replace what I was draining away. It would kill her if I kept trying to suck the energy away from her.

There was a thump, like the side of a house falling down. Kaothos.

Tullah's energy stopped feeding the lock.

The strand I was focusing on thinned. Broke.

I chased the end of the strand, sinking *into* it, hunting it down, down into the knot.

Another broke. Another.

Suddenly it wasn't a knot. It had no complexity, no chilling beauty. It was a scatter of hot neon worms, wriggling away in the night, fading into nothing.

And I was looking straight into the dragon's eye.

Time lurched.

My heart stuttered and fired again. I fell back onto the ground with a grunt, my body twitching and twisting as if the worms were crawling all over me.

"Amber! Amber!"

Tullah knelt over me, shaking me.

I pushed her back.

"Crap, that was fun," I groaned.

I spat and drank from the water bottle in my backpack to clean out my mouth.

I didn't need to ask if it had worked. Kaothos was all around, invisible but humming like overhead power cables. The pines shivered around us, their branches bent and tips thrashing with the passage of a wind we could not feel. Little dust devils kicked and spun in the starlight.

Tullah's face and hands flickered as if she were shedding static electricity. She was jumping and shouting with happiness, then coming back to me and asking if I was all right, thanking me and then going back to jumping and shouting again.

Kaothos? You're stronger than before.

I am.

We have a deal.

For a minute, there was nothing but the ebbing rush of wind through the trees.

If you survive, you will bite Tullah? You will provide her the prions that allow the channeling of more energy?

My turn to pause, but Tullah had told me that was what she wanted too.

"Amber?" Tullah was peering at me. "You okay? You're looking spacey."

"Yeah. Just thinking through what I need to do."

When I know what I'm doing with my bite, I said to Kaothos. *Not before. Do we have a deal?*

We have a deal, Amber Farrell.

It all hurt.

It hurt because, after all that had been almost within touching distance for me—the Athanate, the Were, the Adepts—it felt as if I was deliberately pushing it all away or sabotaging it. I was in trouble with everyone. Tullah was one of those who still believed in me and supported me unconditionally. And I was lying to her in almost exactly the way I'd warned Kaothos about. I was risking her friendship and providing the worst possible example for Kaothos. And while I was sure Kaothos could come in and kill me and Diana to prevent us from being used by Amaral, I wasn't sure that Kaothos and Tullah would survive the reaction when the Adepts realized there was a dragon spirit guide among them.

It hurt because I felt alone and committed to rescuing or killing Diana, whether or not I survived, because I had no faith that Naryn would be there in time.

I couldn't see a way out of where I was at the moment.

So I got Tullah to stop jumping, hugged her and sent her on her way.

I had my HK and a change of clothes in my backpack. Binoculars and a tourist map of Taos. Water and high energy bars.

I was about eight miles away from the town center as the crow flies. There was enough light for my wolf eyes, and I had a flashlight if it got darker.

Getting into the town was the easy part. Figuring out where Amaral had Diana, in the time left—not so easy.

Just something I would have to do when I got there.

I pinned Mary's marque-hiding bouquet onto my backpack and hoped it was still working.

Then I trotted down the old Spanish Trail, my body falling quickly into the rhythm.

Despite everything, it felt *good*.

I missed the running. I'd been able to run most days when I was still just a PI.

The Athanate needed my body to exercise more than I had been. Even my wolf was quiet, enjoying the feel of running. The echoes of discharging Tullah's lock were still eddying pleasurably through my mind—the pain was gone and a glow of achievement remained.

For once, all parts of me were living together and liking it. It lulled me, diminished the problems, let me just *be*.

That struck me with such a force that I stopped.

I clutched at my necklace, but of course it wasn't there.

I could still feel it, though. The subtle bumps and grain of the stones underneath my fingers. The paths that weaved through them. The patterns. That damned message, always just out of reach. Always...

Like the trail beneath my feet. Going a place I needed to be, full of twists and turns I could not see, and yet the way I needed to follow.

And suddenly I sank to my knees in the middle of the trail.

I knew the first pattern that Chatima had laid in the necklace. *Knew it*, like it was something carved into my bones.

I will choose my path.

Not someone else. Not the curse that coiled in my belly, not the Athanate rogue that bit me in the jungles of South America, not the damage that Obs had done in my head. Not the madness that everyone told me was inevitable from being hybrid.

You will have no guides but yourself.

Speaks-to-Wolves had told me that in my spirit-dream.

And I cried, tears vanishing into the dust, because I knew I had taken another step on a path, and because Chatima had warned me that all my paths held death and pain and sorrow and loss, and I cried for all those who would know the effects of my choices, who were bound by me on a wheel that turned without regard for them.

"But I've chosen my path," I whispered into the depthless night.

And I began to run again.

Chapter 47

SUNDAY

The first place I visited was the site where the new Warders' laboratory had been scheduled to be built. It was deserted, and the chain-link fence that surrounded it was padlocked. In the chilly pre-dawn I could see that only the foundations had been laid. No work had gone on there for at least a couple of weeks. It certainly wasn't Amaral's hideout, and neither were any of the houses in the immediate vicinity.

From there it was straight down into the town of Taos.

The town itself was built around the old plaza. The shops made me think I'd stumbled onto a movie set for a western—adobe two-stories with exposed beam ends and Spanish gables. Looking at the businesses themselves, the mix felt touristy—restaurants and upscale art galleries and expensive shops catering to outdoor activities.

The town was gathering itself for the ski season. Hardy holdouts were still intent on cycling and hiking. For everyone, it was just another early winter morning, with people going about their business—eating breakfast, drinking coffee, opening their shops.

But the entire town was also the center of a paranormal hum those people weren't feeling. I was. Without being able to pinpoint where it came from, I got Athanate scents, fragments of Were Call and a continual tickle of Adept working.

I was still in my dark running clothes, and I jogged the length and breadth of the town without anyone turning a hair. Great cover.

What was I looking for?

I might stumble across an Athanate with the Amaral-Romero marque, or a Confederation Were. Or maybe someone with a big *'follow me'* sign on their back.

More likely David and Matt would find something on the internet that would lead me straight to Amaral's door, and all I was doing was displacement activity while I waited.

Then again, there might be more mundane clues. If Amaral had just gotten here last night, and had Confederation Weres joining him, how was he accommodating them? Unless he had a huge barracks and a stockpile of consumables, he had to have people down in town buying in bulk—food, bedding, camp beds, tents. Either I'd catch their scent, literally, or I'd see someone suspicious.

Grasping at straws, murmured Tara, without offering a better idea.

I set up a jogging circuit that took me past all the main stores every half hour.

A group of twelve Japanese were loading up a little fleet of three SUVs with bikes that cost more than I made in a quarter working as a PI. Some hikers had come in from the hills; they'd decided their ultra-light tents were ultra-cold and were upgrading. A pair of nuns in full black and white habits and sensible shoes were loading a rusty pickup truck with a heap of basic groceries, including dozens of trays of canned beans and five sacks of rice. *Yum.* Behind them, a large family struggled back to their people carrier with three grocery carts full of supermarket food and far too many sugary snacks for the kids.

I was distracted by a Were scent that lingered around a camping shop. I went inside and pretended to browse the shelves while I sniffed.

I was too late; the scent was old, maybe a day old, but at least it seemed to validate my theory—supplies would have to be bought. I paused in front of the maps and guides. I needed a map with more detail than the one I'd gotten in Santa Fe.

"Hi, can I help you?"

The assistant was eighteen or nineteen, dressed in a red lumberjack shirt and baggy brown work pants. He was tall and skinny, with sandy blond hair. And he was horny, the way only late teen, small-town boys can be. His eyes had locked on my butt the moment I'd come in.

"Oh, I needed a break from running, and I'm looking for some local info."

"It's cold out, eh?" He grinned, looking at my lightweight running clothes. He nodded back at the counter he'd abandoned to come stalking me, while bouncing on his toes like a puppy. "There's a heater back there. I'm Frank. What're you looking for?"

"You could tell me about the big houses around here," I said. "I mean outside of town. I'm interested in old architecture. Or point me to a guidebook, if you don't know."

He puffed up. How could I suggest that he didn't know the town?

I guessed he wasn't going to offer me a book.

Another shopper waved from the counter.

"I gotta look after the till," he said. "Come sit. I'll go through the best old houses to see. I was born and raised in Taos, and I know them all better than the guidebooks."

"I'd like that," I murmured, and fluttered the eyelashes. *Blink. Blink. Blink. Mwah ha ha, you are in my power, weak human male.* Maybe I'd get a coffee out of it as well.

Never quite mastered the eyelash flutter.

"Something in your eye?" he said as he rang up the customer's purchases.

When they'd gone, and only after a lot of nudging him back to the point—away from where I was staying and whether I had a boyfriend in town with me—he turned out to be a good source of local knowledge. So much so, I had to buy a hiking map, pen and a notebook to take it all down.

There was Taos Pueblo, which I had to pretend interest in because it was old and large. Then all the tourist places, the museums and hotels, the old church and the Martinez fort. And finally, there were the ranches and farmhouses. Places with acres of ground. Places that were at the ends of roads, difficult to get to. Some of them held by the same families for a long time.

Too many possibilities, even when he mentioned those where he knew the families and I could eliminate them.

He was running out of ideas when Tullah called on my cell.

"I just have to take this," I said to Frank. "Was that all of them?"

"Come back after the call," he said. "I'm sure I'll remember a couple more. I'll make us coffee."

I ducked out. It *was* cold outside after sitting next to the heater.

"I've got a list of possibles for the Amaral hideout that Matt and David came up with," Tullah said.

"Shoot."

She ran through their list and I checked it against the one I'd gotten from Frank in the shop. Between us, we eliminated everything but four ranches, with a couple that I held in reserve.

The trouble was, they were all in different directions.

How to get to them quickly? It would take hours to run. I was sure little Franky would drive me around, but that would mean waiting until his lunch break. And I'd spend all my time fighting him off. It wasn't really fair, either, not least because it might suddenly become dangerous.

I could rent a car, but if Amaral had this place staked out, he'd get a warning.

A cab? Tullah had most of the cash from the poker game.

I'd strolled half-way back to the main plaza while Tullah and I talked.

There was a battered pickup truck across the street that caught my eye. I'd seen it earlier, loaded with food. Now it was empty.

It meant nothing. A second errand for the nuns, something forgotten earlier.

It had always looked odd to me, a nun driving a car, let alone a big ole pickup like that—somehow out of place. Which was a stupid thought: how did I expect them to get around out here?

There'd been two nuns before; now there was only one. A store employee was helping her load her new purchases. And I was interested to see what those were. Toilet paper. An entire pickup full. I knew they'd been buying beans earlier, but this was too much.

"Tullah." I cut off her one-sided debate about the merits of one remote farmhouse over another. "Is there a convent in that list? Or a monastery?"

"Yeah, but I mean, it's a convent. Hardly—"

"What have you got on it?"

"The address, size, ownership—let's see," she mumbled. "Been a religious retreat for over twenty years, Eastern Orthodox Christian, fifteen nuns…"

She came to an abrupt halt while my mind freewheeled.

Fifteen nuns? That was a lot of supplies for fifteen people. Of course they'd need to stockpile supplies for the winter. Maybe they got a good deal for bulk buys. Maybe the road to the convent got closed by snow regularly. But still…

Tullah broke back into my thoughts.

"Oh, my God," she whispered. "Oh, my God."

"What?"

"The convent…they're an orphanage as well."

I immediately saw the same connection and felt ice forming in my belly.

I flashed back to the McIntire-Harriman ball. Ethel Harriman taking my arm. What had she said? *"I know Señor Matlal does good work with his orphanages and so on, but I find I can't warm to him."*

And the report on Matlal that Matt had compiled for me—part of Matlal's public persona was that he 'supported many orphanages in Mexico'.

Where the children at Bow Creek had come from.

Matlal didn't support orphanages—he ran them as blood banks.

Not Amaral's hideout. One of Matlal's network. Not stocking up for winter. Loading in supplies for a large group of Confederation Were that had just joined them.

Amaral had been dealing with Matlal directly all along, and now he was here, using Matlal's network to hide.

Frank was upset at how focused I was when I came back. I was in too much of a hurry even for coffee, but yes, he did know the place.

"Sure, I didn't mention the old convent," he said, radiating hurt feelings, "'cos there's no point going there."

"Why?"

"You'll never get in. Those penguins don't even speak to each other. Hardly anyone gets inside, and you need to arrange it, like, a month in advance."

A silent convent, close enough to town and yet completely isolated from it.

My gut was sure.

"You haven't drunk your coffee," Frank complained.

He was laying it on thick. He wasn't as upset as he made out. And he had a nice line in flirting to go with all those raging teen hormones.

My jaw throbbed and my Athanate wanted to tease him.

"I might come back with my girlfriend," I purred, "and I promise we'll take you out, maybe for coffee."

"Oh. Oh, my God. *Girlfriend*." He totally hammed it up, going all doe-eyed, before murmuring: "My mama warned me about big city girls like you."

I laughed.

"Look, come back at lunchtime and I'll drive you to the Fieldings' place out on the Angel Fire road," he said. "It's awesome. Jus' chill, have a look at the town this morning. Forget the convent. You won't get in there."

"I'll take a look from the road, then."

"You won't see anything. They have like a wall, all the way around it."

Yeah, I bet they do.

Chapter 48

The convent was set well back from the road, and shielded from view by walls twelve feet high. Added to that, on the inside, the place hid behind a mixture of dusty green cypress and desert willow trees.

The entrance to the convent was barred with heavy iron gates set between thick square pillars. There was a security camera on the left-hand pillar and a sign on the right-hand one—simple stamped letters on metal.

I wasn't going to get close to that security camera, but it didn't matter; I could read the sign from the shelter of the trees fifty yards away.

It said *Orfelinatul de la mănăstirea - Sfanta Vasilica* with the translation below—*Convent and Orphanage of Saint Vasilica. Admission by prior appointment only.* Frank had it right.

The road was the low point, so the ground sloped up behind me and I climbed until I could just make out some of the main buildings inside the compound.

They were a blend of Spanish colonial and old adobe styles. Pitched roofs of terracotta tiles shaded dusty pink walls studded with vigas, the wooden beam-ends that jutted out. It had been a farm, in frontier days, when the building had doubled as a fort. It had two stories, with only a few narrow windows facing the outside. From my vantage point, it looked to have been built around two courtyards, laid out like the figure eight on a digital clock.

In the middle of the side facing me, the main entrance had been reconstructed in quarried stone. It was a circular tower, about thirty feet wide and ten feet taller than the walls. At the base, it had a deep arched passage wide enough for a pickup.

Above that main arch, there were two smaller arched openings onto what looked like a covered walkway. They bracketed a large black metal cross set into the wall.

Whatever the architect had intended, it made me think of a face, with the main arch forming a mouth opened in an endless scream.

As I peered at the cross, something stirred in my memory. It wasn't the standard Christian cross; it was an Orthodox cross: ornate, with bulbous ends like a three-leaf clover, and two extra crossing elements, one above and one below the main horizontal bar. The one below was set at an angle. I remembered from my schooldays that it was intended to represent a footrest.

But fragments of the comparative religion lesson evaporated when I remembered where I'd last seen one of those crosses.

Matlal's Diakon, Vega Martine, had worn one to the McIntire-Harriman ball, on a silver necklace.

Maybe this wasn't Matlal's hideout, but Vega Martine's.

Movement at the entrance distracted me.

A drawback of designing the old farm like a fort was that any loading or unloading of deliveries had to be done from inside the courtyard. There were no major openings in the outer walls except the entrance. And the width of that meant it was restricted to one vehicle at a time.

A loaded pickup was being driven out as an SUV was being driven in.

It wasn't a real problem—a moment for the incoming one to back up and then both were through. But it gave me enough time to train the binoculars on them and see the logo on the side of the SUV going inside. It was a grinning wolf cub. I couldn't be positive, but it looked the same as the logo on the van that the Confederation had used when they came visiting in Denver.

Great. The gang's all here. Or at least, they were gathering.

Ten minutes later and from half-way up a tree on the east side of the property, I could see a row of pickups and SUVs parked on a paved area, most packing full loads.

Someone was getting ready to move.

That could be good and bad.

The bad part was that, if they moved, I'd need to find out where and I had no method of tracking them. I guessed I could hide my secure cellphone on a vehicle. That might let Naryn track it as long as there was a signal, but it'd leave me out of touch.

And there wasn't room in these pickups for me to hide myself.

On the other hand, there's no time better for covert infiltration than when everything's in chaos, preparing for a move. Security systems get turned off. Doors get left propped open. People get taken off guard duty to help.

Naryn had tasked me with finding where Diana was. This was *probably* the place.

But I wasn't sure, and recon sometimes had to change mission on the fly.

I climbed down and thought it through as I headed for the back of the property.

Going in by myself would be extremely difficult and dangerous. I might find Diana. Even with the disruption of moving, the last place security would be relaxed would be the guard detail for such an important prisoner. I'd done a dozen hostage rescues in Ops 4-10, but that was enough for me to know that this would be nearly impossible for me to carry out single-handed, even with my full equipment.

On the other hand, if I did free Diana, the chances of getting out might be much higher. She was formidably powerful.

Or I could just sit and wait for Naryn, and hope Diana wasn't being moved.

I had no idea what Naryn would do when he got here—he hadn't shared anything with me.

I was sure he'd have a plan to get in and kill Amaral. But he'd arrive with a team, and the larger the team, the more likely they'd be spotted. And what would stop Amaral from killing Diana or using the threat of that to make Naryn hold off?

Going in alone and undetected *might* be the best chance of getting Diana out alive.

Should I listen to my instincts and risk it?

Asking myself questions about what I would have done if this had been an Ops 4-10 mission didn't seem useful; there were paranormals inside that fort and I had almost no equipment.

Not that kind of mission, Tara said.

She was right. There was another kind of mission more suited to a single person.

Assassination.

What would Naryn say? *Kill Amaral or Diana.* Either way, the threat would be neutralized.

I texted Naryn the location of the convent as I crept around to the back, then I sent him some pictures. The layout would be difficult to assess, but between this and the internet, he should be prepared.

Behind the main house, the ground rose. There were greenhouses, vegetable plots and fruit trees. The convent looked to be partly self-sufficient. Some cottonwood indicated they had a source of ground water; maybe there was a small stream running down off the hill.

There was one discordant note in the pastoral simplicity—an area had been levelled and converted to three tennis courts. Was I being too suspicious? If nuns could drive pickups, they could play tennis. But why three courts? I peered through the binoculars. There were floodlights on one side only. No nets or net posts. And why were there fire extinguishers racked alongside the floodlights?

Not for tennis. The convent had a good-sized helipad.

One other thing looked odd. Between the buildings and the fruit trees, there was an area screened off with black fabric stretched between metal posts.

Some kind of plant protection?

Then, as I watched, a couple of guys came out of an opening in the screens, carrying camping gear.

I'd found the Confederation's troop barracks—tents behind the convent, hidden by screens.

There was more movement at the side where the vehicles were parked. A few last things being loaded. A convoy was ready to go.

They might be moving Diana.

I made my way back as quickly as I could.

If they were moving her, how would they do it? Someone down there probably had the sort of military training I had for moving sensitive prisoners.

Put the prisoners in the middle vehicle, out of sight.

When moving onto heavily trafficked roads, stop to ensure the convoy would not become separated. Preferably with someone to hold up traffic.

That would be difficult on public roads in the US, but I was sure they'd stop at the gate to the convent, waiting until everyone was ready. It *was* a point of vulnerability. People wouldn't be fully engaged in the task, wouldn't be expecting trouble while they were still in their base.

I couldn't take out a convoy with a single HK handgun.

I might delay them, shoot out some tires, though neither hunting me down afterwards nor fixing the tires would take very long. Or...

I shuddered. It would be an opportunity for a strike. Ten rounds into the back seat of an SUV in less time than it took them to get out and kill me. A reasonable chance that Diana would be dead.

And if I didn't kill Diana here, they could take her anywhere. This might be the only chance.

I made it down to the gate undecided, my heart in my mouth, uncertain what I should do, or would do.

I hid in the scrub and watched.

As it turned out, there weren't any SUVs in the convoy, and they had no convoy discipline. The gates were opened automatically and there was no one on the road to halt any traffic. It was just a stream of three or four Weres per pickup and a stack of equipment in the flatbeds.

The Confederation were moving their camp, but they weren't taking Diana at the moment.

Just as they finished pulling out, there was a holdup on the narrow road. A convent SUV and a beat-up box van were trying to come into the convent.

The road was an old donkey track; there was barely enough room to pass. To let the convoy get by, the incoming vehicles had to ride up into the scrub that lined the way and stop there.

Which gave me plenty of time to see Frank from the shop down in town, sitting in the SUV. He was unconscious, his head back and his eyes closed. I couldn't see his hands; they were behind him. The way they'd be if he'd been tied up by the nuns who accompanied him.

Shit. I'd put him in real danger just by talking to him.

The convoy was nearly clear and the SUV began to ease out impatiently.

I didn't spend any more time thinking.

The back of the box van had clearance. The driver couldn't see anything behind him.

I slunk through the scrub and dived underneath the back of the box van, where I clung like a limpet as it drove past the security camera and into the convent grounds.

I could sense more Were inside the van. Not Santa Fe, Albuquerque or Gold Hill, and I didn't think they were Confederation. Very scared. I guessed that probably made them Ute Mountain.

I didn't want to think about it. They weren't my concern.

As the van drove next to the walls of the convent building, I dropped to the ground, rolled away and started to concentrate on how I was going to get inside and get Diana out. And Frank, if I could.

Chapter 49

The fortress design of the convent walls, with high thin slits for windows, worked well for me so long as everyone else stayed inside. I ducked below the windows and made my way around the side where the convoy had been parked.

I sent photos of the two remaining SUVs to Naryn. There would be a chance that he could track them just from that.

As I hoped, they stored gasoline near the parking area, in a shed against the wall.

If I needed a diversion, I knew where it was going to start.

And the shed helped me in other ways; from its roof I was able to jump up and catch hold of a viga. From there, a little overhang-climbing technique got me onto the roof and I crawled over it like a spider.

As I'd seen from outside the compound, the building itself was organized around two square courtyards. The one in the front was bare and filled with gravel. It provided parking for vehicles, and it looked as if the business end of the convent faced onto that courtyard: kitchens, storerooms, a dining room, offices and so on.

I guessed that left the rear courtyard for accommodation.

The middle section was a later addition—stone rather than adobe. A featureless building bulging out into the courtyard. Maybe the church, if they had one to maintain their illusion of a religious retreat.

The box van and two SUVs were in the courtyard, but there was no sign of anybody.

I took some more cellphone photos and sent them to Naryn. I decided against checking his responses. He'd only be asking me to do something I couldn't.

This courtyard seemed deserted. In fact, with the eighteen or twenty Were in the last convoy, the Confederation seemed to have moved out already.

Where to? And why?

After a long time looking and straining my wolf ears, I could hear nothing nearby. It was time to get inside.

The overhang on the courtyard roof was less than on the outside, and the second story had a balcony with railings running around three sides. I swung in and grabbed a balcony strut, hauling myself in.

I knelt against the wall, heart pounding. The maneuver had been completely exposed. One casual look by anyone and they'd have seen me. I was fluctuating between scared-stupid and stupid-confident.

The rooms had windows onto the courtyard. It looked like they were originally offices, but everything had been shoved aside and the space used for camp beds. The beds were bare. There was nothing else in the rooms.

I did a quick estimate of the numbers of Were that had been here.

Two hundred in the convent? More if they used the common areas like the dining room and church. Maybe another hundred in tents outside. I had no way of knowing if this was the only place that the Confederation were gathering, but I carefully texted more photos and my estimates to Naryn.

As I was doing that, crouched down in one of the offices, sounds reached my wolfy ears, travelling through the fabric of the building itself.

Shouting. Female and male voices.

And, very faintly, screams.

Shit.

I had a mission. Those screams weren't Diana. They weren't my business.

It didn't matter. I couldn't turn away. I had a terrible feeling I knew what those screams represented.

I found a staircase and slunk down. I was in a hallway on the ground floor. The staircase ended and a separate one went on down to a basement. And that was where the screams were coming from.

Unfortunately, before I got there, the door to my left opened. Two Were, armed and surprised. And *not* Gold Hill—Confederation Were; Iversen's Wind River pack.

I ran through a door on my right, more to get some time to think than through any plan.

Bad move. They'd have me, or they'd have someone coming the other way. Windows were too small or only opened to the courtyard. I needed to get *out* of the building. *Now.*

I could hear one of them, yelling into a radio.

I fired. The sound of the shots would carry, but it was better than him calling in and pinpointing my position.

The second Were fired back. I didn't duck. One day, one would have my name on it.

Tap. Tap. Second Were down and I was out the opposite door.

The next room was a storeroom with no windows.

The next was full of nuns running toward me.

Not the peaceful, billowing habits and prayers type of nuns. These three had lost their cloaks and wimples. What remained turned out to be close-fitting, charcoal-gray PJs, a bit like the uniform that Bian sometimes wore to fight in. But they weren't carrying katanas or guns: they were carrying bō, dark wooden staffs about five feet in length, tipped with silver.

Ah. That would make them the Silent Order of the Kung-Fu Ninja Athanate Ladies. Or something.

My finger froze.

Women. Not armed with guns.

My brain overrode the impulse, but by that time, one of them leaped up and did a showpiece kick and spin, landing with the bō jabbing toward me.

In real fighting, there was only one reason for showy moves like that: distraction.

I jumped to one side, narrowly avoiding the bō-strike through the doorway behind me. She came through, overbalanced by the weight she'd put into the attempted blow. I kicked her in her ribs and tried a quick stamp on her bent knee, but she was already twisting away.

The show-off was closest. I grabbed the bō as she swung it at me, and dragged her forward. As she fell, I took her by the collar and belt and lifted her off her feet. I was still holding the HK, so my grasp on her belt wasn't good. It was enough to lift her.

She could be as strong as a linebacker, but now she had no base to use it against me.

I used her as a shield and battering ram, running straight through the other two, and then tossing her at the third.

The silver tip of her bō wacked my leg and I stumbled.

Crap.

Those bō were frigging Tasers. Unfair. Not traditional at all.

I lurched into the next room.

Windows!

I just needed a couple of seconds to get out through them.

They weren't giving me any.

The nuns were right on my back, even the ones I'd hit.

They weren't armed with lethal weapons.

On the other hand, they were probably going to hand me over to a laboratory where they'd run experiments on me.

Tap-tap. No time for the three shot. One down, gut-shot.

They were too close.

Tap. Missed.

One of the bō slammed against my left arm. Excruciating pain exploded in my head. I leaped backwards, arm flopping uselessly. Slammed into the wall.

Tap. Missed.

Bō coming. Turned, slid the silver end past me into the wall and kicked. Good contact, but weight wrong. Arm making balance difficult.

Another bō, crashing into my chest.

I didn't even see the one that got me. I was aware of it hitting my head.

There was a flash like lightning.

Falling.

Silence.

Darkness.

Chapter 50

I came around gradually, not sure of the point where I went from unconsciousness to being aware.

I couldn't see. I couldn't hear. It smelled as if I was in a toilet. I could taste my own blood.

It was freezing cold, and instinct made me move. I tried getting my hands underneath me to push me up, but they were behind my back, tied together. More rope pulled my upper arms together so my shoulders ached. There were loops around my neck and waist as well. My arms were immobilized. Even part-changing to wolf wouldn't allow me to get my hands free. Whoever had done this, had done it to a werewolf before.

Not a happy thought.

Struggling made me groan, and I discovered my ears were still working.

I wasn't blindfolded, but there was nothing, not even a heat source for my wolf eyes to see.

I hurt. Every part of me felt as if I'd been beaten hard with sticks. Then again, maybe I had.

My face told me the floor was damp, rough concrete. I was naked, and wriggling around to sit told me I had bruises and wounds over all my body.

Sitting wasn't any better than lying down. My head spun and my stomach lurched. I held on grimly and waited out the spasms.

I spat to clear my mouth.

Finally, I got my legs under me and managed to get to a kneeling position. More minutes passed, as I had to wait out the heaving stomach again.

How long had I been unconscious? There was no way to answer that at the moment.

And why was I alive? There were no comfortable answers to that.

I made it to my feet and turned cautiously around in a small circle. Nothing.

I thought of making a noise. I wasn't a bat, but I should be able to get some idea of the type of room I was in. But if they were waiting for me to regain consciousness, maybe they'd hear. I wanted to know more about where I was before they came to get me.

I edged forward. One step. Putting out a foot for the second, I hit a wall.

Okay.

I turned my back to it, felt it with my hands. It was just a plain, bare-brick wall.

I edged to the right and found a corner.

Keeping a shoulder brushing against the wall, I took careful steps until my toes found a wall in front of me. Three steps.

Stop, turn, walk. Three steps. Sensations under my feet I did not want to think about.

Stop, turn, walk. Three steps.

Not okay.

This room was about three yards on each side. No door, no features.

The first trickle of panic skittered down my back.

I pushed it away. *Think.*

Smelled like a toilet. People had been left down here. *Cell. Dungeon. Oubliette.* The words skittered across my mind.

I thought of nothing but breathing slowly for a hundred breaths.

There had to be a trapdoor above to get in. And *out.*

No panic.

I made a noise, as quietly as I could and still get some feeling of confirmation for the dimensions of the room. It echoed a little.

No one came to investigate the noises.

I tried to reach out using the Call, and there was something there, but it was ugly and I recoiled.

The box van I'd used to get me in had been bringing in Ute Mountain Were. Not all of them, just the females. And the Call I was sensing was Gold Hill.

That screaming I'd heard was Gold Hill raping the women.

I didn't know how long I'd been out, but it was still going on.

Sickened, I tried to reach out with eukori instead, seeking anything but the taste of the Gold Hill Call. There was nothing.

Time to take stock.

I was tied up, but I was relatively healthy. I'd taken no lasting damage from the bō-Tasers. I'd been unconscious, but, as far as I could tell, I didn't have a head injury beyond the nausea and dizziness. In fact, as my wits returned, my mind felt clearer than it had before.

Unfortunately, that just gave me a clearer view of how much shit I was in.

Thinking it through…

They wouldn't have bothered to strip me and carefully tie me up just to leave me here to die.

And making a prisoner naked and cold in disgusting surroundings were standard softening-up procedures. The darkness was another. They'd know I'd come around disoriented. The lack of anything in the room was intended to prey on my mind. I'd been trained to deal with these techniques.

Training and reality are different.

But I was not going to panic. I was *not* going to panic. The walls were not pressing in on me.

I had advantages over the time I'd spent in Obs and when I'd been strapped to the gurney in the Max. I made myself go through them.

Able to move, apart from my arms.

Legs not tied.

Fully awake.

Not drugged.

I had control of myself. Not great control, but enough.

So what had they kept me alive for?

A bargaining chip against Skylur? Felix?

Neither of them would give a two dollar bill for me at the moment.

Experimentation? What would interest them? My Athanate Blood or my hybrid status? I shuddered.

There was no way of knowing for sure.

After a while I settled myself into a lotus position and started going through Master Liu's forms in my mind.

Strive only for peace and control.

I am not cold. I am not uncomfortable. I am not scared.

I am not vulnerable.

I am not here.

I endure.

And as I went through the forms and the words, the image of Chatima's candle returned to my mind.

Instead of sand, I now visualized flame passing through my body in a stream, flowing out in every direction.

The energy that flowed out of me flowed into something and some subtle message came back to me, like sound traveling through water.

About all I could think was that there were Adepts nearby and workings. Maybe Diana wasn't far away.

Maybe she'd escape and be the one to rescue me. That'd be ironic.

There was nothing I could usefully do about that.

To divert myself, I tried to think about everything else.

Gradually, I came back to the ritual for Olivia.

Last time I'd seen Martha, something Mary said had been churning in my mind, and it came back again: *Everyone has a connection to the energy, even humans. A million people in the broad daylight who believe you can't change into a wolf would make it difficult for a Were in the middle of Denver.*

Were the packs getting it wrong? Were they the cause of their own problems?

People were more distanced from nature all the time. Jobs and cities, cars and houses, movies and web surfing—everything about civilization, one tiny step at a time, was leading everyone away.

Weres immersed themselves in nature. It didn't stop them from living in civilization as well, but more and more people had a barrier to being able, even temporarily, to abandon all the things that isolated them from their own nature.

That wouldn't cause it all by itself. All it would do was raise the numbers who had difficulty.

Maybe the real problem was that packs had responded to that difficulty with support: the whole pack turned out. The number of failures went up, and gradually, like water dripping on stone, their attitude toward any halfy who had a problem was eroded. Like animals in the wild, they sensed the failure like a disease and subconsciously turned their backs on anyone who couldn't manage the change.

If I was right, the packs themselves were the main cause of the problem; they didn't believe the halfies would make it, and that prevented anyone who had even a small problem with changing from succeeding.

But that wouldn't have been something that Speaks-to-Wolves had to deal with. Martha had said she took Were out to try changing alone.

So, would any ritual she had used work now?

Had Chatima known this?

A helper to seekers, she'd called the necklace. *Make anew*, she'd said of the ritual. And *not quite lost.*

Some of the old ritual mixed in with a new one?

I fell into half-dreaming, imagining a ritual. What would it need?

Four and a half hours passed before the trapdoor above me opened with a crash.

A powerful flashlight blinded me. I had to close my eyes and look away.

There was the sound of a shell being chambered in a pump action shotgun, then someone shouted: "Stand up!"

Using the wall behind me as support, I struggled to my feet, making it look much more difficult than it was. Better to have them underestimating what I could do.

"Stand still, bitch." A second voice.

I swayed. It wasn't that hard to look weak.

The second voice was Lance Evans, the guy that Zane had sent back to Gold Hill, and that wasn't good.

I kept my head down, away from the flashlight.

From the shadow it cast, I could see something was being lowered into the basement. Before I had time to react, a metal hook had slid under the ropes binding me and jerked me off my feet.

All my weight went through the main points where I was tied. I nearly blacked out as pain like a blade sliced through my already abused shoulders.

That was just the beginning.

I was left dangling.

The loop of rope around my neck had also tightened, choking me.

I tensed my neck, grunting with effort, but the blood and air weren't getting through. Someone was shouting. The hook started swinging to and fro. There was a roaring and bright light like I was standing in front of a train at night.

Then my body started to convulse and I couldn't see anything.

Chapter 51

Senses returned as I was lifted out, thrown on the ground and kicked. I barely felt the blows. As soon as the crushing grip on my neck had eased, my whole world had been concentrated on coughing and gasping for air.

A bag went over my head. Hands grabbed my legs and I felt rope fastened around my ankles.

"You fucking idiot! You could have killed her."

"Yeah, but I didn't. She's alive and we'll have no trouble from her now." That was Evans.

"She could barely walk anyway."

"You listen to me," Evans yelled. "This bitch needs to be shown how it's going to be. You two dumb-fucks lift her out without precautions and she'd have gone for you."

"I'm so scared. She's tied up and all I've got is a fucking shotgun."

There were slaps and punches to my head and kidneys; hard, soft, hard. Not disabling, but enough to hurt. It's difficult not to cringe when you can't see where the hits are coming from and can't predict how hard they're going to be. That was the entire point of the bag over my head.

"Yeah, you blow her away, you asshole," Evans said between punches. "Smart. What you gonna tell Amaral?"

He stopped hitting me and grabbed under my arm to haul me to my feet. Blades of hot pain stabbed my shoulders again.

I managed to bite down. I wouldn't give them the pleasure of hearing me cry out. They'd have enough confirmation from my panting and heart rate, which were more difficult to control.

"Well, if you got her, I'll go. Still some Ute bitches need —"

"Shut the fuck up, and concentrate on this."

Evans was dominant, but it felt edgy, out of control. He didn't know how to handle it, and his dominance was feeding on the ugly emissions from the nearby Were. The second speaker, the one who'd started to say something about *Ute bitches*, he was one of the rapists—there was a sickness coming off him like the smell of gangrene.

Their argument stopped and a second hand went under my other arm. I was dragged between them. The rope around my ankles had been left with enough slack to allow me to take small steps, but I wasn't going to cooperate.

Even through the pain, my wolf was taking note of the marques around me. Guy on my left: House Romero, now Amaral. Behind me: Gold Hill pack—the rapist with the shotgun. Denver pack on my right—that was Evans, and he was the one who'd kicked and punched me. The one who'd lifted me slowly to ensure I choked.

He was a dead man walking.

The building was quieter now than it had been earlier, when I'd been scouting. No screams, I thought for a moment, and then there was one. The Gold Hill Were heard it too. I could feel his reaction.

There was a change to the sound. It'd been screams of pain earlier. Now it was lower, the voice ragged, exhausted. More a cry of despair.

I opened myself to the Call and tasted the foulness that was Gold Hill, the fading desolation that was Ute Mountain.

Gold Hill were *all* dead men walking.

I slammed my senses closed again. I couldn't do anything yet.

I was pushed and pulled down a corridor, into an echoing room.

They let go of me and, as I was falling, a powerful blast of water hit me on my chest, pushing me backward. The bag was snatched away and the water aimed at my face.

It was freezing cold, but by the time they lifted me off the slick tiled floor, I was clean.

I was gagged and the bag was put back on again. Then I was dragged outside and dropped on the ground.

Keep focusing. If you lose track and just wait for the next thing to happen to you, you're half-way to broken.

I thought I was in one of the courtyards—there was a sense of space around me, but enclosed.

I could hear a fountain, so not the front courtyard, which was a bare gravel quadrangle.

And a man having a conversation on a phone. Amaral. I recognized the voice. He was keeping it smooth and confident, but he was pacing back and forth.

Overshadowing all of that, a working, so bright in my mind that I could barely hear what Amaral was saying. A hugely powerful working. It buzzed. Colors I couldn't see pulsed and writhed like electric snakes just out of sight.

I wasn't sure whether it was the head trauma, the constant pain of my arms or the unsettling working that I was sensing, but I had to struggle to keep from vomiting.

I couldn't allow that.

This was all part of the deliberate process of breaking me down. The nakedness, the beatings, the cold, the disorientation from not being able to see. My defense was to keep as much dignity as I could and stay focused and aware of my surroundings. Any knowledge about what was going on was useful.

Think of it as one of Ben-Haim's training games.

I could almost hear him. *You've made mistakes, yes. You're where you're at. Put it behind you. What are you going to do next?*

"I understand your concerns perfectly, House Ibarre, because they're mine as well," Amaral said.

Ibarre. Athanate House in Portland, Maine. One of the dozen long-established Houses in the USA that weren't directly associated with Altau. Affiliated through Panethus, but not associated by oath to Skylur. One of the proud Houses whose independence had been under threat from Skylur since the Assembly.

In the relative quiet, I strained to hear Ibarre's words.

"Proof?" Amaral said. "Yes, I have proof. Earlier tonight we captured the Altau assassin sent to complete the destruction of House Romero. She was attempting to kill me and Diana Ionache."

"Captured?" Ibarre's question was clear.

"Yes, captured. I will present her, or her body, at the meeting," Amaral said. "It's not known if she'll survive her injuries at the moment."

That wasn't reassuring—to hear I had life-threatening injuries.

Ibarre spoke again.

"No. Not Diakon Trang. As I said in my earlier broadcast, it's the hybrid abomination, Farrell. You asked for proof and I have her. It was a suicide mission, apparently. Altau must have been hoping to clear up two problems at once."

A longer response from Ibarre.

"Yes, Ionache will be there too. She's..." Amaral's voice hesitated dramatically. "I can't explain how badly Altau's betrayal at the Assembly has hurt her, devastated her. I'm also not sure what part she will be able to take in the meeting, but I assure you we have her full backing, and I must stress again, it's vital that you put all communications with Altau on hold until we speak with one voice."

Ibarre, as far as I could tell, was taking it as gospel.

"So, I can count on you. Excellent. The necessary information is being sent to you."

The conversation ended.

"Call the Diakon at House Prowser next," Amaral said to someone. "Schedule a conversation with Amelie Prowser in fifteen minutes."

Prowser. Old House, even older than Ibarre, even earlier in the US. Big city mantle. Chicago? Or was it Detroit? Prowser was another of the unhappy independents.

How many had he spoken to? How many had he convinced?

I heard Amaral's footsteps approach. The bag was jerked off my head and the gag removed.

His face was dominated by bushy eyebrows, which gave his eyes an appearance of staring. His neck was thick, his lower lip fleshy. He hid his evil nature under a pensive expression.

"Your lies are going to run out soon," I said. Talking hurt; my lips were bruised and swollen.

"Too late for you," he replied. He turned to Evans. "You. Evans? What reason do you think I might have for keeping this woman alive?"

Evans hadn't been expecting to be noticed. He had his own plans that involved keeping me alive for a while, but he was just about smart enough to know that wasn't what Amaral was asking.

"Ah. You could build up the rumor that she can help halfies change." He shrugged. "Might get you some Were allies when you need it."

"Not a bad thought." Amaral laughed. "My Adept allies tell me it's complete shit, of course. No, no, she's part of something much better. Much bigger."

He looked at me.

"You're the key I needed," he said. "You probably can't even understand why it needs to be done, but, in your own way, you're going to be the one responsible for bringing down Altau. All I need is the backing of four other Panethus Houses and I can call a Convocation. That's just four out of the dozen Houses that are unhappy with Altau, in this country alone. He'll never survive a vote."

He was probably right.

"They may be unhappy, but you'll never convince them," I said, my voice was hoarse and my throat painful. "You won't even be able to get them together to call the Convocation."

Amaral laughed. "I don't need to get them together. Such is the wonder of old laws written in Athanate, before the concept of video-conferencing. There is nothing to stop us from meeting virtually, and then issuing the call from just inside Altau's primary domain, which he has conveniently made the whole state of Colorado. As to persuading them…you're right. I couldn't do it alone."

He turned and gestured. "Bring her."

The convent's church was the building between the two courtyards. The main entrance was on this side, where smooth circular steps rippled down from wide double doors.

At a sign from Amaral, his guards opened the doors fully. Evans and the Athanate dragged me over and deposited me on my feet in front of the steps.

This was the source of the working.

Just inside the church, the pews had been cleared and there were about twenty children sitting in two tidy rings around an old woman sleeping in a chair.

Two men and two women, Adepts, stood at the compass points, outside the rings of children, facing inwards toward the old woman.

The old woman raised her head—slowly, painfully—and opened her eyes.

It was Diana. The shock of recognition burned through me. I could barely recognize her. Her hair had gone gray and her face was lined.

Every child mimicked her actions in unison, their faces vacant of any emotion. The four Adepts stood as if statues, locked into their working, only their eyes moving.

Diana saw me and her head dropped again, as if the effort had exhausted her.

I twisted to escape, but Evans' grip on my arm was too strong, and moving sent jolts of agony through my shoulders.

Amaral was laughing again.

"Give me the right lever and I can move the world," he said. "Ionache, you said I wouldn't be able to bring the right lever to bear on you."

He walked across to me, gripped my bound wrists and yanked them upward behind me.

This time I couldn't help but scream at the pain.

"I've hardly started," he said. "You understand that it will be far, far worse than this."

Diana lifted one unsteady hand. The movement rippled through the children.

"You want me to stop? You agree to broadcast a message of support for me?"

Diana's head nodded slightly.

"Good," he said smoothly. "Much better. And you." He let go of my arms and took a handful of hair instead, shook me like a dog. "You need to see the consequences of any attempt to escape."

He made another of his gestures at the Adepts, hand raised and held up.

Diana's back arched and she screamed. She screamed and screamed as if there was never going to be an ending to it. The children screamed with her.

"Please," I shouted. "Stop."

Amaral's hand dropped slowly, and the screams died. Diana slumped back into her chair, looking even older than she had just minutes before.

"Just so we are quite clear." Amaral shook me again. "Those children serve two purposes. They're sustaining your Mentor, and providing the energy of the working that holds her. They're not just imitating her—they feel what she feels. She dies, they die. Understand?"

I felt sick. I didn't dare open my mouth—the things I wanted to say to him would come out whether I wanted them to or not.

I just nodded.

"And rescue? Kill one of those Adepts and the working will kill Ionache and the children."

Amaral threw me down on the ground.

As he turned away, Diana raised her head once more to look at me.

Some Athanate were rumored to have the ability to communicate telepathically. It wasn't a conversation with words—everything was done by shared meanings. It was called alectic dialogue.

I certainly didn't have the ability to do anything like that without Kaothos nearby to relay messages. I suspected Diana and Skylur might have. Sometimes they just looked at each other for a few seconds and then announced the decision that they'd agreed on.

Alectic dialogue or not, when she looked at me, we both knew completely and utterly what the other was thinking.

She'd had to refuse until Amaral presented a threat that had some hold over her which he thought was credible. That had been me. If she'd said she would cooperate earlier, he would have been suspicious.

If I'd said I would cooperate without the threat to Diana, he would have been suspicious.

He thought he had us completely in his control.

He was wrong. Wrong about both of us.

Whatever either of us said or did, whatever hold we pretended that Amaral had over us, it would be his last mistake to make a live broadcast to the Athanate of Diana's support. Diana would never betray the vision of Emergence and Panethus that she'd built with Skylur.

Instead of supporting Amaral, with her last breath, she'd invoke all her support within the entire Athanate world to kill Amaral and put their weight behind Skylur and his plans.

I'd die. She'd die. The children would die.

I had till the broadcast to find a way out of it.

Chapter 52

I heard them first, of course. A helicopter thudded overhead and landed on the tennis courts. An alpha. Before he even entered the convent buildings, I could feel him like a winter storm front.

This wasn't Gold Hill. He had to be one of the Confederation alphas.

Amaral was on the phone to Prowser as the alpha led his wolves into the courtyard.

O'Neill. Wind River pack. I recognized his face from the information packet Alex had given me. Iversen's alpha.

This isn't good.

O'Neill was wearing bulky work clothes, heavy tan jacket, jeans and shit-kicking boots that would have looked more at home on a construction site.

Behind him were five more Were; all big, rough guys.

All looking like trouble.

The alpha scanned the space, passing his gaze over Amaral with a snarl, and coming to rest on me.

Oh, shit.

Evans half-turned to face him as the Wind River Were marched over to us. O'Neill just looked at him and Evans scurried back out of his way.

O'Neill stood right in front of me, hands on his hips.

"This one? She's the one that killed my wolves?"

"Yes, sir," Evans replied, his shoulders hunched.

I felt the alpha's dominance press on me as if he were trying to push my head down. Nothing personal; it didn't feel as if he was testing me like Zane and Cameron, but he sure as hell expected me to buckle anyway.

I got my feet underneath me. I was shaky, but none of that was because of O'Neill.

I'd had enough of alphas trying to show me how powerful they were. Playing dominance games. Expecting me to shrivel up before their magnificence. But I was an alpha, too.

It seemed a long way up, but I stood.

He was taller than me, of course. Six-four. Maybe two-eighty. Neck and shoulders like a buffalo. Eyes like a winter lake.

Pissed. Pissed that I'd killed his wolves and pissed that he couldn't dominate me into cringing at his feet, but angrier than that. Far angrier. Angry in a sort of churning whirlpool that I could sense was being whipped to a frenzy by the foulness of the Gold Hill Call. An anger that needed desperately to find a way out.

So he lashed out at me, a backhand to the jaw.

I saw it coming. There wasn't a lot I could do to block it with my hands tied, but I was moving as he hit, rolling with the blow. I let it spin me around, and ended up staring right back into his surprised and furious face.

"That make you feel better, asshole?" I said. The side of my face had gone numb and the words slurred.

"Shut the fuck up!"

"Yeah. Just shut up and take it. Like the Ute Mountain women that your men are raping."

"We're not!" he shouted at me.

It wasn't a complete shot in the dark, and it wasn't everything he was furious about, but it was good enough to work with.

"Just standing by, then," I said. "Minding your own business."

That got through to him. Old-style werewolves are paternalistic assholes, and they didn't come any more so than the Confederation founders, including Wind River. Female werewolves were rarer than males and the crusty old alphas would be hugely overprotective of their females.

From the evidence here, outcasts like Gold Hill went a different way.

The behavior of Gold Hill to the Ute Mountain women was unthinkable to the Wind River alpha, and yet, here on territory he'd agreed belonged to Gold Hill, he clearly felt powerless to stop it. That Gold Hill Call felt sickening for me. For him, it had to feel like someone sandpapering an open wound.

I didn't know the Ute Mountain women. If they were outcast, it was entirely possible they were as bad as the men. But I'd had some experience of the results of this kind of behavior from my missions with Ops 4-10. In one instance, we'd saved a group of women who'd been rounded up for 'medical inspection and re-education'.

Mass rape wasn't something that only out-of-control werewolves could do.

And the length of time it had gone on here, some of the Ute Mountain women would be dead or dying.

If I took a couple of backhands for them and managed to stop it, I was fine with that.

Another helicopter came in low overhead.

"Just standing by," I said again, yelling over the noise and downdraft. "How's that gonna play in the rest of the Confederation when it gets out? What're the neighboring packs going to think about it? About *you*?"

He might have hit me again, but Amaral hastily concluded his call and intervened.

"You," Amaral said to Evans. "Go stop that business right now." He made an impatient gesture to send two of his Athanate guards along for muscle.

Better late than never, but his intervention didn't go the way he expected. O'Neill turned on him, with all that anger still seeking an outlet.

"You said you had control here," he yelled at Amaral. "It's a fucking disaster. I screwed with Iversen to get you the timing and you've completely fucking blown it."

"It's not happening exactly as planned, but things are well within param—"

"Can that shit!" O'Neill said. "The Albuquerque Weres ran you out of town and killed most of your Warders. You can't even show your face in Santa Fe. Just how is that *within parameters*?"

"*You* failed to provide all the teams you promised."

This was great—enemy alliances falling apart. I could listen to it all day, but I needed to see if there was something I could do to help Diana. The Adepts were still there, maintaining their lock on her, but the Athanate guards were drifting in to flank Amaral and balance the five angry Wind River Were behind O'Neill.

I edged toward Diana, but I was stopped by nuns coming out of the church.

Two of them that I'd fought were carrying the one I'd wounded. They passed me with no more than a hateful glance. Two more stood in front of me, idly spinning their bō, bleak-eyed and looking at me as if they wanted another round.

What now?

I heard voices behind me and looked over my shoulder. Three more nuns had just come in on the helicopter. All of the nuns were in their slinky charcoal-gray uniforms, but the arrivals were armed with top-of-the-line military weapons—HK MP7 and G36 assault rifles.

I turned to face them.

They surrounded me, just five of them, but effectively cutting me off from everything else.

One of them was carrying a spare cloak. She put it around my shoulders and fastened it at the front.

"Thank you," I said. I wasn't sure why I was being polite to them, but it seemed better than getting my jaw broken by O'Neill. He'd just shouted at Amaral that half his force was tied up making sure Taos didn't fill up with New Mexico Were, and he couldn't spare any more to secure the meeting site.

"This doesn't seem to be going well for them," the nuns' leader said, her eyes flicking across to where O'Neill and Amaral argued. She was old Athanate. A voice like satin, and brown eyes, oddly soft.

I snorted at her comment. And then winced at the pain that caused in my face.

"And you are?" I said.

Her ninja-nun outfit was complemented by a slimline black tactical vest, a Beretta Px4 handgun strapped to one leg, and an MP7 to the other. She was carrying a comms-enabled black battle helmet under her arm. Her dark hair was held back in a ponytail. Her face still had smudges of camo.

I didn't know which war she'd just come back from, but these nuns took their fighting seriously.

"Mirela Tucek," she said. A slight smile skewed her thin mouth. "I'll drop the 'Mother' now. It's served its purpose."

"You aren't upset by their problems," I said.

"Let's say that their path isn't necessarily our path." She glanced over at the arguing men. "We've traveled together. They may yet reach their destination, and it may yet serve our purposes, but it's not essential."

I was keeping my guard up and at the same time trying to sense anything from them with eukori. They might as well have been wearing mirror shades over their minds.

But one thing I did sense: we were related, Athanate-wise. These nuns were Carpathian.

"Whose purposes are those?" I said, afraid I knew the answer already.

"The purposes of House Lazar."

"Carpathian," I confirmed. "I guess that means you answer to Vega Martine."

She looked surprised, and a genuine smile broke across her face.

"You *are* well informed about some things," she said. "We do serve the Lady."

I heard the capital letter and only just managed to stop my throat demon from passing a comment about her Ladyship.

Tucek saw it and laughed easily.

I had to admit, she was a lot friendlier than I would have been to someone who'd shot one of my team in the gut. Then again, I was the one who was trussed up like an oven-ready chicken.

If there was a choice, I'd take her over Evans and Amaral.

Was that what she was offering?

"You and the Lady are closer in mind than you think," the nun to Tucek's right said. "We believe in Emergence. We're not fools like Correia, who believe we can hide forever."

"And neither are we backstabbing psychopaths like Amaral," Tucek said. "Who's plotting his betrayals even while he negotiates his friendships and alliances: Romero, the Albuquerque Were, the Warders, the unsettled Houses in the US, the Confederation. Who's next?"

The part about Amaral was right on. But Vega Martine and Emergence, that didn't make sense, surely?

"Vega Martine supported Matlal," I said. "Basilikos—"

"Basilikos and the Assembly would have supported Emergence if Altau hadn't destroyed the Assembly in his grab for power."

Well, they would put their spin on it. Were they trying to convince me that we were on the same side?

"Which he did while getting Matlal locked up, too," I said. "I guess it's hard on you that Matlal is a prisoner of Basilikos."

Tucek smiled. "Not anymore. I put him on a helicopter in Santa Ana not four hours ago. We'll be joining him and the Lady soon."

Crap. She and her ninja-nuns have sprung Matlal from Basilikos. But why? He can't be worth anything to them now.

Despite everything, I was feeling some grudging admiration for Tucek and her 'convent'.

"It's not about Panethus and Basilikos any longer," the second nun was saying. "The real division is Altau on one hand and everyone else on the other. Not even Altau's new allies, Theokos, really believe his line that Athanate and human are equal. It's amazing he's kept Panethus together, but it can't last."

She was right, in some of that anyway. Arvinder had given me the dummies' introduction to Theokos. They believed that humans should worship Athanate.

"Panethus can't last now that the Warders have been dismantled," Tucek said. "The Assembly, and its artificial division of Panethus and Basilikos, is gone. Whatever replaces it will have to include the unaligned groups, and we don't agree with Altau, let alone with what the Empire of Heaven believes."

"So you claim," I said, but I was arguing with Athanate who knew much more of what was going on than I did. How *did* things stand now that there was no means to maintain the Assembly?

Were they so bad, these ninja-nuns? My paranoia twinged. They were putting a lot of effort into talking to a prisoner.

The mental clarity that had seemed to linger after the shock from the bō was ebbing away now. I needed to be thinking of…what?

Tucek came closer.

"But really, you need to be thinking on a more personal level," Tucek said. She ran one gloved hand gently down the side of my face. "I'm not the Lady, but I can sense the turmoil inside you. Were and Athanate, fighting each other. It must be exhausting, even without *this*."

It felt like she'd switched on small light inside my head. Monsters prowled my mind in the darkness. Within the weak glow of the light was what remained of my strongbox—the place I'd kept the things I didn't want to get out.

"The Lady can cure all this," she murmured.

No. Something very important.

Dungeons.

That's it. Something about dungeons. Not how nice the nuns were being to me. Dungeons in the basement of the convent. Dungeons that had been used recently. That stank of fear and despair.

Yes. That's what I needed to think about. What they had been using the dungeons for.

"You used the dungeons downstairs to *discipline* the children, didn't you?" I said. "To break them, until they did whatever you wanted."

Tucek's face went suddenly blank, and the strange feeling of admiration for the nuns disappeared.

"Mother Tucek, not trying to walk off with my prisoner, are you?" Amaral eased his way into the circle. He was smiling, his voice almost jovial. Underneath, he was primed like an explosive. His Athanate were right behind him. O'Neill had stomped off, hopefully to make sure the assaults on the Ute Mountain women had stopped.

"She turned me down." Tucek's voice matched his light tone.

"You'd have been second in line." Amaral jerked his head after the Wind River alpha. "But she's not available anyway. She's mine. I have important uses for her."

Tucek smiled and casually stepped back.

Locked into some invisible signal from her, the nuns moved. It looked random, but suddenly they were all facing the Amaral Athanate.

Please. Let them all kill each other.

Amaral and his men shifted, unconsciously responding to the threat they hadn't really registered yet.

Tucek's lips thinned. Not a smile. Not quite a sneer.

"House Amaral, we're leaving now. Consider this building as a gift." She tilted her head thoughtfully to one side. "I've been here nine years, and though I'm no more a nun than you are, it *has* provided me with a chance for contemplation. I urge you to think on its message."

Amaral blinked. "Deception?" he guessed.

"Oh, that too. But there's another, one that was laid down in the bones of the old farm." She tapped her foot on the flagstones. "This place was built from the foundations upward on the premise that you don't really have what you can't hold."

Amaral blinked again, an understanding of the precipice beneath his feet gradually dawning on his face. His team picked it up. They were good, too, much better than I'd given them credit for. Without any sudden movements they were spread out. Hands strayed closer to guns and the tension ratcheted.

Then the moment was broken.

Another couple of nuns came in, supporting Frank, who was pale and stumbling. He'd been beaten when they kidnapped him. Now, his neck was bloody with bites. His hands were still tied.

But behind the nuns, four more Amaral came in, these dressed in combat gear and with assault rifles already in their hands. The balance shifted.

"Ah. The bait we brought in from the town," Tucek said, as if nothing else had happened. "Redundant now. Is he *yours* too?" She raised an eyebrow at Amaral.

Frank's dazed eyes found me and he jerked in shock. The look of hope that dawned in his face was like a punch in my belly.

"He's just a store clerk," I said. "Blank his memory and let him go. Please."

Amaral ignored me and shook his head, his mouth pursed in distaste. "No interest here. Take him with you."

"For in-flight snacks?" She laughed. "We'll all be strapped in, flying at treetop level. No chance for entertainment."

Amaral jerked his chin. One of the guards raised his gun.

"No!" I yelled.

"No." Tucek raised her hand. She smiled at me. "You're right."

She walked to Frank. "No point in waste."

"No, please," I begged. I'd gotten him into this, however inadvertently. *Death and sorrow and pain and loss.*

"Too late, Farrell," she said. "You had your chance."

Frank overbalanced as Tucek grabbed his shirt. Before he recovered, she'd bitten his neck. His scream choked off raggedly and his knees folded underneath him. She lowered him smoothly, the fangs tearing his flesh but staying buried in him. He started to struggle, giving another thin, bubbling scream that almost covered Tucek's grunts of pleasure.

My hands were tied. I was hobbled.

The wolf burned like acid inside. My view of the courtyard *twisted* and the sound I made didn't come from a human throat. I lunged toward Tucek's vulnerable back.

There was a searing explosion in my skull as the bō hammered against my head, and darkness followed like a falling blade.

Chapter 53

When I came around, I was slumped in the back seat of an SUV.

It was an improvement over the last time—no toilet smells and I could actually see. And I still had the nun's cloak fastened around my neck, although it wasn't doing much good, twisted and bunched underneath me.

Without opening my eyes, I knew Evans was sitting next to me.

Given that I was tied up and mostly naked, that wasn't good.

I pretended to be unconscious still, but Evans wasn't fooled. I could feel the weight of his look, the touch of the sickness in his head. Joining Gold Hill had twisted his mind with shocking speed. His marque was still from the Denver pack—it should have been comforting and familiar to me. The fact that it wasn't comforting at all was a double blow.

There was a subliminal growl from the front of the car.

Two Were. Wind River marque. One concentrating on driving nose to tail behind another truck, and the other turned around and snarling displeasure at Evans.

I let myself relax one degree, no more.

Wind River were the enemy, but they weren't like Gold Hill, and I was relatively safe while they were around. If Evans got me on my own...

I swallowed painfully, my throat dry.

If Evans got me on my own, then I'd do what I'd been trained to do in Ops 4-10.

It had been one of the few times they'd split us up by gender.

I blinked at the memories crowding my mind.

Top is standing at the front of the room, his hands behind him.

'You come to us as a product, in part, of the culture in which you were raised,' he says. 'A culture that reacts differently to capture depending on whether you are male or female.'

He rocks up onto the balls of his feet. 'I will challenge that,' he says.

The women got Ben-Haim. He had us strip naked and tie each other up. We didn't dare laugh, but there were some sly winks and nervous whispers. Then he put bags over our heads and made us stand for hours. Men we couldn't see strolled through our ranks, making obscene threats and laughing at us.

And behind them, Ben-Haim walked, so quietly my ears ached to hear where he was. He touched us or slapped us painfully at random, without reason or excuse.

I could hear his voice, like a gray knife sliding under my skin:

You will smile and sing lullabies if you have to. You will do whatever it takes to make your captors believe they have the upper hand. Whatever it takes, because there is nothing more important than staying alive. Nothing. Not your dignity, the sanctity of your body, your morals, your ethics. Nothing. Dead women don't get away. You will survive.

That had only been the softening up.

A dozen women left the unit without passing that test.

I wouldn't have passed, without the strongbox to lock things away.

Something touched my lips and I jerked in shock, but it was only the guy from the front, holding a water bottle for me.

I drank thirstily.

"Thank you," I muttered hoarsely.

His mouth was a thin, hard line and he wouldn't meet my eyes. He'd probably been assigned to this truck randomly and once we reached our destination, he'd have other duties. Evans was the one who'd be guarding me. The Wind River Were didn't like it.

I couldn't say anything else to him.

I would endure. Evans would make a mistake. Eventually.

The guard reached into the back and tugged the edge of the cloak from under me. "Sit up," he said, and I did, letting him pull it around me.

Which meant I had a great view of what happened next.

The lead truck slowed. I craned my neck. There was a metal barrel in the middle of the track.

Oh, my God.

The second truck wobbled and ran into the back of the first without braking. The rest screeched to a halt.

"What the fuck?" the driver swore.

I twisted and dived into the footwell.

The windshield shattered with a bang. The driver shuddered and collapsed over the steering wheel. The barrel in front of the convoy exploded. There was another explosion behind us, and suddenly there was a wave of dark shapes breaking over the trucks.

The freaking cavalry was here.

Evans was half-way out of the truck when the door slammed back into him.

"Don't kill them," I yelled, keeping my head *down*.

Even if they knew I was here, an accidental bullet is still a bullet.

Shots were fired. There were shouts and screams, and then, abruptly, it was all over.

"Amber?" a deep voice boomed.

I looked up carefully. The gathering gloom of evening seemed to pool into one huge figure at the open door of the car.

"Silas?"

"Yelena," Silas yelled. "She's here."

He lifted me out gently. I groaned at the stabbing pain in my shoulders as my weight came to bear on them.

Yelena ran up, pulling out a knife to cut my ropes.

"Stop," I said. "Don't cut them. And keep that bastard alive." I kicked Evans' unconscious body.

"What?" Yelena and Silas were frowning at me. *Head injury*, I could see the thought hit them both.

"Give me a minute," I said. "I'll explain."

They watched dubiously as I hobbled around the SUV. The driver had been hit by a hollow point round, right through the chest. He'd been dead before his head hit the steering wheel. The guard who'd given me water had gotten out of the car, but he was dead too, and I was sorry for that. He'd ended up on the wrong side and he'd have handed me over to whatever Amaral had planned for me, but he hadn't been evil like Evans.

Yelena had followed. She caught me carefully, trying not to put pressure on my arms.

"Slow down. You're okay now," she said. "Let us help you."

"No," I said, putting out all the House authority I could muster. I pulled gently away from her, and she released me, frowning again.

Silas had joined us, and behind him another Were. For a moment, I thought it was Ben. Right marque, wrong man, wrong level. This was the Cimarron pack alpha, and I became aware of more Cimarron behind him.

"Ma'am," he said. His voice was measured and growly. "You're safe now. Let us get those ropes. They look damned uncomfortable."

On him, the crusty Were paternalism was kind of sweet.

"Believe me, I'd like nothing more," I said. They had no idea how true that was; I'd had a hell of a day and I didn't look forward to making it worse. "But these ropes have to stay exactly the way they are. I know where Diana is. She's in Amaral's camp. And I need for Evans to escape with me as his prisoner, so that little shit can take me right to them."

Chapter 54

They tried to talk me out of it, but I wasn't taking 'no' for an answer. And since neither Felix nor Naryn was here, there was no one who could make me.

More armed Were gathered around: about twenty Denver pack to balance the Cimarron. Mary was there as well, pushing through the barrier of bodies, the tail end of a working drifting around her like a veil. Probably she'd helped conceal the marques of the ambush party.

Yelena moved behind me, massaging my shoulders, while I made my speech to the gathered Were.

"Diana Ionache is one of the most powerful, most influential Athanate in the entire world," I said. "She's being held captive by Amaral and his pet Adepts—under a kind of compulsion." No time now to explain the intricacies of Diana's position and the Adept working. I took a deep breath. "While we're standing here, Amaral is putting together a broadcast in which Diana will be forced to come out in support of him—and it will look like she's doing that voluntarily. We have to get her out before that happens." Or before she refused, and was killed. But they didn't need to know that part. If they thought she would refuse, they wouldn't see any reason to go in after her.

The Cimarron alpha, who Silas had introduced as Don Stillman, narrowed his eyes thoughtfully. "Begging your pardon, but this sounds like Athanate business. Not Were."

I closed my eyes. Time was ticking away.

"It's everybody's business," I said, trying to keep the frustration out of my voice—and my eukori. "Amaral's going to use that endorsement to sway Panethus Houses that are on the fence over to his side. They don't know he's allied with Basilikos. If enough of them support him—and they will, if Diana comes out in his favor—he's going to cross the river into Colorado and issue a challenge to Skylur. That was the whole purpose of claiming both sides of the river for Gold Hill. Panethus will split, Altau will fall—and Basilikos and the Confederation will start a war throughout North America. None of us want that."

I looked directly at Stillman. "I appreciate you coming here more than I can say," I told him. "Now I need to ask you to back me on this. If I get Evans to take me in there, I can disrupt the broadcast and free Diana. All I need is a team to get me out once that's done. Will you do it?"

I held his gaze, and for a minute I thought I had him. Then he shook his head, a tinge of regret in his eyes.

"I brought my wolves here 'cos we owed you," he said. "You put yourself in harm's way to help Ben, down in Albuquerque, and I reckon it might be my great-nephew's alive 'cos of it. I also got a bone to pick with Gold Hill." He grunted and shifted his shoulders. "But attacking the Confederation is crazy talk, almost as bad as taking on Gold Hill while they got the Confederation right here at their backs. I'm sorry about this Diana lady, but I ain't convinced that a few words from her is gonna bring Panethus down, and start World War III."

"You let the Confederation get a foothold in New Mexico," Silas said, "and they're going be your neighbors."

"So Felix told me. But see, we're plains Were and their name, well, it's the Central Mountain Confederation. I don't rightly see that their ambitions would extend to the Cimarron territories at all."

From where I was standing, he sounded more hopeful than convinced on that point. But he was adamant in his decision. "I'm not saying I like it, but I reckon we're even. You go back in, Amber, and I say that's your choice. I won't put my pack at risk to get you out again." He rubbed his hand on the back of his neck. "Now, I shook hands with Felix, and he treated Ben well. He's a good neighbor, too, so I have to stand by him on the Colorado border." He squinted. "Ain't so good a neighbor as I'd cross it for him to fight some Athanate battle."

Having him preventing Amaral from crossing that border would be a big advantage. Silas and I knew it. We didn't want to risk that by arguing, until we had something more to persuade him.

"Been a pleasure," Don said. "Thank you again, Amber, and I wish you luck."

He assembled his Were and they trotted off into the gathering darkness.

Damn.

We couldn't just stall Amaral; he would only move and try again. We needed to stop him here and now.

When Plan A fails, you move to Plan B. And C, and D—all the way down to Z if you have to. I'd learned that in Ops 4-10. Time was slipping away—and my shoulders were killing me.

"Gather 'round, people," I said. "We have about ten more minutes before O'Neill is going to start wondering what happened to his convoy and come looking. I need to get into Amaral's camp and take him out if I can. Then I need to break the lock on Diana. Finally, I have to get her out of the middle of House Amaral, the Confederation and assorted Adepts. How much backup do I have?"

"Not much," Silas admitted. "Our pack is squatted across the river from Amaral's camp, but there aren't nearly enough of us to take on everything he's got. Not if Cimarron and Cheyenne won't play ball—and they're not."

"Cheyenne?" I asked.

"Naryn took your advice on helping Cheyenne," Tullah said, walking up with Julie. Julie had a rifle slung over her shoulder, the long sinister barrel sticking up. I guessed it'd been her precision shooting that took out the drivers.

And was that you, lizard? The exploding barrels? I asked.

Yes. Tullah made your fertilizer bombs and I lit them. Such pretty little explosions. We could have made them even prettier with your help.

I smothered a chuckle.

"The problem is," Silas was saying, "Cheyenne won't move beyond Altau's domain without Naryn. And Naryn's still on the way."

"Look, we should call Felix," Julie said. "We need to report in and, who knows, Naryn might have caught up with us."

Sound tactical sense, but I itched at the delay.

Silas had a military radio and within a few seconds, he had Felix on an encrypted channel.

Besides the Were, Felix had representatives of the Denver Adept community with him, led by Weaver. My House was there, too, apart from Alex, who'd gone with Bian to look for me in Taos, and would need to be recalled. Weaver had been invited because Amaral had Adepts as allies. But Weaver wanted to parley, not fight. His people had agreed to mask the packs' presence the same way that Mary had done for Silas's team, but that was the extent of their contribution so far.

It seemed like Naryn was my only hope.

"He's still a couple of hours away," Felix said, his voice crackling over the radio. "Is there some way we can delay this broadcast?"

"Parley?" Mary suggested.

Silas grunted. "About what?"

My mind started clicking. "Border access," I said. "Look, Amaral can't call a Convocation without physically being in Colorado. That's why he had Gold Hill announce that their territory overlapped the border—so he could call in the Confederation to protect him in his ally's claimed area *in Colorado* while he issues the challenge to Skylur."

"And Gold Hill's claim infringes our territory," Felix said. "If we dispute it—tell Amaral that we're not letting the Confederation or their allies over the border—then he'll have to talk to us."

"What if he just decides to do his broadcast and then fight his way in?" Silas asked.

"He can't issue the Convocation challenge in the middle of a battle," I pointed out. "What about offering him temporary access if Gold Hill's claim is retracted? Once you've told him that, say the parley will resume in an hour, to give him time to discuss it. Then we come up with another problem. Anything to hold him up until Naryn arrives."

"I don't like one-plan strategies," Julie said. "What about a diversion as well? Or something to get more people into Amaral's camp?"

There was a moment's silence. I was shivering in the cold and time was ticking on. Julie's question was good, but we didn't have time to gold-plate.

I opened my mouth to suggest we move when Tullah spoke, fingering the necklace.

"What if we offered to do the Were-changing ritual?"

Everyone turned and stared at her.

"Why would Amaral be interested in that?" Felix asked.

"He wouldn't," Tullah said. "I was thinking about the Confederation. What if you told the Confederation alpha that we know how to do the ritual, and if he withdraws his support from Gold Hill and leaves Colorado alone, we'll share it with him?"

"Do you think he'd believe us?" Mary asked dubiously.

"Say you'll show it to him," Tullah said. "A full-blown ritual should take up plenty of time."

"But we don't know the ritual," I said.

"And I can't put Olivia through that," Felix added. "I have her here, where I can keep an eye on her, but making her vulnerable in that way is too much to ask."

"Then do it on somebody else," Tullah said impatiently. "Someone who can already change. How's the Confederation going to know? It's just to buy us time, and to get Amaral's allies arguing with each other."

"She has a point," Felix said. "It just might work."

"Okay, then," I said. "We have Plan A and B. We've got to get this moving."

They couldn't disagree. Night had fallen. The convoy would be overdue.

Mary and Tullah came and hugged me, carefully avoiding my shoulders.

Kaothos. We have a deal.

We have, Amber Farrell.

The lizard sounded somber.

After Tullah was Julie.

"I'm staying on this side of the border," she said, and patted the rifle. "Plan C."

"The place will be crawling with—"

"Crawling with amateurs. I'll be fine. You're the one in the fire." Julie didn't do kisses, but she tried a hug and then left at a run.

The part of the story that still needed completing was Evans; he needed his memory scrambled to the point where he thought he'd managed to escape.

I took a step toward him.

He was awake and aware of what we'd been talking about. He cringed back against the side of the SUV.

I had no idea what I needed to do, but I'd almost compelled my sister once. Maybe it was an instinctive thing. Before I could try anything, Yelena pulled me back.

"I'll do it," she said.

I could hear an eagerness in her voice.

"Just what's necessary," I said. "Don't screw him up any more."

"Yes, Boss, of course."

"And..." I frowned. Was I getting too complicated here? "Convince him it was the Santa Fe pack."

She grinned, hauled Evans to his feet and shoved him into the driver's seat of our SUV, forcing him to push the dead man away from him. In seconds there was blood all over him.

He struggled until she bit into his arm, her fangs piercing his coat and shirt.

His eyes grew dazed and his limbs flopped.

She stopped biting and arranged him, kicking and shoving his unresponsive body until he was sitting with his hands on the wheel and his feet on the pedals.

I climbed into the back and crouched in the footwell again.

Yelena reached in and started the engine.

I could feel her eukori reaching. It had felt so pleasant when I'd sensed it at the airfield, but now it had a harsher edge.

"Had to get away," she whispered. "Getting dark. Attack on the convoy. Driver was shot. Guard got out and he was shot too. Got in the driver's seat. They were coming in from all sides. Santa Fe Were. So many. So confusing. Had to get away. The bitch was in the back. That's what was important. Had to get her to Amaral. Had to go, fast as I could. They were shooting at me. I kept my head down. Foot full on the gas. I drove around the other trucks."

Evans was staring out the front windshield without really seeing anything. His mouth was moving.

His right foot was on the gas so the engine was racing.

"Put it into first gear," Yelena said.

Evans frowned. He pressed the clutch and shoved the gearstick forward.

Yelena closed the driver's door quietly.

"Ready," she said. "Now, go!"

His left foot lifted and he jerked as if he'd just come around after being stunned.

Yelena leaped away.

The SUV lurched forward and suddenly he was swearing and spinning the wheel, weaving between the remaining trucks too fast.

It'd be a hell of a way to screw it up if he crashed.

But luck was with us. We slithered up the hill, past the burned-out first truck of the convoy, and then back down to the track. They shot at us and I heard rounds striking the SUV and piercing the light bodywork.

Easy, guys. I'm in here, remember.

And then we were around the next bend; Evans was punching the shattered windshield out and thinking he was some helluva hero.

Chapter 55

The plan held up well through the guards around Amaral's camp.

They let us through without delay, and redeployed to face an attack from the Santa Fe pack coming in from the south.

Evans played his part, blood-spattered and wild-eyed. Almost too well—Yelena's work in his head seemed to have pushed him further over the edge.

"You fucking bitch," he shouted at me, laughing. "They tried to get you back and they failed."

The Confederation had parked their convoys off the track about half-way up a hill. We stopped there.

Evans dragged me up the rest of the way, taking every opportunity to jerk my arms until I almost passed out from the pain. He was enjoying it.

"I get to keep you after Amaral's finished with you tonight," he hissed in my ear. "I'm looking forward to all the fun I'm going to have."

"I knew you were a sick shit, Evans, but you're stupid as well. You think Amaral can afford to leave me alive?"

I might as well have been talking Vietnamese for all the effect it had. When we came to it, I tuned him out to concentrate on what was happening in the middle of Amaral's camp.

Stars blazed above us. It was full night now; the air was clear and the temperature was in free-fall.

The hill flattened out into a meadow and then became broken ground before falling into a gorge. There were braziers in the meadow, not burning brightly, just glowing with embers that provided sufficient light for paranormal eyes. The Confederation reserve was camped there, waiting while they were deployed or sent out on patrol.

The hillside was rocky; the biggest stones looked like old, weathered faces sunk into the earth. The ground was streaked with pale fingers of a light snowfall. The wind wove its way through tall ponderosa pine and stirred the snow like ghost hair.

It was flat at the top of the hill as well, where I was.

Here, Amaral had set up a windbreak in the shape of a U, using the sheets of black fabric I'd seen at the convent. The fabric billowed and waved in the wind.

Inside the break, he had a freaking conference table set up, with chairs. And behind that, I could see Diana surrounded by the children and Adepts, exactly as she had been in the convent. Her head was down and her eyes closed. I could feel the working hissing balefully at the edge of my consciousness.

Amaral himself was sitting at the table talking with an Adept. He was dressed in a business suit, ready for his appearance. Guards stood in loose groups inside the shelter of the windbreak. Too many for me to get anywhere near Diana.

They had diesel generators behind the break, thumping quietly in the night and powering a full mobile recording studio—cameras, lighting, the whole works—with operators and assistants rushing around. From the look of it, they were getting ready to go live any time now.

Come on, Felix, time to start the distractions.

Screens came up. I recognized a couple of the faces from meeting them at Haven.

One of the screens was focused on Diana, zoomed in close and cropped tight so that nothing of her surroundings showed.

If she wakes up and thinks the conference has started…

Not quite yet. Amaral realized we were there, and he and the Adept walked over.

One of the cameras followed Amaral.

If that went live…

My wolf growled.

Kill. Kill.

I wouldn't need my arms, just my jaws. That'd look good on Athanate prime time—me getting shot by Amaral's guards while I tore his throat out.

Felix, where the hell are you?

Amaral was focused on the upcoming conference. He barely listened to Evans' story, continually glancing over his shoulder.

Another screen came up as another House came online. That made eight. There were probably four in there that would support a Convocation.

But there was a more immediate threat. The man with Amaral was Taggart, the leader of the Taos community of Adepts. A man who thought he might be as good as a Truth Sensor. He was suspicious, asking questions that Evans couldn't answer.

Felix? Come on.

But plans have a way of not surviving contact with the enemy.

Evans was focused on Taggart. Amaral's guards were behind him. I had a clear path.

I tensed myself, felt my wolf salivating.

Kill Amaral. Hardly a perfect solution, but maybe the best we could do.

Then O'Neill was running up the hill, shouting. And Liu removed the shielding he'd been holding over the Were on the Colorado side of the gorge. Their Calls were sharp and hard as ice knives in my chilled mind.

Suddenly every Confederation Were on the hill knew there were three large packs facing them across the state boundary, and a little night maneuver had changed into a possible pitched battle.

Chapter 56

Amaral felt the shift, even if he couldn't feel the Calls. "What's going on?" he asked sharply.

Evans was forgotten.

"Denver," O'Neill said, glaring at me as if it were my fault. "Cimarron and Cheyenne."

"Cheyenne? They're part of the Confederation. Is this some kind of trick, O'Neill?"

"No trick. I don't know what they're doing here. Something drastic must have happened."

The absence of an immediate assault was confusing O'Neill.

There was just the vast, deep night and the Calls from across the gorge.

Hell, even the hair on my neck was standing on end.

"What do they want?" Amaral said.

O'Neill was still looking at me, when another Were came sprinting up the hill.

"Parley," he said, panting. "They're rejecting Gold Hill's territory claims."

Amaral stood stroking his jaw and looking back at the screens. A ninth screen had lit up. I could almost see the gears grinding in his head. He wanted to go on with the conference, but if he started and had to stop because of fighting, that'd make him look weak. Or stupid. That was *not* a way to win arguments with Athanate.

"Fine," he said shortly. "We'll meet them down at the river."

The Were who'd played messenger sprinted back off to arrange it.

I held my breath, hoping he'd leave me near Diana so I could have a closer look at that lock.

Taggart was muttering in Amaral's ear. He turned and looked at me. "I don't trust her up here," he said. "Evans, bring her along. It may be useful to show we mean business."

Ten minutes later we were all down in the Toltec Gorge next to the shallow Los Pinos River.

Felix headed the delegation. Don Stillman stood on his left, his face impassive. A third alpha I assumed to be from Cheyenne was on his right. Behind them, Liu and Mary. I wondered how they'd managed to keep Weaver out of this.

Facing them were Amaral, Taggart and O'Neill.

There hadn't been time to bring the Gold Hill alpha, so Evans was deputizing. He'd been told to shut up and let O'Neill do the talking.

Felix was eyeing Evans in much the same way O'Neill was eyeing the Cheyenne alpha. I could smell *lots* of delays brewing. Good.

I could also feel workings prickling along my bare arms: Taggart on this side and Mary on the other. This was no Assembly with Truth Sensors; we'd have to rely on our wits to tell us when people lied.

Amaral made a politician's smooth opening.

Felix ignored it.

"That's a member of my pack you're holding there," he said, pointing at me. "You have no right."

It was O'Neill who answered. "She was in Gold Hill territory and she was acting in Athanate interests for Altau. We're treating her as Athanate."

"I'm not interested in Athanate issues at the moment," Felix said. "Gold Hill don't have a territory, and you certainly aren't anything to do with them."

Amaral held his hands up. "Leaving the Were territory issues to one side, there are Athanate reasons I'm holding Farrell, and maybe we can discuss her return when those are complete. But I state that both House Amaral and the Confederation have ties to Gold Hill, and support their territorial claims."

"So, where's the Gold Hill representative?" Don asked. "This man?" He pointed at Evans and raised his eyebrows in disbelief.

"Evans is deputizing as an observer," O'Neill said. "But as the senior Confederation alpha present, our constitution allows me to answer for Gold Hill."

That argument took ten minutes. That was less than I'd hoped and Amaral wouldn't hear of delaying until the Gold Hill alpha arrived.

Felix wasn't finished arguing about me. "Farrell may have done some things for Altau," he said, "but her main reason for being in New Mexico was to acquire a talisman to conduct a ritual to help Were who have problems with the change."

Taggart and O'Neill leaped on that, but the more interested they got, the less Felix would say.

Another ten minutes went by on that and then O'Neill tried to find out what Cheyenne were doing there and got similarly stonewalled.

Don and Felix stomped down every mention of Gold Hill.

Twenty more minutes. Forty minutes and they hadn't made any progress.

I was freezing. I closed my eyes and imagined a map with a marker labeled 'Naryn' inching closer and closer.

When they'd stretched the discussion to breaking point, Don reluctantly suggested that, if it was just some Athanate crap that needed to take place on Colorado territory, maybe he and Felix would allow Amaral access for the time it took. Maybe. So long as no Gold Hill Were came across.

Whatever his unwillingness to get involved in a fight on New Mexico territory, the Cimarron alpha made a good ally for Felix in the negotiation.

And Amaral was interested.

O'Neill objected, but I got the impression it was for show. Amaral was getting impatient and pressuring him to accept. If O'Neill agreed, we were done and Felix would be expected to let them cross the river.

Felix sensed it too, and came back in with a refusal on the idea of a crossing unless there was also an immediate official withdrawal of any Gold Hill claim to any part of Colorado.

"The Confederation stands behind its members and their claims," O'Neill said stiffly. "And you'd be best served joining the Confederation soon, Larimer. It's only a matter of time. You, or your successor, will realize that. You can't stand against us for long."

A thinly veiled threat, considering how many alphas the Confederation had deposed.

I had to rein my wolf in from responding.

Felix was more in control. "In or out of the Confederation," he said evenly, "Gold Hill's claim is a complete fabrication. They don't even have recognition as a pack. Not from *any* of their neighbors."

Evans forgot to shut up. There was a snarling match between him and O'Neill, but the Wind River alpha was overwhelmingly more powerful.

Another five minutes used up, but I could hear Amaral and O'Neill shifting. For the Confederation, whatever gave them an excuse to be in New Mexico was useful; the size of the territory was irrelevant. For Amaral, it was simply a mechanism for him to be protected in Colorado for the time it took to issue the Convocation.

If they could get what they needed, they'd fold on Gold Hill, but O'Neill was reluctant. The Confederation couldn't afford to get a reputation for not backing members' claims. He had to have something to balance that.

Felix upped the ante. "So, what would it take to get you to withdraw all support from Gold Hill and agree to leave Colorado and the bordering packs alone, O'Neill?"

O'Neill frowned and started to shake his head. That was even worse than not backing their claim—to abandon a new member pack. *And* step back from the natural direction of growth for the Confederation.

Felix knew it. He brought out Plan B. "What about a way to help Were who can't change?"

"The ritual you talked about earlier?" Taggart said. "It's a hoax."

Mary spoke for the first time. "It's not. We've recently rediscovered a shamanic ritual—"

"Shamanic?" Taggart sneered. "Completely unreliable."

Mary went on, ignoring him. "—a shamanic ritual passed down from Amber Farrell's great-grandmother." She paused, her eyes holding O'Neill's. "Her Arapaho name was Speaks-to-Wolves."

O'Neill started at the name, and he looked over at me, his eyes narrowed speculatively.

I wondered how old he was. Had stories of what my great-grandmother did spread along the Rockies? Could he have heard of her?

He turned to Taggart. "Is she an Adept as well?" He jerked his head toward me.

Both he and Taggart came over and stood close.

I felt Taggart try and press in on me with a working. The cold made it difficult to concentrate, but I pulled in my eukori and sought out that elusive feeling of the energy flowing through me; the feel of it passing undisturbed, without gathering information.

Taggart grimaced. "I can't see anything."

Mary had seen something when she'd first met me. Even Felix had sensed something. Either I was getting some skill at hiding it, or the injuries I'd done to Hana were obscuring any potential talent I had. Or Taggart wasn't that good.

"You may not be able to," Mary said. "But she is."

Amaral had had enough. "Taggart, you're a Truth Sensor," he said. "Ask this woman outright if there's a ritual that'll work."

Taggart turned to Mary.

Both of them had maintained some kind of working that made our paranormal senses duller.

They squared up and I could feel the pull as their workings tested each other out.

Mary's face was serene.

Taggart thought he could get through enough to question Mary. "Is this woman, Amber Farrell, an Adept?"

"An Adept in training, yes," Mary said.

"Can she successfully perform this Were ritual we have been speaking about?"

"Yes," Mary replied without hesitation.

I held my breath. Technically, I could perform some ritual. If I did it on a Were who could already change, it would 'work'.

Could you fool the Truth Sense that way? Or was Mary strong enough that Taggart couldn't see through her defenses?

I could see Taggart wasn't convinced by what he sensed.

Amaral fidgeted. "Well?"

Taggart shrugged. "Apparently, she believes it," he said. "Whether it's true or not is another matter."

O'Neill tried to dominate me. I'd had enough practice recently. I held my ground.

We'd succeeded in wasting another ten minutes.

A messenger waded across and muttered something to Felix.

"A break for private discussion," Felix said.

"Ten minutes," Amaral agreed, glaring at his companions.

We made our way off to the side, Evans still jerking my arm at every opportunity.

"I think we should consider their offer of safe passage," Amaral said. "We can't wait around for the sun to come up. I need to issue the Convocation tonight, and we need to get out of here before someone calls out the National Guard." He studied O'Neill, who was looking into the distance, eyes unfocused.

"That ritual," O'Neill said. "I want to see it."

Amaral pursed his lips. "Evans," he called him over. "Leave Farrell with us. Go get your alpha. We need him here. Hurry."

And Evans went off at a sprint. Bonehead—they were only getting him out of the way.

I sank down on my knees as if I was exhausted. It didn't take much acting.

There was silence until the sound of Evans' running faded.

"I don't give a damn about wolves changing or not changing," Amaral said. "I need my conference back on track and access to Colorado in the next couple of hours, without fighting through three packs of Were."

Taggart and O'Neill nodded, O'Neill still looking distracted. Good. We had him going on the ritual—the idea of finding a way to stop losing Were who couldn't change was irresistible. Now I just had to hope he'd refuse to ditch Gold Hill unless he could make sure it was worth his while.

"It is only three packs?" Amaral prodded O'Neill. "Cheyenne isn't going to be joined by Medicine Bow, or some other pack you've lost control of?"

"There must have been a challenge," O'Neill said defensively. "That wasn't the alpha we installed."

"I don't care about your excuses," Amaral snapped. "I need to know what we're facing over there, if anything goes wrong."

"It's just the three," O'Neill confirmed. "With no common purpose. They definitely don't have the cohesion to attack us." He paused, eyeing Amaral, letting the tension build. "I wouldn't recommend crossing the river without my backing, though. If they decide to turn on you, you'll need my pack."

"Without your backing?" Amaral said. "Look, Larimer's only keeping out Gold Hill's allies and associates. Just get rid of Gold Hill. They're dead weight, and you'll have to deal with them sometime anyway. You saw their behavior in Taos; they're one step from rogue."

O'Neill shook his head. "You're the one who suggested the plan with Gold Hill. We recruit packs by offering them the support and protection of the Confederation. If we renege on our promises to Gold Hill, it could undermine the confidence of every member pack, present and future. I'd need a damned good reason to take that risk."

Amaral saw where this was going, and he snorted with impatience. "This ritual," he said. "Are you telling me you won't back me unless I delay my conference for a damned Adept circus?"

O'Neill said, "If it works, it's worth getting rid of Gold Hill." He looked like he'd be glad to—he just needed a good enough reason.

"And if it doesn't?" Taggart asked.

"Larimer could lose control of his pack." O'Neill shrugged. "If that happens, their alliance comes apart. Even if he keeps his position, he's exposed as a fool in front of the other packs. They're not going to be in any state to fight."

"Fine," Amaral said. "We concede the Gold Hill claims. Larimer gives me an ironclad guarantee on safe passage. They do the ritual." He pointed a finger at O'Neill. "But if it doesn't work, you agree the Confederation will force the crossing and push any Were on that side back far enough for me to issue the Convocation. I'm not going to hold everything up for nothing."

"Agreed," O'Neill said.

Taggart said, "Even if this farce works, how do you know Larimer will really share it with you? It seems that he'd gain more from keeping it to himself."

"It doesn't matter," O'Neill said. He returned his gaze to me, cold and calculating. "If it works, I'll get it, one way or another."

Of course. He'd be thinking I went with the ritual. Regardless of what Amaral had in store for me, O'Neill had no intention of letting me go.

I didn't care what he thought, as long as Naryn arrived in time.

O'Neill spoke into his radio. Evans was recalled to hide what was happening behind the scenes, and the rest of the Gold Hill pack were quietly detained.

"I'd film the ritual, if I were you," Taggart said, looking contemptuously at me. "Even if he doesn't lose his position immediately, Larimer's credibility will be destroyed."

And you'll have another weapon against shamanic workings. No wonder Chatima was on the run.

"Fine," Amaral said. "It's nearly time. O'Neill, you'll need to keep Evans in line when we go back down."

O'Neill nodded. He knew what he needed to do.

Amaral turned to me. "Remember, Diana's life is on your head. Don't do anything that would jeopardize that."

Evans came scrambling back into the gorge and he couldn't believe his luck. The alpha offered him a position in the Wind River pack.

He forgot to jerk my arm as we returned to the parley area.

He was still a bonehead. I doubted he'd last the night, whichever way it went.

Chapter 57

"We agree to your proposals, with conditions," Amaral said. "O'Neill…"

The alpha went through the sequence.

Something had happened during the break. Felix had become edgy. Don was nervous. And Tullah was there—standing in the shadows with an escort of Denver Were.

What the hell?

Mary was watching me. Choosing a moment when Evans was distracted, I mouthed, *Naryn?*

I got the tiniest headshake in return.

What then? Had Weaver tried something on Tullah?

Felix was nodding. They'd come to an agreement, both sides lying through their teeth. This part of the delaying tactic was over.

"What do you need?" O'Neill asked. I could feel the excitement and anticipation building in him. The Confederation must be really suffering from new wolves inability to change—or he was even more power hungry than I'd thought.

Felix gestured at me.

"A dozen, maybe fifteen others." My teeth were chattering so I could barely speak. I tried to concentrate, but all I could think of was a warm fire. "I need a bonfire in the meadow," I said. "And everyone else to clear the hell away."

"I'll be observing," Taggart said. "To verify the authenticity of the working."

I didn't have the energy to argue with him. It wouldn't matter—I only had to fake it until Naryn showed up. It couldn't be much longer.

"The necklace, of course," I said.

"Of course," sneered Taggart. "We'll need to inspect it before you do the ritual."

"Fine." I turned to Felix. "Who's the candidate?"

He looked into my eyes. "Olivia Todd," he said quietly.

I barely caught myself. He'd been adamant that Olivia wouldn't be put through a fake ritual. Unless…

"How close to crisis is she?" I tried to sound cool and analytical, but my wolf was scrabbling inside. *Help her. Help her.*

Felix's voice was clear and steady, but I could see the effort. "She's very close. If she doesn't change within the next couple of hours, she'll die."

But I had a couple of days to work on it, I wanted to shout. This was supposed to be a fake. I wasn't prepared.

"Who else do you need?" Felix asked.

I had to get myself together. I had to figure this out. I'd promised Olivia. Everyone was depending on me. Diana, Skylur, Felix. Now Olivia.

"Ricky." I said, my voice strained.

Felix nodded. He'd expected that.

Who else? Maybe I could really try something with eukori?

"Yelena. Nick."

Someone to comfort Olivia. And one for backup.

"Martha. Tullah."

One more. One who'd shared something with me.

"Ursula," I said. "And about a dozen cubs," I added without really knowing why. It felt right.

Felix frowned. He'd expected me to ask for the best fighters, to get them closer to Amaral's camp. And I would have, if this had been fake. But now it was real, and something deep inside prompted me.

"She'll need to be freed to do the ritual," Mary said.

Amaral strode across to me.

"You know what will happen to Diana if you run," he said.

I nodded. I had no intention of running away.

At Amaral's curt nod, Evans cut the rope.

For all my determination not to show any pain, there was no hiding it. As my shoulders were released from their unnatural position, I groaned. My back and arms felt like every joint was made of broken glass. I slumped down while Evans hacked the hobbles from my ankles as well.

Martha was first to arrive, and she massaged my shoulders gently.

Then the others I'd named came, one by one, until finally Tullah moved to join the group.

Taggart blocked her way.

Could he sense Kaothos?

A wisp of voice came to me. *He cannot sense me, Amber Farrell. He feels something, but there are none so blind as will not even look.*

A hiss of laughter.

"Give that to me." Taggart held his hand out for the necklace.

Tullah offered it up and he snatched it away.

He ran his fingers over it.

Best of luck.

"This isn't a talisman," he said, sneering. "Not even an heirloom. It's dime store junk." His voice slowed. "Though…"

My heart thumped against my throat.

"Someone has imbued it with workings." He frowned, rubbing the beads between his fingers. "They have no structure, no form. Meaningless shit, that just—"

"It can't change Were?" Amaral interrupted him.

"No. I told you, that's ridiculous. This junk is exactly the kind of thing that needs to be destroyed, along with the people who made it, and the mumbo-jumbo they peddle. It's dangerous using the energy with so little grasp of what it might do."

I could see energy coiling around him, ready to attack what he could not understand.

"Break it and the deal is off," Felix said.

"Taggart," Amaral said.

The Adept leader threw the necklace back at Tullah in disgust, and she plucked it out of the air.

Careful.

"I will need everyone who's not participating to clear the area," I said, and made signs for Mary and Liu to stay.

Taggart and Amaral whispered urgently. Amaral was shaking his head.

"You didn't say those Adepts," Amaral said. "They can't stay. We don't know what workings they might try under cover of the ritual."

"I need them," I said stubbornly, "I'm still in training."

"You can't need them both," O'Neill said. "Speaks-to-Wolves worked alone."

Damn. He did know about her. I should have known that'd come back to bite me.

I needed Mary and Liu, close enough to work on Diana's lock.

Mary stepped forward. "You only need one of us to help you," she said, and she turned to Amaral. "I'm willing to offer myself as a hostage, to ensure the others' good behavior."

I had to admire her balls—and her strategy. If they took her up to the camp, she'd be right where she needed to be.

I could see Taggart liked the idea of having Mary under his power. O'Neill didn't argue. He'd see the benefit of another captive.

But Amaral refused the bait. "No. I'm not having an experienced Adept in my camp."

He looked at Tullah instead.

"This is the woman you had with you in New Mexico?" Amaral asked me.

We froze.

Shit. What now?

I nodded.

"Someone you care about. I'll take her," he said.

"No!" Mary strode forward and suddenly the air was charged with violence.

"Stop!" Tullah leaped in front of her. "It's all right, Ma."

Did Mary know I'd freed Kaothos? Was this acting?

Calm. Kaothos' voice whispered in my head. Liu reached out and pulled Mary back.

At a sign from Amaral, Evans took Tullah's arm and led her up toward the top of the hill.

"I'll take good care of her," he hissed as he passed me. "Maybe she'll like it enough that she won't want to go back."

Tullah handed the necklace to me before letting herself be taken.

The necklace felt smooth and heavy in my palm. Still hot from Tullah's touch.

I put it on and sank down until my head touched the ground.

Don't take Tullah.

I had to press my face into the rocky surface, concentrate on the sharp edges cutting into my skin. Roll my shoulders. Anything to get the pain to blot out my thoughts and stifle my hysterical laughter.

Oh, no. Don't take Tullah and Kaothos right into the middle of your base. Oh, hell, no.

Chapter 58

"Amber." Martha touched my arm.

I looked up. There was a group of about twenty young Were, led by Ben.

I blinked. I'd said I needed some, but I'd forgotten what I was thinking.

My hand came up and stroked the necklace.

What had I been thinking in the dungeon beneath the convent? That most of the problem with changing happened when the pack didn't believe a halfy could change.

That's why I needed youngsters.

They hadn't had as much time to get into the negative mindset.

Ben was grinning and nearly bouncing on his toes. No negativity there.

"My sister," he introduced the Were behind him, and she was looking at me with a sort of wide-eyed hero-worship. No negativity there either.

They were perfect. I pointed them across to join Olivia.

The next three I rejected. Two Denver pack, one Cheyenne; I tasted their minds with eukori and found doubt. And most of the rest. Four more from Denver, three from Cheyenne and one more from Cimarron in the whole group of cubs were what I needed. Young, fresh, willing to believe.

Gullible, snarked Tara. *Only joking, sis.*

I guided them up to the meadow and got them gathering pine needles and broken branches to make a bonfire.

My fingers traced the necklace.

I will…

Martha dropped an armful of branches on the growing pile and put her arms around me.

"You have a duty here, Amber," she said.

I sagged against her, shivering.

"I don't know—"

"No path is known until you reach the end," she murmured, and gave a breathy chuckle. "Amaral has done his unwitting best by picking us a sacred area. Whatever it was that she did, Speaks-to-Wolves always took to these places."

"Is it really?" I said. "This place is sacred?"

"Shh. Listen…" She held me, rocked me gently. "Listen with your whole heart."

The wind hushed through pine and teased little snowtrails. It was like a song, like an old memory of something heard in passing. A meaning that always just escaped me.

My fingers traced patterns in the necklace.

The rest danced away from my fingers. The beads spoke a language that murmured words in my head. The second pattern felt similar to the first. The same start. Then different words for the same thing?

I will... I will...

"The song is strong tonight," Martha whispered. "Many are called."

It's just the wind.

I will choose my path.

That was the first of the patterns that Chatima had laid in the necklace. I'd chosen. I'd taken one step after another that led me here. And I could feel the cost of my choices wheeling above in the night sky. Death and sorrow and pain and loss hung like vultures circling above me.

My fingers tried the second pattern again.

I will...

Chatima had faith in me. She thought I could do this ritual.

The embers from one of the braziers were dumped in the pile and the fire caught. It was low and smoky, but it felt right, and I needed the warmth.

Martha left me while I warmed up. She moved across to Olivia, looking worried.

I could get them to dance. That felt right.

Olivia was trembling now, even more than I had been earlier.

I had no time left. I went to her side. She was wheezing with pain, tremors shaking her whole body.

"Too late," she groaned. "Kill me."

I flashed back to Alex showing me through eukori what had happened to his girlfriend, Hope. She'd screamed, tearing with her nails at her flesh, bloody foam bubbling out of her mouth and nose. *Kill me*, she had screamed, *please kill me.*

No. That will not happen.

I held Olivia's head in my hands and forced her to look right into my face. "No. Trust me."

She did. Half blind with pain, she still reached out to me with her trust.

Pain. Something in the necklace. *Need* pain? *Want* pain? It wasn't in the patterns; it lay beneath, a shadow swimming in the depths.

I reached blindly to the people supporting us.

Ursula was there, solid and dependable. She trusted me too. It was like having a harbor wall shielding me from the storm. And beneath that, another heavy responsibility on me. A secret of hers that I knew. I hadn't made a promise to her like I'd promised Olivia, but still...

I pulled her into a hug and rested my forehead against her for a second, breathing in the steady thump of her heart, the odd familiarity of her marque, caught half-way between Felix and me, between what she was and what she wanted to be.

On the other side, Martha. Light to Ursula's darkness. No burden of expectation to place on me, simply a willingness to help, and a deep well of compassion.

"I need your help, both of you. Just hold Olivia for the moment, calm her. Let her go, Ricky."

Should I send him back? I could feel the despair leaking out of him.

No. Keep him.

"Yelena, I need you next to Olivia too. I need us to touch even if we get far apart." I tapped my head and sent a sliver of eukori toward her.

She looked surprised, but she nodded.

They were half-believing. Even Ricky kept a tiny spark of belief. It was buried deep in their minds, underneath what they knew from what had happened so many times before, but it was there.

I just needed something to divert their thinking minds, hide the disbelief away and let the belief catch and flare, like the bonfire.

I will...

"We're going to dance," I said.

Puzzled looks. But not from Nick; a slow, thoughtful breath from him, steaming into the cold air.

"Do the Chippewa dance, Skinwalker?"

He grunted. For a second, the image of his bear seemed to suck up the darkness of the night and hover around him.

"We dance," he said.

"Then dance me a spirit dance, Skinwalker. Dance the stars down, dance the earth up into the sky, dance the spirits out of the air."

He grunted again, a deep sound. His head lifted as he tested the cold air.

He turned, shucked his clothes and began clapping and stamping.

"Yelena."

She laughed. "I am Dancing Girl. Yes." She looked at me. "I dance. I get naked too? This is like club in Denver? They put dollar in my g-string?"

I gave a tired smile. "No g-string allowed in Were dance."

She laughed and pulled me in to kiss my forehead.

"You will do good," she said, giving me the strength of her belief in me.

Then she shed her clothes and spun away to begin stamping and clapping behind Nick.

The cubs stripped and joined in. Lightness in their step. Strength in their youth.

The wood on the fire had too much green. Smoke billowed out around us, but at its heart, it burned.

Olivia was staring into the flames, shaking. She seemed past caring what happened to her.

Martha and Ursula took their clothes off. Olivia allowed herself to be undressed. They pushed her gently into the group. She stumbled, but managed to catch a little of the rhythm of the dance.

Nick completed a circle of the bonfire, picking them up in his second pass.

Stumbles wove their way into the step. Nick stamped and twisted and wheeled. Buffalo, bear, eagle, wolf, salmon, cougar, elk. He started chanting. The words were Chippewa, and I doubted anyone else understood them, but it wasn't the words they needed.

The rest of them joined in, carrying the sounds.

I felt a storm of derision from Taggart, a hundred yards up the slope. Flickering disbelief and hope from across the gorge. It didn't touch the dancers. It wasn't directed at them. It was directed at me. I let it pass through me.

And behind it, I welcomed in the beat of the spirit dance.

It unwound its way through my head.

The heart beats forward: da-DOM, da-DOM. Nick's chant turned that around: HEY-ya, HEY-ya.

I will…

I joined the dance. Every step jogged my shoulders, and the pain built and built until it seemed the sky was red and I forgot myself. Beyond the pain, I became clumsy, calm and dreamy.

Nick led on. We stamped and spun through the drifting smoke and the flickering firelight like phantoms of an earlier age.

The spirits weave in and out of the world. An eagle wheels through the clouds; a ghostly wolf chases the shadow through the forest. The bear leads them. Their steps are thunder, their breath is the terrible wind that bends the trees.

A dancer changes. A human lifts a foot, a wolf strikes the earth with a paw. I hear the song of his change and it rings through the circle. His mind brushes against us, fevered with hunting, running and fighting.

Hold. Hold. Not yet.

Olivia was lost. She moved like a stick on the rapids, her eyes unseeing. She was carried only by the power of the dance, flowing through the weaving pattern of phantom wolves, and the deliberate tread of bears.

I felt Yelena's eukori pulling me, allowing me to reach Olivia, increasing the strength of my connection to her.

Now all I needed was something to send.

What had Noble said when I asked about the first change? *Imagine your wolf running.*

She feels what I feel. Our hearts beat together. I remember for her. She sees what I see; herself, her wolf, racing through the forest. Faster and faster.

Flying. Running. Closer and closer.

Energy crackles through me.

Pain-Pain. Pain-Pain. Pain-Pain. Can't think. Feel.

Wolf and bear. Wolf and bear.

My hand pressed the necklace against my skin. The beads felt hot, painfully hot.

The pattern in the beads.

I will master my way.

That's what it says! That's the second truth. Burned into my body.

I screamed it into the night with words that felt strange on my tongue. Words I did not know I knew.

I will master my way.

Wolf and bear.

More wolves change.

Dive like the hunting eagle. Down. Down. Down.

SLAM into the running wolf.

I smacked into the ground. I hadn't even felt myself falling.

Dizzy. Too much smoke. My eyes streamed. There was too much noise to think straight.

I crawled away from the fire and the wind changed, drawing the smoke away.

All the wolves had changed. I staggered to my feet, my legs uncertain under me. The wolves were leaping; not around the fire, just in one spot, one huge ball of struggling, tumbling fur right in front of me.

Olivia! Oh, my God. NO!

I'd failed. This was the mercy of the pack. They were killing her.

"NO!" I screamed. I stumbled forward, grabbing the wolves nearest me and hurling them back.

I was bitten, again and again.

Their bodies cannoned into me, buffeting me from side to side, as they snarled and spun and jumped into the air.

I wasn't being killed. The bites weren't breaking skin. They were nothing more than excited nips. Not a mercy killing.

The wolves were dancing.

The tangle of furry bodies parted and I fell onto my knees.

In front of me stood a beautiful red wolf. She swayed unsteadily, looking startled and proud and self-conscious, all at the same time.

I threw my arms around her neck and hugged her to me.

"Olivia," I sobbed into her fur, letting my heart open to the soaring song in the Call that told every Were for miles around what had happened. An explosion of joy answered from the far side of the Toltec gorge.

And then from the swirling smoke, monstrous shapes emerged, rumbling a sound so deep I felt it rather than heard it.

A large, cold nose was pressed into my side.

I blinked. My sight seemed to come and go like a faulty light. Was I seeing double?

Two Kodiak bears.

Wolves swirled around them, binding them into the celebration. None of the wolves cared that they were bears. Or skinwalkers.

Ursula butted me with her shaggy head.

The secret that she'd kept from the pack for so long: an aching certainty that she was more inside her, something different.

"This wasn't me," I stuttered.

She butted me again.

"I can't show you what I don't know."

But I had formed some kind of bridge. My experience in changing to wolf had gone to Olivia. Had I channeled Nick's experience of changing to bear through to Ursula?

Whatever had happened, it had left me a shambling wreck.

Feet and hands clumsy. Legs wobbly. Eyes blurry.

I had to get it together. Time was up; I couldn't wait for Naryn any longer. I had to free Diana.

The night wasn't over yet. Not by a long shot.

"Go," I said, hitting bear and wolf on the shoulder. "Back across the river. Until we get Diana free."

Chapter 59

I started up the slope, feeling great, except for the fact that every part of me was hurting and my head felt like my brain kept shorting out. Just a little while longer.

And then, behind me, as if an orchestra conductor had just raised her baton, a new Call came sweetly up the hill.

The ritual had worked in a way that none of us had expected. What had been a discordant confusion of Denver, Cimarron and Cheyenne Calls before had now blended.

I could still sense each pack. There was no submission of one pack to another, but a new, stronger harmony, and a sense of shared purpose that lifted me up.

They were united. And they were coming.

Amaral couldn't hear it; he was deaf to the Were Call. But he still wanted control of me.

"Get hold of her. Now!" he yelled at his guards.

But as his men turned to run downhill, they were caught in a surge of heavily armed Wind River Were with O'Neill at the head. *He* wasn't deaf to the Call from across the gorge. Neither was he deaf to the reaction in the Confederation Call. It suddenly sounded like a cheap brass bell with a flaw in the metal.

O'Neill was getting ready to run.

"Santa Fe have attacked. We can't hold them here, it's too exposed," he was shouting, waving his arms. "We have to withdraw. Get the trucks closer."

But there was purpose in the apparent random way his Were moved, preventing Amaral's security from reaching me.

The Wind River alpha knew the balance had changed. He had no commitment to Amaral's plans, not now when he had a much better way of achieving the Confederation's aims.

He wanted me for the Confederation.

Diana was no concern of his at all; he'd want to take me and escape as quickly as possible.

The Wind River Were formed an impenetrable wall between me and Diana.

I stopped.

Kaothos! I called, but it was too far.

Luckily, Tullah saw it too.

There was a moment when everything lurched.

Tullah yelled something at Amaral. Amaral's guards looked confused and raised their weapons, but they were hopelessly outnumbered by the Were.

And even though I wasn't consciously feeling for it, I sensed Kaothos shed her masking. Her presence, like a ground tremor, rippled through the energy. Taggart's head whipped around.

Even the Were felt it and halted.

I took the chance and sprinted forward.

"Get that bitch *now!*" O'Neill shouted. He jumped on top of one of the big rocks so he could see over the heads of his Were and direct them to me.

And then his head exploded.

Julie, you star. M24 sniper rifle, 7.62 NATO round, two hundred yards or more, at night, in a crowd. Straight through his eye. Freaking A!

The Wind River pack went berserk, but there was no way they'd be able to work out where the shot had come from in time to do anything about it.

I ran around them, heading for the black windbreak where Diana was.

Everyone was shouting at once. Amaral was surrounded by his security. He was screaming at them to get me, to take Diana, to shoot the Were, but they couldn't hear him in the pandemonium.

Not everyone was bugging out, though. Evans spotted me. He had been standing guard over Tullah and he leaped up to intercept me.

He hadn't tied Tullah up because she was only a girl. Mistake. *Fatal* mistake. He had a hundredth of a second to regret it when she grabbed his jaw from behind and twisted his neck. I could hear the crack from where I was.

A little part of me cried for Tullah. There is no right time or right way to learn that you can kill people with your bare hands.

I darted inside the windbreak, carrying the infection of chaos and panic with me.

The conference scene had been set up to project an image of calmness and rationality. A place where sober, measured decisions were made.

Except now, there was me. I didn't have time to see their reaction to me appearing naked and filthy on their screens, swearing as I heaved the camera intended for Amaral around until it pointed right at Diana. Live. No cropping. The entire montage with Adepts and children.

The camera assistant tried to stop me. Not Athanate. Someone's kin.

I threw him out of my way into a stack of audiovisual equipment. There was an explosion as fuses blew. Half the screens died right then.

So close.

Were guards charged at me, but they were still in shock.

I broke a boom mike over the first one's head and stabbed the second with the broken remains.

While he was clutching the metal sticking from his stomach, I took his gun and emptied it at the remaining guards.

Closer.

I stumbled. Blinded. This close, the working wasn't hissing. It was howling in the cold night air. It made my bones ache and my eyes blur.

Diana was sat close to the back of the windbreak, head down and eyes closed. Around her sat the children and on either side of her stood an Adept. Two more stood in front. All of them completely consumed in their working, unable to move.

Careful. Don't kill the Adepts yet.

Kaothos?

There was fighting outside. She was too far away and there was no time.

No time.

I'd lost track of what was inside me and what was not.

No sound in the physical world, but my ears were full.

The fabric of the windbreak bowed in. There were faces pressed into the material. They sang. They screamed. Theirs were the voices in the wind, the cold voices of the uncaring stars wheeling above, the spirits rushing over the bleak hills.

A candle guttered in the darkness of my mind, its flame swaying through my head.

The energy flowed through me, pouring into the sink that was the lock around Diana.

Energy flowed from Diana, through the children and the Adepts, still frozen into their stations to hold the lock, and down, down into the ground.

I could see it right in front of me.

A precarious balance.

Maybe I didn't need enough strength to break the lock. Maybe all I needed was enough to tilt the balance.

I reached into the tightly woven strands that formed the lock and tried to pry just one end free.

This wasn't like Tullah's lock. The Adepts' minds were there, inside the lock. They fought me. It felt like the strands were slithering and slipping away from my fingers, tensing tighter wherever I touched.

Slithering like nightmares wriggling in my head.

I saw Diana sitting in a chair.

Then floating, held in place by a mass of writhing snakes.

Then me. Strapped down. A windowless room. Screaming.

I caught one strand and tried sinking into it like I had with Tullah's lock.

The energy flared through me, sucking away from the rest of the lock, burning through me like acid.

Pain.

I screamed and reached for a second strand.

Taggart was here. I felt him running to the defense of his community's lock, his eukori livid with fear. He was shouting for help.

I ducked instinctively, and the empty rifle he'd swung at me struck across my shoulders.

More energy flared through me. The pain was unbearable.

I dug into a third strand.

"Stop her!"

Taggart dropped the rifle and wrapped his arms around me, trying to get a strangle-hold.

At his touch, I felt ice cold. Calm in the eye of the hurricane. The Athanate in the storm of wolf.

Hello, I said, and laughed.

My jaw melted. Reformed. Wolf fangs, not Athanate.

I sank my teeth into his arm until I felt bone.

He screamed, shaking violently, desperate to get himself free of me.

My Athanate made my saliva poisonous.

Taggart felt it. Razor blades dragging through his veins. The pitch of his screaming going higher and higher, till it blended with the spirit screaming I could hear outside.

I was aware of Amaral and his security team bursting in through the side, ripping through the fabric of the windbreak.

Kaothos! Help!

I took strength from Taggart's eukori. My cry for help was deafening.

Equipment exploded, and as the studio lights went out, one of the assistants started screaming to my left. "Look! Look! Look!" Over and over. Hysterical fear.

"Oh, God."

Above our struggle, in the great bowl of the black sky, the uncaring stars began to disappear.

I could feel her manifest. Not as the smoky illusion that passed through walls and ceilings. A solid, sinuous shape, poised in the air, blocking out the starlight.

All the screaming merged into one, endless, wordless song in my head.

I felt her presence flowing through me. My spirit hands were like great claws latching onto the buzzing substance of the lock.

More explosions.

Huge scaled wings crashed down on the windbreak, collapsing it. Buffeting winds threw all the remaining equipment over.

People running. Amaral running.

No, not him. He is mine!

White fury in my head. The entire energy of the lock collapsing, *burning* through me. I couldn't take it.

Kaothos *pulling* it through herself instead.

Fire in my veins. Me screaming. Kaothos screaming. The whole Taos community of Adepts scattered around the hillside, all of them, screaming. All of us bound into this one, hideous pain.

White. White. White. Burning my eyes.

No lock. No Diana. Just a ball of flame like a sun going nova.

Then no energy going through me. All of it feeding into the sun.

No pain.

Taggart falling into the sun, struggling.

His mouth and eyes open in terror. No screaming. Instead, a sound—a single note so deep I could only feel it.

Children floating, falling. Eyes closed, drifting.

And then my face was pressed into the ground. Blood and dirt covered me.

I heard a shout from down at the river, a huge cry echoed in the throat of every Were in the three packs, and echoed in the Call they raised.

Hunt. Kill.

Shots were fired, but I could feel the Confederation buckle and run.

What was that stench of burning?

Nightmare? Memory?

I knew I'd smelled that before. Human flesh burning has an odor that you never forget.

Hunt. Kill.

That was my Call too.

They were sweeping up the hill.

I rubbed at my eyes, wiping the muck away.

The windbreak was gone. Tables and chairs were splintered. All the audiovisual conferencing equipment was broken and scattered, tossed every which way.

The smell was coming from the four Adepts who'd been maintaining the lock.

They still stood rigidly in their places. Their heads were on fire, the flesh melting as I looked. Faces fixed in shock and pain lost their features and collapsed into unrecognizable ruin.

The children lay dead or unconscious around Diana.

She was slumped on the chair, her front bloodied.

Taggart was dead at her feet, his throat ripped open and his face fixed on his final moments of horror.

No sign of Kaothos. No sense of her. No sense of the spirits that had swarmed over this place. My mind was eerily silent and empty.

Except for the Call.

Hunt. Kill.

Amaral, I screamed. *Amaral. Mine. Mine to kill.*

Life simplified down to that one thing.

Chapter 60

Death comes to all. To some it's a blessing. But few get to choose the manner of their passing.

He struggles. He is getting weaker, but there is life in him yet.

He is old. Old. I can taste it in his Blood.

We have danced his last dance on this cold hillside, but the final steps can linger. Pain and fear. So sweet.

Eyes that first saw New England in 1757 from the rigging of a Yankee whaler are growing dim.

My jaws ease. There is a little life in him yet. He knows his death nears and he is so afraid.

Good.

"Amber. Stop it."

I heard voices around me, but they meant nothing to me.

He'd run. The loss of the Wind River alpha, Kaothos' sudden appearance, the death of the Taos Adepts and the great shout from the packs swarming across the Los Pinos River had broken the Confederation utterly. With only his Athanate security to protect him, Amaral had run.

I'd caught them halfway down the hill.

His security weren't Ops 4-10, but they were Athanate and they'd been armed.

It hadn't mattered to me.

I'd howled a challenge and felt the wolves racing in from all directions, passing like ghosts through the pine, flying over the uneven ground, faster than the wind that bore the first icy fingers of snow. Spirit and physical forms like black and white ribbons had mixed until there was only gray.

Every way bears death and sorrow and pain and loss.

I have chosen.

Amaral would not get away. I'd seen his death in him.

Hands touch me. I growl. There is a bubbling sound in his throat.

Slowly. Slowly.

Dance a little longer.

There had been death all around. The cloud of fear and confusion. One of the Amaral guards in front of me. The taste of his Blood. The feel of cartilage crushed in my jaws. The sudden end to screaming.

Huge wolf, Silas, attacking the last group of guards. Others fighting.

Then Amaral himself.

I'd changed back briefly. I needed him to see who it was that killed him.

My body was painted in blood.

Amaral carried no gun. Too arrogant. Too well protected. Not anymore.

So he'd attacked me the way he thought was his strength.

Icy daggers in my head against a wall of my anger.

Then fighting hand to hand and mind to mind at the same time.

I'd never practiced that. Hand to hand I could beat him, even if he was stronger than me. Even if the damage to my shoulders made me scream in agony.

Mind to mind I could defend.

But I couldn't do both.

He got a grip on me, and I wasn't going to be able to break it.

I spat blood and poison into his eyes.

Not enough.

His attack was battering at my mind like a sledgehammer.

So I let him through and he shared my mind.

Memories I'd locked away, like fire rising up inside me, and he couldn't let go. He couldn't let go.

Betrayal and despair so strong they shatter your mind.

This is what it's like, Amaral.

This is what it's like to be strapped down unable to move while they break your arms and legs and cut and burn your flesh so they can test how long it takes you to heal from your injuries.

This is what it's like when you hear them talking. Let's try it with drugs this time. Let's see if more injuries slow the rate of healing of individual injuries. Let's see if starving has an effect on healing. Is she viable for reproduction?

This is what it's like when it's your own side doing these things to you and you wake in the middle of another experiment and scream until your throat is raw and someone says the subject is distressed and then there's cold streaming into your veins and you can't scream but you can still feel.

And then my wolf came and took me, and Amaral's mental and physical grip faltered and I seized him by the throat.

Don't die yet, Amaral. I'm enjoying this. There are still things you haven't seen.

More movement.

They're not here to save you, Amaral. You're mine. Your death is my life.

A bang. A smell of burnt oil and nitro. Then my jaws are clamped on dead meat.

He was mine! I crouch over the body and snarl at the figures around me.

Mine to kill, however I wanted.

I will kill and kill. I need to kill so I can stop seeing the things that are in my mind.

Alex was there.

Thought was difficult. I didn't want to think. If I thought I would remember.

He flowed into wolf form, took a careful step.

Snarl.

But I can't fight him. He is my alpha. I have accepted him.

I let them drag Amaral's body away, my lips quivering with more snarls, but my head sinking down.

Alex stood with his head high. My lips drew back, but I didn't snarl at him.

Every way bears death and sorrow and pain and loss.

I had chosen a path that ended here. Diana was alive. Panethus might survive and forge links across the entire paranormal community. Olivia was alive. The Confederation would stagger; the survivors of tonight would return to their individual packs bearing the virus of doubt and the Confederation would turn in on itself. My pack was safe for the moment. My House was protected. Amaral was dead.

For everything, a cost.

Even in wolf form, under Alex's dominance, I could feel the madness in my head.

The irony. In the end, it wasn't the Athanate driving the Were rogue, or vice versa. It wasn't trying to be an Adept. It wasn't the curse twisting in my belly.

It was the things they did to me in Obs before Colonel Laine rescued me. The memories they hid in the places I had prepared for such memories.

The walls that I had built, and that they had strengthened, had finally burst.

My wolf gave me some protection from it, but without Alex around, the killing rage would return. It would be worse if I changed back and let the Athanate take over. The thought of drinking Blood was making my wolf tremble with eagerness.

I closed my eyes.

Oh, yes, I'd bite. Deeper and deeper. Feeding on fear and despair. Uncaring.

My body pulsed with the thought.

Rogue. Rogue. Rogue.

Chapter 61

A crowd was gathering around us.

Through it came my House.

Not mine any more. Not mine. I shook with anger. Naryn's House.

Safe. Better that way.

Mine!

A warning growl from Alex calmed me in time for Jen's arrival.

Alex tried to stop her, but she knelt beside me and hugged me to her.

The snarling died in my throat and became a whine. Alex was pushing between us to get Jen away from me. I snapped at him.

Ricky pulled on Jen's shoulder. "Jen, she doesn't know what she's doing. It's too dangerous."

"She won't hurt me." Jen buried her face in my fur and refused to let go.

Kin. Mine.

"Come back to me, honey," she whispered.

I whined. It hurt to not shift.

My kin's desires are sacred to me.

No. It's safer to stay wolf, let Alex keep me under control.

My lips drew back in a silent snarl again.

She kissed me on the head, rubbed her face against my jaw and hugged me tighter.

She was smothering my senses in her. Her scent, her touch, her sound, her taste. Her eyes held mine.

Kin. Love.

"Come back," she whispered again.

I shook, but she wouldn't let go.

"You can't stay wolf. You need to be both. Wolf and Athanate. You need to balance them."

Pia tugged at Jen. "You can't do this. If she turns back she'll want Blood."

"And she can have it. She knows she can."

"Just wait for Diana."

"And when Diana isn't here? *We* have to fix this. You told me I have rights as Amber's kin, Pia. I'm exercising them."

Danger, I whined.

Alex shifted to human.

"I agree with you," he said to Jen. "We do it, but it should be me. I can take more damage. She won't know what she's doing."

"No." Jen wasn't having any of it. "That's the wrong way. She needs to know she can control herself, even with me, at the worst time for her. That's what we need to prove. After that, everything gets easier."

With Alex in human form, his dominance began to slip away.

I felt the pull from Jen. From Alex.

I changed and fell over.

"Too dangerous," I croaked.

"Yes, honey," Jen said and lay down beside me.

Someone was wrapping me in a survival blanket, but the trembling wasn't because I was cold. It was because I felt the need. My jaw ached. I squeezed my eyes shut.

I tried to talk, but nothing came out.

David was stroking my head.

He'd found the necklace that I'd dropped when I changed.

Olivia, back in human form, wrapped in a blanket herself. She put the necklace back on me, a look of worship on her face.

I tried to tell her to stop it, but the words came out mangled.

Jen, her body so warm against mine, pulled my head down so my lips rested against her neck.

"Can't," I stuttered. "Dangerous." The words were muffled against Jen's sweet, rich skin.

Her pulse beat an excited thump against my lips.

She was murmuring lines I recognized from Pia's writings: an Athanate oath, more of a love song from a kin.

I am your pass through the mountains,
And your track through the wilderness.
I make this gift with love that we both may live.

Time slowed. My jaws felt as if they were melting, but the groan that escaped me was all pleasure. The Athanate fangs and the blood channels, the *taryma* as Athanate called them, manifested, followed by an entire network of Athanate organs in the throat and chest dedicated to one thing: taking Blood.

"I love you," she said.

My fangs throbbed in time with her heartbeat. Her flesh just seemed to dissolve beneath their pressure. We both gasped. My fangs slid into her neck, doing what they were superbly designed to do—find her Blood.

I took my first taste. It wasn't like swallowing. The taryma rippled all the way down in my chest. It felt more like inhaling.

Blood. Joy.

It was exquisite. Pleasure exploded in my fangs and cascaded down the taryma into my chest. It was so powerful, my back arched and my fangs slipped free of Jen's neck. I moaned. The air was too cold against my fangs. I needed Blood, more Blood, warm Blood, more than anything. *Now.* The need blotted out everything else. I gripped her and strained blindly upwards with my mouth gaping, frantic.

"Gently, gently, gently," Alex was whispering. I could feel him pressing down on me. Body and eukori both.

Kin!

I loved them. Both of them. Alex. Jen. Gentle.

Our eukori mingled.

They could feel what I felt—the need, the urgent need.

"I love you," Jen breathed, pulling me back to her neck. "Oh, yes," she groaned as my fangs slid into her neck again.

Gently.

I could take this step. I could choose this way.

Like the pack, I will be the sum of all the things I have ever done.

Vasana. *I will do this in love.*

I sipped, so carefully. The rush came again, like a wave breaking over me, crashing into me. Only this time Alex and Jen were with me and it broke over them too.

No more.

I wanted it. I wanted to feed on Blood until I was sated. Jen wanted me to feed.

I will choose my path.

I tilted my head back and my fangs came clear of Jen's neck. They still ached for more.

I had to heal her neck. My duty as an Athanate to my kin.

But Bian was already there, and Pia.

Jen, limp and giggly between them, while they licked her neck. I could smell the aniatropics being slathered on her.

"See," she said. She still held onto me, refused to let go.

Then Alex. My alpha wolf.

He kissed me and rubbed his face against mine, wolf-style.

I could sense his Blood, thundering through his body.

I twisted and pulled him closer.

"I love you," he said as I bit him.

Oh, my God. Pleasure.

He tasted different. He tasted of wolf. Male, strong, alpha.

I could feel the shock of his Blood all the way down into the Athanate organs in my throat and chest. I didn't care what the Athanate told me, I could live on this Blood.

I *pulled* again, pulling his Blood into me and feeling the delicious shock detonate through all three of us.

And stop now.

Beautiful.

My kin are pressed against me, and I'm never going to get up again.

They're worried.

The necklace burned against my skin.

I will choose my path.

I will master my way.

I will…

The words were unfamiliar. Not in any language I knew. Joy. Existence. Something joining them all together.

"Okay?" Jen wiped my face with her shirt sleeve, peering into my eyes.

My mouth moved, but no sound came out.

Complete. Enough for now. Peaceful. So wonderful.

Both kin worrying. Alex's wolf wants to come out. Nuzzle me.

Go ahead. No reason to worry. Everything is good.

Warm. Wonderful.

The third truth is floating to the surface. Stop reaching for it. It will come.

Slowly. Unfamiliar words, not in English. They mean…

I will exult in my being.

Tears ran.

Someone was cleaning my face. All the blood and dirt. I needed a bath, not a wipe.

I will exult in my being.

I didn't need to fear my wolf and my Athanate. The two parts of me had learned to work together, not each driving the other side to rogue. They'd flexed their dominance and found the good in each outweighed the bad. They had found a balance.

But that wasn't enough. The insanity in my head was something else entirely. The part Chatima had said: *patterns others have written on you.*

I withdrew from sharing with my kin. I wound my eukori tightly around all the madness that was leaking from me.

I can't let anyone else feel this.

More and more people gathering. Athanate. Were. Adepts. Noisy. Joy and sorrow blended together.

My House were worried. They formed a ring around me.

Felix's sister, Martha, has somehow found her way to my side. Silas stands behind her like one of the Lyssae statues in the basement at Denver, impossibly perfect, his face unreadable in the starlight. They are holding hands. There are more behind them. So many more. A silent part of the crowd.

Martha bends down and kisses my forehead.

Cold lips.

Fingers trace my cheek.

She's so cold.

Silas bends over me. I can't hear him. I can read his lips. Good hunting, he says.

Martha's head is tilted up as if she hears something, far away.

Her lips move. Listen, she says. Listen to the song.

The look on her face. Joy breaking like dawn in her eyes.

I try to say her name. Martha.

I chose a path. For everything, there is a cost.

They were bound by me on a wheel that turned.

Death and sorrow and pain and loss.

I can see their wolves more clearly than I can see their faces. Listening. Listening. Then running. So many of them. Running out into the depthless night. Following the song.

"Is she all right?" Jen said, her voice sharp with anxiety. "She's not talking."

"She's…fine." Diana said. "She's gone into Blood rapture. Not the most surprising thing that's happened tonight."

So that's what this is. Blood rapture. Floating, in a sea of sorrows.

Martha? Silas?

Nothing.

I blinked.

"She'll come out of it slowly," Diana went on, sounding exhausted. "You have to stay with her."

Diana's hands on my head. Real hands.

Fingers, spirit fingers, sinking into my head.

Not good. Darkness. Make my eukori tighter. So tight nothing can get out.

Words. Arguments. Fear. Darkness in my head.

Wrap my eukori tighter and tighter. I can't let anyone see this.

"I can't do anything now," Diana said. "I will try as soon as I can. But we've had an order from Skylur. I can't refuse. Neither can Amber. We have to join Skylur in Los Angeles *now*."

"She's in no state to travel."

"We're in no state to disobey."

Chapter 62

Helicopter. A sensation so familiar I couldn't tell where reality stopped and flashback started.

Faces bent over me. They didn't fit.

"Tell Top I'm sorry," I said. "I lost them. I lost them all. I'm sorry, Top."

"You're not making sense, honey." Jen, worried. Face pale.

Had I been talking aloud? Where were we? Not in South America.

I should ask.

I kissed her instead. Lost myself in the sensation. Alex and Jen were crushing me between them. Their hearts beat in time with mine. It didn't matter where I went in my head. The thumping of their hearts was like a beacon in the vastness of the night. I'd always find my way home.

Hold this moment. Hold it. Precious.

The thudding of the helicopter blades faded beneath the whine of the turbines running down.

Angry voices. Urgency. Smell of aviation gas.

I turned my head and breathed in Alex's scent. Wolf. Pack. Calm.

A looming shape. A jet.

They tried to strap me in.

No! No! No! I'm screaming. I'll never get out of here.

I slammed the door closed on my eukori again.

I ended up on the floor, squeezed between my kin, trembling violently.

Never let it out.

Doors close. Pressure changes. Engines spool up.

The lights dimmed.

The plane smelled of new leather and air fresheners.

I couldn't shut my eyes. I couldn't. There were nightmares waiting. Nightmares. It *did* matter where I went in my head, because there were places I couldn't return from.

"Rest," Jen whispered.

We're flying.

Floating…

Floating down the river of night toward the city of dreams.